ARRAKEN

JOHN OWEN

Prime Seven Media
518 Landmann St.
Tomah City, WI 54660

Printed in the United States of America

*Dedicated to the Chivalrous use of
Sorcery everywhere.*

TABLE OF CONTENTS

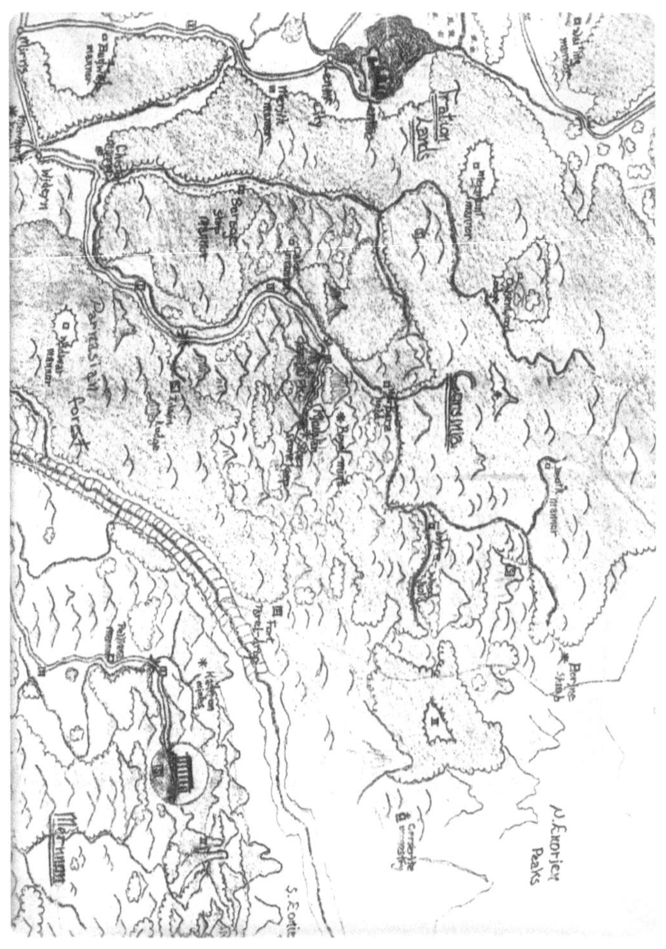

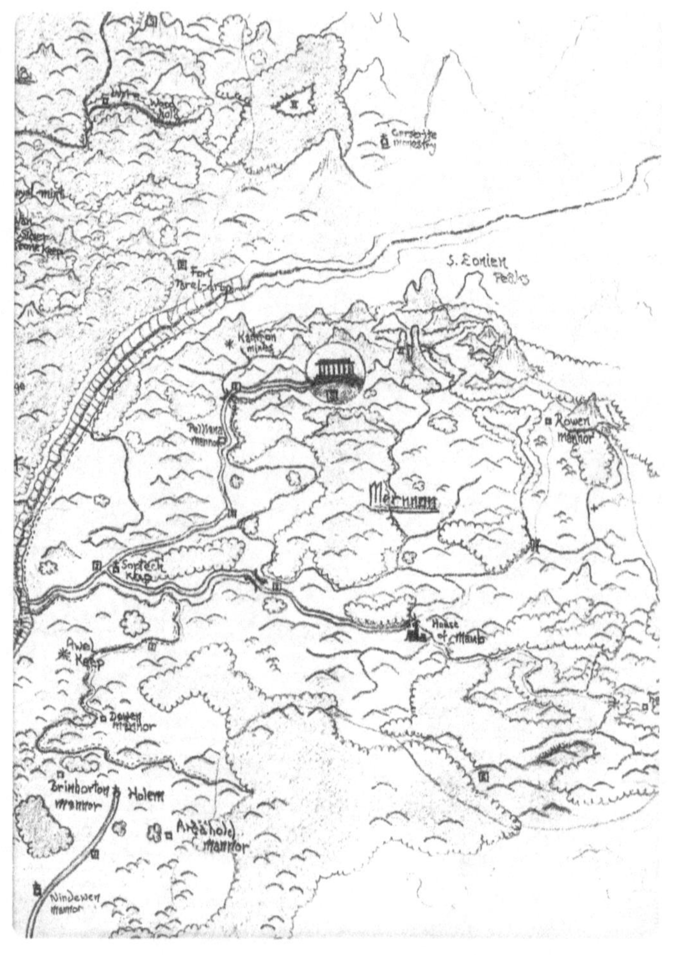

Wood Hall
Corsenthe monastery
S. Eonien Peaks
royal mint
silver Stone Keep
Fort Threldrop
Kenron mines
Pelliana manor
Rowen manor
Mernnan
Sortock Keep
Awel Keep
House of Maub
Dowen manor
Brinborton manor
Holem
Argahole manor
Nindewen manor

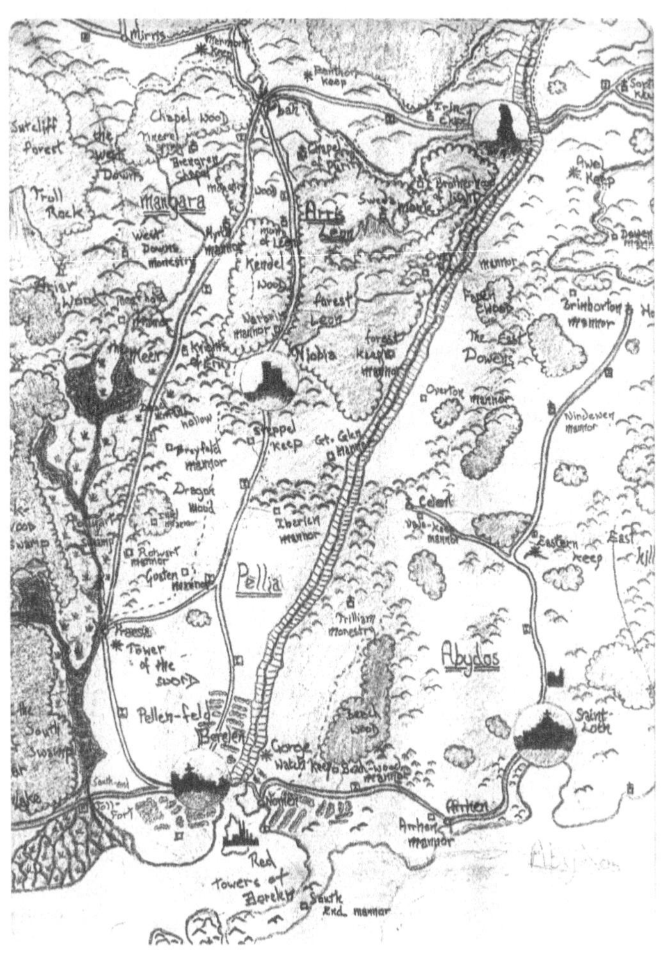

Mirns
Chapel Wood
Sutcliff Forest
the West Downs
Troll Rock
Manbara
West Downs Monestry
Friar Wood
Bergren Chapel
Arra Leon
Kendel Wood
Forest Leon
Niobia
Forest King Manor
Manor
The East Powers
Brinborton Manor
Nindewen Manor
Overton Manor
Stappel Keep
Gt. Glen Manor
Celon
Dragon Wood
Iberian Manor
Vale-Kal Manor
Eastern Keep
East Hills
Pellia
Trilliam Monestry
Abydos
Tower of the Sword
Pellen-feld
Borelen
Gorge Watch Keep
Sand-wood Manor
Saint-Loth
South Swamp
Toll-fort
Red Towers of Borelen
South End Manor
Amhon Manor
Arren

PROLOGUE

The age was old, it had been three thousand, three hundred, and fifty years, since the coming of the Ellendei. The thick timbers of their boats, felled in forests far from the land they now inhabited, wore thin over the generations of exodus. Tales and legends orated, each dusk, heartened minds and spirits over great wanderings, reworked, still clung to shreds of their people's collective histories.

Where they landed their crafts, the local denizens urged them ever on. Serving for a time as mercenaries and sailors, never finding home or hearth to call their own. They traveled. Aboard the slow, swaying vessels, those wise in the ways of sail and oar, became the chiefs of these homeless navigators. Calling themselves the Ellendei, they forgot the land from whence they came. Forgot, the legendary desolation that had birthed their nomadic ways. Forgot, the ancestry of their names and titles. Their crafts bore them ever on, hailed by the residents of beech and shore, when greeted, and shown compassion, they imparted expertise, to the rude societies they found.

Early cults and religious practices, faded replaced by the loudest voices of each ship. Thence they, argued, captain against captain, each ship against the other; who cut the swiftest keel, which, boasted the ablest warriors.

The disagreements and bragging, were countless, endless bickering to fill the miles. And when the arguing became tiresome, then there was strife. The wanderers threatened to destroy themselves, fire flung between ship toward kin and ally, sent many of the noble husks of Ellendei sea craft into a deep watered grave.

Restricted in the cramped galleys, punts, and dromos their orators fought the steady and rising darkness that had taken root in their souls, an erosion of the people's spirit, an erosion that they felt and feared with each oar stroke.

Replacing the eternal warring of their spirits and boastful clan gods, the priests and storytellers turned their people's thoughts inward to a worship of the One. They replaced the brutal sacrifice and warrior worship of the dark rising cults, with, the care of virtue and noble aspiration. To combat deadly rivalries, that, sprouted between men, and, abuses that threatened to destroy the floating union, the Holy commandments of the Ellendei, a law governing actions, and discourse, a scripture concise and elegant in its clarity, was compiled. This scripture was then carved into the stern of each of their many vessels and the voyaging continued, now baring a sacred mandate.

The tenants of the faith grew from the ten visions of the Corse Wrights, a guiding principle defined from the truth of their clarity. A blessed people the priests then did, call them, and, indeed, for a time their voyage brightened and the dwindling ships once more flourished, adding new and improved craft each generation to the next. And the aged were seen to look skyward, when far out at sea, and with eyes moist they declared, "We art truly a blessed people, lord... Yea, hear in thy glory how we now flourish... Yet when lord will we have soil to call our own... and hearth, hovel, hamlet, field, mount, and stream? "Then the young would know that their work was not done, and muscles would strain against rope and wind, and they knew that not till a land was found to rule and call home would they rest.

Then, it came to pass, that after many generations in the time of the Ellendei, their ships found the coast of a wild and sparsely populated land. A jungled peninsular that though wild and full of indescribable beast, foul lizard and man-eating plant, provided timber and valley unclaimed, by nought but, a rare and un-supposing people. A bronze race of sun worshippers. Here the Ellendei dwelt trading lore and art, battling wurm and great lizard with their new friends and allies.

For a time, they called it home and from here they explored a series of islands devoid of people, and rich in resources and timber for their boats. Great mountains towered from the steaming jungle. These they populated, for they had always been a people to overcome hardships, and creatures of the sea had hardened them to those they found on land. Cyclops and giant ran before the massed weaponry of this new people.

Aricia, they named their greatest port, located at the apex of a long island bay, and honoring the worship that had saved them from oblivion, they named their greatest clergyman pontiff, supreme bishop of the One. In Aricia, he enthroned himself, and plentiful were the fleets and captains that brought him tribute there.

To the north they found a second people old and wise, Mernnon was named the citadel, and glad were they, to accept the Ellendei, for hobgoblins, and foul creatures threatened the eroding power of their dwindling empire. The Kadron's they had called themselves, and mightily had they ruled, till the dark tide that, thus, they yet fought, had swept their land asunder, and now, they clung to a single mountain enclave, the last of a dying race.

Mernnon divided the Ellendei as they populated the low lands that grew beneath the mountain chains of that land. And they flourished, with the new people, turning their hardened minds to farming and cultivation, beating back the foul brood of beast that descended from mountain, to devour their flocks and lay waist to their fields. Then it was that their crafts were their undoing, for low it came to pass, that many sold the secrets of the people, both Mernnon and Ellendei alike, forsaking the covenant of the One, and building kingdoms for themselves. It was whispered amongst the good, that a malignancy had crept from the mountain peaks to enter the hearts of these power seekers.

So, it was, that lodges sprang to protect the people from darkness, councils of the wise, and unions of good. Seeing the need, the Faerie revealed themselves to man, a race of power surpassing even the Ellendei in the art of craft and lore. It was they that spoke of a dark enemy, he that dwelt beneath, seducing the soul. Shaitan, the pontiff of Aricia named him, yet the race of Faerie, and forest, that the Ellendei named Elf, claimed him to be the Imprisoned One, condemned to lay till eternity within a rocky tomb. It was from he that the Faerie claimed corruption was spawned, and foretold that the Ellendei were to be the people of Three Thousand Wizards, subjects to the Imprisoned One and yet those who were destined to fight his machinations beyond all others.

A great denial sprung within the peoples of the One, and a shunning of the fairies, who in this way warned and worried the Ellendei. And who's strange and powerful ways were unsettling to the new comers. The warnings were refused and the lodges and councils faded, forgotten, ignored, for fear of the very doom they threatened.

This was the time, that the first wizards walked the land, using power and craft for their own selfish ends. The Ellendei fell under the sway of these converts, and the cults that had been quashed by the worship of the One returned, their members, the mindless servants of the Imprisoned One, replaced hearth with pyre, foul fumes clouding the fertile land of their settlements.

War again claimed lives as these sorcerers vied for lordship one over the other, and each over all. The Ellendei fell, as the power of the Wizard Kings grew, the continent swamped by the reach their evil. For a thousand years they raked the land with sorceries, defeating each other in battle upon battle, until only five remained, ruling the land in an uneasy peace. Parnassus, Ergedh, Gaobel, Idawin, and Traites, carved up the freshly cultivated lowlands, marking their boundaries with scorched and burned mountain tops.

The foul twisted forms of their monstrous allies stalked the stunted and blackened woods that clung to the slopes of wizard peak and valley. Few were the Ellendei that survived, huddling around nomadic hearths, mumbling the words of the supreme pontiff of Aricia, too distant to be a relief in their despair. Mastering weapon, sword and armor they cleaved a fragile life from the warped escarpments and blackened growth that had been their home. Aided by the stout smiths of Derem Goria, a stunted race who named themselves Dwarfs, the Ellendei sea farers steadily adapted to warcraft.

In the years, that followed, the Ellendei, eked out a meager and brutal existence, the oaths of warrior rising beside the words of God, to govern their ways. In the foot hills to the north, in a land called Norcadia there was then born the warrior Arraken to an Ellendei, Delri and her husband Aserel. As the warrior grew, he showed great skill in weaponry, soon commanding the respect of the arms masters. With a ring of chosen soldiery, he came to protect many in the lands South of Norcadia.

Parnassus the Wizard king, plundered much in these lands, his foul denizens patrolling the hills unceasingly and claiming them for their lord. Arraken took it to mind, to defeat Parnassus, but knowing the sorcerer to be hundreds of years old, and wise in the way of hex and deomer, he felt it would be a task great in the time of men, to defeat such a one. Just as it had taken time for the wizard to come to be, so then it would take time to destroy the Hex King of Parnassus.

Then it was, that the warriors of Arraken took the Oath of slaying. Calling themselves a knighthood, they swore to protect the faith of the Ellendei, to guard all persons from harm, and to spend their lives working toward the destruction of the Wizard Kings, and, the ill they had wrought.

Arraken was anointed sovereign to the fighting orders. When the knight was in his hundredth year Parnassus the Sorcerer Lord slew Arraken during a direct assault on the wizard's Peak . The liege's son Arraken II carried on the fight, and, over generations the knights grew in might and number, aided by Faerie, Derem Gorin Dwarf, Norcadian, Gnome, and Mernnonian they defeated the Wizards slowly one by one.

Traites and the fire worshipers fell first, followed by Gaobel. Idewin converted, turning to aide in the battle for Ergedh. Parnassus and Ergedh were the last to fall, filling the land with sorceried brood from their bottomless pits of incantation and breeding. Ergedh spawned gigantic wurms, dragons of all types, beholden to his lieutenant Clortherregge, a red hewed drake, who had grown long in the coliseum of his lord, feasting on the flesh of many an Arraken knight before he turned the countryside, glades and valleys into his foul reeking playground.

Spewing ash Cloretherregge rekindled the devastation of the Ellendei, taking unto himself, the lordship of wizard and man. He descended to inhabit Old Nede, with his flaming serpent swarm, streaming behind. Not till, Serderan Elf lord of Thornbreak, sovereign of his people long before the Ellendei beached their wooden craft along the shores of Demain, Lord of the seared Pools of Shaidra, came again to aide and council the Ellendei, did the hope of Arraken return.

For it came to pass, that Eorowin, Elf of the host of Serderan, brother to the Elfen lord, gave his heart to Enerille Gunarson the beauteous Ellendei princess. Hearts were glad, Man, Elf and Dwarf, saw the hope of their victory in the union of faerie lord and human princess. Fair beyond measure were the couple and thence did the daunting devastation of Cloretherregge lessen in minds, replaced by the resplendent beauty of young love.

The Dwarfs of Derem Goria, turned to their forges, and, taking to themselves a tooth of Cloretherregge, wrenched from the Drakes jaw it had been, imbedded in the Door of Aseren, Gateway to the faerie kingdom. A great fiery immolation had Cloretherregge vented upon the loss of that tooth, and pursued as he was by knight and Faerie lord he had fled. The Dwarven smiths toiled long and wrought a blade of enamel, white, blessed with wards and guards of lore, runes imbued with ancient craft know only to their artisans.

On the birth of Enerille and Eorowin's first child, a son, who they blessed with the name Torechel, there was a great muster of Man, Elf and Dwarf, and with festivities, the sword was bestowed on the boy child. A union of three peoples.

Torechel, chose his mother's name, Gunerson, and his farther, Eorowin, who was to be Lord chief Justice of the Ellendei, protected him wielding the sword, until he should come of age, and take his place among the knights of the Arraken, King. Thangbite, was it called, for it did hate that from whence it came and the spawn of Cloretherregge trembled in fear before it.

When it came to pass, that Torechel had slew many of the foul broods of wizard and witch; he was knighted, held as first among the vassals of his king. It was he, that challenged Cloretherregge, sending the dragon hence with many a sortie to the wilds of Nede. After his foe had flown, Torechel turned, leading his host, to lay siege to the halls of Ergedh. Before, Cloretherregge returned from his fright, the citadel was opened, and Ergedh slain with the tooth of his dread lieutenant.

Torechel was then by the Ellendei declared Duke of Drake, first beneath the King, to stand shoulder to shoulder, with the Earls, alongside the sovereign. Carel Eiadawen, daughter of the king, was betrothed, and in time bore him a son, Atol Gunerson the first, grandfather to Herigar Gunerson.

Coretherregge, yet lived returning to declare himself supreme emperor of the land, spreading his seed from Nede. The lizard spawn drove Arraken into the strong stone castles, and citadels, so again did fear rule.

For a century the war raged between the forces of Coretherregge, and Drake backed by the Arraken crown. Many fell in the scorching onslaughts that issued under the plume of Coretherregge's flames. Widows and orphans, wandered the kingdom, homeless from the devastation. It was in this time, that Parnassus now supreme in the art of wizardry was defeated. An alliance of Ellendei barons and the little people, the Gnomes that the wizard had used as his servants and minors, the skilled tinkers worked from within to afford access to Arraken knights. Thus fell the last of the wizard kings.

Torechel tiring of the bitter conflict, donned his thick Derem fashioned plate mail, and taking Atol as squire rode to Nede to face the lieutenant of Ergedh, Thangbite burned at his side longing for blood from its spring of birth.

They found the wurm sunning its hide before its mountain throne, and unable to run from the draw of the blade, Lord and dragon smote each other. Atol returned to Ergedh with Thangbite and the tale of his father's death. So came the passing of the wurm, and the dawn of the age, the Elfs call, the Time of Three Thousand Wizards. Serderan, lord of Thornbreak, seeing the pain of his nephew's death, in the eyes of Eorowin, Chief Justice of Arraken renamed, his brother, Eorowin the Cursed, carrier of the doom of man. Thus, was it to faerie, that Eorowin lost his right to lordship over Thornbreak, that before that time was his as it had his brothers before him, in accord with in the genealogies of his people. Cursed he is, to ever see that which he loves wither and die before his immortal eyes.

The visions of the ONE; the commandments of the Corse Wrights.

1. Thou shalt keep to the ways of the Wrights
2. Thou shalt not bear false witness
3. Thou shalt not act from hate
4. Thou shalt not waste
5. Thou shalt not kill
6. Thou shalt not steal
7. Thou shalt not commit adultery
8. Thou shalt not covet
9. Thou shalt not take the name of the One in vain
10. Thou shalt not worship the Imprisoned One

CHAPTER 1

CORSERITE COUNCIL

The rain beat steadily as Thomas wound his way down the slope. He pulled the heavy coat across his wide shoulders pausing as he did so to take in the view. The sky was dark, yet he could still see deep into Corsinia, raged peaks surmounting forested valley floors. The horizon disappeared into a dull gray and brown. Summer had left these high mountain passes as soon as it had come. Thomas thought of the monastery beneath him then, sighing deeply, he continued his long trek.

The Elder Ones had reached their decision quickly and there was little more to be said. He would leave at once for the northern court of Aterrol Aterrolson, Treathbaron of the Ellendei, lord of Darkmore Keep. This was not a journey he welcomed, the mountain road to Darkmore was over a hundred leagues and treacherous even in the height of summer. These were dark times and it would be difficult for him to leave his responsibilities at the monastery in the hands of a lesser. But the council had been right, no other Corserite monk had a personal relationship with Aterrol, and it was he who knew the secret passes through the Karonccacks.

Thomas wiped the rain from his eyes and began a prayer to lessen the winds effect. "qudrall etherol nondrelleth…" He mumbled the ancient words under his breath singing the final phrases. His eyes closed as the spirit of Enruth, the One God, coursed through him. When they opened, the wind had abated, and, Thomas continued his downward journey.

It was getting dark, but he knew the path well. Twice a month for the last forty-six years Thomas had made his way between the Hall of the ancients and the monastery. It was steep, traversing the western side of mount Quetheron, and, disappearing into a ravine below the bare granite summit.

From here the path wound its way to the east and then up to a small cave entrance. The barrow of the Corserite. There, a few hundred feet from the summit, the High Abbot of the monastery held council with the spirits of his predecessors. Their bones and carcasses lay on adjacent mantel, entombed a long a sinuous passage. Once each year on the mid-winter, the Corserite congregation followed their Abbot, traversed the narrow Northern gorges of the Enorian Peaks and climbed Mnt. Quetheron to hold a communion of the entire order, past and present. It was many months since their last pilgrimage. The packed snow of solstice made the upper climb more arduous; monks had to use their craft to watch for each other and avoid mishap. His current trek was not as grueling, still he looked on to the gentler paths bellow.

He griped the rod of Corser, a four-foot-long staff of gold, iron and hard wood. With his order since the first Ellendei colonization it was rich in Corserite power. The wood from the land of Brahil far to the south, the iron from the hills of Niobia, and, the gold that emblazoned its side from the royal mines deep below Corsinia. We are going to have our work cut out for us old friend, thought the abbot.

His prayer protected him from the strong winds of the ridge top, and with morning he descended into the warmer clime of the Enorian divide. The first bell of prayer rang out dully as he rested above their valley.

From here he could see the small monastery in its entirety. Its outer walls covered in a thick vine that was forever being cut back by the order's novices. Thomas watched as the monks filed silently into the chapel of Enruth, home of the morning song.

The first words spoken each day were the Quenderoth, the blessing of the land. It was said that this prayer had been taught to the first priests of Arieon by Posalymo the water spirit soon after the great cataclysm.

As the ancient words reached his ears Thomas remembered the advice of the ancestors in the cave. Tiron Wateron had been amongst the first of the Ellendie priests to colonize the main land and warned that the Imprisoned One had been here long before mortal man. Even before the Mernnonians ruled Kadra the Great Enemy dwelt here. He knows the ways of beast and mountain, Tiron's spirit had warned, trust in the waters.

For a man who had never traveled on anything more than the Dwarfen barges of Corsinia or the Tratian river boats this was hard to accept. The lake of Lemarr was a daunting enough obstacle for him, the vast oceans of the Ellendei migrations an empty ordeal, a distant memory of his monasteries past, he felt no personal ties with the sea.

Thomas looked at the ground below his feet. If the dark one wanted land he would have to fight for it. Thomas was not going to relinquish that which, they had fought over for ages easily. It was on land he felt comfortable and it was there he was going to stay.

Besides Aerion was surrounded by water and it had not escaped the machinations of the Dark One. It was the ghastly news of its corruption that Thomas was to take north. He for one would trust in the land for a little longer.

As Thomas sat listening, the distant sounds of the Quenderoth intermingled with the whistles of mountain blue birds, the sun finding a gap between thick clouds warmed his cheek. Yes, thought Thomas, our lord still rules the land. Tiron may be wise but I foresee that the heart of man will be easier fodder for the Enemy than these creatures of the One. He stood and stretched, then continued his dissent through the heather toward the birch trees of the valley floor.

It was already late in the afternoon, Thomas sat, his head in his hands, fatigue finding deep crevices in his face. Bardoth De Ghent Presenter of Corser and cousin to Ruik Warder of the White Plains held the floor. Thomas had stressed the need for haste in this matter, but it was Corserite tradition to reach decisions unanimously, and through open discussion, so, the whole monastery sat in the hall of words listening to the thoughts of Bardoth. It was his contention that Thomas should not travel to the north alone, but, with another, and he seemed willing to keep the whole monastery in council for days if he had to. Bardoth had a strong deep voice, and, today it echoed painfully. As the abbeys choral leader Bardoth carried a great deal of influence with the younger monks, it was essential the abbot gain his support, but why was he always so strong headed?

Thomas allowed his eyes to wander around the room resting his chin on an upturned palm. He was tired from his night on the mountain and the prayers of the last few days.

Bardoth continued slowly, he was recounting his early days as a warrior priest among his brother's knights; the goblin wars and the battles with wandering giants. Presumably he was making a case for his own inclusion in the journey north. It was true that the presenter was probably the most skilled warrior among the monks, but it was precisely for this reason that Thomas wished him to stay. If the events of the last weeks were anything to go on, the Corserites would need every able-bodied monk they had. No other had the skill in military tactics of Bardoth De Gent.

"....just as the spirit of the lord speaks though our brother Thomas....the code of war is carried within me.... If he travels alone we risk his discovery by the eyes of our enemies ....It is said that two travelers are less suspicious than one and my sword will dissuade many... thus we may keep our strengths hidden.." He paused, listening to his own echo, then, after making direct and steady contact with his audience, he went on. "For if we call down the might of the lord... the Ellendei will.. talk .....From the innermost Halls of Arien to the villages of the Ridge, spies will twist these stories into their own, turning our works of God!.... into the works of the enemy....The farmers of the Ellendei have become soft and stupid. If we reveal ourselves to them Simmon the snake... chief archbishop of Berelan......... Lord of the inquisition!...defender of the one!" He spat the phrase out with sarcastic contempt. "Will soon have the Corserites excommunicated." He paused again. "We will be outlaws among our own people hung and burnt for Witch- Craft....An outlaw monastery! Is that what we wish to pass?"

The dull afternoon light of the meeting hall was worsening Thomas' fatigue. He rubbed his forehead pushing the hair back off his face, grimacing and opening his eyes wide. Their gaise wandered over columns carved with scenes of the early Ellendei colonization's and the great wizard wars, these formed a natural circle within which Bardoth spoke. Thomas sat, listening, behind a large stone table at one side of the round hall, his monks surrounding him. Marble met the table at each of its short sides, an ancient vein whose source deep below them rooted the table to the bed rock of Mount Quetheron. These four columns depicted the particular history of the Corserites themselves, recording their development from a small cult of studious wanderers, during the migrations of the Ellendei sailors, to the quiet serenity of their present wilderness abbey.

"We must keep a low profile if we are to have any chance in the war that is to come." Bardoth's voice was compelling, he had slowed his speech and the care of his delivery convinced its listeners. "Our friends of the north have warned us for years that powers are moving to the West...... The imprisonment of the enemy has had its toll on the Land... The waters of deep wash have bread corruption since before the time of the wizard wars, and, now Berelan itself!....... If we must travel, let us be armed heavily, and not, rely on defenses that will reveal our true identities".

Bardoth paused momentarily his slow metered tones left a gentle reverberation in the chamber, arms hung loosely at his side. "If I were to accompany our Abbot any trouble could be dispatched with the sword. Our monastery is small and we are few. If the snake discovers we are organizing against him he will destroy us... Our only hope is secrecy, we must hide behind the sword."

Thomas prayed under his breath "Lord give me the strength to see through this day and accomplish the tasks you set for me "He said the prayer in Ellendei avoiding the high speech for the moment. Faith restored energy to his tied body.

If, he had the time to discuss the consultation with the dead, and, the event that had precipitated this journey, with Bardoth alone the present discussion may have been averted. But, private discussions of monastic matters had been frowned on before, and it was not until he had communed with the spirits that he knew who to trust.

The Corserites prided themselves on their open discussion of all issues. When Bardoth had begun his diatribe, two monks were already standing, silently waiting to be heard. They stood sometimes for hours, until their turn to speak finally came. Their stamina heartened the abbot in his exhaustion. While, Bardoth held the floor five more monks had got to their feet. Thomas shook his head; it was going to be a long day. If he stood to speak now many of the monks would sit anxious to hear his words, but, if there was more to be said, as often there was, the discussion would only be lengthened.

Thomas' mind thought more clearly now. He watched as Bardoth concluded the speech and returned to his seat. That large man would certainly be an asset on any journey. There were strong well used muscles behind that lose habit, and the head beneath those short black curls was one of the best military minds the priest had ever met.

The spirit of saint Adrian had been able to tell Thomas that none of his officers were infected with betrayal, this alone, did not rule out the probability that Simmon had friends amongst his order. He trusted Bardoth, Archnold, and Robert. Archnold Thomas' circature was not at the meeting, he was busy investigating the corruption they had found within the visitor from Berelan. Even during his time as a wizard's apprentice, Thomas had never seen anything like it. Some form of parasite, grown, he had little doubt, for a foul, and, hither to unknown purpose. He definitely needed to consult with Archnold as soon as possible. The meeting was going on far too long. What could he do? Unfortunately, he would have to miss evening prayer, again. This was important he simply had to confer with his officers before they wasted more time.

The monk now taking the center was known as Noldarn. He stood straight and walked with a steady stride. A forest elf from the land of Thornbreak, his long gray and silver hair reflected in the cold steal of his eyes. He was the youngest of the nine Corserite elves, although, wise long before Thomas was even born. The saint marveled that such an ancient race still acted foolishly proud on occasion, never the less, Noldarn would make a mighty traveling companion.

His voice lacked the melodic accent of so many of his people. He spoke plainly and to the point. More like a Mernnonian the abbot thought.

"If the illuminated one must make this journey I will accompany him." He paused "Bardoth should not worry I will not be noticed "Noldarn met Thomas' gaze with sparkling gray eyes, smiled, and then, returned to his seat.

Thomas felt thankful, at least the elves were on his side. He was not planing to ask any to accompany the quest, they attracted too much attention, but, at least they were with him.

Frederick Blackhand strode to the center of the hall; the son of Haldrick Blackhand, his grandfather, William Blackhand had been Lord Blackhand baron of Cirwen. However, Frederick had never accepted his place among the Ellendei royalty. His farther, a well known Knight defender of the crown had become a wanderer after Ottar III ascended the Ellendie diadem.

Frederick had learned much from his baron father. Before entering the monastery he had been called Frederick Giant Bane, named for the personnel war he raged against the family of Barrenrock giants that had killed Haldrick. These giants had the unfortunate luck of attacking a wagon train that Frederick and his farther were escorting across the Thornbreak pass. The following fifteen years of Frederick's life had been spent hunting and murdering giants in the wilderness. As the years had passed Frederick's grief cleared and he began to see humanity within the faces of his foe. Leaving his weapons and armor in the wilderness, and after traveling four hundred leagues unarmed, the baron's son found him self at the steps of Corser monastery.

He was now in his 56th year. A tall dark Ellendei with shoulder length hair and a thin beard. He showed little sign of age, exhibiting instead the High Ellendei propensity for long life. Frederick had become a quiet man since he had donned monk's garb. Thomas could not remember the last time he had spoken during council. He stood silently surveying the hall with dark brown eyes. After waiting a number of seconds, he cleared his throat.

"I know the Ellendei of Arraken........ and ...I... have traveled, through the lands west. There is much of the song of Enruth in that land." Frederick paused; he was not used to public speaking. "The land of Thornbreak is deep and dark.......... home of Noldarn and his people.........", a fragile hand pulled a brown wisp out of his face. "The voices of the spirit can be heard in their homes. The empty lands north and south are large and beautiful............. It is the lands of men and the lands of the Deepwash river that are full of the works of the enemy.... We must look within ourselves to find the source of life. It is our own sin that is bringing about these events not an outside force. In our hearts we should fight the devil not in others. If we resort to open warfare, we accept the ways of death.... Let us preach the war of peace to the minions of our...... enemy......"

Frederick stopped talking, the pain of his own guilt evident in the quick movements of his restless eyes.

"What gives us the right to kill ....it is not for a Corserite to judge another soul even if corrupt ..." He pulled the hood of his cloak around his ears and returned to his seat.

Thomas doubted that he would talk more this day.

The next speaker was Sally Seondry, a monk who had originally come to them from the Corsinian town of Khulalan. She shaved her head, as did most of the female Corserites. Her gold within green eyes shined about the hall.

"I too like Frederick believe that violence is no answer. We must protect the sanctuary of our monastery. If the Ellendei are to fall into the snares of the Imprisoned One then there is bound to be war. How can we halt the inevitable. The Ellendei are warlike.... have they ever truly known peace? It is often those who strive to thwart the plans of Enruth that aide his greatest works...It is for us to look to our faith. We must safe-guard the teachings of The One. If there is to be another time of dark then who but the Corserites...will be the memory of light... Let us be that memory. The Corserites survived the long years after the fall of the white lodge and the time of the Wizard kings. We can survive this."

As Sally returned to her seat another monk took her place. And so, it went on throughout the afternoon. Many of the monks preached that passivity and caution were the best strategies, others, that an organization of the forces of Enruth was in order. A small number of the Corserites including Robert of Darkmore, Thomas' sacristan felt a crusade, preached throughout the Northern baronies of Arraken, the answer. They argued that a mobilization of the north would interfere with the spread of the inquisition and act as deterrent to the War of Thornbreak.

The Duke of Drake, Herigar Gunarsson, inheritor of his families title of Dragon Lord kept a standing army of 4000 men with 100's of knights. Heregar laid claim to the elfish land of Thornbreak through, his great grandfather Eorowin Nolkien an faerie lord, that had loved the human princess Enerille Gunarsson. Immortal, Eorowin, was now Arraken's lord chief justice, he and many of his followers distrusted Serderan the faerie king with the Thornbreak elves, trusting instead, the weak-willed mortals that they had little trouble dominating. They supported Herigar in his claim to the throne. Since the Duke's baronies increased his own force by four-fold, Drake was certainly a force to be reckoned with.

At this rate, the council would last well into the next day. Should he stand and speak now? He could perhaps speed their dialogue, but unable to count on Bardoth's support, he may create a divided council that would take days to resolve. It was better to wait, during evening prayer he would meet with his officers. Feeling uneasy about going behind the backs of their brotherhood, and breaking the integrity of open council. The slow murmur of the monastics caught within indecisions reconciled him to his choice. He sighed, following the flow of the central columns up to where they met the buttressed dome of the Hall of song. Fragmented blue, yellow and red beams, broke thorough the seasons grey cast, compounded into a rainbow of light by a ring of stained-glass window. Color's danced on the grey habits as they spoke.

It was evening and Thomas was in his Chambers, a modest divided room, that comprised the top story of a small towered turret, projecting precipitously from the north wall of the monastery. Through its single tall window Thomas could see down the valley to the border woods, along forest of oak and evergreen that crowded the foot hills of Northern Corsinia. The sky was darkening. Sometimes, in the evening, he caught a glimpse of the large bear, Rorouth, he knew its name, as it wandered up to the fir slopes of Corserite mountain. But not tonight, tonight there was no moon and the wind whistled around the tower all seemed bleak, desolate. Thomas shivered involuntarily. Autumn was not the best time to travel.

He closed the shutters and turned stoking his fire till the coal spat flame. When ablaze, he pulled up a stool and warmed himself, patiently waiting for his guests.

As expected Archnold arrived first. The efficient saracen's stern expression told Thomas that he was troubled with what they had discovered. He paced the room slowly thinking to himself. Wrinkles furrowed his brow, flexing as he walked, tufts of gray framing the expressive skin of his head.

They had first noticed strange behaviors in their guest during the second week of his stay. It was unusual that he had been sent at all. The Corserites were considered an eccentric group best ignored, important historically but little more. Since the appointment of Archbishop Simmon as Primate and the restructuring of the church bureaucracy, however, that had changed. Now, Berelan decided to take an interest in the wilderness abbey and its order's Mythological significance. They were to be bought in line with current doctrine.

Thomas and his advisors begrudged the meddling clerics of the south and their attempt to further consolidate liturgical power. Joining the archdiocese of the north, they resisted the Cathedral of Berelan, relying on their own faith over Simmon the Snake's empty pontifications.

The crown traditionally acted to protect the rights of the provinces, or, it had until the Ascension of Ottar the Dandy. Ottar, a forgiving fellow, was a weak king politically, and, with his appointment of Illid Friz Ansculf as the realm's chancellor Simmon's influence had increased. Illid always sided with the primate, favoring a heavy hand in the enforcement of church doctrine, and its strict ban against the free practice of wizardry.

Thomas had been informed by primal decree that a visitor from Berelan was to arrive and observe Corserite practice. The message, delivered by a caravan of dwarf traders on their way to the Derem Gorin Mnts up from Wyre-Wood hold, sighted, an increase in influence of the dark enemy, witchcraft, and the worship of his allies as reasons behind the visit. Thomas chuckled to himself it was not the Corserites who were falling into the snares of the enemy.

It had become increasingly difficult to accept the legitimacy of the Berelan primacy. Simmon, known to the north as the snake, had managed to outlaw the practice of virtually all but his own school of clerical magick's. Claiming that a secret order of deamon worshipers was undermining the sovereignty of the kingdom, he had many innocent Enruth worshipping magicians burnt, maimed and tortured. Pushing a number of laws through Berelan's Crown Hold, its seat of government, he and Illid had tightened the shackles of their tyranny.

The orders of magick that survived the onslaught escaped to the tolerant provinces of the north. The realm's barons were happy for the wealth and technologies that these escapees bought with them, enriching the lands of the less affluent north. Tratia and the West Ridge were now home to many of the ancient guilds and secret societies of Arcane lore. Berelan, no longer the sensuous, cosmopolitan, center of the arts, that, Thomas remembered from his youth, had become an empty bleak, repressive husk. A depressing dark capital. Only Old Berelen, the cities guild hexeture, held any of its well reputed charms.

Fifty years ago, he had walked through the gates of that, teaming city, for the first time, there to study the word magic of Iandiar the Fleet. The charms and delights of Berelan had been a delusion for him, then, the stench of those bitter streets still flamed the inside of his face with memory. Thomas imagined that the smell was all that remained of the wondrous Berelan. It's golden domes and ornately carved frontages stained with the blood of The One, canals choked with the minions of the Snake.

Yes, Sally was right, the Imprisoned One was ever powerful. It pained him to consider the vibrant street life of the capitals markets, crumbling under the empty ritual of the Berelan primacy. The Dandy's complacency had costed. Even during the civil war the crown had shown more presence. Though there had been much debauchery on those streets that did deserve attention, Simmon's clergy had subjugated that which was good, its freedoms, whilst still protecting their own forms of degradation.

"Well, it's all well and good you sitting there dreaming. The spawn of Deep Wash could be amassing north of West Ridge..... for all we know....... or care... by the looks of it. "Archnold stood within the frame of the portal he was obviously tense.

"I examined the corpse, as well you know, and, that thing that came out of it...Uhg I have never been so disgusted....lets see...some kind of crustacean as far as I can tell......It had a hard exoskeleton ..... In side.... it's cavity... was filled with... a tissue ....It ......er...It .... appeared to be a ...brain .....Yes..brain-like...... I had Seletrall look at it ...He, of course, said very little."

Archnold, a stout and restless man, had a short gray beard and white hair that he kept in a tidy pony tail sitting well back of his bald scalp. As he talked he paced back and forth about the small room, his hands dancing eloquently to the sound of his voice.

"Seletrall and I discussed the way it must have used its eight articulated appendages and its mouth in unison to enter the body at the base of the skull...." He touched fingers to the back of his neck and shivered. "In the name of Enruth I've never seen such a thing.... Seletrall said that there was no mention of anything like it amongst the history the Fearie ...and I have certainly never read of anything even remotely similar to it in any of the bestiaries."

Thomas studied Archnold from where he sat.

"Well...... What are we to do?......Oh.. Seletrall noticed these little...... cilia... all over it ....He seemed to think that it could control the thoughts of its host..."

Archnold stopped pacing the room to examine the map of Arraken that covered the rooms interior wall.

"Who knows how many of these things there are out there? Perhaps we have already lost."

"I refuse to believe that!" Thomas snapped, he quickly lowered his voice and continued. "As I announced during open council, I plan to travel north to consult with Aterol Atrolson our Treathbaron. You will be in charge of protecting and running the monastery. When Bardoth gets here we must persuade him to stay here, there is simply no time to discuss these matters in open council and you will need him here to defend the monastery."

"This corruption may cause unneeded conflict." The Saracan, spoke from his final resting place by the fire. "if it be demonic in seed ...we will have time..... the Astral realms move by clocks far slower than our own. I pray this corruption has not bread..."

"You and Seletral will investigate further. Perhaps there is a way to discover whether one of these beasts is inside someone."

A knock interrupted his train of thought.

Robert stepped into the room followed by Bardoth. They wore their brown robes with the hoods thrown back. Robert his usual self, hadn't shaved in a number of days, his eyes flashed with a dark quiet intensity.

Bardoth spoke first, darting between the other Corserites, his steel gray stare revealed that war was something which he was familiar with. "We must mobilize the northern provinces against the Primate of Berelan." He was about to step to the map when Thomas stood in his path.

"We must needs plan the campaign!"

"Yes." replied Thomas "The Ellendei however are best left to themselves. .....Anyway ..I called you here to discuss something far more pressing than the unification of the north... The Treathbaron is far more suited to mobilizing the people than you or I." He placed a hand on Bardoth's shoulder.

"As you know, before I left to the Council of the dead I was attacked by the primal emissary. A number of our brotherhood had noticed unusual behavior in Stephen of Niobia.... so I chose to question him on matters of the faith. As our debate intensified, he attacked me with a concealed blade. Thankfully..... the will of our Lord was with me... I defeated him." There was sadness in Thomas' voice. All this you know, what you don't know is that there was something living inside the villain. A form of parasite."

"Archnold and Seletral have been studying its carcass. Apparently, it could control the thoughts of its host. It seems likely that these things reproduce and infect new bodies. The emissary was with us for a little over three weeks before he attacked. We must consider the possibility that more of these beasts are among us."

"I do not know what the creature has to do with the corruption of the Clergy, but, its presence does not bode well." He turned to Bardoth. "I must hold council with the Treathbaron and quickly. We will carry the news of this north. If war is the answer, although, I pray that it is not, Aterol is the only one who can legitimately question the authority of the Arraken crown. And we all Know that the high king Ottar the Dandy is Simmon's puppet. Could it be that our realm is governed by such beasts?"

"So, I find myself undermining our open council and talking to you privately." He gave Robert a hard look." I feel that the parasite should be kept secret and in lew of the seriousness of this problem.... I should not travel with you Bardoth." The abbot leveled his silent question with his gaze. "Although under less extreme circumstances I would."

"I will travel with one of the younger monks. You three are all needed here... Bardoth you must get word to your cousin and organize a defense of the monastery."

Bardoth nodded slowly, he was readjusting to Thomas' words.

"Archenold will be in charge of the monastery. Robert you will work with the Keepers to protect our northern lands from the enemy. Tomorrow, if we all support the same plan, council will conclude early, and, I will be on my way. If not, we could be delayed here for days."

Thomas examined the worn faces before him. Their life in the mountains was hard. Many creatures of Darkness had made this wilderness their home and the thought of war was nothing new to the monks. Even Robert of Darkmore looked serious.

"I am tired and I must sleep, if we are all in agreement I can leave tomorrow after council."

Robert and Bardoth nodded while Archnold scratched his head and tried to smile in agreement.

Council ended early the next day and Thomas managed to depart before mid-morning prayer. He and his companion Eothan the fair, a Norcadian warrior who joined the Corserites after the distruction of his clan, had made good time traveling from the north Enorien peaks well into Border wood. Eothan Thomas knew well as he was often called on when the Corserites needed a scout or mountaineer. He was a hunter and tracker for his Norcadian clan. Following his path finding, they moved quickly, they should reach the ruins of the Karash-Yan before dark.

Karash-Yan was the Norcadian name for an ancient temple that stood in the center of the forested Corsinian boarder lands. Built by the Kadron's, a people who populated the lands of Arraken before Thomas' ancestors had colonized the shores of Daquin. The Yan gently influenced the land about it.

To the south its builders' descendants ruled the north west province of Mernnon from an impregnable mountainous citadel, still worshipping and building shrines to their many deities as they had done for countless generations. Far less populous than the Ellendei, a powerful Pedocracy united the race, protecting the faith of their gods, and ruling through a series of traditional laws. The house of Maub, the Mernnonian family of princes, represented the barony within the Ellendei feudal structure.

For half a league about the ancient temple tall lush grass created a fertile field within the woods. Travelers often rested beneath the Yan's soothing marble columns, where an air of peace had stayed many a broadsword. It was said among Eothan's people that no blood could be spilled within the field of Karash-Yan.

Thomas hoped they were right. If things were as bad as he expected, anything could happen. Corsinia was a wild place, controlled by dwafen barons who had pledged their fealty to the Arraken crown during the wizard wars. Settlements were sparse and brigandry rampant.

The baron of Corsinia, Rand Lakedwellar, an efficient and honorable Ellendei knight, spent most of his time lording the royal mint, leaving the policing of his barony to his predominantly dwafen vassals. In spite of their self-proclaimed vigilance, smugglers controlled much of Corsinia's ruggedly mountainous terrain, apparently with the active consent of these same vassals. Secret societies had many save houses tucked away in the inaccessible wilderness. The Dwarfen sub lords were ever happy to base friendship on gifts of gold and silver.

Thomas did not fear the arm of the primal bureaucracy as far north as Corsinia. Clergy had little influence among its interracial populations, that worshipped Kadran, and Derem Gorin gods, alongside, their lord Enruth. It was more ancient and subversive groups, the secret government of Ellendei devil worship, the Kingdom of Wicca, for instance, that Thomas feared most.

Eothan stopped suddenly, he crouched examining the ground in front of him.

"This trail has been traveled recently." he said. "Looks like armored goblin Kin.... Twenty.... Hobgoblins from Enoria, if they are of Gour Gareth's tribe then they too will observe the peace of Karash-Yan."

Thomas prayed that they hailed from Gour Gareth, all he wanted now, was a bloody confrontation with warlike goblins. During his early days at the monastery many monks had been killed by hordes of Kalthrek Trolbrand a mighty goblin king. Thomas had been a young man at that time and was forced to kill a number of goblin soldiers himself. War continued until the Norcadians caught Kalthreck and a band of his goblins in the Enorian pass. The northern clansman impaled Kalthrek on cold iron, butchering scores of his smaller kin, and leaving their carcasses for the mighty Enorian buzzards.

More recently, a large tribe of these hobgoblins had migrated from the south. They worshipped a lord, or God they named Gour Gareth. Thankfully, the group was less warlike than their smaller cousins. Indeed, Thomas' brethren had managed to convert some of Garath's hobgoblins to the worship of Enruth, at least, so it seemed.

"How far from the Temple are we?"

"Not far .... half a league. "Eothan spoke over his shoulder.

"Good if we can talk to the goblin people we will." Thomas inhaled the damp sent of the forest. "They may have news of the north."

In silence they continued, the trail heading west and then turning toward the north. There were no pine or spruce, as there had been on the lower slopes of Corserite mountain. They were on flatter ground, now, the boughs still held to their leaves; the colors of late autumn had not yet taken hold. There was bushy wide-reaching oak and tall elm and roan, then along a drainage the white truck of birch. He detected a thinning of the trees and more bush and shrub spouted up where light was able to reach the forest floor.

"We are nearing the edge of Karash-Yan. "Eothan beckoned, crouched low and ran off the trail. Thomas followed. They ran from tree to tree until they reached the edge of the wood. From there they could see the Yan. A large marble and stone building less than half a league from where they stood. By stooping and crawling they approached, concealed behind the long grasses.

Hobgoblins were sitting on the steps in front, and, moving shadowed within the dark of the cool stone. Large and man-like, wearing chain mail shirts and open-faced bassinets; the silver of their metal, bright against the dark hair and cloth that covered their hides.

At the base of the Yan, they had built a pyre and were busy roasting animals. The smell of which reached the hidden monks. Hobs each stood as tall as an Ellendei but stepped heavier, with a stooped gate, their long arms, as thick around as Thomas' legs, hung to their thighs.

"If they are of Gour Gareths tribe they will honor the peace of the Yan"

Thomas wished the words true; he didn't fear these creatures, he needed information. If they chose not to trust the monks it would be hard to learn anything. Thomas decided not to leave it to fate.

"Qudrall etherol nondrelleth cantor nellindon im uon nosh ethek.... The High Ellendei words felt thick on Thomas' tongue. "......... Imtesh toaken Yar-em eth. Meneth nantok......."

The Rod Corser was warm beneath his hands. A light of silver and white flickered under his fingers. Traveling up his arm it disappeared into his chest. Thomas inhaled; he felt power. The light of Enruth was in his eyes, twinkling. He spoke the rest of the prayer under his breath.

When finished Thomas turned to Eothan.

"Follow me." he said. His soft compelling voice hard to refuse.

Standing, a halo of silver and white formed around his form. From his eyes it radiated out. Slowly, he walked towards the hobgoblins. Calm serenity radiating out. It was hard for Eothan to keep from laughing, a broad smile covered his face, as if peace had become a tangible and immutable presence in the air about them, he was happy.

As they approached the group the hobgoblins hurried to their weapons.

"Halt and identify your purpose" growled a large hob from the steps. The Ellendei common was spoke with thick accent, the words obviously difficult for his canined, forward protruding mouth.

"Put down your weapons we come in peace. "Although, foreign to these creatures, they understood his every word.

The hobgoblins looked around in bewilderment.

"Spell slinger, watch 'im "shouted another in their low guttural mother tongue. A hobgoblin near the fire, pulled a heavy ax over his shoulder and readied to throw.

"Wait my friends" continued Thomas "We bring you the comfort of Enruth, the One. "Thomas held his left hand flat out in front of him.

Their large war contoured faces softened with the touch of his eyes.

"Friend you" muttered the closest hobgoblin as he lay down a large notched two-handed sword.

"That is right" replied Thomas. He continued "I am Thomas, Abbot of the Corserites. We would speak to you of the north."

"We know of you "It was the hobgoblin from the steps of the temple who spoke.

"Gour Garath smiles on your work among us. I am Roeck chief of Yareck peak .....come we will speak. You have the golden eye; you will talk truth. Come.

Roeck motioned for Thomas to approach the temple.

As the hobgoblins returned to their fire, Thomas spoke to Eothan.

"Stay with the others, tell them of the One and the songs of the land."

Eothan nodded in agreement. He had seen Thomas' effect on the hobgoblins, their happy hearts would be open to words of peace.

From within the temple, the tall iron-clad leader beckoned Thomas to follow. He stepped beneath the cool granite roof of the Yan as the hob spoke in a deep low voice.

"A new sorcerer walks among us. He orders our shaman as if they were his slaves. Talchaus of the Ourth stood against him." Roeck's whisper betrayed the characteristic rasp of his people; his talk slow, dark eyes carried the decisiveness of a great warrior.

"As leader of the Ourth, Talchaus challenged the sorcerer's kin right. Soon Talchaus became sick and stupid. We bought him to this place for healing. "

Roeck motioned toward an altar at the back of the temple.

Behind a large marble block stood the dull tarnished statue of the temple's goddess. Her serpentine body stretched around the back wall entwining the Yan within her constricting length. Eight outstretched arms each carried a sprig of spring growth. She smiled benevolent from beneath a weathered crown.

The hobgoblin shaman lay on the floor his feet pointing toward the statue. His eyes were open and periodically he blinked. With each breath, his lips curled back exposing a set of formidable teeth. Thomas noticed the lose leather loin cloth so common among the priests of Gour Garath. Their shaman refused to ware clothing, instead protecting themselves with charms of bone and rock enchanted and then bound into their thick hair protecting them from harm. Judging by the number of enchantments about his body Talchus was a powerful in his craft.

"What happened? "Asked Thomas "How did this condition develop?" He knelt beside Talchaus examining the shaman's eyes. They focused on an unknown point, imperceptibly fluttering.

"After challenging the sorcerers kin-right Talchaus became silent. He ate little at the evening kill. The blessing of our meat was weak. Over many days he spoke less........ until three nights ago he spoke no more. The power of the sorcerer grows among us. If he halts the tongues of our priests, what can we do? Ireg nak uyo yarll! "Roek cursed in his own language. "I will eat the enemy of my kin's heart "He translated the curse roughly, under his breath, for Thomas' benefit.

Thomas put his hands on the shaman's shaggy chest. They rose and fell with each inhalation. Meditating he cleared his thoughts in an attempt to hear Talchaus' mind. Monk and shaman began to breath in unison. Thomas grunted, synchronized to rhythms that came from the humanoid. Then he found the reason for the affliction, something consumed and occupied Talchus' intellect. The shaman's brain was working overtime, solving, and resolving successive thoughts, that swamped the conscious mind. A never ending puzzle that became forever more complex just as the solution was reached. That which seemed the end, was merely, a forever more complex, penultimate, conclusion, to an ever expanding puzzle.

Feeling his own mind being consumed by the same thoughts, he pulled his hands away from the shaman's body and scanned the inside of the temple. As he did so his bearings returned. That was close, he thought.

"The shamans mind has been coaxed into an extra dimensional vortex of some kind. He no longer sees the world around him, but is trapped within the quasi reality of your sorcerer's spell."

"To save him we must undo its fabric..... "Thomas thought for a moment. We can alter the spell but we cannot negate it. If we introduced the ideas of another powerful reality into the reality of the spell's own universe, we should draw his soul into a different fate. One located in our reality. At present the universe of the spell is drawing him towards death, the land beyond. .... a fate you wish to forestall."

"With the grace of our lord, and, the blessing of the Yan's growth spirit, we can fuse the fabric of this spell with the fortunes that Enruth and the temple deamoness foresee.........In theory it will work at least."

Thomas held the rod of Corser by the middle of its shaft and placed it to his forehead. Silver light flooded the temple, echoing between marble and granite, flickering upon the crown of the life serpent, reflected in eye gems.

Eothan and the others climbed towards it, casting deep shadows in the gathering evening shade that reached out into the rays, flooding the field of the Yan. Happy was he that the light of the One shined freely, without, rising the suspicion of their enemies. In the populated lands of Arraken the miracles of saint Thomas would have to be more subtle.

As the light flashed and dwindled, it sparkled back golden from the eyes of the goddess.

The darkness had been lifted from the shaman. He blinked, his pupils moving erratically around the inside of the temple, they came to rest, finally, on Thomas.

"A spell of the realm of Illusion I believe "Thomas offered as explanation. He seemed almost surprised that his prayer had worked." I myself know some sorcery."

A heave relaxed his body. "I studied it during my youth."

The great brows of the hobgoblin furrowed and a hiss escaped between its sharp teeth.

"you are .... our ...kin. "

It was hard for the shaman to speak, but nevertheless, Thomas felt power behind the blessing.

He repeated "..you do the work...of Gour Garath among us......we are kin."

Thomas saw understanding in Talchous' gray browned eyes. "The Ouroth is yours." Thomas replied

"You know our customs Corserite?" The leader asked. He stood at the edge of the alter surveying the field of Karash-Yan.

"The dark peoples of the Under Mountains are restless ....." he paused searching for the words. "The shadow of sorcery walks among us and ....the names of the ancient master are once again spoken ....How are the princes Arraken and the soft fleshed kin fairing in these times?"

He turned a puzzled look toward the abbot that softened with understanding from the abbot.

"Signs of the ancient enemy can be seen among the Ellendei "He acknowledged.

The hobgoblin worried. The great protuberances of his forehead quivered with tension, a weary fear, as that of a strong force pressured into final action. His prognesive face flexed, into a canined grimace, and air escaped through his clenched teeth.

"Come let us return to the fire. I would talk further on this." Thomas patted him reassuringly on the shoulder.

Eothan slept as Thomas and the Hobgoblin discussed the peoples of the north, the Traition Lands, Corsinia and the Tribe Clans of the Lands Beneath with their complicated treaties and feuds. As Thomas had feared, the Imprisoned One's influence was everywhere. Ancient treaties from before the times of the Wizard Kings had been reestablished. Once more, an Under Mountain hierarchy, that established ruling races and slaves, with the worship of the Imprisoned One, had come to be. The tenuous peace of Arraken looked doubtful. Thomas could only hope that some of the goblin peoples would resist the ancient vows of the Imprisoned One and stay with their own gods, as this group had.

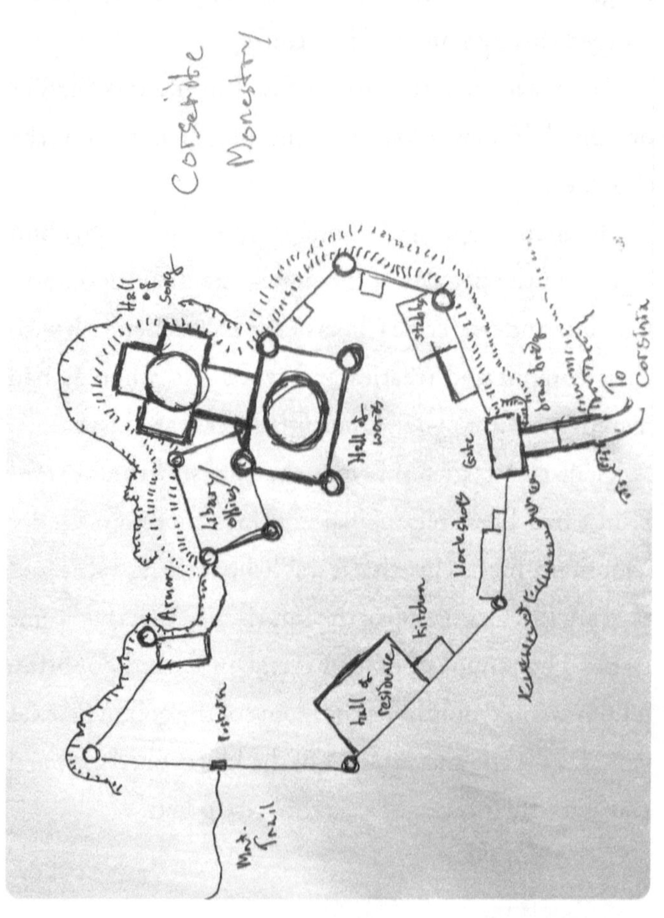

Corselithe Monastery
Hall
Song
Library/offices
Hall of words
Armory/
Chapel
Workshop
Gate
draw bridge
To Corsinia
Kitchen
hall &
residence
Kennels
cistern
Mnt.
Trail

CHAPTER 2

CORSINIA

It had been two days since they left the safety of Karash-Yan for the rugged land of Corsinia. The saint wore his plain habit covered by a wool cloak tight against the cold, Eothan, the traditional skin and fur of his people. They had made good time, traveling against a thick drizzle that blew up the valley of the Mourn. Thomas used his craft sparingly, doing little more than keep himself and his companion warm against the approaching winter.

Eothan the Fair moved in front bobbing between brambles as he found a way down the steep mountain gorge. He jumped lightly from side to side pausing, only fleetingly, to choose the path of least resistance. He carried a moderate spear which he relied on as a walking staff or stick, point upward, he pushed the base it in front, holding his weight at times as he controlled his descent. The easy agility of his descent belied his size. Over a hand and two paces, he was among the tallest and largest of the brotherhood. He carried his wooden shield slung over his back, a light strong rope hung at his waist, and his long sword was wrapped and packed along with bow and quiver. Thomas remembered the day of the youth's initiation ceremony five years earlier. He had worn animal skin, then, accepting the faith with a cold sincerity that had reminded the Abbot of his own initiation into the sorceress society of Iandiar the fleet.

The muscles of the barbarian tightened, as, he jumped from bolder to bolder. Thomas marveled that such a huge man could move so quickly. It was all the abbot could do to keep up with the youth.

The previous night they had camped at the edge of Border Woods and had spent the next day following animal trails up the slopes of mount Brelldia. By evening they reached the high pass that led down into the valley Mourn, their gateway to Corsinia and the King's highroad.

Thomas still felt stiff from the unforgiving rock of their lofty bed. Earlier in the morning, during a break in the steady drizzle, they had climbed swiftly down into the valley.

The head streams of the Mourn, swelled by Autumn rains, bounded and crashed beside Thomas as he struggled after the acolyte. He hoped he could keep up the pace, if so, they would reach Wyre Wood hold by late that evening. From there they were to travel down river, deep into the Kingdom of Arraken and then to procure horses, or a Tration longboat for the trip north.

Eothan disappeared momentarily, obscured by the deep undergrowth of the stream bank.

"I've found a trail of some kind." His voice came back clearly from the thicket.

Thomas stopped and approached slowly one hand grasping the rod of the Corserites. The hawthorn and brambles pulled at his cloak as he pushed through, against their tearing snarls.

The trail took a perpendicular turn, at this point, to run parallel to the stream. Eothan had already begun to follow.

"Wild boar, "he said over his shoulder, as, he stooped under, yet, another thicket.

Judging by the size of the hole the Boars stood as tall as a man. Not the small domestic boars they keep at Wyre Wood Hold, but giant feral boar.

They followed quickly and quietly, hesitating, to listen for sounds. In case they disturbed the trails patrons, Eothan unslung a long wooden spear from a back pouch and carried it poised on his shoulder.

The trail was smooth and easy to follow. By midday they had traveled out of the mountains into the deep forest of North Corsinia. The trial, still visible but far less pronounced in the scant undergrowth of the deep forest. At times it would branch winding back and forth between the hills on the north and the river on the south. They avoided the paths that lead to the impassable thickness, choosing instead a way less cluttered and over grown. Eothan catalogued changes in the trail, declaring that he saw Dwarfen tracks here and human tracks there. Apparently, they were getting closer to Arraken as, the evidence for boar thinned out.

They kept up the pace till lunch, stopping to eat bread and cheese beside a large fallen oak. The sweet seasoned smell of their faire attracted the attentions of an old badger hunting for grubs in the bark beneath the rotting oak. He gave them a gruff unfriendly glance, and thinking they were hunters, retreated to his den. While they ate, Thomas spoke soothingly to this old forest native in the tongue of beasts. Within a fraction of a glass, they had persuaded him to join their meal outside.

Eothan watched as Thomas questioned the badger concerning rain, the early winter, grubs, and, finally, when they got around to it, forest traffic. Apparently dwarfen and human woodsmen used the trail frequently, perhaps as much as once a day, but animals were by far the most common travelers. With fox and wolf, the primary concern of the badger.

"Best when 'em boar's round see..t' wolf..they say right away then....Much more deer on, path then....... Yea" Said badger.

To Eothan his talk consisted mostly of low barks and gruff grunts. The tracker was careful to note the speech's structure. Being familiar with the language of bears and wolves, he forever longed to learn more forest dialects. All animals conversed in the generally known forest speech, yet they, each possessed such strong individual accents, that, unless they intended, it was impossible for all but the most fluent to understand them. Being unversed in the dialect of badger, Eothan contented himself studying its cadences.

After lunch, they continued west, with Eothan, again setting a fast pace. Responding to the change in terrain, Eothan had unpacked bow and sword locating them on his belt and shoulder. He still carried his spear. The forest rolled from oak to elm and beech and back to oak. Individual trees old and large allowed little light to filter down through their ancient canopy. The undergrowth which was sparse, on the floor below their expanse, involved little more than a scattering of fern and grass in the occasional clearing.

The earlier yellowing leaves of rare horse chestnuts stood out within the green. As the Corserites walked on, Thomas began listening to the voices of forest birds.

Though hard they were to see, their chatter filled the air, flitting between the branches, busily preparing for the coming winter. The many furiously squabbling voices, each seeking its own ends, mad in discord. Distracting. At times the sound appeared deafening, as, he attempted to translate its drastic intensity.

The first warning of impending danger was their sudden, abrupt silence.

Eothan half way across a small wet clearing, before, he could as much as shout a warning.

It was upon them.

With the speed and accuracy of an eagle, the beast, swooped down from above the trees north of the clearing, bellowing loudly as it came.

The ground beneath their feet shook with its growl.

Eothan leaped desperately trying to roll out of the way as two great lion-like claws dove towards him. His warrior training, saved him from the monster's impact, the grass cushioned his role.

Thomas watched as the monster, now standing on damp grass, lunged at Eothan with its head. A massive canined jaw, that's empty bite cracked sharply about. Its front half resembled a giant lion, while, its hind quarters that of a goat. Two huge wings grew from behind its fore shoulders and a billowing main told that its sex was male. Wind gusts from the wings blew past the Saints ears.

The two giant wings beat the ground hard as its head lunged for Eothan again. He managed to dodge. But, as the beast's maw snapped shut, its head crashed into his back, sending him flying.

This time, his wrist twisted painfully as he hit the ground, yet, he managed to continue the roll, ending back on his feet. He still gripped the shaft of his spear, remaining crouched, he prepared.

"Querator Kouthak Queoar "Thomas spoke the words as quickly as he could, the ancient rod of his order transforming in his hands.

Caught between the creature's wing and jaws the barbarian monk found no escape. Instead, attacked; Swinging to his feet he thrust the spear towards his foe's head.

The goat like back legs scrambled for footing on the wet grass. It let out another roar, then, its head, readied, lunging for him again.

Thomas, running, echoed the roar, hoping to divert its attention. Monster and saint vied for the very air about them, the sound rang his ears, straining at his throat.

Transforming! The rod Corser, became, Der Aaeth, the heavy dealer, flail-staff of Saint Thomas the young, cold, prepared, it was in his hands.

Eothan deflected the bite with his spear, the point digging into flesh of its far side jowl. The weapon's shaft caught in its maw. Mighty jaws closed splintering the weapons wooden length.

Seeing his foe distracted! The Norcaidian ducked and leaped towards its underbelly drawing his dagger. This keen Dwarf blade would cut deep.

He stretched upwards, as the beast rose on a strong flap of its wing, missing its underbelly. Two heavy talons strafed the warriors back. He staggered, managing to save himself from falling. Pain sheared throughout his body, threatening his conscious mind with blackness.

Beside the brute now, Thomas brandished Der Aaeth, preparing a flail swipe.

Their enemy was quick, three strong beats propelled it out of reach. As it continued to rise Thomas got a good look at its hind quarters. The back legs, and hind quarters were, those of a giant goat, but it had the long spiny tail of a dragon or wurm. Climbing out of the clearing it began a banking turn to the south.

"We are sitting ducks in this clearing."

Eothan nodded, swiftly changed the grip on his weapon, and threw it after the retreating underbelly of the beast. Hitting it pierced the inside of one of the goat legs, there it stayed, venting blood.

Eothan dropped to his Knees, blood gushing from the deep wound in his back. Pumping, viscous red awashed his thick firs. Ignoring the pain, he bit his teeth, and stumbling pulled his long sword from its scabbard.

Thomas reached him and knelt examining the damage. Hardened Norcaidian leather had been sliced to ribbons, shredded about the warriors back, dark red blood blackened the Saint's hands.

"The Chimera is returning," The warrior monk muttered. ".... I.. I see flame ."

Thomas placed the pommel of his flail against Eothan's back and prayed for the bleeding to stop.

"....... We must ..." the Norcaidian choked. Thomas could feel Eothan losing consciousness, he had lost a lot of blood.

Glancing up he watched as the Chimera transversed a long arch in the air. The air around it rippled hazily with a self emulating heat, like sun on the desert.

sand.

The Abbot prayed for protection as the beast bore down on them. Sitting ducks! Their only projectile weapon, Eothan's spear, lay shattered at their feet. Claws were stretched out in front of it, massive wings folded at its side, all its weight focused behind its two lion talons, the red and gold of flame crackled around the outside of its body.

Stepping in front of Eothan to take the blow Thomas gripped his flail with both hands. The bleeding had stopped and staggering Eothan tried to stand, leaning heavily on his sword.

Der Aaeth radiated a dull defiant white.

Suddenly the chimera's head wiped to the side and it let out a below of pain, a large iron spear lodged deep in its neck. Reeling in the air it cut off its dive, searching the forest at the clearing's far end, for its new foe.

Thomas grabbed his acolyte's shoulders, hastily dragging him toward the trees, away from the crashing branches behind them.

As they reached the edge of the wood, he turned to see the chimera battling amongst the distant trees. It was hard to tell, but, their new alley did not look human. Too large. Returning to his patient, he guided Eothan in amongst the Oaken trunks. Then, clutching Der Aeth he headed toward the fight.

Running, he followed bellows, snarls, and growls of pain. Catching sight of it, between oak stumps, wings beating resoundedly as it again took to the air. A second wound visible along its flank, a long gash, stained its light brown hide red, where the lion and goat quarters met.

The massive face contorted in anger, rising above the forest in a bellow. It was hurt, but, not mortally. Its lion head looked around with surprisingly human eyed anger. Then with two wing beats it disappeared to the north . Toward a lair high up in one of the neighboring mountains, Thomas suspected, from there, it could nurse its wounds whilst it watched the entire valley for prey.

He had seen chimera before, both wild in the wilderness north of the Abby, and in captivity, with, the old wizards of Berelan. The Chronicles of the Corserites recorded a mighty Chimera named Belerophon, who, had the head of a fire breathing dragon, a goat and a lion. Three headed it was, one of the creations of Wizard King Ergedh.

Responsible for the untimely death of Lemion first protector of the Arraken knighthood, the beast had finally been dispatched by a Corserite brother Orean. Orean had anointed the Ellendei's first Treathbaron, Torelle Atrolson soon thereafter.

The wizard pet from his youth had been nothing in comparison to their present enemy, a mere five paces in length and, its entire body, that, of a lion. Still, at the time even this small specimen had frightened the young Thomas.

The Chimera that had attacked, had like the Berelan pet, only one head, that of a lion, but it was big, about ten paces in length. Corserite scriptures were full of references to these and many other fell beasts.

Thomas remembered transcribing an account written before the migration. It traced the lineage of all malignant creatures, beginning with the known spirits of the Devil, the Dark-One, the primeval Archeaon spirits, their transformation to the Fallen Angeles, and, then, following their decent through many lineages, and generations, to the earth bound beasts and monsters, that now plagued mankind. He did not know whether that ancient priest's manuscript had been accurate, but it did give the explorer an idea of what to expect. It's sections pertaining to Deamon lore were well known for their reliability. So much so that precautions to prevent theft by would be deamon worshipers had to be taken.

When, he was sure the Chimera would not return, he ventured out into the clearing, looking for the warrior who had saved them. All he found were crushed and broken branches. No one was to be seen. The battle had left obvious marks, but no victor.

He called a number of times into the wood, and after, getting no reply, he returned to Eothan the Fair. The Norcadian could decipher the traces of the battle, better than he.

He found him, leaning against the trunk of an oak. Alert, he moved easier, having recovered somewhat. The prayer had stopped his bleeding, filling the deep gashes in his back with a soothing white energy, knitting together the wound. They would have to be dressed properly, but that could wait. The two monk's tangible faith in the One, bound his severed tissues, affording his body the time it needed to heal.

The young monk rose and walked the clearing, he stopped here and there. Twice he lay to the ground and smelt the earth. On reaching the trees, he crouched and placed his hand to the soil, feeling its deep cold moistness.

"Our savior was alone....... A large man. "He sniffed.

"A mighty warrior indeed, to battle a chimera single handed."

"Yes..." Eothan walked in amongst the trees, his eyes darting along the ground as he went. "

"He left this way............" he paused looking closer. "He walks without shoes but the prints are that of a man not goblin-kin."

Thomas followed as they tracked their benefactor further into the forest. The trail eventually led them to one of the boar paths. Eothan trailed the prints till they were lost, covered by those of the boar.

"Too many boar....... I can not tell one from the other....I am sorry Lord Abbot." He again sniffed the air. "....A whole heard must have passed through here since the battle. "he spoke slowly and again examined the trail. "The ground is wet its secrets read easily...."

"The heard numbers twenty, "he continued "Giant mountain boar....enough to feed the monastery for months."

He stood continuing to walk, scanning for prints. They hadn't seen the sun at all today, the sky remaining dark and overcast. Under the trees, the dense oak and hawthorn added to the dullness creating an environment of near night. Last years, rotting leaf fall smelt rich, earthy, a softness underfoot, its loam a rich bed. A renewed steady pattering around, told them of ensuing rain.

"No use........ I see no man tracks "Eothan spoke softly. "He either left the trail or his tracks have been erased by the passing of the boar."

"Perhaps he used magic." Thomas looked up into the canopy above their heads. Clouds, visible through the thick colorful net of autumn touched leaves. The rain continued to grow in strength. Large leafy droplets of clean northern water felt good in his dry mouth.

"Possible." Eothan grunted in reply.

They turned, and continued to follow the boar trail as it meandered back toward the river. Steadily, the rain grew into a down poor that clattered amongst the foliage wetting them. Thomas' magic kept in the dryness and warmth, but the ground became slippery, mushed, signs harder to detect. Soon water pooled, frustrating, Eothan no end. Slowed, their pace became a crawl.

"Forget ...the task "Thomas said reassuringly. "As long as we reach Wyre Wood by tonight, I will be happy." Thomas patted Eothan's massive shoulder and in silence they walked on. The Abbot had never known him to lose a quarry and choosing their destination over a methodical hunt they continued the trek.

It was many hours later when they finally caught sight of Wyre-Wood Hold. A welcoming light through the trees. Night had crept upon them as they walked; the dark of the forest becoming the night. At one time, they had both seen lights toward the hills, but, knowing it not to be the hold they pressed on.

Finally, they emerged from the forest and crossed a muddy pasture land toward the village's outer rampart. Thomas heard the faint sound of Dwarfen music. They made their way past pens of pig farmers, to a gap in the long wooden stockade, the timber construction protected the up-river side of the town. Guarding the gap were two stout Dwarfen warriors in chain-mail hauberks that reached to their knees.

They wore their beards unbraided, in front of their armor, as was the custom amongst Corsinian dwarves.

Wirery tufts that reached to their leather belts.

"Halt 'ow goes there" said one of the guards as he poked a long halberd toward the intruders.

"We are travelers "Thomas said, as he spoke he drew energy from the Corserite rod.

"We are safe you need not fear us. Quelderoth Naren Tor. We come in peace."

Eothan felt the same easiness he had felt before at Karash-Yan, this time it was less pronounced.

"Yea all right ye seem safe, in yea go then. "The guard gestured over his shoulder toward the hold.

Thomas and Eothan filed passed into the village. A collection of small wood and rock houses scattered about the inside wall of the stockade. Beyond these, and, across an open grass common sat a small church. Behind the church tower a dark stone outer wall of the hold itself shined with the faint light of the villagers' hearths. Through a large gate house they could see the interior keep, a sturdy round granite structure. It shadowed the small tower of the church, allowing its masters a vantage point overlooking the entire village. Doors were wide open, music, fire light, and the smell of burning pig filled the stockade. Resisting the pull of the tower, the food and warmth it offered, Eothan followed Thomas toward the river.

Next to the docks they found a small barge station and the house of Beoran Sterwight. Beoran, an aged dwarf, had been a friend of Saint Thomas for the last fifty years. The descendent of Derem Gorin mountain dwarves his ancestors had migrated to Corsinia after its annexation into Arraken one thousand years ago. The Derem Gorin dwarves were longer lived than their Corsinian cousins, their kings were known to live for up to five centuries.

Beoran had begun to show signs of age, a graying in his enormous unrestrained beard. Thomas guessed him to be about two hundred or so.

As barge guild representative of Wyre-Wood, Beoran Sterwight carried a certain amount of prestige in the village. Unlike many Dwarves he was married and had children. Meramere, his wife, a Corsinian dwarf, was a well known and accomplished herbalist. Her family had been in Wyre-Wood for generations vassaled to the lords of Wyre-Wood hold, the Strongbows.

The Sterwight home had the reputation of being the largest and best provisioned residence in the village. Built out of a smooth gray stone quarried up stream, it sat close to the bank of the Mourn. On the hold side it sported a small, diverse garden of bush and flower, colorful. The brush added a background of green, the flower's a vivid glory.

A climbing rose crested the door and covered half the front wall. Two white blooms blossomed among red to greet weary travelers.

It was Meramerei who answered the door.

"Yes, who is it who calls so late, and on such a dark night." She peered from behind the large iron reinforced wood, her blue eyes twinkling in the light of the house.

"You know me Meramerei, "replied Thomas . "I am Thomas . We are Corserite monks. It has been long in the reckoning of man but I did not think that your people forgot so quickly."

"Oh farther Thomas, is that you? Come in father... Oh.. and your friend. Beoran is in the study, I'll get him. You can wait in here by the hearth "she gestured for them to enter the kitchen of the small house. It was hard for them to stand up straight in the hall way, but being tired they quickly obeyed.

"No it has not been long really, not if you think about it." She said as she scurried off down the hall in search of her husband.

The ceiling in the kitchen was thankfully high enough for them to stand erect. Corsinian dwarves had to build to accommodate humanity. Although, they constantly complained about the draft that the added height caused. Thomas had heard from some of his brethren's northern wanderers that the strong holds of Derem Gorin dwarves were not so spacious.

There was a fire smoldering in the hearth, and, the gentle tart smell of coal intermingled, with, the aroma of fresh bread welcoming the monks. Eothan crossed the room and knelt before the fire warming his hands. A thick stew slowly bubbled above his head. The aroma grumbled his empty stomach.

Thomas stepped to the kitchens low wooden table, and surveyed the many fine crafted cupboards. He smiled. It had been far too long since he had visited these friends, he thought.

"Is that you .....you old god peddler ." The deep gruff voice filled the room. Beoran stood at the door way his hands resting on his hips.

"It's about time you drug yourself into town. I thought the mountains had swallowed you up."

The two friends exchanged a long glance.

"And who's this, a barbarian monk by the looks of him....I thought the Norcaidians had their own gods."

"Yes, well we have managed to attract some to the worship of Enruth. "Thomas smiled.

"Haven't you heard that the Ellendei god will drain your heart and coffers... bare!" Beoran chided playfully, as he shook Eothan's arm. "He has here at least...."

Thomas raised his hand to silence the protest he could see beneath the warriors brow.

"You know as well as I Beoran that the primate and King do not speak the will of Enruth. It is they that take your taxes, not I. The pope of Aricia is old and has little support within the feudal halls of the Arraken."

"All I Know is that our taxes go up every year. And the Chapel priest has begun to talk of forbidding unsanctioned magic...... Unsanctioned magic...umph... Next thing you know, we'll hear of unsanctioned worship ....I tell you my friend ..all this talk of the one god ..your priests are trying to take our gods from us." While he spoke Beoran pored three large mugs of dark ale that he quickly handed around.

"Derril's men delight in harassing the traditional dwarves.." he went on.".. they see anything from the north as a threat to their lordship." He raised his mug.

"To your hearth and home."

"Things are bad everywhere my friend. I fear that the deceits of the old enemies are again working themselves among us." Thomas took a hearty swig of his brew, deep and nutty, not a bit like the honey mead of the monastery.

"What about me old hart ... do I get forgotten in my own house." Merimere spoke as she scampered from the door to the table, a mug out in front. Beoran shrugged to his guests and turned to fill her a mug.

"Now tell us how the monastery fairs." Merimere said politely happily looking at the top of her mug, and its cresting head. Then she examined her guests faces.

"I hope he hasn't been grumbling..........He has hasn't he?..."

"I was just bringing our esteemed friend up to date on the political environment of Arraken Merei.... The difficulties we entrepreneurs are forced to face these days. But don't worry I'm going to the pantry now to get some bread and cheese for Saint Thomas and his companion. I'm sure a bowl of stew will do them some right good just now."

Eothan nodded with hunger as Beoarn left the room, gruffly chuckling to himself.

"Of course he's right, times are bad, but we should say hello before we start solving the woes of our village, don't you think. Now tell me have the leaves of the upper Mourn turned yet and who is this tall golden haired friend of yours. Not an Ellendei, surely, but some barbarian?" She looked for an answer in Eothan's face nodding to her self as she did so. "A Norcaidian perhaps?

Female dwarves were rare, males being the most common of their people. Three out of every four dwarf children were born male and since most dwarfs favored their vocations over personal relationships this suited them. That is not to say they were loners, quite the contrary in fact, Dwarves loved ruckus and revelry. They merely preferred to put their time and energy into careers, not families.

The few women, there were, commanded a high status within society, not only were their particular careers deemed important, but any family aspirations that they should have were to be venerated by the males they chose as mates. Dwarf husbands and their male relatives were expected to shoulder a great deal of the burden of the household, this ensured that the wives' trades did not suffer. Honor, also, very important to Dwarves increased with the profession of the mother, the single most important measure of a Dwarfen family's esteem.

Not to say that Dwarfen society was harmonious, far from it, a proud race they were prone to feuding and strife. The practice of slavery on their kindred races, was common, in particularly against Gnomes. Dwarfish cities of the Derem Gorin mountains each kept a colony of imprisoned gnomes, that, executed the cities less honorable tasks. Outlawed in the Arraken's principality of Corsinia slavery was not condoned, although the kingdom's more tyrannical barons treated their vassals and serfs as slaves. Indeed, most of the Corsinian dwarves would be treated as little more than slaves if they themselves should travel north. Derem Goria did not look kindly on foreigners of any race.

The norm in Arraken was feudal servitude, this, in many parts of the kingdom was a form of slavery itself. Feudal life had changed much since the early oath of the Arraken wizard foes, for a greater part the traditional reciprocity of lord to vassal still remained but, the respect for common citizenry, liveried, or free, had disappeared, altogether. Only to the North were Arraken's barons still trustworthy. The king was all the common people of the south could look to for justice and his agents made the most of it, playing the poor against the barons for their own profit. Some of the local liturgical courts were truthful and fair, but the closer you got to Berelan the less that was the case.

The Sterwights, being freemen, honored the traditions of their own people without racism. And, as syndic for the barger's guild in Wyre-Wood. Beoran kept a number of friends and co-workers who were gnomes. Allendweselldar, the forgotten, the most note-worthy of these, something the traditional dwarfs of Derem Goria would not approve of.

Allendweselldar, who had grown up in the Pinnacle of Parnasuss, the former strong hold of one of the great wizard kings, acted as the guilds scribe and accountant. The Gnomes of the Pinnacle had delved deep into its secrets and grown proficient in Parnassuss' arts. Its many vaults and catacombs were filled with all manner of arcane lore. Having learned from their many years of torture and servitude at the hands of the great mage, they now used his magick to protect their own people, unifying them against threats of slavery from Derem Goria.

Allendweseldar, himself, had been known to cast a spell or two at times, especially at parties. Beoran's most trusted friend and advisor, he was often invited to the Sterwights for tea and companionship. Beoran, unlike his friend, frowned on frivolous magic, and the two argued long and hard on the subject. Most of the village longed for the pyrotechnic displays and illusions that Allendweseldar could conjure, so, there was ample opportunity for their discourse to air.

It was not until Eothan had explained his whole history, the death of his family at the hands of a rival Norcaidian clan, his journey and adoption by the monastery, and after Beoran had served the guests two bowls of stew and a number of ales, that, Meramere finally let the conversation drift toward the worrying matters of the present.

"So." Began farther Thomas, his voice signaled a change in mood." Your priest is curtailing magic..... the precepts of Simmon the Snake travel far north these days. Must Rand Lake-dweller capitulate to Berelan or does he still receive orders from the Red Towers?"

Merimerei broke the short silence." Oh... he's much the same as ever, from what I hear. He openly defends the rights of his vassals and the free peoples of Corsinia to practice religions as they see fit. Of course Witch Craft and the worship of the Dark One is strictly forbidden, as it always has bin."

"The best defense against the great deceiver is wizardry and worship," interrupted Beoran. "If we are all free to explore the arcane arts then we are less likely to be controlled and seduced by its powers."

"Your local vicar preaches against the use of magic completely? "Thomas asked.

"Yea.. that is right...... He started t'other month..So I hear .....We used to go to church every week when old farther Richard was vicar but he's been dead well on forty years now. He was a good sort ...was Richard .....talked about the spirit moving in everything... Often mentioned our deities and the ancestral spirits from which they grew. Now all you get is a bunch of pig swill. All this talk of the One God and the importance of a strong church ....more like a political speech than a sermon. It's that Simmon's doing. He's rewriting Ellendei history taking out all references to the many manifestations of the spirit of Enruth and replacing them with this vindictive One god. The Ellendei peasants are far to short lived to know the difference but take it from me I've seen t' changes with me own eyes.......Why in my youth I remember Ellendei priests openly preached the words of Chorack Gar and some of the other non-human deities...They saw them as all part of the same force moving the land, but, not today I tell yea."

"There are many ways to interpret Ellendei scripture," Thomas conceded. "The church of Berelan is far more interested in consolidating power than in embodying the Lord's spirit." Thomas shifted forward, his hand swept in a small arch suspending itself in the air.

"Enruth called the world into being, his spirits soon descended from the heavens to work their will on its surface. There were many battles with the enemy and many peoples and races were born and died. Over time these spirits changed, became the gods and deities that we now know and worship. They adapted to the world they found, forged by it. But it is the will of Enruth, the one who was before all, he conceiver of creation's dance, that fills our beings with light and life energy."

"According to Ellendei tradition it is believed that the dark enemy was born of the darkness within the soul of the world itself. That he was here in the land before the spirits of Enruth descended, and was carried with our early ancestors on the ships of the Exodus. The Elf, however, claim that he was the great deceiver, a spirit born of Enruth, who, turned against his creator, appearing in the land to thwart and pervert the work of his master."

"Be that is as it may, the machinations of corruption and strife are alive among the teachings of the high church of Berelan." Thomas paused and added almost to himself. "I can feel it."

"Well, there's not a lot that Beoran and I can do about that farther." Merimerie shook her head and looked worried." Beoran says we must not attract attention... what being foreigners and so on. No we need to maintain our stature in the village."

"Yes, you mustn't worry, nor do I expect help, the church is very powerful and solving its problems, has nothing to do with you. Friends, we would simply like a place to sleep the night and friendly faces with which to exchange the gossip of Arraken. I will be the last to ask you to get involved in Ellendei affairs. But if not too great a burden, perhaps, you could find us passage on one of your southern bound barges."

"That would be easy enough to arrange. "It was Beoran who spoke. "I'll talk to Allendweselldar in the morning, he should have a barge leaving in the next day or so." Beoran scratched his beard in thought and then went on. "But what do you intend to do? Surely you cannot expect to change the primacy single handily. And what of these chivalric orders ...they are barbaric... I've heard say, that if Ottar was a stronger king t' church wouldn't have all this power."

"No, the problem is far more serious than that. Many southern orders of knighthood pledge themselves directly to the primate, and, Ottar needs the church's support to keep his own vassals in line. I plan to travel north to speak with Atrol Atrolson Treathbaron of the Ellendei. There is more to these acts of liturgical aggression than meet the eye. As overseer of the Nobel courts the Treathbaron will know what is to be done. It is he that has the power to challenge the king. If the Ellendei keep to their oaths all will be well."

Thomas leaned back in his chair stretching his legs. He was tired from the already long journey. His eyes sunken deep lines in his face made him look his age.

Eothan spoke for the first time since he had told the story of his past. "Farther Thomas should be in bed."

"Yes, we shouldn't keep you young fellows up so late." Beoran chortled. "I'll prepare your beds." And with that he stood and left the small room.

Eothan and Thomas were given beds in the eastern corner of the house. Shuttered windows opened toward the river; they could see the barge house with its small dock. Thomas chose the bed by the door. Beoran had said, that this particular room was the only one with beds large enough for their taller friends and as he drifted out of consciousness Thomas recalled the comfortable familiarity of its bed's downy, firm softness from an earlier stay.

Eothan sat by the window for a while watching the river from this second story vantage point. His mind wandered through the barbarian villages of his early childhood. The moon, already high in the sky, cast a silver sheen on the river, reflecting the forests beyond. Close to full, it lit the night with its half-light. His breath floated in the early autumn air. A long time passed before he finally turned from the night and made his way to bed.

Thomas thought he was mistaken, but, the sound came again. A dull thud. He blinked his eyes against the darkness and slowly turned toward the window. The shutters were open and against the night he saw two silhouetted figures moving toward the beds. Then he caught sight of a tint of steal. Assassins!!

Thomas rolled away from the first lunge and toward Der Aaeth. At about the same time a shout from the other bed, told him that Eothan had been hit.

The blow meant for Thomas buried harmlessly in the night sheets. He pulled Der Aaeth up to swing, as he jumped out of bed toward the door.

The assassin leaped across the bed at him.

Thomas dodged sideways turning the momentum of his movement into a sweeping blow with the Heavy Dealer.

The assassin, attempting to regain his footing after his leap, was quickly caught in the head and neck. He let out a deep groan and fell to the floor near Thomas' feet.

Thomas stepped over the body and ran naked across the room toward Eothan. The second assassin was already escaping through the window.

He knelt beside Eothan. His body awash with blood. Multiple stab wounds had turned his chest into a mass of flesh and bones. The saint would have to work fast if he was to save his friends life. Thomas placed his hands above and below the wounds and preyed. His breath had ceased and yet Thomas could feel that Eothan's spirit had not yet departed.

"Stay with me my friend." He spoke. Then he began the prayer" Qui

In Dereth Kall mouk nan dindedran. Am nickral shack Quidneral shwaderin shoook Falbreien. I call thee back from the edge of the dark kingdom, for yours is not the time to sleep."

Thomas stopped Eothan's bleeding and patched the gashes in his chest with the white energy of their mutual faith. Then he placed his hands gently over the wounds and coaxed Eothan's body back to breath.

"Breath." he repeated to himself.

The barbarian convulsed and went limp, then he exhaled with an audible breath that erupted from the bottom of his lungs.

"Relax ," Thomas soothed. "You've been through a shock....We were attacked by assassins........ Sleep." And with that he stumbled back toward his own bed. Picking up Der Aeth, on the way, it transformed, becoming the rod of the Corserites. Tired from his miracle he draw energy, as had many predecessors before him, from the rod Querature, gardian of his order.

Succored, he searched the room. The space at which the assassin fell was bare. Where had his body gone? Worried for their hosts he looked to the door. It was still closed, and there was a faint smell of sulfur in the air. Thomas focused, praying to Enruth for clear and truthful sight. He scanned the room to see if the intruder had become invisible, finding nothing.

The assassin had most likely escaped using a gate, or teleport spell. The sorcery had left the smell, thaumaturgy or cabalism perhaps?

Thomas pulled a small leather pouch from the bundle of cloths at the foot of his bed and began to pace. He loosened the draw strings, sprinkling a fine gray powder around the room's perimeter. It sparkled gold and blue within silver as it floated in the moon lit night.

As he muttered the ancient words of the incantation, he remembered his boyhood amongst the wizards of Berelan. Eddies within the dust caught his eye, and, the feint crisp touch the magic bought to his nose, sent his mind reeling into the past. His master had taught him this Kadron ritual of protection after the completion of an important errand.

Thomas remembered that difficult trek well. From the main kingdom of Arraken over the western pass, to the great Asserenn Gate. From there he had traveled through the Elfen forest of Thornbreak and across the Platered Hills, a region filled with the serpent spawn of the great drake, and into the Fairy forest known as Hervan Mierel. Within Hervan Mierel, he consulted with astrologer Gordel Erandill concerning an item of power, that, his master was to build.

His Highness Gordel, great grand uncle to Ottar, was considered the greatest astrologer of the land. It was he wizards consulted before the constitution of any enchanted devices. It was traditional, if not, compulsory to get the renowned astrologers advise before starting any major work of magic. Like men, major magical devices of power lived and breathed, recycled their energy with the ebb and flow of sun and moon. As such, knowing the sign and aspect of the item's birth was an obligation to fate, a necessity before their construction. To forego such advice tempted disaster.

An items final enchantment, its synthesis, was completely impossible unless its particular fortune was researched. This step of manufacture would ensure some success in the final product. Thomas' master not wanting certain failure had sent his apprentice far to gain the advice of the reclusive astrologer.

Gordel lived in a modest tower within a small keep. Hervan Mieral broke into rolling hills around his home, peopled with fairies, little people and their kin. Thomas liked the place and passed a number of weeks waiting for the peerless star sorcerer to complete his research and agree to meet.

Their conference had been mostly technical talk, Thomas taking copious notes, but, near the end of the meeting Gordel had pushed back his large brimmed hat, and, peered probingly over his reading spectacles, and said, "You're not to be a Wizard you know......No my boy.....Your fate lies far closer to the word.......But, I must not give away secrets must I."

At the time, Thomas had been upset by the astrologer's presumptiveness. What had the little fellow meant? But, on the way back through Thornbreak he picked up the writings of the monk Corser and unknowingly began his life of worship.

Now he stood in the center of the room finishing the rare Kadren phrases of the ritual he had been taught so long ago. Gordel had been right of course, and standing, now practicing magic the astrologer's words came back ever more poignantly. What was to be their monasteries fate? Would it be the Saint's doom to be the last Corserite

Abbot? He knew not. Perhaps, he would meet Gordel, again, one day.

Beads of sweat had collected beneath his eyes, and in the crevice of his naked back. Thomas was tired from the ordeal and the incantation. He panted into the night. Having no time to reach the rod of Corser, he had used his own energy to heal Eothan.

He let out a deep sigh, and walking to the bed he laid down. The spell would protect them till morning then they would leave on a barge, quickly. The saint had not expected so much trouble. And so soon. Were their foes Corsinian, or had Simmon more allies than he had expected?

The rain had stopped for the time being, and Thomas stood close to Eothan warming them both. The barbarian was alive but, leaned heavily on a staff they had borrowed from Beoran, his insides ached and moving was difficult. He held a thick bear skin tight about his shoulders and neck. Considering he had almost died the night before he showed great fortitude. At this rate his full fighting capabilities would return within a few days. Of course, the damage to his chest, the flesh and bones, would take a month or more to heal, but the power of the spell would keep him together till then.

It was a cold day even for autumn and the early morning light was further muted by a thick bank of clouds. Beoran and his advisor Allendweselldar the Forgotten were busy seeing that the barge was in order.

The guild had not planned on shipping down river for another day or two, but, as top official for Wyre-Wood, Beoran had changed the plans. He and his assistant watched as cargo was loaded aboard by human and Dwarfen dock workers. Allendweseldar kept track of the goods in a large leather-bound book. He sat near the gang plank, the ledger nestled on his knees, a faint, yellow, green light floating above illuminated the pages in the early twilight.

He had the characteristically long nose of his race and his hair, red, and, voluminous, marked him as a Gnome, from the Pinnacle of Parnassus. Thomas marveled at the amount of that hair. Although, tied back and beneath a hooded cloak it still threatened Allendweselldar's vision. The Gnomes of the pinnacle invariably wore their hair free, in vibrant contrast to the tightly bound style of the Dwarfs.

As Thomas held the Rod of Corser and watched this jolly fellow doing his job, the gnomes features began to shift before his eyes. The nose becoming more petite and the wrinkled skin smoother. Thomas turned away and looked down stream toward a point where the Mourn disappeared amongst the forest. Then he looked back to Allendweseldar.

He saw two images that of Allendweseldar a middle-aged male gnome and more clearly now as he concentrated the figure of a young female gnome with the same curly red hair. Allendweseldar was an illusion projected as some form of disguise.

Thomas wondered who this Gnome woman was and why she lived in disguise. She was young for a Gnome, and, must be important to possess such powerful magic. Thomas was impressed, it took intelligence to wield thamaturgey so convincingly.

As he stopped concentrating the image of Allendwesseldar the guild advisor returned.

"We have it all loaded now. "He spoke in a clear high voice.

Allendweseldar left via the short gang plank as the crew unmoored the barge. When they were under way, Thomas took Eothan below deck. Comforting, to feel the water moving beneath them. If all went well, they should reach Widern by early tomorrow. From Widern coach, horses or Tration long boat, all made the trip north to the Karonkacks in only a matter of days. The passage through the mountains north to Darkmore took a full month, or more.

Thomas hoped to travel quickly through the lands of men and get into the wilderness as soon as possible. The latest developments told him that his enemies were closer, and, more numerous, than expected. If, Berelan had spies in the Wild lands of Corsinia, the populated lands of the Ellendei princes would be at least as dangerous.

Pulled down stream by a large barge guild stallion, they moved silently on.

Wyre-Wood Hold

CHAPTER 3

CALOR MANOR

The hold of the barge was spacious, designed with the simple practicality of Ellendei craftsmanship. Equipped with a steel strong box, protecting the load's more precious items. Luxurious firs from Northern Corsinia, Dwarfen trinkets of great value, the rare metals the region was famous for, all lay hidden securely behind padlocks and iron.

Around about lay bulkier goods, goods that could not be carried in the open air, with, skin protected Corsinian timber. It was here that the bargers carried whares acquired from the Derem-Gorin mnt. Dwarves; ornate furniture, silver utensils, for, the rich markets of Niobia and Berelan. Outlawed for the bargers, or any of the other guild, to trade in weaponry there was, nevertheless, a thriving illegal market for Dwarf built arms and armor throughout the kingdom.

Within the hold, near the back, adjoining the keel, three rooms provided comfort for the crew and any passengers. Here, Thomas guided Eothan to one of the bunks and examined his wound.

The cavities in his chest were large but the prayer had worked well, there was no bleeding. A pool of yellow white filled in the mangled flesh providing a matrix built from faith, allowing Eothan's tissues time to rejuvenate.

"I feel well. "He said.

"Better rest all the same. "replied Thomas. "It will take time for your body to grew back. You are strong but even the mighty must rest. "

And with that he cast another spell from his old days as a wizards apprentice. A spell of the spoken word, a spell of sleep. It took time to cast the spell, which, he knew only in Dragon Tongue, a thick and clumsy language for people to speak. He remembered each symbolic gesture and word, being sure there was no mistake. By the time he had finished, its guttural and rasped consonants, Eothan snored deeply. Patched together with a number of the Saints prayers already, there was nothing Thomas could do to aide him with any further injuries, not without the time his body needed to heal.

Thomas turned and made his way into the barger's kitchen, and, sat at its small table. He reflected on their pleit. If the stories were true, Berelan had changed much since his youth. It worried him that their enemies had struck so suddenly. He expected trouble only in the south, if at all. Now vigilance would be their key.

A steady patter on the roof above told of the returning rain. He was familiar with Corsinia, its unpredictable weather, and the fierce independence of its people. Traffic should be steady this time of year, merchants and farmers busily finishing their barter, before, the onslaught of winter.

Corsinian winters were known to be harsh, the rain turning to snow with little warning. Last year Kululan lake had frozen deep and many of its indigenous fish had died. This year's early rain promised more of the same.

More snow. More death!

Darkmore, their destination was inhospitable in the height of summer, its winters legendary in their severity. He felt time passing, it worried him. They needed to get through the passes before this month passed. Their northern trip, dangerous enough, was soon to become impossible.

"May the winter treat us kindly, as is thy will" he offered.

If free to use normal means of transportation, Thomas had hoped to leave the kingdom by the end of the week. After last night, he presumed the stage coach lines and the Tration long boats would be watched. Safer to avoid the population centers, he thought. Perhaps a longer route?

Yes!

Thomas remembered rightly, a distant relative of the king, and, a vassal to lord Wirkael Ciradan owned a keep north of Widern. Finding horses there, they could travel by back roads through the Tration Lands. A longer route, but their trail would be far harder to follow.

In a large wooden chest on the floor next to the food cabinets Thomas found a map of the Corsinian barge routes. There was indeed a manor, about, three leagues north of Widern and on the Traition side of the river.

Wirkael Ciradan, Marquis of the Traition lands, was a well-known adversary of the Berelan clergy. A staunch advocate of freedom. He refused to outlaw the practice of magick as primal edict warranted and looked to the bishops of Geldron and Toulon, for spiritual guidance, not the corrupt ministry of Simmon the snake.

The Ciradan's, a Nobel Ellendei family from the time of the great alliance, would certainly follow the word of the Treathbaron. Customs of honor and knight hood coursed deep in their veins; Thomas looked forward to reaching the safety of Wirkael's demesne.

Corsinia was a wild boarder land full of brigands and cults, its people indifferent or openly hostile to the machinations of Berelan. There was no telling what connections Enruth's enemies had with the thriving Corsinian underworld, if last night was anything to go on, they were extensive. Best keep undercover until the bargeman dropped them off in Traitia. No sojourns ashore. Although independent, Corsinia was far too corrupt a place to trust.

Thomas put away the map and went up on deck to find the barge master. The stout old dwarf was behind the wheel, two human companions sat close repairing the harness, and ropes to be used on the return journey. Corsinian barges traveled down river with the current to be drug up stream by massive barge ox. These beasts were born, raised, and, housed outside the town of Widern. A pleasant, if he remembered rightly, free, town of rivermen.

"There's been a change in our plan," began Thomas. "We wish to be dropped at Cheston Manor inside Traitia."

The barge master studied him and scratched his beard. "Please ye self. "he said. Then after a pause he added, "Widern be a nice town...lots o'pubs an' that ...... Cheston only village........Don't smell of Ox though." His slow brown eyes went back to the river.

The Mourn had widened out considerably since its birth in the mountains above the monastery, it's water reflecting green and calm, not the crystal clear rocky bottomed mountain course that they had followed a day earlier. Slowly navigating a series of bends, the dwarf kept the barge close to the north-west bank, compensating for the river's increased flow. Thomas counted numerous submerged and inundated trees. At times the banks had crumbled, the river overflowing and swamping small strips of the narrow valley. Forested hills rose sharply on either side, disappearing into a low cloud. Visibility now only as far as the next bend. The vapors closed in framing the swollen river in a blanket of mist. The steady motion of its water moved ever on.

Spotting the surface of its water, the steady Corsinian drizzle made the day seem long and dark. Thomas stayed above deck for a while and watched as the wild land drifted past. The road that followed the opposite bank was high, built well out of the way of the rising waters. Accommodating the barge ox, for, its long up stream trek, the guilds livelihood depended on its maintenance. When no stops were scheduled, it took only a day and half to reach Widern. The upstream trip was considerably longer, taking the greater part of a week, dependent on oxen and availability.

As Thomas watched he noticed a lone rider on a brown pony slowly making their way toward Wyre-Wood Hold. The horse was tied, but made better time than would an ox.

".....hear things are getting ugly down south." It was the barge master who spoke. His eyes gleamed dully reflecting the hazel waters.

"Yes, if one believes the rumors." Thomas answered. "But the will of the Ellendei has always been strong."

"'ear they burn all 'ho does as much as mention magick.... On'y people allowed to cast a spell is t' priests of Enruth. "His eyes settled on the abbots cloth.

"We do not all follow the precepts of Berelan."

"Yea, 'at's good t' ear..... don't care much up ere none fer em priests any 'ow, present compni' cepted... Tell ye the truth primal edict's bin good fo' trade...All these spell slingers movin' away from Berelan ...'n that.... they bought a lot of business with 'em. A rich bunch ye know."

The barge keeper fell silent again. Listening, Thomas heard the rhythm of the ancient river, in his speech. After some time, he ventured his question.

"Have you noticed an increase in brigandry over the last year or so?" venturing the question, the saint pulled up his hood against the rain.

".. always 'ad brigandry on river..." He replied.".... an' a lot more on it an all..." Accept for his pipe the dwarf remained quiet. The saint watched until the rain reached through his habit to the skin, then, tiring of the Corsinian gloom, he climbed down into the hold and slept.

There was a practical wisdom to the rustic Corsinian.

By the time Thomas awoke the barge had stopped. Eothan sat at the table, looking much healthier, he concentrated silently. The saint presumed he was listening to noises outside the cabin. Adept at the laws of hunting and trapping, Eothan knew the minor magicks associated with forest law. He projected his ear, hearing distance, sounds, as if, close at hand.

"We have stopped at Silver Stone Wash." he said." Goods are being unloaded for Kululan..... fir and Derem-Gorin brandy."

"Making good time?" Thomas spoke, pulling himself up to his elbow.

"Yes..... It's dark but not late..... We will reach Widern tomorrow."

Thomas stretched, his arms were sore from last nights skirmish. I haven't fought in some time he thought.

"We must talk.... Since we have enemies abroad, we will avoid common forms of transport.......I asked the bargeman to drop us off at Cheston Manor. From there we can travel by back road."

"Our path was to the north." The young warrior monk shook his head. He was not at ease among Civilized people. They were far too deceitful. Besides, after last night, their chances were better in the wilderness than here amongst treachery.

"How long till we are underway?"

"The master is readying the barge, the others loading goods....... we will be gone....when they finish."

As Eothan relayed the events, Thomas found some food in the cabinets. They ate quickly and quietly, each man lost in his thoughts.

Soon the barge got under way. Thomas took out Der Aeth, and, knelling, they prayed. Eothan repeating the saint's familiar phrases in his head.

"Que' ethal lenderi ....."

"Enruth "replied the warrior.

They sat for a while in silence, before, Eothan left his abbot to join the crew on deck. Finding the men playing dice near a small can fire he drew his sword, and, settling down into the darkness against the barge-rail, he sharpened the blade. The red glow lit their ruddy faces, while, a lantern, illuminated the boards and cabin between them.

"Ye owe me another copper", They grunted, exchanged coins then continued the game noiselessly.

Eothan leaned against the rail, by the smell of the wet, earthen, river bank Eothan knew that it had not rained since early afternoon. It was a mild night for Corsina, the clouds had kept down the days heat. Relaxing he could hear the men cursing to each other.

"They sound like Gour warriors," he said to himself. The smell of their brazier and the sent of their clothing reminded him of the hobgoblins at the Yan.

The men soon stopped dicing, and, instead, began telling stories. They talked of the great cities to the south, the markets and concubines of Thaine, the lizard people of Torcassa and the exploits and intrigues of the Ellendei royalty.

So many people, thought Eothan, how could they tell each other apart. By chance, they did not wish to? hiding from each other in their sheer numbers?

Most of the names were unfamiliar. He recognized the King's, Ottar the Dandy. These Corsinians gave him the more friendly title of Ottar the Forgiving. To them, obviously, a protector from the Primates inquisition. Thomas had once told Eothan that the Northern Ellendei were much more resistant to the precepts of Berelan than their southern relatives. It was the Northern Knights who still held to the oaths made during the war against the Wizard Kings. This bias reflected in the stories told on the boat to pass the time. They denigrated the Dragon Lord, Duke Heragar Gunarson for consorting with hell spawn, and, claiming lordship over Thornbreak.

Arguing, they boasted of Aterol's and Wirkael's swordsmanship, declaring, finally, the Treathbaron to be the greatest warrior of the kingdom.

"Ottar may be king, but Aterol Aterolson is Treathbaron." They would say, then share a draught of wine. The dwarf keel's man kept to himself, steering the barge.

Eothan watched the night as it drifted passed. The tall pinnacle of Chazebel peak and the metal rich valley of Kulalan, were shapes in the dark moonless night. The royal mint, was only a day's march up the vale from where, a single watch tower over looked the river, a testament to Rand's watchful eye. Brother to Illid Ansculf, Rand, did not share his brother's love for primate Simmon's authority.

Within the dark night the brown and white crevices of thick cloud above, were lit by the hidden moon. The men slowly settled into a peaceable silence, leaving their thick ale as the only reason to speak.

In the distance, the lights of a settlement twinkled into view. From conversations at Silver Wash, he knew the next village to be a place called Calor. Around a distant opposite bend, its lights came steadily closer. Then Eothan noticed a dark shape moving toward them on the river, far closer to them, a wooden boat of some kind.

He kept an eye on it while he walked toward the barge master. At this distance it was hard to tell, but it looked to be manned by dwarves or some other small humanoids. He crossed behind the bargemaster stringing his bow. This time I will be ready for trouble, he thought.

"Sir there is a boat off to our right."

Just as he spoke a voice hailed from the night.

"Ahoy there ......barge men ! "went the shout. "Ahoy there!"

The boat, propelled by four dwarfish oarsman, headed to intercept the barge. In its prow stood a short creature, dwarf like, but, shorter than most dwarfs and broader too. It was this creature who shouted, cupping its long spindly hands around a shrill resonate voice.

"Ahoy!!" It cut through the night.

As they drifted in closer, Eothan noticed its wide face, and leathery folded skin. More goblin than dwarf, its mouth revealed a set of sharp pointed teeth, smiling broadly.

"Merklings ." The barge master hissed under his breath. "Dirty li'le creatures... a lot petty trade around 'ere..they do... remind me a' cunning muskrats.. 'ave to trade with 'em..Ye know...'cause somes of their friends is fairies see....an if we don't keep em 'appy we get bad luck."

"Are those dwarfs with them?"

"Oh yea... Probably thugs frum t' streets a Kulalan.... Be careful these things drive a hard bargain."

"I will not trade with them." replied Eothan. He kept his arrow notched, playing with the tension, as he, eyed the approaching boat suspiciously.

"We have many fine beads and pelts." the merkling lilted when he got closer, the rise in his voice an invitation to trade.

Tying up the wheel, the barge master went to the side of the boat to meet them.

A flash of yellow and orange, lit the boats, and, the Merkling with two of his assistants, dwarves, floated toward and over the barge's side. Bowing deeply, they paused in midair. There hands and arms swept out and down in gratuitous gestures of greeting, coming to rest on the timbers near the master and his passenger.

The Merkling wore a red and blue cloak. Its large eyes blinked almost lizard like darting to and throw around the boat, they rested on Eothan, momentarily, then, jumped to the barge master where they stayed affixed.

"We have many things to show you." He giggled as he reached into a hidden pocket to pull forth a small stool and writing book. Although, small, both, items were too large to be concealed within the robe. The Merkling must be carrying an extrademensinonal space, thought Eothan, sorcery of some power.

He watched as the dwarf and merkling haggled, occasionally it produced articles out the thin air. Usually small replicas of the product being discussed, Eothan was not sure if they were real or illusory. A forked tongue flashed around its mouth punctuating speech.

Nodding expectantly, the two barge workers joined the haggling, Yelping, when they saw an item of interest. Their ale flushed faces beamed, and laughed at the merkling's pyrotechnic display.

Then the murkling's images began to change quicker and quicker. Eothan saw objects within objects. A cornucopia of wares. Soon he found himself caught up in them. Their constant shifting, interchanging. They began spiraling, changing colors. Vibrating as they metamorphed: A multicolored spiraling rainbow, that, suddenly, filled the expanse of his vision.......

When he awoke his head was spinning, as after images plagued his vision, he blinked, and, shook his head, opening his eyes again to find himself starring at the floor boards. Thrown to the side, the barge had tilted sharply, loud cracking sounds echoed about.

The hull was ripping apart, the mourn dragging them down stream along the bank. They were beached, trapped by water pressure, as, the swift current steadily crushed the craft. Boards and planks were split up and thrown outward under relentless momentum.

Eothan looked toward the wheel.

There was no sign of the Merkling nor his guards, but next to the fallen figures of the dwarf and one of the men, Eothan saw a new figure in a lose dark robe. Crouched with back toward him it examined the bodies. He looked around for a weapon, but, both his bow and sword were missing, a pang of loss shot through his stomach as he vowed under his breath to recover them. With him since his youth, he would not part from them easily.

He rose to his knees, silently creeping toward the intruder.

The figure stood, from crouch and began to turn. It wore no shoes.

Another shudder ran through the barge and they both staggered, Eothan recovering quickly launched an attack from behind. He grabbed the figure over the neck and arm and twisted to the ground flipping its body over as he went.

The move worked perfectly and he ended up on the intruders chest pinning them to the floor. His arms went instinctively to the neck.

The young Corserite found himself starring into the face of an Ellendei woman, he guessed her to be in her twenties. Accept for her open robe she wore no clothing. Her body was large for a woman and her muscled shoulders told him of her strength, very solid. He felt two large thighs beneath his legs. She was still, and had yet to struggle.

Nudity did not bother him, it was a thing Norcadians were familiar with, but, it seemed strange in an Ellendei, which, her dark straight hair and angled features showed her to be.

"Who are you!" He said.

She met his stare with soft deep brown eyes, blinked three times, and, before he could speak, smashed him in the side of the face with a blow from her left fist. He reeled sideways to the deck. Rarely had he been hit so hard by a berserk, even. She must be must be a demon, to carry such strength, he thought. Not mortal at all.

Amongst his tribe there were women warriors but none as strong as this.

The deck was now at a steep angle and Eothan's role stopped against the barge's gun whale. He rubbed his jaw and shook himself out of a concussion.

As the woman moved toward, him her torso stretched and widened transforming as it did so. She became a beast, metamorphosing. Her neck thickened growing hair and large tusks erupted from her mouth, as, her jaw protruded outward.

"My name is Taresa." she said. Her voice gravely, more a husky grunt. "I am a subject of the kings."

Besides her appearance, there was something friendly about her.

"Who are you? "She trotted and stumbled to where Eothan lay.

A shape changer, he thought, perhaps a priestess. Eothan had met shape changers, before, and, knowing how self-willed they were, he was glad that this one was vassaled to the king. Not an alley of Simmon's at least.

He rolled to a sitting position.

"I am a Corserite monk." he replied." He could see now why she wore only the robe. It could accommodate the change.

The boar Teresa was much bulkier than her Ellendei counterpart. Her arms had become cloven hoofs and her large breasts had shrunk into her torso to become teats, barely visible. Hair covered her body. The robe that was once lose now stretched snugly about her front legs and shoulders. A strange tunic for the beast that she now appeared to be.

She looked him up and down with what were now wild boar eyes, a snort accompanied flaring nostrils. She assessed the Northan's monks scent.

"My farther said there were two of you." she grunted.

"Thomas! "Exclaimed Eothan. The wereboar was not aggressive, so, he stood and clambered, frantically, toward the hold. Tarese followed on cloven hoofs.

"I already checked below." she said.

Eothan ignored her and climbed quickly down the ladder. He found it, already, partially full of water. The barge was at a steep angle and had sprung leaks. He swam against his clothing across to the sleeping quarters. Here, in the cabins, there was less water, and, Eothan was able to stride at ease. He found no trace of farther Thomas nor Der Aeth, there was a faint odor, perhaps burned gas or sulfur.

Sorcery again.

There had been magick down here! and recently too! He cursed himself for being so stupid about the Merkling, why, hadn't he impaled it with an arrow, when he had the chance?

Worried, he climbed back to the ladder. As he climbed out, he looked for signs of what had happened. Without Thomas, there was no mission. Would he have to return to the monastery alone? How could he explain himself? A hollow in his stomach filled, threatening his mind with memories from the loss of his family. I could return to Norcadia.

Alone again, he pulled himself back out of the hold; the barge was still sinking as the mourn drug it into its depths. Cracked and popping about him, it scraped between bank and flow, more pressurized timber erupted from the deck.

Looking over the steeply angled barge to the shore, Eothan saw Teresa, the boar standing on the bank among the bodies of the bargemaster and one of the men. He climbed over the side and leapt to meet her.

"Did you see the other man?" he shouted over the river. "He wears priests cloths."

"No."

Eothan fell to his knees, his head in his hands. Where was Thomas? Kidnapped! He had failed at his charge. Without Thomas there was no quest. The pit in his stomach widened. Tracks! There must be tracks.

"Do you know where we are?" he asked looking up to find the shape changer in human form standing close. Her sweet Elllendei oils flamed his nostrils.

"East bank of the Mourn near Calor Manor." she said. With her large robe around her. Only her head was visible, long black hair pulled tight beneath the thrown back hood.

"There are dark sorceries in these woods," she gestured toward the Corsinian forest, that, lay about a league west, "and the old Manor is the home of brigands." She stepped closer and knelt beside him. "Genru Star Born told me to look out for you."

Of course, now he realized, the spearman in the forest and the boar tracks. He turned into those brown eyes again.

"How far is this Manor?" Did they take him there?

That was it! The Merkling had been a distraction.

He stood and stepped in front of Teresa to the bargers. They lay sprawled on the river bank in a form of enchanted sleep. He began pacing. The sleeping men, they were one short, why was one missing? An agent of their enemy? Treachery, he cursed.

"I must find Thomas. You say there are brigands at the manor. If the missing man was a spy.... then... a band of thieves are our enemy.... Do you think they have taken saint Thomas to the manor?" With out waiting for a response he continued, "We must find out. Saint Thomas the young cannot be lost."

And with that Eothan turned and ran at a jog toward the distant woods. Teresa pulled the bodies into a small thicket for hiding and followed. In boar form she quickly caught up to the warrior, following behind at a safe distance, she loped. Her hooves soft on the muddy ground. He ran smoothly, easily maneuvering in the moon lit night. Lithe for a young man carrying so many burdens, I already like this Northern warrior, she thought. Her farther had told her to watch for the right man. She admired his sleek and strong form.

They ran east toward Calor, and as, the forest neared, they found a small unpaved road, following it, Eothan picked out a distinct trail. Panting, he rested with his back to a sweet chestnut tree, till he caught his breath, and, then, with a great exhale, he heaved up to continue the jog.

The boar Tarese smelt the deep loam of the wood around them. She had run in these woods much as a child, but more recently had taken to the dense forests and mountain peaks of northern Corsinia. The wild mushrooms and giant fungus were left to grow in these higher climbs.

The land here was hilly with lush wooded valleys, and the occasional grassy fern clearing. Silver had been mined in these hills in the early days, but now only farmers and forest dwarves remained. The scent of their fires and livestock filled the air, polluting her nostrils.

Snorting it out, she filled her lungs with a clear breath.

Eothan examined the road at several instances during his run, fresh tacks told him that a party of humanoids had passed through the area, and recently too. Some dwarfs by looks of the boot prints, and a goblin or too, something smaller, the murklings!!! His blood raced.

Something large as well. Eothan shuddered, a troll most like.

He had only once faced a troll in combat, a huge mountain troll of the Bogwood Stolenfist tribe. He stood against its force and even managed to wound it, a stab that penetrated the beasts rocky hide, before it knocked him unconscious, with, one blow of its great fists. He had woken up in the monastery, head in bandages, saved by the two Corserite elves who had luckily been his companions at the time. All he saw in memory of the experience was the trolls huge tusk filled maw, and, the surprising eloquence of its tongue.

These prints were large and wide even for troll, Eothan guessed water troll, because of their muddiness, their sloppy outlines, but, so far from the river? And the rain had stopped. If it was a water troll only magick would give it the confidence to travel so far from water. Enemies upon enemies he thought.

As they traveled, he found the trail easier to recognize. It followed the edge of the road keeping close to the tree cover. Whatever they were, they marched in single file. He calculated one large troll, a collection of goblins, and some dwarves, the four thugs from the row boat, most like, and finally, the small, but, long prints of that spell slinging merchant, the merkling.

They followed on for two leagues paralleling the road way. Then veered right making a bee-line toward the north, and a steep hillside.

At times, Eothan could hear the great boar in the woods beside him, but often she would tire of his pace and disappear to explore on her own, using her nose as a guide, she covered many leagues in front and around on her cloven hoof.

Eothan kept his eyes down, crossing, and, following a number of game trails as they pursued the ambushers. The tree cover lessened, climbing out of the valley floor. Then, at the wood's edge the trail split in two; the merkling, troll, and the dwarves headed west, whilst the goblins, followed the hills up to the north.

He placed his head against an oaken trunk and again rested. The night had darkened, and, it was cold. His heart pounded in his chest, and his warm breath shone in the night. He leaned back and looked about him deciding which way to go.

Distant hoof beats told him that Teresa was approaching from the hill. She slowed transforming into human, standing upright as she came.

"There is a troop of goblins up that hill. They number over two score, some of the group we followed are among them."

She paused and studied Eothan. Her cloak, the sweat in her bedraggled hair, and the intensity of her soul penetrating eyes, reminded him of a wild human banshee in the night.

He shuddered, returning her stare. The women at the monastery always kept their hair closely cropped, and did not perfume their skin, as this young woman did.

"Did you catch a sight....... of the other group." He managed between breaths.

"Yes your friend is there, I could smell human. The others went on the low road down the valley"

"Then that's the group we should follow!" he replied.

Taking no time to discuss the matter, they, ran back down into the valley along a small hunting trail. Tarese confirmed Eothan's fears.

"I smell troll." she said, then, metamorphing back into a boar she disappeared down the trail in front.

He shook his head. This transforming was something he found hard to get used to; her curved very human body dissolving into that of a quadruped. Blech.

The path lead along a small stream, large, now with the recent rain. It will soon be morning, thought Eothan. He was worried for Thomas and the monastery, but, happy to have found a companion.

Looking ahead down into the forested valley, the night about them had lightened. From this height, he could see a clearing within the canopy below. A manor and collection of village lights reflected upon a small lake.

He knew that daylight effected lycanthropy, and wondered how Teresa would react. He hoped she would become human for a time, with Thomas gone, and the mission in jeopardy, it would be nice to talk, especially to someone his own age.

It was morning by the time they reached Calor. Early dawn bird calls had slowly grown to the present feeding swarm. The path had led them around the lake to an outer masonry, without nearing the village. They lay in tall grass not far from the wall resting, not wishing to crawl closer to the battlements for fear of being spotted. It had not rained since yesterday, though, the grass was still wet, with a thick dawning mist, that still clung to the valley floor. Late swallows swooped above them gobbling down a biting horde of insects, there was still warmth in the valley, though the sun had not yet burned through light cloud.

He had been right about shape changers, since mourning Teresa had remained human. He wondered how in control of the change she was. There were legends amongst his people, but in these stories the change had been uncontrollable, a wild curse. A wolf man of his tribe had been put to death for the hideous crime of murdering his own family. Their bodies had been found half eaten; the house drenched in blood. The elders had the tribe's warriors hunt and shoot the wolfman with silver arrows, then, decapitate it with a ceremonial sword.

He glanced toward the attractive Ellendei in the grass next to him. Her dark brown hair glinted with maroon in the morning light. Her eye lids fluttering with the visions of deep sleep. Then, he remembered another story of a great warrior, a hero who assumed the shape of a bear during battle. It was told that these shape changers were immortal and could only be harmed by magick.

His eyes returned to her; robe now securely fastened about. Her chest rose with steady repose. They were both tired. It was hard to imagine that this Ellendei walked in the shape of a wild boar at all.

Eothan shook his head, the quest was more important than this young lady. Did Thomas lie imprisoned in the keep before them, or not? What was to be done?

The smell of her wet hair filled his senses. His mind becoming full of their proximity. What was that oil they used on their skin? I hope this shapechanger has learnt to control the boar spirit within her, he thought.

They had decided to rest and approach the manor from the village. Teresa knew Calor and felt it easier to go through its main gate. If turned away, they could return later under the cover of darkness, and, break in.

Before the dawn got too old, Eothan woke his companion, and, acting naturally, a couple of field workers, perhaps, they walked around the manor at a distance. They kept in the long grass. A small gate looked out on to a lot of land separated from the village by the moat. The single church and blacksmithy lay to the manor side, the village's homes and farms, were reached by an arched bridge. The newcomers walked out of the grass and along the edge of the moat, on the forest side. A liveried yeomen fished off the bank, his son, excited by unfamiliar faces, pointed enthusiastically, he was scalded, into, an abrupt silence. The fisher nodded, smiling in replay, as the two moved on.

The church and grave yard cut off view to the manor momentarily, and, seeing it again, Eothan thought it would be easy to climb the walls. Toward the village they were a mere 10' in height, and, as the moat extended around the church there was plenty of land between it and the wall on which to stage a silent assault.

The village, itself, stretched along both sides of a gravel track. A mixture of houses, barns, chicken pens and pig sties. To the south a wooden stockade protected it from the forest. To the north there was no protection other than the moat.

The cloudy sky began to break a little and Eothan felt the warmth of the sun on his back for the first time in days. The heat of summer gone from its bite, it still rejuvenated the tied monk. Approaching, as they did, they entered the village arround the edge of a mill and without having to climb a wall, or, enter a gate. The land to this side was open and tilled. Peasants spotted the fields, here and there, busily gathering the last of the summers crop.

Being mid mourning, most of the village's men folk were in the forest hunting or tending pig herds. Children, both dwarf and human filled the village with a noisy game, in which, spherical rocks were pushed back and forth with long oaken rods, they stopped the ruckus to stare at the newcomers.

"My family name will provide us lodging at the manor." Said Teresa. "If I remember rightly there is only one Inn here and it lies at the other end of the village. They have beds, but, not many..... besides, we needs must get inside....and strangers are uncommon here.

"If we sleep in the manor, we must stay alert. Our enemies are amongst its guardians." Eothan, contorted his face, and, turned, glowering at the closest of the nosy children. All scattering, they vanished, howling with joyous fright.

"Yes, Calor, the lord is an ancient Dwarf and tires of the affairs of the world. Undoubtedly, someone close to him is in league with the troll. I know that Brigands haunt the woods south of here, but my farther considers Calor to be harmless, he speaks well of him."

"He has grown short sighted in his age?"

"Yes perhaps, I know he has a son, Calor the second."

"The sooner we search the manor house the better, if we are to rescue we must act!" Tarese recognized the strain in Eothan's voice, his master's mission now lay squarely on the novice's shoulders. Amongst the Ellendei, Norcaidians were considered little more than barbarians. She wondered whether Eothan could continue alone and what his quest entailed.

Was it brigands or trolls they were looking for? Her father had often surmised that the brigands of these woods found protection at Calor Manor, but, how much, and, from who? Their stay at the manor should be interesting, to say the least.

They made their way across a second bridge, and, toward the manor's gate house. It was wide open, two liveried dwarves stood guard at its mouth. Richly emblazoned on their shields, they bore the coat of arms of Calor's house, the red gem and silver bolt. Eothan noticed another guard topping the gates tower, and, the silver glint of sharpened pike, told him there were more.

Tarese halted unthreatening.

"I am Tarese de Ghent I request lodging for myself and my companion."

There was a pause during which the two dwarves eyed the strangers, and glanced back and forth between.

"My farther Genru de Ghent is a friend of your lord," she added, and a close relative to the king she thought to her self.

One of the dwarfs watched the new comers, as the other disappeared into the court yard. He returned with another, far better dressed dwarf carrying a walking stick; extremely ornate, it boasted a large gem stone as its pommel. He wore his gray beard braided and walked with the proud air of a Derem-Gorin mountain dwarf, slow and stately. Ethan presumed him to be the manor's doorward. Looking the new comers over, quickly, he cleared his throat, and, began to speak.

"I welcome thee to house of Calor. It is rare our house be graced by Nobel guests." He paused, eyeing them cautiously. "Thy king is my king, thy hearth is my hearth." He spoke the Ellendei welcoming, and, then went on. "It be long since thy farther visited our hearth, I pray all be well?"

"Well yes." She managed.

The chamberlain turned and led them across a small pathed court yard, following close behind, Teresa explaining, that they had been traveling from Kulalan, when, their barge had run aground and sunk. She told the story well, adding, that the recent flooding had been to blame.

The Chamberlain, for that was the name given to the castle keeper amongst the Ellendei, appeared politely concerned. He ushered them into the hall of the manor's keep, and, hurriedly began to find quarters.

They waited in the small hall decorated with frescoes from the Derem Gorim mnts. Around, them, on large dark wooden panels, dwarves worked for centuries carving halls out of the ancient mountains. There was a brake at the chamber's opposite end, where two iron enforced doors split the story of the Derem Gorin frescoes in half. An ornately carved tree reached up between spreading its branches as it reached for the ceiling above. Its trunk housed a grand metal door who's hammered finish carried the bark motif of the tree's wooden trunk.

Eothan was flabbergasted, the panels would have taken the finest of craftsman years to complete. He had heard that Derem Gorin Dwarves were skilled craftsmen, but, never had he seen any of their work. The frescoes were exquisite. He turned a full circle taking in the life like faces that surrounded him; expressions of conquest, joy, and, pain. The crude work of the Corserite Hall of Song was nothing in comparison to this. Scenes within scenes, generations lived, died, fought and delved. Halls, castles, mines, bridges, and, cities rose and fell.

There was power in the work, a quiet sublime power like that of their massive mountain homes; a surprise, indeed, to find work of such unsurpassed beauty in an out of the way place like Calor. The primitive stamped metal patterns and torques of his own people were simple in comparison.

The chamberlain had disappeared through an unseen door in the wall next to them. Eothan presumed that it led further into the manor's keep. Above the door and extending around the hall and across its long back wall was an open walk way. Two servants, both dwarves carried what looked like baskets of linen along its length. Their chatter filled the chamber, as if the ancient walls themselves were taking.

Tarese was uninterested, choosing instead to imbibe a small amount of enchanted powder that she kept concealed within her robe. This will fight my fatigue she thought.

The Chamberlain returned with a servant to show them to the quarters he had found; a chamber in a small tower jutting from the manor's north western wall. It was large, especially for a Dwarfen structure, encompassing the tower's entire lower floor, curtains divided it, into, a living area and three sleeping nooks. Across from the door, providing the chamber with exterior light, a small window overlooked the moat and out into the clearing beyond.

The Chamberlain left, leaving the servant to wait on the guests.

Eothan crossed and stared out of the window toward the hills. It was mid-day and the sun was still shining. He thought he could see a trace of the trail they had followed through the wood. With his eyes, he found the near portion, crossing from the edge of the wood, ending against the northern most of the moat. Only a trained tracker could have even recognized such a slight path from this distance. Tracing its course, from its end point, across the moat to the manors wall, he found, at water level, a grating of some kind.

At a stiff angle from where he stood in the tower, it looked to be the exit of the keep's plumbing. Eothan knew that dwarves were handy builders, perhaps the manor had a sewage system. The abbey had a meager sewer of its own, that during the summer months, the novices worked hard to keep supplied with water.

Tarese was asking the servant about old Calor, trying overly to appear polite, he thought.

Suddenly he had a frightening thought, perhaps the water troll lived under the moat somewhere. The hair on the back of his neck stood up and he felt a shudder within his bones. Then, he was sure of it, there was something hidden beneath the stower formality of this dwarfen hold. He could smell it in the air. The Troll had friends among Old Calor's household. He was sure of it.

Tarese took parchment and wrote a note of introduction that she wished taken to Calor the elder. She stood beside a tall writing table, up against the inside wall, near the door. Eothan watched, as, she finished her note, returned the goose quill and added her seal, handing it to the servant.

After, he had left, Eothan beckoned Tarese to come to the window.

Showing her the steal grating, he quietly, whispered into her ear that they could trust no one. She nodded and then went to one of the sleeping nooks.

Her powder wore off quickly and before he could discuss their next step, Teresa was fast asleep. Not feeling comfortable he resisted sleep himself, building a fire in the rooms hearth. He looked around again, and missing his familiar sword and bow, he contented himself sharpening his falchion and checking the straps of his small wooden shield.

The Dwarfen servant returned with food and an invitation to feast at the Old lord's table that evening. Eothan considered asking some questions about Dwarfen architecture, but instead, dismissed him choosing the familiarity of his faith to the company of a complete stranger.

The sound of chattering dwarves filled the air. Eothan and Tarese were seated on the guest side of Calor the Old's table. The mighty carved tree rose behind them. The Dwarf lord wore a heavy brown and gold ceremonial gown. Within a golden lattice, a fist sized amulet hung loosely around his neck, its center an exquisitely carved red emerald glowing dully in the touch light. The smells of pheasant, pig and, brandy mixed with those of boiled leek, carrots, and, yam.

Old Calor had spoken briefly as the meal was being served, but now he was far more interested in the roast boar on his plate. Ancient even for a dwarf, the years were beginning to take their toll. If the way he struggled with his knife and fork was anything to go by Tarese doubted that he had much say in the running of the manor. Even a dead and broasted boar could get the better of him, what could he do to stop brigandry?

Eothan gobbled down his own food pausing only to rip off large chunks of dwarfen bread.

Tarese ate slowly, she was never very hungry after a full moon. The Corsinian woods boasted far too good a supply of root, and, truffle.

Calor the younger, seeing her hesitation as an invite, began to talk. Tilting a wrist, he offered her a jug of wine from where he sat, opposite.

"Have you visited the royal court of recently." he began.

She remembered her last visit to Ottar's court and the head ache that had ensued. Ceroth the Good had given her an elixir to relieve the pain, but, her puritanical instincts had worked to dissuade her from spending too much time within the open debauchery of Ottar, and, his court of royal revelers. The memories of that flamboyant stay still haunted her dream time.

"No, I'm afraid not" she replied, "I do see the king when he comes to the lodge, but that has not been for many months."

"Yes, your farther is the warden of the kings hunting lodge. And how is that old dandy?" continued Calor. He must mean the King not my father, she thought. His gray Dwarfen eyes searched for something within hers, there was a hint of sarcasm in his voice. "Here we always have good boar hunts." he added.

How much did this nosy Dwarf know of her family. The Hidden Lodge had grown with the Arraken crown, as, a society of royal magicks. Behind, its cover as a hunting lodge, the Hidden Land of Idiwin taught and protected the use of intoxicants for their innate magickal properties. The kings of Arraken had been traditionally taught this form of sorcery since the Ascension of the Eidawin's, after, the fall of the Great Drake 500 years ago.

Ottar the Dandy was far less serious than most of his ancestors, preferring the intoxicant aspects of his art over its more practical applications. Though, proficient in the arcane arts, he rarely visited the secret lodge, and, when he did so, was far more interested in the persute of boar, than, the mystical persutes of the unknown land.

Tarese quickly concluded that she did not like this young dwarf. He was not a bit like his farther. He wore his beard far to short, and, tightly breaded, more like a Niobian merchant, not Dwarfen at all.

And he was rude.

Soon after, she had awoken, Eothan had told her that they were to be expected down stairs at the feast. She had only time to wash before this young rascal had arrived in full mail, sword carrying, dwarfen regalia, to escort them. A little much for a simple evening feast, she thought.

"I've only been to the royal court a few times" he went on. "They don't spar enough for my tastes rely too much on magick. Dangerous stuff. "His eyes explored her. "Of course they have a lot of fun, don't they?"

She turned back to her food and eat, using her full mouth as an excuse not to talk. The young dwarf went on. His talk was plain enough, but, somewhere underneath something was going on. His eyes were far too forward and the candle light in the room was dancing distractingly around his bejeweled gauntlets. Was he trying to enchant her in some way? Cast a dwarfen charm of trust?

She felt like standing up and drawing a circle of protection, that's how obnoxious he was being. Glancing over towards Eothan, she saw the warrior, already, devouring his first plate of boar, and, eyeing a helping of broast pigeon. She wondered which of the local herds their feast had belonged to.

Fighting a wave of disiness she kept eating. Yes there was definitely some magick in the air. A juggler had begun to perform a routine in front of the table, and, Calor the younger turned his chair from her to watch. Eothan thankful for such a hearty feast laughed appreciatively.

"After we've eaten perhaps you would like a walk in the garden?" It was young Calor again. He turned his head, his voice suddenly sounding softer and more inviting. Tarese was surprised, she had almost said yes without knowing it.

"No ." She managed after a pause , "I'm happy here "Their eyes fenced quickly and then she managed to pull hers away, creeping back into herself.

"Have it your own way.... but you really should see.. we have some of the most beautiful family grottos...Deep down under the keep?"

Tarese coffed on a piece of bread, finally, managing to wash it down with a glass of thick wine. She felt tied again. Definitely a form of charm at work. This has gone on long enough.

As she drank her wine, her left hand to slipped into the arm of her robe and unseen she extracted a protective drug her farther had left with her. Resisting another urge to agree to the young dwarfs offer, she slipped a dose of the dark red and gold powder into her own drink. With a toss of her wrist, then drained the goblet in one quick motion.

Her father's magick coursed through her body making her giddy, but, simultaneously restoring her energy and will. Feeling protected her face lightened. Now she could enjoy the meal.

Turning to meet the dwarfs expression, she felt much stronger, her grin widened.

"No thank you M Lord I find grottos a little dank myself.....Depressing!" She added, with an Ellendei giggle.

The younger looked pained, surprised and a little hurt. He quickly returned attention to the entertainment.

The juggler was joined by two dwarfen acrobatics and a small human playing the drum and horn at the same time. The noise was defening, although, the total effect was amusing. Eothan had, by now, satiated his appetite, and, plied himself with enough dwarfen brew to loosen his stiff northern tongue.

"So" He said "When do we head on."

Teresa thought a moment he was obviously trying to make them appear as normal wayfarers without exposing the sensitivity of their mission. She gathered this from the way his eyes lingered in hers, as if, he meant more than he said. She was happy for the distraction. The Calor family was one of the oldest dwarfen emigrates from Derem-Gor and she knew the Derem-Gorin's to be well versed in gem and armor magicks; perhaps some of this lore was at work here.

"Well..." she smiled and pleasantly accepted a bouquet of summer flowers from the Juggler.

"I think my farther expected us to arrive last night or early this morning.....though I do not think they will find things amiss until next week. I am often longer on journeys than I expect to...be..."

"So you appreciate traveling do you, M' Lady." interjected the Younger."

He cleared his throat and continued. "I've done a bit of traveling myself, especially southwards. I remember the beautiful domes of Berelan simply smashing architecture, considering they were built by human, of course ..I wonder, have you ever seen our Northern cities of Derem-Gor by any chance?"

"No I have not" She retorted rather harshly, but then she lowered her voice and leaned towards him, adding. "But was not the pinnacle of Parnassus built by your people?"

Calor was taken aback.

"Gnomes!" He spat, "It was Gnomes who built the Pinnacle, slaves. That Pinnacle stood long before even Parnassus caught sight of it. No humanoid built that........... Of course it is an impressive piece of stone, but Gnome architecture is not pretty....No.... Not at all...... Far to much filigree...they have no sense of beauty...none!"

Eothan finished the last of his draft and pushed himself up to his feet.

"I am tied from our night without sleep!......". He announced.

A dwarf retainer stepped forward.

"No I will find my own way........thank you"

Waved away, the dwarf stepped back toward the wall again.

Old Calor also stood, a retainer on each side. He had spoken very little during the feast and had eaten even less, after the defeat with the broast boar he had eaten only fruit. Tarese had noticed him nodding in time with the music earlier but now he was falling asleep, the retainers could barely keep him up.

The younger watched the older leave, then, turned back toward Tarese; his empty smile whitened his well-groomed face.

"Hark, Tarese De Gent niece to king Ottar.... and daughter of Genru, warden of the kings hunt, my bard will sing you the ballad of Kalerbron the house of Calor." And with that he clapped his hands together four times sharply in concession.

The horn and drum stopped, and a younger dwarf with tall brown boots and a bright blue tunic strode to the center of the hall. He paused glanced around the room, raised himself up tall and announced in a loud voice. "The Ballad of Kalebron."

He then began to recite, act, and mime the long convoluted and very dwarfen story of the house Calor and its migration to Corsinia. She found some of the events of the wizard wars interesting, especially, the oaths between the family and the kings of Arraken before the battle of Parnassus. But, the long winded and thoroughly exaggerated exploits of Calour's various heirs she could do without.

Calor himself smiled, laughed and made comments about his relatives. Tarese was polite but soon his probing lustful eyes began to tire her. She felt herself continually resisting the pull of this Dwarf, although, she personally found him repugnant.

She expected that some form of passive spell slinging was at work, her father's powder protecting her. She reminded Calor how tied she was from the unexpected trek. And, when the performance had ended, quickly found her leave from this young dwarf and his confusing Derem-Gorin ways.

The room was quiet except for Eothan's deep breathing. She sat for a time listening to the keep fall asleep around her. Then she patted across to Eothan's bed and kneeled beside him. He was fast asleep his huge shoulders and chest naked and uncovered. His ribs expanded slowly with each breath. She thought of her father's house and and her days of chore work with the apothecist. Why was she helping this Northerner. She knew not. She knew nothing of his quest. Nor, his distant monastery. Why were these two Corserites so far south? And why had her farther been so interested?

She stayed quiet the night about them, listening to his sleep.

When all sound from beyond their chambers quieted, she woke the young warrior-priest with a quick shake, and placing a gentle hand to his mouth, whispered in his ear.

"The house is at rest would you like to search for your friend."

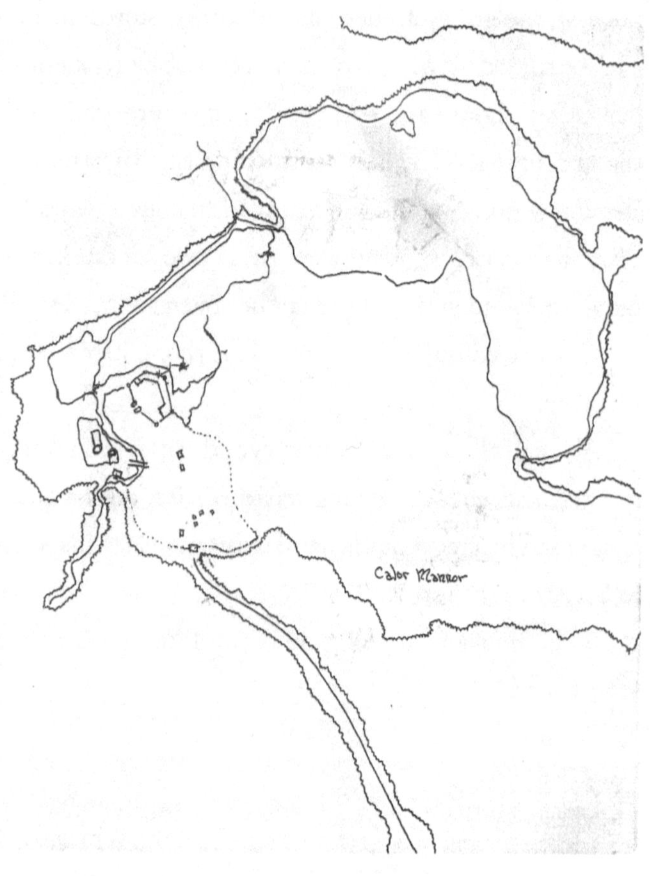

Calor Mannor

CHAPTER 4

MNT ELLENDON

"Human's." Noldarn curst. He spat the words out from under his breath. "By the Watcher of the pool's we are lost."

If Saint Thomas had chosen us, this mess could have been averted. He contained his anger for the moment, and, crouching to the ground, he considered, creeping closer to the group. Already strained his energy was being used to remain hidden.

"Curse...that spell using troll and his minions." He whispered to himself in his own tongue. Shamen or witch he is a formidable opponent.

The troll stood tall, apart from its companions. He moved heavily as did all his race, carrying a cunning and surety that belied his size. The bag slung across his back easily large enough to contain a body, possibly Thomas' or perhaps Eothan the Fair the abbot's companion.

It was from within the large group of goblins making their way up the hillside, that the elf sensed Thomas' presence. Noldarn reached into his tunic and pulled out his bars of divination. Their carved and gold inlayed surfaces shinned dully in the darkness. He had made them when a boy in Thornbreak over three hundred and fifty years ago, they were unworn, as vibrant as the dawn on which he finished their enchantment. Four weeks of intense meditation and fast, it had been the culmination of years of research.

Gathering the correspondences of which this, his focus had been constructed, had taken three decades, the enchantments themselves another year. He tossed the rods thrice determining the direction, distance, and elevation of his charge.

They agreed with his intuition, the small group winding its way up the hillside contained Thomas. Strange since he saw nothing the size of a body among them. More sorcery he expected. He cursed again. The time of the thousand wizards was, indeed, drawing nigh. As the keepers of the pools had prophesied.

He considered the duke Herigar Gunison, his claim to the throne of Thornbreak and shuddered. The Ellendei were getting powerful. Too powerful. As his kin faded into their forests and glens, retreating from the world to the land of faery, man was forever eager to take their place. He tried not to think of the vaults of power hidden under Ergedh, the dutchies capital. Mighty catches and troves stored there by the wizard king Ergedh. It was Torechel Gunersson, husband to Carel Eiadawen, great grandfather of Herigar and the first wielder of the Dragon Bane who finally defeated Coretherregge, the great wurm, to claim Ergedh for himself. The wurm had out lived its master by over 200 years, replacing the despotic wizards rule with rampant destruction and devastation.

The two groups had separated. The water troll, the bag over his shoulder, retreated down the hill with what remained of his companions. His grey faery eyes could see clearly in the dark night,

Noldarn crouched low and began to pursue the ascending group. These Goblin kin, were larger than most, probably hobgoblins or their taller kin, bugbear. Not having time to examine their tracks and make a more accurate determination, their particular tribe or species would have to remain unknown. They were goblin-kin, and to Noldarn, that was all that mattered. Obviously up to no good, the missing saint hidden somewhere among their number.

He could sense Thomas, but not being able to see him, couldn't pin point the cleric's exact location. Knowing that magick was at work, he began to creep cautiously toward the enemy.

There were six in the group, two rear guards carried heavy iron wrought halberds, sharpened blades gleaming silver and red. They lopped along in an unconcerned fashion, unaware of the enemy at their backs.

Without a sound, Noldarn strung his bow. He moved in on the group. The four closest wore leather and chain with smooth conical helms protecting their heads. The front members of the band were hard to see, but he sensed power and magick.

Loading the first arrow he let it fly, three more followed in rapid succession. They buried deeply into the backs of the last two hobgoblins. Who fell to the ground, with, little more than a groan. It took more than chainmail to stop arrows from an elf's bow.

With a great shout from the front, the two closer hobgoblins turned to face their assailant. They brandished a long ugly scimitar, and a mace, with shields on their left arms.

In a single motion, Noldarn slung his bow over his left shoulder, drawing his bastard sword from its scabbard. In his youth, he had named the blade Noretrell, and often it had soaked in the enchanted pools beneath Thornbreak keep. Now, in the presence of enemies, its blade radiated with a dull blue light.

Down slope of the Hobgoblins, instead of charging, he began to close the distance, moving to the right and working up slope.

The hobgoblin brandishing the scimitar screamed roughly into the sky above, then turning his gaze on the elf he charged head long toward him. Noldarn pulled back his blade, preparing a blow. The hob led with its shield, intending to knock Noldarn off his feet, to bash him with the weight of body and armor.

The elf waited, hefting his sword in both hands, he smiled to himself, preparing the mighty blow. The doom of his kind was upon him. Saliva dripped from its canines, its eyes burning with hatred. At the last moment Noldarn leapt to the right. The shield ricocheting of his left shoulder. Reeling backwards, he used the momentum to spin full circle delivering a two-handed chop into the assailant's back.

He felt a biting pain in the back of his leg, the hob's scimitar had connected, slicing into his calf.

Noretrell had dug a deep wound into its enemies back, but, as the momentum of the charge carried it further down slope, Noldarn had no way of Knowing whether his foe had been wounded critically, or, weather its armor had saved it. Having no time to think, the second foe was upon him.

It growled deep, and, low. Then, lunging, it struck at him with its mace.

Ignoring the pain in his leg, he parried the first blow. The hobgoblin was strong, but the elf moved aside the mace with his large sword, counter attacking. He struck its shield squarely. The metal dented but held.

Jumping straight back he avoided another lunge. He smashed the hob's shield, keeping it busy. Out of the corner of his eye he, again, saw the scimitar, as it descended toward him, sweeping red in the moon light. His first enemy had returned.

He dodged, twisting, inside its guard, and still wielding Noretrell two handedly, brought the point upwards thrusting it deeply into the hobs stomach. Retracting it with the speed of the finest Ellendei warrior, the elf was in time to parry, another blow from the mace.

As it struck, Noldarn dropped to his knee, and ducked. the blow sailed over his head. He stood, instantly stepping forward, and, delivered a resounding pommel strike to the nape of the creature's neck. Sent forward to its knees, the elf looked around for his remaining foe. In the distance, two shapes scurried up the steep slope above.

The hob had gotten to its feet, and turning it rushed him, with, shield out in front. This time the young elf was up slope of his opponent. He again waited preparing to dodge, holding his sword in his left hand, the point faced the ground. Brave at least, he thought.

At the last minute he stepped to the side, slashing downward slashing hamstrings as it passed. It fell, Noldarn leaping to its back. He grabbed around its neck with his free hand. Putting it in a choke hold. Noldarn pulled backward, arching its body toward him. He questioned in its own tongue.

"Where is your prisoner?..... Speak or you will die."

"We got no prisoner........"

Noldarn tightened his grip and the thing choked.

"Speak or die"

"You ....stink of .....the.....forest...I....eat the intestines of your kin!"

The elf snapped its neck with one swift move. In no mood to talk, he hissed into the night through clenched teeth.

"The dark enemy has worked power into this tribe."

Sick to his stomach from the carnage, it had been too long since he had walked in the gentle forests of Thornbreak, and, talked through many nights, with his friend high lord Serderan. These times were fell, the seeing pools had lain dark for many years, and much of his peoples' work came to naught. Even the Ellendei were succumbing to the sways of the Dark One. Coverns of witches thrived in Arraken's major cities, and, honest wizards were put to death as accused devil worshipers. What has happened, he thought, to the virtuous orders of Ellendei knighthood, the Lodge of White, and, other Ellendei order's that protected all from the misuse of arcane lore.

The pain in his leg bought him back to the task at hand. He bent down, repeating from memory the phrases of an ancient spell of healing. A dweomer old in the lore of his people. Touching his fingers to the wound, the bleeding ceased. It healed from the inside, blood vessels reforming under the ancient elfish words. A deep gash, not long, a chop wound, to heal it completely, he would need to cast another incantation.

Deciding to conserve energy and time, he sheathed Norretrell, the second healing could wait. He turned and hurried up the slope as the quarry crested the top of the barren hill side. Two figures, silhouetted light against the dark and cloud covered sky.

There was a moon, its light unable to penetrate the black northern canopy, only the southern clouds refracted its diffusion.

As he continued, there was a flicker of pure white between them. Noldarn involuntarily inhaled, magick fire he thought. I only hope that the adept who created it is not overly powerful. He touched his fingers to the divination rods, and repeated the long spell of protection, creating a movable invisible shield about himself.

He continued the upward climb.

A distant screech like that of a giant vulture filled the air. Then, as if in reply, a bolt of magick flew upward from the hill top. Noldarn quickened his jog. He would soon reach the top.

As he reached the hill, he slowed, and grasping the divining rods cast a spell of concealment. They were goblins. Not as large as the soldiers he had left down the slope, but, a kindred race.

The larger of the two wore a light leather jerkin, sitting on his haunches, by the pool of magick fire, he warmed his hands, his eyes were not registering, instead, he stared blankly into the night. Noldarn crept forwards from the hill. The smaller of the two stood, arms raised, as his movements levitated a spherical ball of the magick fire.

It floated in a globe about a foot wide; flickering, and, pulsed, as it changed shape fighting the wizard to fall out of the sphere it was constrained to. Concentration visible in the sharp angles of the goblin's face, sweat beaded along his forehead, and above his lip. It wore no cloths, but, charms of bone, rock, and body parts were mattered into its thin short covering of hair.

Colors danced, within the fire, highlighting the brown, and, greens, in its skin, two gold and red eyes burned brightly beneath thick eye brows.

The screech came again, but this time louder. The goblin once more sent up a small ball of the fire, while, his companion, worked to keep more ready. Then he saw it! Between, the fire wielder's crouched companion's legs, there lay a large leaden flask, with silver cap. The lead glittered white with the light of the magick. An enchanted flask! These spell slingers had stolen saint Thomas' soul. So that was it. It must have been Thomas' body in the bag. His life essence lay imprisoned before them. Now, things were complicated.

Reaching into his tunic he found the divining rods. Rolling them back and forth gently he learned, that the crouched figure was older, stronger in the ways of lore; the other, the fire thrower, young, and yet, burned with a certain intensity. The air around them shimmered, they too had set up a circle of protection. The circles of two wizards together were stronger than those of one alone. He would have to think fast.

Looking around the sky, he scanned for the beast that had made the noise. There, just below the cloud line. It glided down toward them from the north. A wyvern, and a large one at that. It's long neck and reptilian head, pulled back by a massive harnessed bit.

It screeched again, as it began a long banking curve to the west. Noldarn looked out from the hill top. To the north he could see Chazebel Peak, its sharp pointed crest protruding up through the thick bank of cloud. Foremost among the mountains surrounding Kullalan and the Royal Mint, they were far from the safety of Rand Lakedwellar's fire warmed halls, nestled securely at its base. To the south his elfish eye marked the sprawling forests of southern Corsinia. Over the forest, and, through the distant rain, he barely perceived the ancient wizard peak of Parnassus; the fire from its gnomish gondola silhouetted the top in gold.

The wyvern turned toward them in the sky, now far closer to the hill top. It's head and neck pulled forward against the harness, as it scanned the approach.

Against the dark of the cloud cover Noldarn made out a black robed figure amidst the reptile's red emblazoned saddle. It rode hunched, hood pulled up against the rain.

Noldarn started, "Glamawer." he muttered under his breath.

"Glamawer the Damned."

There was no other it could be. Still holding the divining rods, he began to cast his spell of growth in reverse. It was a trick that had taken him months to learn, and had proved useful ever since. He was careful, spending time remembering the enchantment, then, repeating the backwards slowly in his native tongue. He made sure there were no mistakes. With all these wizards and sorcerers about he did not want his own incantations noticed. The magick cost energy and he was concentrating to disperse the ripples it made on the Ethereal plane.

As, Noldarn well knew, Glamawer, high priest of the Hidden Lodge had many spirits and friends who dwelled on the outer and inner planes. All the lone elf needed, was for one of the Damned's allies to notice, and report his presence to their Lord, Glamawere, the Eternally Damned.

The incantation worked, and all around him grew, as he shrank. When dwarfed by the short-tufted grass of the barren hilltop he began to cast a second spell, a conjuration of transportation, from his early youth, an abjuration of flight. At this size the smell of the Corsinian mountain heather overpowered him, watering his eyes. He concentrated, flying up above the grasses. Expectantly, the goblin spell slingers vigilantly guarded their charge. Their necks craned toward their approaching lord.

Noldarn waited, as he watched the mighty reptile approach, he remembered from their last encounter in the wild lands north of the Enorien Peaks, that this beast of Glamawer's carried a poison. Its tail tapered into a lethally envenomed sharp scimitar shaped barb. At that time, he had been accompanied by other Corserites, and not wishing them harmed, had resorted to mortal combat. This time, he hoped to avoid it.

The great beast soared silently below the black of the Corsinian cloud. Then with a flick of its rider's wrist it banked, and came about with a mighty flap. Snorting, it exhaled a plume of red and yellow fire that lit the sky around it, as it came. Glamawere sat motionless, as its head, and neck reared back allowing its massive hind quarters to brace for landing. Taloned feet clenched expectantly, and then opened, as the beast, thundered to the ground. It let out a screech, rocked forward with a step. Wings beat against its momentum, buffeting the elf, before they settled, with a crumple, dormant against its flank.

Having no forearms, it sat on its talons, a razor tooth maw slavering with the smell of fresh prey.

To Noldarn it seemed that the whole hill side shook as the great beast landed. The sickly-sweet smell of its hide mixed with the ashy brimstone of its breath; fire licked around the edge of its nostrils. It leaned further forward resting its head on the ground in front of the two cowering sorcerers, eyeing them with the amused intelligence of its race.

Prostrating, themselves, they gibbering feverishly. Noldarn smiled. Now was his chance, he spoke a charm of warding, and, his enemies distracted, slipped unseen through the edge of their protective circle. Then, flying to the leaden jar, he hid along the vessel's side.

The wyvern's neck and jaw were massive to Noldarn, he watched, as its cold icy stair flitted from side to side.

He noticed what he took to be a smile pass across its features.

"Where isss........ the ......Jar." Hissed Glamawer from the beasts back. He sat forward in the saddle his long-stooped form leaning heavily on its pommel. He had thrown back the hood of his black cape and eyed the pair with burning red within steal eyes. Unnaturally thin, his skin stretched smooth and leathery over the frame of his skull. Long silver hair was worn loose, wafting thinly in the Corsinian wind.

As neither spoke, he sat back surveying the land scape.

"Well!" he hissed again. "Have thou forgotten sspeecch"

"ere ..... she be...... M lord." stammered the older of the two. He picked up the jar and held it out in front of him as he bowed.

Noldarn hovered close to the jars side, keeping it forever between him and the Damned.

"Hum..." he coughed, and, with a twitch of two right fingers levitated the leaden jar toward him.

Noldarn followed close behind, and, when within Glamawer's grasp, he flew underneath the steed, concealing himself amongst saddle's leather girth straps.

"Tell Hogmire Dwarf-Bane......he ..weeill...... ..beee... rewarded."

Then, with left hand, he pulled forth a brown shrunken head from the fold of his robe, pointing it toward his two subjects. Gem stones one black and one red glowed, lighting its eye sockets, as he silently mumbled a phantasms ancient phrase under his breath. Their eyes steadily widened, as a pile of glittering silver appeared slowly before them. A small fortune in coin, the ransom of a marquis or viscount.

"Now go and spend ....quikely....my friends......for in seven days and seven nights thisss gold will beeeee..... no more."

The elf curst to himself, that silver would come to no good.

Glamawer, pulled his hood back over his head and with an order spoken low and in the speech of the dragon kind took to the wing. His parched skin barely noticed the wet chill wind, as it once more bit into his face. The wyvern looked hungrily down at the two goblins scurrying from the hill top, no meal today it thought.

Glamawer turned the great lizard to the north, flying over some of the most uninhabited land in Corsinia. He stayed well clear of Kullalan and Silverstone Keep. The Elf climbed slowly from his position beneath, over Glamawer's stirrup and up into the baggage of the damned. Amongst a pile of cleaned and enchanted bones lay the leaden jar. Noldarn counted thirteen skulls; a sizable body guard for a witch. Glamawer must be a prince amongst his people, royal within the kingdom of Wicca.

Finding a place behind the jar he again concealed himself as best he could, the Damned's sleeping skeletal guard surrounded him. He resisted an urge to use magick, choosing instead to suffer the moist cold of the heavy cloud bank. The reptile coughed against its harness, turning sharply in the cloud, then they were clear. Glamawere kept his beast low, soaring only feet above the bank.

They flew north for twenty leagues until shadowed by the colossal Caroncrack mountain. This great peak rose to the height of four leagues carving a wedge between the cultivated land of Traitia and the wild sprawling forests of Corsinia. Now, they flew higher still. The Crag's base obscured by the thick bank. No longer dark, the cloud echoed silver with the light of the full moon. The shadow of beast and ridder, a single dark form, transversed its contorted surface to the melodic beat of giant wing.

The air was cold, but bought a pleasant reprieve from the stale dead air of the tomb that accompanied the Damned, and his unwholesome paraphernalia. This was the smell that accosted Noldarn's nostrils.

Little snow clung to the shear surface of the Crag. The beast began a decent back down toward the silver tufts of cloud. They turned paralleling the mountain. Cloud extended south in all directions. A thick carpet whose wispy silvered tendrils found crevices and nooks around the granite of the mighty peak. As they flew past the Crag's saddle, Noldarn saw out to north into a clear stared sky. From this height he spied the great Orucrop and the sprawling plains of Norcaidia.

Clear was the land to the north, the bank stopped by the mass of this high peak, and its foot hills. Moon light bathed the land bouncing blue from the granite walls. Cold and unmovable the mountain reflected its quiet testimony. The native granite rock peering through from under a shimmering sheet of ice.

They followed its silent wall for a number of leagues dwarfed by the splendor. There was power in that rock. Only the sound of strong wings echoed from the mountain's face to break the silence.

Finally, the wyvern shrieked again, its voice faint in the night. Glamawer turned his beast abruptly, with a strong pull of the reins, to head south east, back under the cloud covered sky. The steed flew along the bottom of the cloud, concealed by its edge, but within the eye sight of the ground.

The land beneath them became more familiar. After, ten leagues of flight the beast landed at a cave opening on the western side of mnt. Ellendon, a giant but lonely mnt., that rose steeply to a single peak from dense forested foot hills.

Folding its wings the beast snorted a fiery plume and hunched enabling Glamawere to climb down. As he searched for the jar, Noldarn quickly flew to the side of the cave. Glamawere turned and carrying the leaden jar he walked silently into the dark of the cave.

As they had once more reached solid ground the Elf cast another illusion of concealment. Such incantations had limited physical range. Noldarn could make them last indefinitely, but if moving rapidly the spell became useless. Following closely behind the Damned, he hoped the wizard's destination would not be far.

The damned reached a seemingly empty, rough section of wall. He placed his hand against its surface, uttering a saying in the secret speech of his order. Noldarn shuddered involuntarily, the syllables crawled inside him, bristling the hair on his back.

After a few moments, the wall dissolved revealing an unseen passage. The damned stepped through, as Noldarn hurriedly flew in after him. He found a tall, but narrow passage that cut directly into the center of the mountain peak.

As the passage behind them closed, a wall of knobbled basalt formed covering its entrance. Glamawere paused, turning over his shoulder. The elf froze, as he felt the

Damned eyes probed the darkness about the portal. Noldarn's circle of protection guarded his mind against the sorcerer's eye.

Glamawere took his time, and when secure he was alone continued his progress down the passage.

The elf breathed his relief into the cold darkness. His small breath twinkled gold and green as it dissipated in the empty passage, then he continued, flying cautiously behind his quarry.

There was no natural light but neither of the two unlikely companions needed it. They followed the passage as it led on for twenty paces. There it reached a steep, narrow fissure. The fissure traced a ragged course up towards the mountains summit. At the point where the passage and fissure met, an ancient stair had been carved, it led straight down deep to the mountains core.

Glamawere paused looking upwards for a moment, then chose the descending stair.

It spiraled towards the left, smooth, dry, and, even. The Damned moved quickly, with no noise. Only the soft swish of his long robe audible in the silence. He cradled the jar in his arm, holding the brown head cradled in his other hand. Its brown and red eye were the only light to break the mountain's black.

They descended for hundreds of feet, Noldarn staying close, until, the stairway opened into the center of a large square chamber. Sporadic torch light illuminated its dusty brown floor, the walls each facing a cardinal position. There were no visible doors in the walls, but by concentrating Noldarn saw at least two. He was not sure if they were true or false, nor weather they carried traps. He waited, the Dammed stood motionless at the base of the stairs.

After moments, that seemed like hours, under the heavy weight of the air in that dank mountain, the dammed began to mutter darkly. Then his body swayed back and forth as if to some unseen beat.

Noldarn flew from his position behind the witch's head to the chamber's ceiling. The damned rocked trance like. His eyes fluttered, his robed form flickering fleetingly. Noldarn had seen this lore before. Glamawere was projecting his spiritual essence into the Astral plane.

The elf stifled a curse, better be careful in this place he thought, no telling who was watching. If there were close to a forest of power, Thornbreak, Wisper Circle, or, even, Herven Myeriel, there were countless spirits of the Astral plane that he could recruit, but, Noldarn knew the deceitful ways of the Corsinian woods all too well. To trust them while in such a powerful place of their enemy's might was foolhardy to say the least. He sat and watched, as the spell was completed. Better do nothing, than evoke Glamawere's wrath in his own den, he thought.

The stooped wizened form of the spell slinger below him convulsed slightly as it began growing, soon there were two Glamaweres standing side by side. The original in a trance muttered slightly, his lips barely moved, as the second Glamawere looked himself over took the jar, and head out of his own hands, before he walked toward the southern most of the four walls, vanishing, through it. Noldarn sighed, he hadn't seen a portal in that wall.

The witch's double below him had finished casting, and stood silently hands placed lightly together in front of him. Noldarn flew slowly and carefully toward the wall hugging the ceiling as he went. The wall seemed plane enough, but as he neared, he sensed it emanating magickal vibrations.

He glanced over his shoulder, and assuring himself that the damned was still engrossed in his spell, he flew, vertical and horizontal axis of the wall. There was no sign of a door, although, there did seem to be a pattern within the brick, a repeating very slight deviation in the surface texture of rock. Yes, there they were, concealed vents, like the ones in the hall way but better hidden. Each carried a well disguised flap of textured metal. But there was something else, an intense magickal energy radiating from the area that Glamawere had disappeared into.

Noldarn flew to center of this area, readying a spell. A short visual and audible ritual for probing and examination. Thinking better of his position he flew above the magickal area, again readying the spell. Then, he began to probe the area. An enchanted barrier beneath the surface of the wall blocked his magick. He could penetrate no further. The whole wall was enchanted. A magickal device of self-generating power, much like the elf's, divining rods, but, far less personal in nature. What was blocking his spell. Enchanted lead! Noldarn gasped. He had encountered lead lined walls and boxes before, but, enchanted lead! This wall had had centuries of work put into it. He found himself impressed. Perhaps a dwarfen artificer from Derem Goria had had a hand in its construction. Surely no human was responsible for such a mass of enchanted metal and rock. There were spells woven within the fabric of the wall, layers of protection upon protection. The diviner in him marveled, if times were different, he would spend days engrossed researching the history of such an artifact. Could he find a weakness in such a device, a chink in its magick armor? Something its manufacturer overlooked? Lead itself was highly resistant to magick this lead had defensive enchantments added to that.

Suddenly, he felt something reflect off the outside of his protective circle. A hex or incantation? The wall was fighting back! Noldarn quickly readied his bow as a protective shield. Any spell the wall threw at him would injure the bow before the elf. Like an amulet of protection, in this way wizards designed layers of magickal defense sacrificing enchanted items before themselves.

Then he saw it! A bolt of rock hurtling from the center of the wall, Noldarn dodged flying downwards. At this size the bolt was ten times his mass. It ricocheted off the top of his circle to explode in a crashing shatter as it smashed into the ceiling. Shards went everywhere, cascading around the elf as he dove out of its path. Those that were not deflected by the circle of protection, did not penetrate the guarding energy of his bow. Then, suddenly a biting pain under his right shoulder. The wound smarted. A rocky fragment had managed to break through his guarding magicks. Groaning, he flew out of the debris' path.

A second bolt flew past him to the right. He glanced toward Glamawere. The witch had already broken his trance. He moved toward the elf, preparing a spell as he came. Deciding not to wait around and see what would be cast, Noldarn flew toward the east where he had spied a concealed door. His eyes had not lied, there was a door, but he knew not weather it was false or true. Glamawere growled, he turned this way and that not finding the intruder.

Triggering a stored illusion from his bow there were suddenly four three-inch high Noldarns, all concealed by his invisibility phantasm. That might confuse the Damned.

"I know thy smell..thy art here.. ssome .....wwhere. "the voice rasped with the emptiness of the grave. "I ssmell thy virtue!!" The damned had produced a wand from within his robes, and staucked across the room toward the enchanted wall.

"What art thou ......aahh ... ELF! "He almost barked the word with anger. "Raagh... Spawn of Thornbreak... musst thee forever... medal in the affairs of man!"

Noldarn, curst himself for not storing an incantation of wall passing in his focus. Now he would have to remember it. Not that he had much use for that kind of thing around the monastery. The high Ellendei in which he had learned the spell came back to him almost as quickly as he could repeat it.

"Elf! thou wilt not go far........Thy art discovered!"

Noldarn looked back toward Glamawere, as he rushed, tracing the gestures for the spell on the wall above the hidden portal.

"Naught but a nat thee bee ...which nat,.... yessss I see thee.....One of these art thee? Corserites .I......Curse thee and thy kin from the unhallowed earth of this our walking grave......... may thy...seed breed corruption!"

The recognizable crackling brimstone of magical fire filled the room. Glamawere's wand spat and sputtered with a gathering flame that issued around him to coagulate in the air. It followed its own eddies and currents cycling about the wand. Until, abruptly it amassed along the shaft of ancient wood. A spherical ball flew toward Noldarn. The witch had pulled magickal energy from the elemental plane of fire. Taking time to materialize, it was the most lethal magickal missile known.

A small ball, it exploded covering Noldarn as it became a sheet of fire. The Damned had targeted bellow, amongst his duplicates, the enchanted circle deflecting the balls indirect fire. Magick splattered around him, then was gone, he remained focused completing the last gestures of his own spell.

Fire surrounded the Damned flowing from his wand to his enchanted circle then back again. It erupted white then gold, filling the darkness of that deep mountain chamber with its blinding rays. As a second, far larger fire ball gathered along the wand Noldarn managed to finish his incantation disappearing through the wall.

Still three inches tall he now flew above the dusty floor of a ten-foot-wide passage. The wall through which he had just passed to his back. An overpowering sickly sweet smell like that of rotting flesh, filled his senses. He needed time to think, and the stench did not help. He grasped his bow, and hoping there were no bats, triggered his transformation into a fly.

Unexpectedly his previous revulsion had turned suddenly to a craving. The tastiness of that smell inundated the sensitive hairs of his new hexipedal form, they vibrated with intoxication. His fly body began involuntarily looking for the source of the smell. Noldarn, himself, fought hard to resist these feelings, and for reasons other than sustenance flew down the hall way. The smell increased as he flew, further titillating him. He buzzed as he went trying out his new wing based vocal cords. Only an increase in the voracity with which he buzzed, belied the frustration which this carrion craving carapace caused.

The passage soon ended in a downward spiraling stair. A slight updraft carried more of the sour sweat odor that the fly found so inviting. Both stair and passage were badly worn, with many cracks and fractures. Noldarn again resisted an urge to investigate the tasty aroma. Instead, he alighted near a fracture at the stairs peak. A plethoric multitude of tinny fleshy fragments littered the rock surface, still toying annoyingly with his hungry stomach. Noldarn himself had not eaten in hours and wishing to avoid the putrid flesh of the corridor he used another spell from his bow to again change form. This time he transformed into a spider. His senses abated, for the time, he crawled into the fracture. There in the dark he finally rested.

It took time for Thomas to realize he wasn't dreaming. All he remembered was the barge and eating. He had felt tired, but this was not an illness nor fatigue. No something more serious. That's it, there had been a spell. And now what? His body gone, incorporeal again! It had been a while. Wizardry, that time too he remembered, Aeo'ostar the Kadron sorceress of Mernnon, a fine-looking woman and well spoken, but a little short tempered when it came to faith. He always felt giddy, like now, no more aches and pains, all those years of work in the foot hills of Mnt. Quenderoth, gone. It was hard, if not impossible to figure out what was happening around you, without training that is.

Praying for guidance, things became more apparent, as if a weight of wool had been lifted from his eye. Enruth was indeed benevolent. Gaseous in form the monk was confined to an enchanted jar, like an imprisoned deamon or effret. So that was it, their enemies had caught up with them. He prayed for Eothan's safety, and for the guidance of his Lord. he had been foolish to travel alone. Bardoth had warned him, but things had never been this perilous. Even during the council of Saint Loth, when Simmon had managed the nomination of primate, there had been no real espionage, not like this. Kidnapped? Imprisoned in a jar? Where was his body?

The abbot's jar was high up on a shelf or mantel, he couldn't be sure which, and these things being as they are, his prison was probably molded from solid lead, a substance impervious to any form of magick. Safe at least for the time being he thought, in a relative sense. Nothing going out but nothing coming in either. At least I'm not dead.

No, not in the halls of the dead.

Few jars there he surmised, my body could be anywhere. Then he cringed remembering the corruption they had found inside the emissary, he only hoped his bodies fate was more benign.

Beginning to get an impression of the surroundings beyond the silver capped jar, he put his own desperation out of mind. Instead, he cleared his thoughts, remembering Enruth and the songs of the land. As he did so visions came to him.

His image heightened.

He was at the end of a long rectangular hall, high up, perched upon a massive stone mantel. A carbite encrusted golden throne stood between the mantel and halls distant wall, its back toward Thomas. It burned in his mind with a sooty golden fire. A figure sat upon the throne, hunched and hooded. Torment, the turmoil of the living tenaciously combating an ever-present mortality was all Thomas could feel. A single spark of gold within a gathering blackness and gloom, the curse of the damned. The captures emptiness held him a while, he had been human once, but now was far beyond the constraints of human morality. A walking reminder of living death, the tomb of damnation. An evil priest! Damned, but still alive.

Smiled upon by the devil.

His Damnation not limited to mere matter of seven years, but a multitude of life times. No, this soul was strong. It would last centuries. The saint felt pain at its tenacious self-identity. He prayed for its forgiveness. No, there would be no easy fulfillment to its contract. This soul was to be whittled down slowly over generations. An amusement to the Devil as long as it continued to outdo its self with its own infernal acts, continually horrific to its own personal sense of conceit. Whichever of hell's angels held this mortal's blooded signature was to feast well, for centuries.

Voices drifted into his awareness.

There were others in the room. They stood at the foot of the throne's dais, divided in two groups by the empty floor at its base. A voice broke clearly through the mist of the Saint's vision.

"....though I be beholden unto you... Glamawere... our duke ties....where lies thy talent?...."

"Don't use that speech with me Arraken knight..... Thy art in the hall of the Damned!" Glamawere rose from his throne and looked down upon the speaker. A tall brown haired Ellendei wearing the Ergedhian's characteristic chain hauberk. Dragon tail and spike emblazoned green, conspicuously on his surcoat's chest. Retainers stood behind him, a squire, Seraious, the lanky lizard worshiper of the Wadeen, the Gunarson's private religious order, and, Sstaithich the priest's tiny reptile companion.

"Glamawere ," the Knight, Davide de Clune, grasped the hilt of his broadsword, shouting defiantly into the hall "Thy be enfranchised unto us.....Glamawere watch least thee be brash.... "His voice carried a warning, a lilting expectation, ".. Thy coven have dipped thy bread in m' lords blood .....All too Oft! Glamawere.....we will haf recompense...for thy feeding....thy charge.! Glamawere ! ...Thy charge be mine!"

Seraus began to pray protections.

Glamawere stepped back he offered quiescence.

"I speak too rashly my friend. To thy Lord Herigar I be indebted.......The warm blood of thine hast oft fed our brood "Glamawere's eyes searched the chamber. Creshmar Goldentooth his woodtroll high priestess stood at the dais' base opposite the knight. Behind the Arraken, Regyurt the young, squire to Davide de Clune, leaned heavily on his characteristically Ergedhen two handed broadsword.

"Thrice three times hast the horde of the Dead drank deep thy gouts."

Yes, they had already tapped the slave pits of Ergedlh over much. The Duke demanded warriors for the coliseum and any blood siphoned to feed Glamawere and his coven costed. Three apprentices of the Damned stood close, members of his coven. Alaghk Ulsha a hobgoblin high priest was nearby. He felt well supported by coven members. Spells took time to muster, however, and Herigar would not be well pleased if more of his minions went the way of the dead. Ergedhian's were the strictest conditioned warriors of the Arraken Knighthood, and, with a lizard worshipper to back them up, Davide and squire could cut deep into his entourage before they were halted. Glamawere was not willing to lose most of his house hold in a confrontation. To assuage Davide's wrath, he would forestall.

"Thou hast been kind unto the deceased, their Kin, and my dark hall, for, the son of an accursed monk, Davide De Clune. What shall we who haf' both drank from the cup Olissria haf such words." He imitated the speech style of the Ellendei Royalty. His hands flattened and widened in friendship.

Davide cringed, resisting a shudder. It was true he had conversed with the Carrion Queen. It was true, the memory of her touch haunted his sleep. But it was an illusion, a phantasm of the knight that Seraus had accompanied through the orgiastic festival of death and reawakening. They had tricked the wrinkled damned. He cared not weather Glamawere knew it had been he or no. Could the wrinkled priest be taunting him?

"Now is not the time for you to depart... we must need converse...in private. thy must carry penciled figures of our script.....that I shall beseech thy lord's eyes withal." Glamawere continued in the style of the Ellendei court speech. It feigned a respect for the Duke's the emissaries.

The knight swallowed his pride for the moment. He took a gauntlet hand from his hilt.

"Lord thy words dissuade the spite of my blade... We wilt have words ont...but low we would to Ergedh town?......"

"Thine charge lies here betwixt us both. .Let it be as so."

He talked with the Arraken, while his mind went to his servant the hobgoblin Alagk Ulsha, "Alagk preoccupy these Gunerson vassals. Gifts of the flesh will feed the hunger of the Wadeen the Arraken knight will take more guile to distract. The coven will convene to have words on this."

Alagk left the hall to make ready.

"All hail...Make way..." Glamawere's herald paced to the center of the hall, a tall Ellendei with jet black hair that started at his golden coronet to fall straight and blanketing to his waist. He wore a black coven cloak lose with its hood throne back. The guild of his tunic sported wealth and bore a coat over its heart that Thomas could not make out. Sound came clearer to him than sight.

"Make way," he repeated again, in a clear voice, to whom in particular it was not certain. "All hail, Alexandra, Herald of the Catacombs, all hail to Ollesria of the Thorned Crown, Queen of the undying. "He struck his cane once resoundingly against the cold granite slabs of the hall. It echoed thrice.

"All hail Ollesria of the Thorned Crown. "The chamber answered in concert, even Glamawere mouthed the tribute to himself as he returned to sit in his daised throne.

Davide and his companions stood silent; gauntlet hands returned to swords. They watched with the unfear that only the eyes of an Ergedhian possessed. Death did not touch their souls.

The stench of death stung their nostrils even before the herald spoke. Ghoul, Davide thought to himself. Oh, that I could dispatch this beast. As the cane's echo died, Ollesria's herald lurched around the doorway. It stood motionless. Then gibbering to its self, it scampered stooping toward the throne on a pair of legs bent backwards by the disease of the ghouls; a baton of gold, silver and red clutched within one of its talonlike hands, a single gold bad encircled its bald head. As it lopped, the baton stuck the ground disconcertingly.

Glamawere studied the herald methodically, as it came to an abrupt halt before the foot of his dais. What did the Deamoness of the catacombs desire now?

It stood up to its full height for an instant, coming to rest in a half-slouched position. It looked about lingering on the full fleshed coven members and the Knights. Then it looked back to Glamawere.

"Iiiiii coome to thee from ssshe who does not sssleep. "It paused to sniff the air and lick its protruding razor toothed maw. It was hard to tell whether it had once been human, or goblin kin, the disease had reached such an advanced state. The curse of the ghouls could only be cured for the first month of its infection. The victim soon became one of the undying, a carrion eater. This victim had been a ghoul for centuries.

Its gaze shifted again and skittered about before it found the shape of the silver capped jar sitting up high and behind the dais.

"I ssssmell the liffe of it. ...." It stepped to the lower stair of the throne, and crouched in a form of bow before the High Priest. It looked around, from here, its glaring stair cutting through the darkness of Glamawere's cavern. No longer humanoid the thin dark slits of its eyes bulged inquisitively. "Olisria wantsss of It! "It spat, a venomous serpent-like tongue probing the air. And speaking out to the ensemble in a search for a response. There was something vaguely human in its face. Its body's disease engorged bone threatened to rip through its tightly stretched green and pink hide. It appeared crooked and powerful, warped, but strengthened in its affliction.

"Wee , sshee wiill have it....You bring us the sauce of the living....As our Queen rules Elledon thy will deliver the sauce of life.... We will have that which isss oursss. Grerrggh" It growled with hunger eyeing the closest of Glamawere's coven. "Give us the Corserite soul. It is Ollisria who rules Ellendon "The ghoul contorted, stretching out a single grouping talon.

"It is not our trinket to barter and sell. "Answered Glamawere from the throne.

The ghoul hissed, moving, threatenly toward the closest of the priest's apprentices.

"Hold fell herald, or, thy life be forfeit" Glamawere began to muster his fire. Issuing from the mighty kiln upon which the jar sat, flames licked around his throne. They coalesced quickly before him to be readied as a bolt of enchanted fire.

The ghoul stopped and looked up toward the Damned. There was no fear in his blackened eyes. Though he knew the fire would be his end.

"Weee will have our recompense....Damned...we hunger... my queen beseeches you!...Tribute You leave usss.....in hunger....too long damned you owe tribute !"

The chamber flooded with an unexpected blue and gray light, as a swirling form materialized in the air above them. Within the blue a writhing of snakes.

"Gorgon wife!" Seraus muttered from under his breath, "Avert your eyes!" Davde de Clune and his squire turned from the swirling. Seraus pulled a small leather-bound book from beneath his cloak and began searching for a spell. A casting so obscure he did not carry it prepared or memorized, but it would ward them from the glare of Glamawere's wife.

As the writhing mass of snakes parted, they revealed, the handsomely angled face of a woman. It floated within the blue and gray light, facing the dais. Brown and red asps, slithered around it. She bared the air of a noble Kadron.

Glamawere stood, fire sputtering in the darkness. He slowly looked up into the face and smiled.

"Love....." He began, apologetically. ".. it has been long mine marrow desires thy temperament. Do thee tire of my absence?.....for lo' thou hast graced us little of late...."

"Don't use the high speech with me Glamawere! Bring me the soul. We hunger for it. My sisters can feel its light...the saint's soul... bring it to us... Glamawere!"

"This be a Coven matter wife. Thy privilege is disenfranchised from my charge." He gestured down to the groups scattered about the base of his throne. "Our duty is not to thee in this! "Glamawere's tone changed as the air about him crackled with increased vigor. He marshalled the fire further using it to punctuate his status in the hall.

"Go consult with thy spirits away.. away , I am in council we will talk no more on't, be gone I say!"

"Husband, you anger with me.... as I swear to walk in Mernnon as Queen .....I swear I will have my will in this. Would thee who has fed my flesh be so harsh. "She pouted and looked about her asps arching and readying a strike. Her eyes searched for those who match her gaze. "My sisters have served thee well...Would we be unlooked for in thy council?.... Mind do not cross me husband... I will touch the glass of thy saint!.....We feel his light..and must feed. Do not we require thine homage. Bring it me It can be thy duty!"

"You anger me. Wife!" The fire writhed about his head and body. "We will talk on thy plea..in time.. Herigar is not to be traitored for thy sovereignty...I tire of thy prattle. Wife!"

Grasping fingers quickly ensnared the jar that housed Thomas hefting it into a leathery lap. Using the distraction, a small pilfering devil of Ollesria's consort had dared the undaring, attempting to steal the Damned's prize.

"The flask!!" shouted Davide. He pointed to where Thomas' soul lay entombed in lead, atop the fire furnace of Glamawere the Damned.

As he drew his broadsword and bounded up the steps of Glamawere's dais he continued, "Thy discourse shall leave our quest ruined.....away beasts of death thy carrion infects....To arms..!"

Glamawere taken aback, turned in time to see the devil, a three foot fiend with horns, tail and forked tongue, open a tiny dimensional door in the air in front of itself and begin to jump in, the jar couched in the crook of its arm.

"SILENCE!!!! THY WILL DO MY BIDDING!!!" The voice seemed to come from deep within the dark mountain itself. It vibrated, ringing in the air, prickling the hair on the back of mortal and undead alike. "OF LITTLE IMPORT TO THEY THAT WEAVE THE FATES ARE THEE! I HEAD OF WOSE HAVE SEEN KINGDOMS RISE AND FALL. WAS MIGHTY LONG BEFORE THE WIZARDS. SHOULD I LAY BY WHILE SOOT BICKERS. THEE WHO KINDLED THE FIRE OF PARNASUSS DO THEE REIGN?

I IT IS WHO COMMAND... A DEATH THAT MAY BITE THEEE ALL.... BEWARE!"

The brown shrunken head had risen from its place on Glamawere's palm, now floating in the air between the glowering Gorgen Wife and the Damned, its lips scarcely moved, while its voice gnawed inside all their heads.

"YOU'RE TIME TICKS ON TO OBLIVION. DO NOT MOVE SON OF ROBERT DE CLUNE. THY BLOOD WILL BE SPILLED AFORE A MORTAL CROWD. THY SHOULD NOT TAMPER WITH THE TRIFLES OF THY PEERS. TO DUST HELL SPAWN!"

With these words the ghoul and devil growled in pain for a fleeting moment to disintegrate suddenly. The flask clattered to the dais, rolling toward Glamawere and Davide who now stood face to face eyeing each other suspecting. They did not move and the voice went on.

"AS MY VOICE IS THINE, SO WILL OUR SANDS GRACE THE SHORES OF STIX ANON, ANON........"

With a flash of contempt toward the Damned, Gorgen Wife's visage vanished.

The head fell silent, floating slowly back and forth. Nothing but the golden white flame of the Damned made a noise. Around the hall, Mnt Ellendon slumbered not.

Hidden Lodge : Hall of the Coven
Glauer's Aud. Chamber
Lodge Quarters
Stair of Concubines
Rooms of Red
Gt. Stair
fire vents
Chamber of the Initiates
Demon sun
Pot. Pis
Temple
Library complex
conjurer
(Gorgon wife)
Glamour's quarters
Wyvern cave
Glamour's stair
Society of Medusa
Prisons (Hall of the Hobs)
hall of the coven
Acolytes of Glamour
hippogriff
Wraith home
Catacombs
Caverns
Offages of the thorned crown
Stair to the lands
Benieth

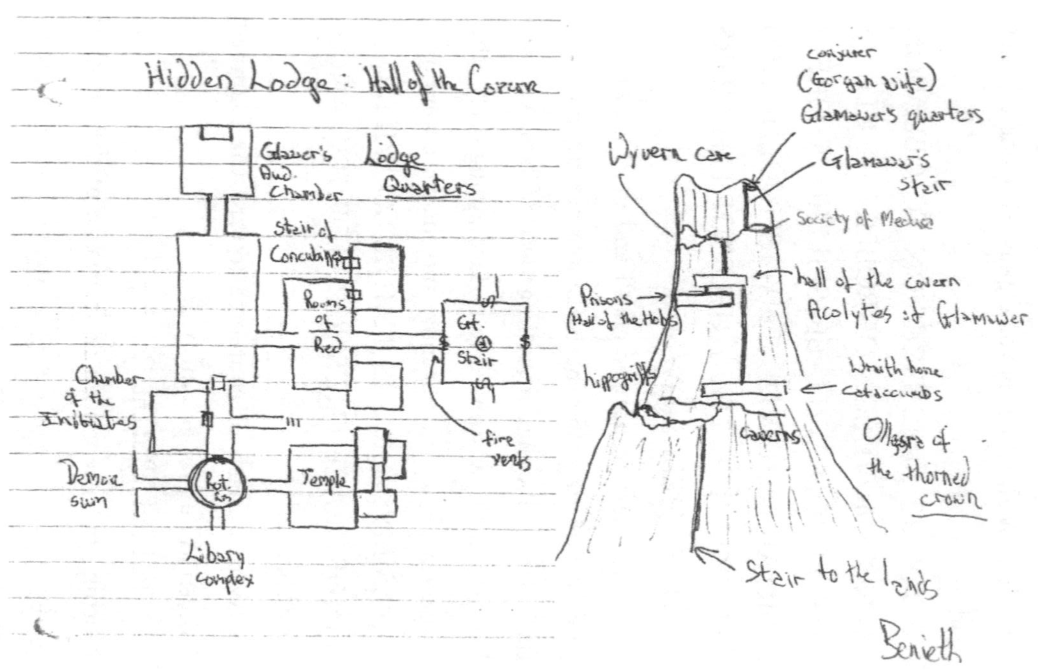

170

CHAPTER 5

WIDENTOWN

The Dwarfen great hall was quiet but for the gentle breathing of servant and hound. Eothan smelt the thick ale of their breath as he completed his search of the manor's upper levels. To satisfy a continued hunger, he grabbed an unfinished loaf from a table cluttered with unfinished food, stealthily steeling out from the thick air of the hall.

Calor was a peaceful village, and the manor its self was not well guarded. Keeping in the shadows he was sure not to linger long in the occasional spill from lighted embrasures.

Tarese waited him at a round view point, the union of their own chamber's tower with the manor's keep. A large iron enforced door, that lead to the keep's crenelated roof stood in its own arched alcove, above. Here she stayed quiet and out of sight.

"The great hall is at rest, there are but two guards." The northern warrior was worried, lines around his eyes carried a hardened look, and his brow was furrowed and tense.

Tarese moved down to meet him. A step above they met eye to eye. He softened to the understanding he found there in her hazel brown Ellendei stare. Placing her hand on his shoulder she touched a single finger to his lips. In the dark, he heard the flutter of her eye lids, as one ensnared the other.

"There is one guard outside the door and two more pacing the battlements." Her breath carried a slight bitter scent that attracted the Northerner. Leaning closer she continued. "I told him I couldn't sleep and needed air."

Eothan exhaled, thinking. "We must get onto the battlements. If it be a water troll, we look for we would do well to search the moat. There is a sewer, I saw its grating from our chamber window. Can we pass the guard unseen?"

"Yes...I have a way.... Eothan the Fair. I will charm the guard into a deep sleep. While he is bemused with dreams of Derem-Gora we will steal our way to the battlement stair." Then she added conspiratorially "Now Corserite see how the worshippers of the hidden land do their work." Still whispering it was now the unusual scent of the Berelan powders mixing with the perfumes of her skin that made Eothan's head light. He remembered the mountain heather of mount Corser.

Tarese pulled her robe tight as she produced a small silken bound package. Throwing her head back with a toss she consumed its contents, swallowing them whole. Her eyes bugged as she grimaced and involuntarily shuddered.

"Yuk I don't like the taste of that one!" she said. Then her lids fluttered and her eyes rolled back as she went momentarily limp. Eothan caught her from falling and as he lifted her to be propped against the wall. She became suddenly lucid. There was a haze in her vision but she spoke with certainty.

"I will charm all I see to a slumber of dreams..." Her hand flinched directing the spells energies "..Open the door."

Grabbing the doors large iron handle Eothan threw the door open with a heave. The dark night welcomed the wanderers. Tarese had been right, there was a single Dwarf guard standing close but looking out from the keep off toward the north, as he turned toward them Tarese stepped past Eothan, her hands held in front palms forward.

"Sleep now my friend... sleep ..rest thy weary bones dwarfen comrade and think on thy gem fields for thy art the keepers of the holly fields of Goria. Inheritors of all that crystallizes. The veins of thy metal run deep within the land and will nigh be spent afore the Imprisoned

One stirs again....Think on't and rest....thy weariness will pass."

Her voice was removed, distant, it carried with it energies from the astral and ethereal planes, and her breath glittered hanging in the cold night.

The dwarf's turn became a spin repeated twice as his legs slumped below him, staggering. He struggled against the sudden weariness, attempting to speak, but then as nothing came, Tarese de Ghent daughter to Genru star born, master of the Irdiwin lodge, Keeper of the Land Unknown, got the better of his will and slumber was a upon him. He lay still, flat on the keeps roof, a gravely snore issued from deep within his stomach.

He was still snoring as Eothan attached the end of his climbing rope to the battlement's crenellations. Its end dangled down toward the moat coming to rest a foot above the grate. Tarese still enraptured by the planer energy she was channeling stood guard on the battlements as Eothan quickly scaled down. Once reaching the grate he managed to lodge himself between two of its iron bars thus staying above the water line.

He concentrated remembering the wilds of his northern home, and, after settling his mind, quietly, in the forest speech, cast a spell of dark sight.

As he had expected this was not merely a piece of dwarfen plumbing but the entrance to a concealed mooring. From where he crouched he followed the water tunnel back under the keep with his eye. He estimated it to be about eighteen paces long, ending in a small dock that had room for two small row boats. As no boats were there now, he guessed that the quarry had already fled.

Pulling his shield from around his back as he slipped between the bars of the grate and then drawing his falchion from its scabbard, he lowered himself into the cold water. Placing the dagger on top of his shield and using it as a float, he pushed it in front as he swam.

The walls of the tunnel were slick with slime from the many pipes that issued rank effluent into the moat, Eothan coughed keeping his head well above the water line. He prayed quietly to Enruth in an attempt to keep pure from the sewer's rancid corruption. Quickly reaching the mooring he pulled himself out of the water searching the tunnels end with his eye, hoping for an exit.

No door was immediately apparent, but after collecting his thoughts he began another dweomer in the forest speech. This spell revealed footprints to the caster, Eothan had learned it from the elf Seretral a year ago at the monastery. He finished the whispering language, as the incantation took effect. Already an excellent tracker, with such bewitchments he could find signs of passage on even the solid rock of this underground hideout.

The chambers surface carried minute cracks and fractures in the large slabs of its construction. After a few moments, with the magick's help, Eothan began to decipher a pattern within these marks, they followed areas of ware. The continual use of the chamber by its inhabitants had taken its toll. Although slight, Eothan made out two general paths of movement. The first and major trail ran straight from where the chamber met the tunnel to disappear under the inside wall. The second, from the chamber's deepest wall to the dock's mooring.

Eothan examined the wall where the first path vanished. His fingers lightly brushed the algae smooth surface. The large dwafen bricks fit close, yet, after examining the work closely he discovered unmistakable signs pointing to the presence of a hidden portal. A clear fissure around the wall indicated that a great section of it would slide back in on itself. If only he knew how it was triggered?

His finger tips probed the gap to no avail. Moving on the Fair searched the remainder of the wall being sure he didn't miss a thing. The precision of the dwarfen manufacture was impressive, he felt sure that if it had been human, he could force it open. But the ancient Derem-Gorin's who had lain these bricks had been skilled beyond the norm. There were no braziers or torch holders that concealed the trigger, nor were there Dwarfen runes or cabalistic symbols, it was not particularly magickal, just plain solid workmanship.

After scouring the whole wall and finding nothing he began to despair, he thought of Teresa, and, the battlements, surely, she would be expecting word. How long would she be safe up there? He looked about the watery chamber, then began to examine the adjoining walls. Near one corner a slimy alga revealed a single bare foot print, obviously not dwarf or human it was either merkling or goblin. Eothan quickened his search, what had become of Thomas?

He started with the wall under which the small fracture path disappeared and again finding no trace of a portal or door, worked toward his original position adjacent to the secret entrance. He wondered what was beyond that fissure in the snug rock.

Whether Thomas was imprisoned beyond its impassability, or as he expected the saint's captures had already fled with their charge? He did not know for certain. Perhaps he expected to find evidence. A sign left by the captures. Could his sword and bow be hidden there? He remembered the two groups of the mountain top and hoped that he had followed the right one. He needed evidence as to where Thomas was being held and by whom. Something that told him he was on the right track.

The second wall proved as fruitless as the first and he began to search the last of the chamber's walls, cold from his water drenched leathers, worry for his friend and teacher wore him thin. He longed already for the company of that young Ellendei maiden and her strange powers. There were few at the monastery of his age and since the death of his clan he was only filled with a longing at the meeting of peers from his own people. A dearth of friendship had resulted. Wishing to return to her gentle comfort he was about to give up his search altogether when he heard a soft familiar voice that spoke from within his own head.

"There is a way in young monk."

"Thomas!" he spoke allowed. "Where art thou."

The voice chuckled. "No but thy art close. It is true I carry some of saint Thomas the Young within me..But alas we are far separate. No Eothan I be Queratuer, Der Aeth, the Death Dealer Heavy Flail of Saint Thomas the Young and Rod of Corser. Thy be not alone my disciple only distant."

"How am I to reach thee."

"The small door way will be easy for thou I will aide thee. It can be levered ..Have faith ..trust to thy own strength Enruth is true to the virtuous, as thy believe so follow thy faith to me.."

Of course, thought Eothan during his last fast on that mountain top, he had seen, or thought he had, no, he was sure; Enruth, in the form of the great hunter had come to him and with words spoke softly in the speech of the wood lands, and in the forest speak, had taught unto him his latest magick. The spell of following he had named it, an incantation to aide in the finding of paths and directions. With Queratuer's presence perhaps this spell could draw then together.

Although it was dark already, Eothan closed his eyes to concentrate, the spell was new to him, far more complicated than many of his more simple incantations and the chance of a mistake carried with it serious consequences. It was the Norcadian mage Alserantur the Shifting who had immolated himself and many of his kin with a miss spoken spell of kindling. Eothan was glad he knew only the innocuous incantations of the forest, for they did not punish their practitioners so harshly for the occasional blunder.

As he finished the forest words and opened his eyes, the path became clear to him. The smaller trail of prints led his way, and he sensed toward the Corserite artifact. Once more he examined the far adjacent wall of the chamber. The door, surprisingly easy to find this time, took some bending and prying with the point of his falchion before he managed to crack its old iron bolts. Ideas came quickly, as he sensed or knew that there would be no impediment to his progress. The hidden panel slipped backwards, revealing an open space beyond.

Stooping he ducked under the lip of its frame, finding himself in a small roughhewn passage that wound to his right and left, presenting two alternate routes. Knowing instantly that he needed the right he crept on. Large enough to accommodate most men, Eothan found the ceiling too low. He adjusted his stance to accommodate, holding his shield outward, the dagger underneath and at the ready.

A small side passage ended abruptly in a metal banded and reinforced door, this told him that he was in a dungeon or prison. Where else would such reinforced portals of such a small size be necessary? He passed two more such cells before the passage opened into a cavernous antechamber. It was empty, but for two passages and a heavy door. More cells could be seen down each corridor.

The air was moist and quiet. Silent, for aurt but, the constant dripping of stalactites, small calcium carbonate fingers that reached stretching from the roof. Eothan thought the cells to be empty. One thing was certain there were no guards and the passages showed little signs of use.

Knowing that his path took him through the door, he inspected the passage and crept backwards towards it. Paying close attention to the iron reinforced cell portals.

Finding the heavy door unlocked, he sighed in relief and cracked it an inch.

Nothing. He opened it further.

The space beyond, was well built of the same Dwafen brick as the manor. A long irregular room containing two other doors, one directly opposite and one to Eothan's right. They were both reinforced but the opposite door was giant a full twice the size of the others, far larger than that of regular Dwarfen construction. A massive key hole gapped in its center, that, Eothan thought to peer down. He imagined the huge key that must fit the lock, and the even larger hand that wielded it. The troll? There was no telling for certain. His magick disclosed that the quarry of his search lay behind the rightward door.

He ignored the large door, finding the other locked, and hearing no noise to indicate that these chambers were occupied he prepared to force entry. First, he made fast work with his falchion loosening the hinges. Surprising himself with his own strength, they soon succumbed. The door itself took three quick but loud bashes till it crashed, clattering, to the floor. He hoped the sound would not travel far through the thick ribs of rock about him. He would not be alone for long if it had.

The room beyond was smaller, oblong in shape. It contained a long table pulled back from the left wall, and a spiraled stair descended into its left most corner.

Carved into the stairs axis stood a menacing marbled Dwarfen lord in ancient Derem Gorin battle armor. Two door adorned the wall opposite; smaller than the last, but, both carried key holes.

The room was dry, sporting a ruddy brown woven rug, and, a portrait of Calor the Young hung conspicuously between the doors. A dusty incense mixed in the dry air replacing the heavy, wet, mildew of the other chambers.

As Eothan hurried across the room he was stopped by a graveled voice that carved through the musty dry with the alienated, distant, authority of the grave.

"Thou wilt depart from hence kin of man.!.."

Eothan froze, the voice rose the hairs of his neck. The room was empty, or so he thought. Then he saw a shadow, a darkness within the dark. Above the stair it moved toward him around the edge of the room. A swallow turned deep in the pit of his stomach.

Eothan lunged toward the door and finding it locked threw his whole weight against it, to no avail. Only a feint snapping somewhere within it gave him hope.

"Thou art a traitor, behold now thy death .

.. For though thy heart think'st thee circumspect...

...Thy blackest thoughts haft thy deeds revealed..

The happy wrigglings of thy bowel sauces..

... here upon my silken point needs must lie..

.Until thy silent head lie severed.....

. my wanton incensed soul shall rest no more!!!!!!. "

Eothan stood transfixed as the shadowy dark within dark billowed, convoluting, then, a gray white within the dark revealed itself. The unhappy visage of a grimace ladened dwafen lord, much like that of the carved stair, glowered from beneath a still forming crown crested bassinet.

A malevolent spirit, Eothan took the silver cross that hung from his neck and praying under his breath held it toward the forming spirit.

"ahhhhhhhhhgh..!!!!' bellowed the ghost.

"This..... thy race's Treachery speaks ill of thee

...Haf't thee not the courage to face my sword."

No, I don't thought Eothan, he swallowed trying to clear a dry lump from his throat, then, holding ever tightly to his cross he spoke out. As a monk he had faced undeath many times over the years. The Corserites had trained him. He had been assigned to accompany a quest to quieten walkers in the sparce villages and hamlets of Corsina. Hopping this was a lone spirit he reached for the blessed Corserite cross around his neck. If he was to face undead, he would rather companion an exorcist or more experienced priest.

"Back restless soul I am not thy enemy..".Words came easily...."In the name of Enruth Lord of the land song you are naught but a shadow to this land...sleep spirit your time of revenge will come."

Eothan turned toward the glaring armed visage and thrusting the blessed cross toward it took a step with all the courage he could muster. The Ghosts voice shook the bones within him filling the young priest with the dread of death's grave. Eothan's hair prickled with its presence.

"I am Eothan the Fair Corserite monk a warrior of Norcadia .." Braven by his words he continued. "My people have no quarrel with thee ...your might is great Lord and I be no Arraken for thy slaughter...Sleep I have been no enemy of thine"

The spirit rose above Eothan as it retreated from the power of his cross. There it floated aggressively brandishing a mighty broadsword the Caldorian gemstone glowing coldly, a dull red, on its shield. It stayed its ground, frowning thickly toward the monk.

The priest kept his eye on it as he stepped back toward the door and prepared another bash. It took five more solid shoulder blows and a swift kick before Eothan stepped through the right of the two opposite doorways. He found a small room beyond decorated with tapestries, it contained a work table, crowded book shelves, a bed, a chest and two urns full of rolled parchment.

Against a book shelf and in amongst a number of other weapons, which included a large bejeweled dwarfen battle axe that caught Eothan's eye, was Der Aeth, Quenature the Heavy Dealer flail staff of Saint Thomas the Young. It looked plain compared to the silver and gold glittering ax that was its neighbor, yet Eothan was gladdened to see it. Grasping it quickly, the flail's three chains hung lose, heavy and, strong solid iron on steel chain. Thrown to the side of the same pile he found his own weapons the barbarian long sword and bow.

The hideous image of the Dwarfen ghost was nowhere to be seen, Der Aaeth had banished it to the Astral plane, from whence such spectral beings came. Caught unhappily in a half-life, they dwelt there, about nexus that linked the astral and prime material planes, consumed by the particular troubled fate that had caused their death. There must be an interesting story behind this specter, a past relative of Calor wronged in death most like, was he murdered in this dungeon? Ghosts were unable to move on to the halls of death, unless offered recompense or resolve. Necromancers found ways to manipulate and profit from death, was this a natural haunt or conjured by the art of an arcane practitioner?

Hurrying through the anti-chamber and out to the tunnel, the way he came, he paused, noticing a high-pitched hum, a fluctuating chiming that issued from one of the prisons nearer cells.

Fearing to spend more time, he denied his urge to investigate and hurried on. He winced, leaving a dwarfen axe of such unsurpassed quality, yet, time demanded they not be encumbered by extraneous items, it pained him to think on't. A weapon like that was worth an entire Norcadian kingdom, and many were they among his people that could use such an axe for good in this fell time.

Finding Tarese carefully perusing the battlement, quietly waiting for his return, she was lucid again, the distant look gone from her eyes.

"We must hurry," She Said. "The guard will soon awaken, should we not be gone?"

Eothan lowered Tarese into the moat and after a short swim they headed into the predawn night. Once within the wood Tarese transformed herself and Eothan had to be content with his own company as he searched for signs of Thomas' captures. Tarese moved quickly on all fours, scouting the forest ahead.

Queataur was not aware of who their assailants had been, but when he attempted to ask the relic with his mind, images of magick and extradimensionallity flooded his consciousness. The weapon surprised him, at times, it was heavy, but, now, as he hurried to keep time with his distant comrade, it was light as if he carried no weapon at all.

Although he had had little training in flail combat, he somehow knew Der Aeth already. The weapon fit well within his barbarian grasp.

Running on through the night, the heat from his body fought the wet cold of his tunic and briefs, their soggy fabric a weight and added burden. A crashing in the brush signaled the boars return. Transforming as she stood upright.

She grimaced broadly.

"You travel slowly." She mused. Eothan bowed his head slightly. "...I have found your friend however........ well-guarded but still in priest garb"

Eothan met her gaze. The stress showed clearly on both their faces. Young neither had tackled tasks of this magnitude alone before.

"Who!" managed the young monk, he was once again exhausted. Keeping up with this shape shifter was a task in itself, wet and tired as he was.

"That troll for one and our friend Calor the younger... They are camped out waiting for something...I got close enough to see your friend. He wasn't tied up ...must have been under an enchantment. The troll sat close.... Three murklings and two Dwafen men at arms. Not far from here...... we could reach them before day break. The west fork of the mourn carves through Corsinia beyond these woods and that is where they camp...Barge stop manor is to the south.... They wait for passage on the river. I know not from whom."

Tarese's robe hung lose and in her excitement she did not notice. Eothan glance slipped down to be caught in the curved pattern of her ribs, her abdomen pulsed with the inhalation of speech. Its lines of muscles shined in the moon light from under a shadow cast by her breasts. Shaking his head he remembered who he was and what they were discussing. He kept his eyes from being drawn in and down. Instead, he lost himself in her gleaming brown eyes and the sweat glistening along her neck.

"What shall we do?...... well come on priest this is your quest!" She almost snapped.

"I'm not a priest." he replied," I be only a monk."

"Well monk....... what now." She held her cloak around her, again, shivering against the night. "With out hair this moon lit night is cold."

Eothan looked at the trees around him. Similar in form to the mighty oak of the monastery. Their trunks carved dark columns into the bright night. Air was cold and crisp; the slow whitening of a morning frost caught their upper branches.

"We must hurry ...surprise them before dawn." Eothan smiled as his eyes returned to hers. Der Aeth kindled the courage within him. "Thomas' quest must not fail."

They ran again, Tarese in the form of the mighty boar as the sky became dark, cloud sweeping in from the south east to blot the starry sky, no moon shone through the thick immovable blanket.

Leaving the wood land they climbed quickly between steep hilly dales before they plunged again into the thick woodland that covered most of Corsinia. As dawn approached the pair drew toward the west fork of the mourn. Eothan recognized the smell of its slow-moving water in the air's sent.

"The river lies close." He said.

They found their quarry busy readying a breakfast in the receding darkness. Unaware of the observers hidden in the downwind trees they made no attempt to disguise the camp. There was no sign of who they were awaiting. The water troll sat close to his companions, large, rotund and massive. He kept an eye on the approaching dawn, and their captive at the same time. His mighty jaw rotated in a slow grinding motion as he gnawed a leg of raw mutton. Above rows of gnarled teeth and two massive lower tusks, his tiny nostrils twitched and twisted to a predawn breeze, that reached it from the water.

It's thick brow and heavily sloped forehead were furrowed with crevices and hardened crystal lumps that made its hide impervious to all but the strongest well directed blade. Seaweed and algae covered its upper torso, hanging lose and in knots. The cloak that barely covered its enormous form had been tossed back by immense arms thicker around than Eothan's thigh. Rune carved rocks and enchanted bone hung on twine from its ear lobes and appendages, and two glittering, beauteous diamonds glinted from its chest with fire light in the predawn light.

The frost had hit hard, that night. Eothan crouched close concealed by hardened grass, The run had warmed him throughout and the ice only cooled his forehead. He noted the groups movements keeping track of their various locations. He watched the troll, a group of around six goblins with murklings lay toward Terese.

A dull crunch followed by a slight movement within the troll's glottis told him that the mutton leg had been swallowed. Eothan saw intelligence in its beady eyes as they scanned the river, hopefully, he thought. Expecting he knew not what.

He imagined plunging his long sword deep within that giant throat ending the troll enchanter's life forever. Oh that it was summer, and, the sun was about to crest the mountains of Corsinia, but the sky was thick with cloud, and the sun may not be seen all day. Even so, a troll of the water was never happy in the light of day and their impending battle could only be aided by the ever-present dawn. Turning from the thick-skinned foe Eothan crawled to were Irdiwin's daughter lay waiting, in human form.

"When the dawn comes it will be hard for me to keep the form of boar." She said. ".. especially if it be that the sun breaks through."

Eothan looked up into the slowly lightening sky.

"The cloud is thick ...that which will aide our enemy will aide us..also...I think there is to be no sun on such as is this day...I had hoped on sun to hinder the trollen wizard.....Now I hope for none."

"Let us not delay least they should receive succor before we strike."

"I will move to the north and attack the troll...... you.. come at them from the south....I trust you are a formidable foe... as is the reputation of your people? Wait till I ready myself..... your attack should come first." He looked to her for affirmation, dwelling longer than necessary in the deep of those auburn brown eyes. Dark in the pre-dawn, he remembered hazel streaks from the torch light of the dwarf hold. The lycanthrope carried much of her people's potency within her, the threat of a warrior, hardened by battle preparing her energies, flickering beneath her gaze's calm.

Eothan made no sound as he carefully crept stealthily through the frozen brush. No early bird had yet chosen to break the cold silence of the pre-dawn. Through the dark, he could barely make out the distant bank of the mourn. He still knew not for who, or what, their foe waited, but any brave enough to kidnap Saint Thomas the Young, were not to be trifled lightly.

After he reached the river's edge Eothan worked toward the group. He hoped to take the troll from behind, thinking that a sudden attack from the water would be unlooked for. Somewhere the sky must be brightening, but the cloud was far too thick to tell.

A voice within his head spoke quietly. "I am still with thee Norcadian." It was Teresa. "I can hear thy thoughts.... When thou wilt I shalt attack the Merklings."

Eothan crouched against the bank, the slowly heaving back of his enemy lay above him. He pushed himself up with his tired knees till he was lying full long in the sod. The melodious high-pitched speech of merklings mixed with deep dwarfen sounds, drifting from beyond the hulking form of the troll.

He prepared to attack readying the powerful Der Aeth in both his strong hands. Its three massive iron spheres hung sullenly on chain, solemnly waiting by his side.

He did not relish a chance to again meet a troll in mortal combat. Especially a spell wielding water troll. Settling his mind he prayed to Enruth, the one. And when, finally, he felt the Land with him, he steadied his grip and replied to his friend through his mind.

"I am ready Terese de Ghent daughter of Genru Starborn." They were both surprised that he knew and used her father's full name.

"My tusks will carry thy quest unto thine enemies!" The boar answered ruffly.

Leaping over the bank, Eothan swung the Death Dealer in a mighty circle about his head. He found the heaving back of the troll, covered in a voluminous red and gold emblazoned cloak, and exposed for his weapon. The attack was silent, but for three massive enchanted balls of Der Aeth cutting through the frozen dawning night air.

Eothan's arms and legs added impetus to that great blow as it smashed into the warlock's back. Each ball landed with a distinct and separate thudding sound, biting their enemy hard. Not waiting to reprepare the flail, the Norcadian shifted his grip delivering a resounding strike with the weapon's metal handle into the side of his opponent's head.

The troll warlock growled as it staggered from the attack. A slash behind its ear spewed dark trollen blood.

"Inginderal asenyak..Kenddareeal..." It began an incantation in the black speech of trolls.

Eothan stepped behind, not allowing its hideous face to meet his. Once more he smote with Der Aeath, the

Heavy Dealer. A shout from the merklings told that the were-beast was upon them. They screamed scattering in the dark.

A rapid upward stroke with the flails shaft parried the trolls gigantic grasping claw as it closed to constrain him. He jumped still remaining behind the warlock.

"ahrwalLLLLLLLLLL ! "It growled in an attempt to continue its incantation. "…….ahrwall in tosh nadral Yarech…"

The night was not clear and dawn would be slow. Again, Eothan struck its mighty back. As each maneuvered, they circled bringing them toward the center of the camp and further from the water. The flail had cut mighty gashes in the troll's cloak and dark thick liquid oozed, drying as it met the cold night the trollen blood hardened quickly. Much of its first wound had healed by the time Eothan stepped back to ready his fourth strike.

Giving up on its spell the troll fumbled beneath its robe. Eothan's hands descended together propelling Der Aeth toward their enemy, again.

The troll's neck creened as he kept a steady gaise on his assailant, the whitened silver of the flail glinted within their reddened glow.

Hunching quickly, and with an involuntary cough, the troll leaped forward on its mighty back legs. Frog like its legs hung in the air before it returned to the earth crashing to the ground near a pile of cloth bags and leather satchels at the camps center. Eothan's blow harmlessly reflected from the ice hard ground, for a moment he had caught a glimpse of the troll's tail tufted with a head of brown wisped hair, now he peered into the night for his quarry.

There was light in dark, the day creeping upon them. He made out bodies lying at the tree line, the dwarfs and murklings he presumed. A distant crashing told him that the rampage of the boar had not yet ended. He scanned the enemies camp and finding a pile of their possessions and tackle, he glimpsed, that which he was looking for, a blackness within the steady brightening dark, the sorcerer!

He would not surprise his enemy again. The touch of Der Aeth steadied his nerves.

The darkness moved, steadily toward the swollen river before them, a sphere, easily large enough to encompass the troll.

The enemy was escaping! He sensed through the impenetrable darkness that St. Thomas was also before him within the dark.

"Thomas! "Eothan muttered and gritting his teeth he ran headlong toward the dark. He swung the flail twice, adding momentum, the sphere continuing its steady pace and as it neared the bank, Eothan bore down upon it, a translucent wall of black that cut off the now visible far bank from his view.

Ice, great shards of ice, erupted from within the blackness. The first crashed into Der Aeth shattering around the acolyte. A second caught him in abdomen sending him back and to the ground grasping for air, as two more flew off above him to crash careening into the forest behind.

Eothan groaned as he heaved desperately trying to catch his breath. He rolled to his back and probed the half-light for the warlock. Nothing! He took up Der Aeth and staggering to his feet he heard a splashing beneath the waters.

"Escaped!" He looked widely about him for a victim on which to vent his rage, and hopping to encounter a merkling or renegade dwarf he stomped gloomily toward the wood.

"Lo.. why so glum Norcadian." Terese stood near the camps baggage; her hands out spread she meditated.

"I lost it! "Eothan spat. "May Enruth damn them! All Spell slingers!"

"All..." She replied.

"All Troll and Murk thing sorcerers!"

"Yes.....There is magick amongst these belongings not much mostly the petty dweomers of the little people....."

Charms, cantrips, enchanted materials perhaps....
useful....and I sense the presence of greater magick..a
presence that has left the imprint of its power amongst
the enchanted fabric of these things."

Eothan fell silent, he examined the early day for a
sign or omen. The shape changer gathered a handful of
the materials before her, storing them within concealed
pockets in her robe.

"The water.... we must pursue. "Eothan stood and
leaning Der Aeth over his shoulder he made his way
back to the water's edge.

Terese followed, the warrior was weary but his
mighty shoulders, wore their fatigue well. His long
golden hair hung mattered behind his head. Her hand
went involuntarily to her own, they could both do with
a comb and brush she thought.

"They were waiting for something....A rondaiview?"
Eothan searched upstream for any sign of traffic, they
had reached the west Mourn a river not as populated
as the east and without an improved ox track. Leagues
downstream lay the river Lener, well known for its
Tratian long boats and being the southernmost port of
the Dwarfen bargers guild.

The water undulated as it passed silent bar the
occasional lapping at its strained banks. Soon they sat
and feeling the cold, they warmed themselves against it.

Terese by consuming a ground mix of enchanted herbs and forest leaves and Eothan through prayer.

"I presume …….you're the troubled friends who called. "The large bulbous head had crested the water in front of them. It bobbed, large green eyes blinking as they swept around their sockets taking in the surrounds. Whiskers on its cheeks highlighted a sensitive motile nose much like that of a horse. Large, it kept pace against a strong current with front flippers and a round tailed body.

They were taken aback. Eothan stepped to his feet.

"Well that's not much of a meeting is it." It went on. "I must say who's helping whom here anyway."

"You are not here to meet a troll witch….a warlock?" Terese asked.

"Troll! I should say not. I am not a minion of Bogwood or any foul denizen…. I merely heard your plea for help…" It paused, dipping its head as its large tail broke the surface maintaining its position in the mourn. "… but, if you and your warlike friend are safe then… we …will be on our way."

"No wait." It was Eothan. "Do not leave…No…You may aide us. "

The new comer grinned, its mouth almost disappearing beneath two flabby cheeks.

"A change of heart…. How can we be of service? "As he talked three similar creatures surfaced up stream.

They drifted toward the companions, their breath calmly floating above the mourn in the cold morning air.

"Er..." Eothan stammered "....I....hum? ...We have lost our priest a water troll sorcerer has kidnapped him escaped into the mourn I know not which way he went."

"I see." Then he turned to the others and with a beat of his tail moved amongst them. After a few moments of grooming and head nudging they came to a silent agreement, then separating they disappeared under the slow undulating water of the mourn.

Eothan looked quizzically to Tarese.

"Manatees, river people she replied. Rare but friendly...... The Murklings eat them..... if they can catch them that is. "

The manatee who had spoken soon returned.

"The evil form you seek passed down stream. The river voices tell that it is on its way toward Widern Town......We know this spirit...many of my people it is that have been lost to its hunger. Widern Town is crowded with the fleet boats of the north.... though man hungers not for our flesh.....If thou wilt ..we shall transport thee hence as water steeds.....sea horses."

"We would be very grateful." replied Eothan.

As a second manatee surfaced Eothan climbed to the back of their new found friend. My prayer will help fight the waters cold, he thought, pulling his northern firs tight.

The manatee pushed out into the current followed closely by Tarese and a second of the river people. The water was indeed cold, their legs warmed by the respective powers of sorcery and prayer felt its icy bight but only superficially; there was no threat in the sensation. The manatee swam at a steady pace, the river bank passing quickly due to the added downward current.

Eothan wondered what they would find in the overcrowded cities of Arraken, and why the troll was leading them there.

The troll and ogre bolstered ranks of the hill giant Bogwood lay to the North.

The smaller west fork of the mourn meandered through the oaken forests of southern Corsinia. Low lying hills and the periodically flooded branches of oak crowding them in. There was no rain but the sky remained overcast. Eothan thought of the monastery and whether they had had their first snow fall yet. It had been only a week since their departure and the mission was already in a shambles. Who would warn the Treathbaron? If he managed to rescue Thomas in Widern they could head north from there and all would not be wasted, lost time was replaceable. What of the tribes of the Lands Beneath, and the oaths of the Imprisoned One? They had little time.

The manatees were fast much faster than the barges of the dwarfs. They followed the far bank passing opposite a small manor with barge dock and then pushed out into the strongest current.

The trees here were predominantly smaller not the massive oak of the northern forests. Periodically the oak broke into large willows whose branches drooped lying limp on the surface of the flooded tributary. Areas cleared for firewood or timber left empty grass covered meadows, and the sense that the forest was not immune to the advances of human kind. Eothan felt a growing unease at the butchered groves that clung to the river bank. They were approaching civilization.

There was little conversation, the manatees did not speak, at least not noticeably, and, Eothan and Tarese conserved their energy to fight the cold.

It was late afternoon when they reached the confluence of the Maun. The eastern portion far larger than its sister swept them away in its ever-increasing flow. Here the river traveled east, but soon it swept south through a long bend. After a day of travel, they found themselves in the last of the day's waning light, floating through a cultivated flat. Ringed to the south by the Boarder Downs, highland that lay between the baronies of Arris Leon and Mangara to the south, and Corsinia and Tratia to the north, there were many villages scattered upon the plain. The Fell, lay to the not distant west, a wild land watched by the strong arm of the Arraken knighthood, separated the duchy of Drake and Arraken's western baronies from those of the east.

With the darkness Eothan's steed became more talkative. He explained how he and his herd frequented the northern reaches of the mourn staying away from the more treacherous southern waters. He being more of a wander had in his youth explored the Lener, where he had found others of his kind in the water of Lener Lake, known to the Ellendei as lake Lemarr.

It had been years, the greater part of a century, since he had made that upstream journey, and he knew not whether they still dwelt there, or no. The amount of traffic on the lower Mourn and Lener had steadily grown till now the trip itself was dangerous. Although, the Ellendei did not go out of the way to hunt Manatees, the hungrier fishermen would not pass them up. Their friend worried for his distant relatives that he had once found there.

Homesteads bestrew the farm land, more frequently as they approached Widern town. The yellow of lantern, torch, and fire sparkling throughout the flat land. The smell of the fires reached Eothan even out on the river, the water doing little to dull his keen nose. Their steeds dropped them close to the Widern barge, bellow the meeting with the Lener, and close, but south of the great pens of barge ox. The distant honk of who's bellowing filled the early night.

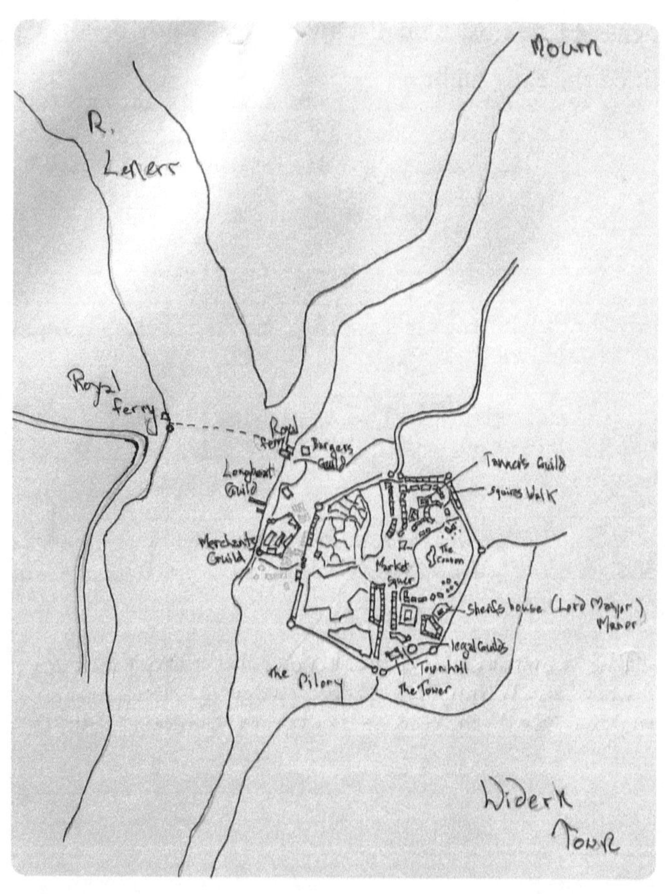

Rothr
R. Leherr
Royal ferry
Royal ferry
Burgess Guild
Longboat Guild
Tanner's Guild
Squires Walk
Merchants Guild
The Croom
Market Square
Sheriffs house (Lord Mayor) Manor
legal Guilds
the Pilory
Townhall
The Tower
Widerk Town

CHAPTER 6

THE HOUSE OF MAUB

The spider Noldarn rested, the alluring smell of the flesh had become a distraction again, gnawing on him, filling his mind with the wish to investigate. Different than fly huger the spider-Noldarn had an urge to hunt to suck dry a living creature, small or large. His intelligence told him that Thomas lay above him somewhere, imprisoned in the age-old granite of Ellendon.

But his unabated hunger told him that all of import lay below. It became too much. He simply had to find the source of that aroma. The enticing stench of meat. The spider scurried out into the hall way descending along the roughhewn stair's ceiling. It passed fractures and cracks that contained far fresher morsels of spidery diet. The unique smell that issued from the depths now urged it on. Where could he find a pristine morsal to drain of its living juice.

Circling forever downward. He climbed, the high-pitched sounds of bats, not a distraction, too brave in hunger to notice. Noldarn now only dimly aware of Thomas' plight could only think of satiating the bottomless hunger of his arachnid's abdomen.

A door of great dark hardwood, ancient and carved, inlaid with metals and enchantments old before the coming of the Ellendei to Arakken sealed the stairs descent. Following his senses Noldarn soon found entrance under its over worn masonry. The years of use had carved deep ruts into the hard rock of its stop.

The spider moved quickly, long hairy legs propelling it along the smooth stone of Ellendon. It passed a litter of lose fractured granite, and ascending limestone slabs. On its eight legs it pulled itself up a vertical surface reaching a masonry plateau.

The smell was everywhere now, and Noldarn knew not how he chose the direction of his progress. He was in a large catacomb, proceeding along the surface of one of its many crypts. From here he got the feint sense of movement. Shambling death within the dark. The soft pat of bare flesh on stone had replaced the squeaks of the distant bats. Still, he moved on. The sound steadily grew.

Creeping from sarcophagus to tomb, grave, and burial, passed crypt and mausoleum, he continued. A knobble green surface of luminescent fungus lit the way. A caustic surface for the spidery exoskeleton dim and unnoticeable at first, it grew in frequency, and population. With its density came the light, a green hewed blue that touched the solid rock right angles of this unholy land. He avoided walking on the stinging fungus, keeping to bare stone. Appendages tapped out their progress to a melody of patting fleshed feet. No other sound.

With the light, the forms became clearer, a shambling mass of silence. Now clothed, now naked, they moved forever onward, like sand in a human hour glass they crowded in their uniform walk. Hemmed in by tight walls they moved massed, ever on.

Cassocks, and tunics in tatters, clung despairingly to bone and canker, the vestments of the dead. Some carried their flesh mummified, desiccated about them, on others it hung fatted replenished and half dead; gangrenous, death adding life to its rot. Still others had been transformed, diseased by malignancies, held in suspensions of half and unlife. Souls encased within the dooms of hell they were. Their imaginations allowed nothing but torment, the fear of what awaited in the hexemery hexetory hexet, the 666 abysmal layers below this portal. Their infinite hunger urged them to action and so they shambled. No thought only the empty need to move. The lower layers pulled them on.

Finding a wall, the spider began to make its way between the clumps of fungi vegetation. There acidic odor stung in the sent fibers of its legs, further warning him that the growths were not benign. The path proved torturous, it took time to pick and choose a way. There were times when the fungus reached a mass that necessitated risking the floor and the crushing weight of the walking unlife. So, he continued, crawling aside and above converging passages of silent death.

The sweet odor had not abated and Noldarn could not free himself from an overpowering thirst for it. His spider senses detected a dull ringing repeated at intervals, a gong. The passage in front opened up and there was a thinning of the luminescent fungus. Yes, it was a gong, he was sure of it. Shaking the hairs of his legs with its reverberations. And more, a new smell, mineral in nature, fire and brimstone. He climbed out and into a massive chamber wrought out of the deep rock in Ellendon's center. No pillars held its roof aloft and nought but the dull blue green radiance from a sparse spattering of fungus gave it light.

Beneath him the dead converged from each side of this their great chamber, an excruciatingly slow-moving mass of humanless humanity. In eddies they caught, paused, to eventually re-animate in their ceaseless momentum. They spiraled about themselves moving to the left in a pattern repeated for eons.

No voices!

Merely the quiet deafening slap of their naked feet on soft stone. Towards the circling's hub, an incline, a declining cylinder, took the throng down and out of site, deep into the bowels of the earth. The spider Noldarn new not where they went. Some walked on bare bone, most on flesh, still others wore cloth or hardened leather footing.

Mortals he thought, a never-ending sea, fleeting sparks that last no more than a mood or humor and then are gone. How the halls of their after death must overflow. And with that thought he returned to his Elfen form and concealing himself with enchantments drawn from his bow, he sat crouched on a natural ledge above corridor from whence he had climbed. Why had he followed these things? Where was Thomas? He remembered the scent of flesh and the overpowering desire to feed. They continued to shuffle on.

After time, the Elf noticed variations in the uniform throng below him. Slight counter currents, that lasted for a time, to be engulfed in the momentum's mass. And more, creatures that moved amongst the dead, ghouls, he knew them named. Humans diseased beyond recognizability, that walked, and leaped, on legs moving backwards, like swamp storks, or cranes. These foul beings searched for prey amongst the dead, clicking, and humming to themselves in a talk of their own devising. On finding a transfixed victim possessing a greater amount of flesh than most, they fell about it, rending the sorry soul between them. Like hungry jackals, they thus hunted and preyed, squabbling between themselves for sustenance in amongst the dead.

Winged fiends, that Noldarn imagined gargoyles and imps, flew above and between ledges, roosting in the crevasses of Ellendon's bowls. Their high-pitched squeaks clattered about the hall, prickling his forest sensitive ears. He needed to find the saint's soul this catacomb was a distraction.

Emerging from the southerly floor of this chamber rose a tier of diminishing terraces. It looked much like the step pyramids of Thrasia, or Nabroth Melzanos, lacking only in size. Yet, it forged a space around which the merging mass of death yielded. Their shambling giving way to unforgiving rock. Upon its summit Noldarn spied a tapestried divine, scattered with pillows. The gigantic gong from which the periodic clang that echoed about the hall and throughout its adjourning passages issued, hung behind suspended between two marble columns. Braziers burnt red and hot at each of pyramids north-east corners.

It stood askew to the caverns four cardinally located entrances, much akin to the brick chamber from above, the figure of a women sprawled amongst the divine, and shadowy shapes moved about her. The winged beasts alighted there often, conducting their foul businesses before leaping to the sky, and retreating to their rocky lairs. A particularly large winged form stood beside the gong wielding its heavy metaled stick. More a mace, than an instrument of music, thought the elf.

But his eyes were ever drawn toward the reclined figure at the divine, she was beautiful beyond compare. Long, black un-waved hair started at her skull, covering her in a shiny blanket of dark.

"The dark of a starless sky." The Elf whispered beneath his breath. He was washed with waves of cool. It was if he was the first of his race spying the dark of the sky, before the birth of the stars. His eye witnessed the black of those first nights, the primary constellations suggested hesitantly with a vague twinkling in her eyes.

The sky immense and softly powerful in its omnipresence, the first stars mere specks within its black. He was lost, lost within that hair that was the nights first sky. A sky before the birth of the multitude, before now, before the time of the thousand wizards, and the Ellendei, before the Gods fragmented into the manifestations of present myth. Those stars that took time to trace their first journeys through the void of their birth. His peoples' astrologers and diviners had had eons to record their tribulations, time to meditate on every change, become aware of its implications. The millions of conflicting and ever-changing constellations of this time made pre-thought difficult at best. It took a human Astrologer like Gordel Erendile to fathom and translate todays sky, its shifting, developing consteller interactions and the godly events that they reflected. He longed for that uncluttered sky of his races birth, a time before humanity, before the Ellendei, before Norcaidia, or Brahil. It was this longing, a yearning for a lost darkness, that the alluring reclined figure awoke in him.

Pale ivory blue skin, thick blood red lips, and thin ellipsoidal eyes, filled with darkened brown that threatened to engulf what little light lay about their edges. She wiped aside the glimmering black of the hair, riveting him in the contrast. He saw no clothing about her, only the cascading black.

To her left stood a thin white boned pedestal, twisting upon itself till it reached a tangled crown of thorns red with fresh blood.

"Ollisria the Mernonian hand maiden of the dead." He thought.

In Mernonian myth she was originally a princess kidnapped by Hados prince of the underworld. Rescued by her lover, she returned to Hados' care when the agreement for her rescue was broken. In Mernonia she was considered the keeper of the door to never ending night. The last to call on in the name of the mortally wounded, or sick, those on their way toward death.

Enthralled by her beauty, he watched as her chest rose and fell under the sheen of hair. She looked upward, distracted, as if lost in some distant thought, then, her gaze fell to the ceaseless throng at her feet. She hardened. He saw her eyes swallow the glimmer of humanity he had caught there, his heart ached, as if he had seen her die, fall within herself. He wanted to fly to her, to take her by the arm, to end her servitude, to say. "Despair not I will fight for thee!" But why should he first born take a mortal's fate upon himself? A mortal with an immortal curse. His race had been old before her race had appeared in Arraken. Why did she command his attention so?

She turned on her divine, swung her legs to the floor. Rising she looked about, from the flattened pyramid top. The giant gargoyle behind her grimaced displaying its canines, and throwing back its head, it gargled deep in the back of its throat, then, turning toward the gong it struck twice. The reverberations echoed, smothering Noldarn where he sat, shuddering him.

There was an answering flurry of activity from the demonic roosts above. Ollesria looked up and lifting the crown she held it aloft, stepping down toward the shuffling swarm. Her thin arms out stretched she stood solemnly, and as the first foray of winged forms fell among the host, she pulled the barbed coronet sharply to her scalp. Spines gashed into the pure silken skin of her forehead.

Then they were airborne carrying skeletal and zombied body with them. Ollesria stood silent her hair shining back in the blue green light of the cavern, as blood dripped from beneath the crown dashing red along the black sheen of her natural shroud. Noldarn watched as tears welled in the distant brown of her Mernnoian eyes, splashing into the pooling blood diluting and cleansing that which it fell upon.

A shadow, blackness in the blued green of the pyramid, moved, it stooped at first, knelt, then upright at seven feet it sprinkled yellow particles at the Queen's feet, vanishing as soon as it had appeared. The particles writhed, growing as they were washed with blood and tears.

'Devil spawn, larva of the damned.' Noldarn thought. His grey and steel eyes hardened. Kernels of those spirits diabolical enough to join the deamon ranks, the maggots from which the imps and their larger brethren were grown.

The maggots lapped at the Queen's feet, each carrying a distorted, pained human head, slurping up the blood and salt water, by the time the maggots had reached the length of Noldarn's foreams, he perceived a number of the dark shapes, emerge along the perimeter.

Seemingly they materialized from nowhere, milling around the edge of the pyramid. Then suddenly, as if by unknown command, they converged on the Queen in unison. Noldarn saw her fall prone, and pushed back to the divine before he lost sight of her engulfed in their darkness, as everything in that cavern froze as if suspended in time, even down to the last insignificant skeleton. The unceasing throng ceased. A single pitched and shrill female scream tore through the mountain, merging finally with the silence.

Noldarn could not think, he found himself half way toward the pyramid without any form of concealment, he had automatically loaded his bow with his finest shaft, and flew as fast as his spell and gravity would cooperate to carry him. The shapes were gone before he could reach her, as were the new grown maggots. The queen lay crumpled, her hair beneath her revealing a slight fragile body, effete, black enshrouded nudity. Noldarn felt as if looking itself could damage her. The tears had washed her person clean of any blood, leaving her silver shining bright, white within the black blanket of her hair.

He alighted and knelling checked for breath. Then he gathered her in his arms, carrying her unconscious body to the divine. The thorned crown had returned unseen to its pedestal, it sat unsullied with no sign of the blood it had drawn from its monarch, waiting in peace for the next ritual.

"First born dost thee wish for thy demise?

Me mace itches to crush thee out o' life."

Noldarn looked to the daemon before him. Red and brown fire licked golden around its silted nostrils. Two mighty bat wings spread behind it. Sulfur stung in the back of the elf's throat. He did not relish a battle.

"I humble my self before thy greatness.

The Mortal one of dragons is not to

find me opposed to his claim on Thornbreak." Noldarn lied. He did not support Duke Herigar Gunnerson or his claim to lordship over the faery kingdom, Thornbreak. The Queen still slumbered. Then he told the truth....

"We be both servants of the same master,

a lady beyond compare, beauteous,

white as the grave. From who we seek respite.

For Ollisria refrain from use of might.

Our peoples have their quarrels. Keep True!

The bond beyond death aswades my race quest.

And whilst me blood boils, for thee I shalt toil.

A refuge of hated beneath thy thorned crown.

A truce from fleshy conquests, bought dearly

upon our undamaged forms, that without
strife may strive to shore up this Queens honor.
Least our many factions, through our seeming war,
erode that self-same strength, a unioned power!
Unrivaled the host of Ellendon we stand.
Do not, by untrifeled boasts, squander that
divisionless front. Least by fractious bandying
and brutish tyranny thee dost dishonor us all!.."

Noldarn stood beside the divine looking up to the daemon that easily stood ten feet at its shoulder. High pointed ears twitched and turned reacting to his every word. He gripped tight his bow ready to draw a circle of protection from its finite source of magick. Amused a smile crept along its double fanged mouth, and flame flickered around its leathery body. A cloven hoof stepped toward the elf, clattering the rock with a stamp they both froze attentive to the other's words.

"You shame thyself with foul cowardice Elf!
This mace boasts a full twenty of thy kin.
Thy heart dost speak before thy courage......Elf!"
What care I for the honor of thy Queen.
My fate be sealed bellow her domain.
For though I beat out hours here, maggots
fatten in putrid lands deep down from hence.
One elf more I see, a noble victim.
Thy head a necromancers wand wilt be!"

With that a beat from his wings, and circling stroke with the mace propelled him toward Noldarn. The Elf dodged to the air using his fly spell he landed on the other side of the divine where he drew a circle of protection in the air about him. The daemons speech had allowed him to cast the first half under his breath, whilst his enemy was preoccupied. He finished the protection ritual quickly, once again, pulling energy from his bow.

"Lord of loam thee fight! Thy cowardice shames me!"

The daemon rose on a leap from cloven hoofs, and as his wings directed the descent toward Noldarn, flame rippled along his sinewed torso. Fire of immolation shimmered the air about in its heat. He rose the mace skyward, again preparing to crash upon the Elf's protective circle.

"In the name of the sacred pools desist.
As Serderan still reins in the land of light,
I forbid thee, thing of despair avant,
cross not my circle, for thy doom is nigh!
Noldarn of the fallen house commands thee!
Halt!!......."

Holding his bow in the center with both hands the elf stood cross like a light watery blue washed from under his fingers. Minute waves soaked to the ends of the bow were they trickled about him reflecting blue in the green light, bolstering his circle with liquid strength.

The hoofs recoiled in their attempt to land, unable to break the natural wizardry of the elf. Instead, they clattered to the pyramid as the be-metaled mace smashed into the circle. Noldarn shifted as it swung past, an answering blast of cool liquid struck back, staggering the fiend toward the gong.

"Who dares offend my sovereignty...? Art thy hell fiends not yet tired of thy marshaled violence?.......Do I of mortal born..who hast served thus three thousand lives more than my heritage prophesied....must I who endues all this....Weepeth for thy pains, a score and more.... betwixed each sun birth, must I thus....be affronted by clamor at my place of rest.....SILENCE I SAY.....least thee be crushed to the dust from whence thee came. "Ollesria sat upright her hair about. Her swoon had passed.

The daemon hissed, returning to his place besides the gong. Noldarn turned and not wishing to gaze into the face of the waking beauty, knelt on one knee, lost for words. He had only felt love once before, over a century ago, in Thornbreak the court of Sederan high lord of the faerie people. He knew not how to put his thoughts into words, and less knew what feelings scorched his soul, was this fate that this doomed mortal should touch him so? Or a cruel enchantment that he knew not of? Reaching for words all he managed was a high stammer.

"I Noldarn high born of my race.... pledge thee
my honor...First born are we, from death immune.
To thee, dark of the starless sky, Ollesria
of Hados doom, my sword for thee shall fall,
or, in thy sight may flourish for thy will,
A faltering light, a star in your night....."
Ollesria rose and crossing she stood above him. His
eyes draw toward her, he kept them down cast noticing
her slim feet, and firm ankle step from under the sheet of
black hair, slender toes gripped the flagstones. Perfume he
thought, a scent of the distant Mernonian heath. Taking
his face, she cupped it toward her gently. Brown probed
deeply into steal gray, and as tears welled in her subjects'
eyes, she bent and without kneeling kissed his forehead.
"Thy shalt serve well Noldarn, first born.
For not now twelve glass falls hence a herald had I
Glamawere the damned and Woes the lord
all to dust they have taken him hence......
In place whereof thy first born servst well
Thee to his staff do I willingly give.
Rise Elf lord Herald to Ollisria.
The Throned crown thee doth tend us well.
To ghoul thy predecessor quickly fell,
may thy blood resist foul curse, doom and hell."
As she spoke a herald's staff appeared in her soft
hands. Noldarn took it willingly, and he rose herald to

Ollisria of the Throned Crown. In the ages since her doom befell her, Ollisria had not appointed a herald from without her Mernnonian clan. The first born would serve her well.

The ceremonies had gone well, feats of skill, feasting, theatrical contests, the blessing of the temples for the upcoming winter. It had been a good year, the rains had come quick and snow capped the Enorian peaks early, still these were not bad, omens, and they added to the splendor of that sun filled afternoon. The air was crisp, it carried a sense of autumn early in these high peaks. From their repose high on the templed peak of Mernnon, the party of Uuk first born to Sarkhen Heathkeeper, grandson to the great traitor, Oritand, relaxed. Litter bearers would soon arrive to carry him down the winding stair to the ruined city of Mernnon. First born and prince to the great house, he was sleepy with wine.

It had been an age since the city had boasted a population to fill those streets, now a religious retreat and manufacturing center for statues and pottery, not the trade capital of the mighty empire it had once been. A mere tenth of Mernnon was still occupied, the once unrivaled city lay scattered, swamped by sand and dirt that had blown along its empty streets since before the Wizard Kings. Yet they still honored the festivals each year.

The acropolis, as ever the most important seat of Kadron religious power, rose from its center. Eroded not it still retained its original elegance and strength. Home to the gold, silver, and platinum, be-marbeled arches which the pantheon of Kadra called home. From here the Oligarchic priests of Mernnon maintained the precepts and relics of their many mythologies, as they had done for millennia before the Ellendei migration and the Wizard Kings.

And so, the princes entourage sat merrily, they had supped bountifully of the years wined grapes, and, the undulations of many a temple maiden, had guided them with the dance of love. Now they laughed and shared a joke in that mountained haunt. Long from hence were the spring's trials and combats, their traditional Mernnonian games, and the jousting of the Ellendei knighthood.

The titanic temple to Kadra the all-powerful, the patriarchal lord of time, and tyrannical overlord of the pantheon sprawled behind them, as they lounged on its steps waiting for transport. During the opening ceremonies, now days hence, a monster, a griffin, half eagle and half lion had flown out of the peaks north of Mernnon, and in homage to Kadra, had alighted upon the temple roof top. The grand priest had rejoiced triumphantly announcing it a grand omen for Mernnon.

The cause way between the many temples, surprising empty for a festival season, reflected the heat of the days sun warming the companions against the mountain air, languid in their mood. The House of Maub had married themselves into the Ellendie aristocracy taking on the name de Vishi, it was a construct, not accepted by the Kadron priesthood who traced the lineage back to the Kadron Gods themselves, Gods who had interbred with mortals creating demi gods and heroes and the now defunct houses of Kadra. Only the de Vishi of Mernnon, the House of Maub still survived. Their own bloody house history that involved matricide, patricide and divine vengeance, was kept out of the Ellendie politics. It was reserved to Kadrons themselves to know the true mythologies and histories of the people.

Ortand the Traitor had declared an independent Merrnon, and fought a war with the Ellendie King over 100 years ago. Ellendie were still considered heretics by Mernnonian and Kadron priests, but they were also married to the first house, and far to mighty a Knighthood to conquer. Merrnon's survival depended on the House of Maub maintenance of a truce and companionship with the Red Towers, and its Primate Simmon Worshiper of the One. So marriages with Ellendie nobility and the adoption of the name de Vishi. Ortand's desperate bid for independence and crusade against Sarkhen and his Ellendie allies had been destroyed. Maub was still the ruling house, and Unk its first son.

Unnoticed, the insignificant, shrine to Helgetei, gold beside its great brother, cast a long shadow across the acropolis, like a sun dial pointing a gnarled finger to the south and Berelan in the afternoon-late sun. Silhouetted, no one noticed the winged worm emerging from a mosaic on its spires east.

Within the goddess' northern mosaic, women-snakes, gorgons, and naga, crouched stone and still as the winged worm stirred. Eyes opening its head pushed out from the metal coated column, hissing as it breathed a lung full of the warm late summer air. Its chest rose with inhalation emerging from the embossed bronze.

Its wings stretched and when aloft it began to grow to its natural thirteen paces. It made no noise writhing southwards to attack the resting party of prince Uuk unawares.

Surprised and without proper armor they had little chance. Brushing aside inebriated nobles, with a flick of its tailed body, the serpent entangled the first prince of the house of Maub in its constricting grasp. And, with a mighty roar that temporarily deafened the company it flew north, disappearing over the snow topped Inorian peaks.

The prince and his captor swept north west, following the wilderness along Arraken's boarder. Sober now, Uuk felt unusually at ease as if something amiss had been righted. His friends, the ambassadors at court, even the Barnakan princess to whom he was betrothed felt distant, inconsequential pieces in a festival game. The serpents tail gripped tight, without causing discomfort, its dragon-like head spurting embers and flame warming him beneath its reptilian wings.

It had no limbs, an articulate body, and tail constricting its prey, with a strong viced jaw and forked tongue. Uuk of Maub recognized the steep sided canyon that for eighty leagues marked the boarder of Mernnon with Corsinia. The enormous ravine stretched beyond his sight to both the north east and south west. Known to the common people simply as the Gorge, it had for ages been a focus of political intrigue. Separating the land of Kadra from the Ellendie new commers.

With the gondola at Parnassus the only public method of passage from one bank to another, the importance of the Mernnonian, Abadosian, and Pellian portage cranes could not be stressed enough. With the river deep and easily sailed, the cranes, bureaucratically controlled machines, determined the rate of trade for this third of the kingdom. The only way, beyond flight or mountaineering, to traverse the four-to-six-hundred-foot cliffs, the cranes were well protected, each with its own militia, and clan of engineers.

They hastened on above the Great Cragg into territory that Uuk knew not, Corsinia he guessed. Mighty yellow and gold autumn forests, and barren mountain slopes. The titanic mountains of the north, barony sized peaks, that his people's priests claimed housed Heaven, the home of the gods, dwarfed their lesser brethren to the south. Uuk spotted the North Enorian peaks the continuation of the range of Mernnon's acropolis. Here the beast turned slightly and descending it approached a single peak to the ranges far west. The land mostly dark. Bellow them only the towering Enorians were visible, a reticent race of granite stone giants, mute witnesses to the passing ages of man, that had settled its more accessible heights. It will soon be night, he thought.

Winging slowly, the worm gently came to ground along the peak's south. The prince stretched flexing his muscles against the sore of the flight's stiffness. Growling, snarling to itself, Uuk did not feel threatened by the beast.

"Lord Uuk, you will follow. "The voice was spoke in the ancient ceremonial speech of his people, and, as if participating in a ceremony, he obeyed.

Two hooded and robbed aspen priestesses ushered him along a well-worn mountain path. Arms hung loosely at their side, their robes reached to the track's dirt where massy serpentine tails emerged, oscillating them forward toward the mountain. The wurm screeched behind, as it once more took to the air.

From his position between the two he saw their hoods undulating, a muffled background hiss warning him of their serpentine contents. Gorgons, he thought, and spying small wings folded on each's back he knew. Gorgons! Kadron myth talked much of these winged deamon forms, and their ability to turn mortals to stone with a glance. Beings of the gods, they were, like, many mythological creatures descended from one particularity famous set of ancestors.

As the first house of Mernnon, the predecessors of the Maub had had dealings with these divine monstrosities. The traitor Oirtand had consulted with a Gorgon before the assassination attempt on King Geldon, and the profit Ollisria had warned of their Deamonic influence. Ollisria of the Thorned Diadem, their house's curse to provide their first born as heralds and confidants, was that the reason behind his kidnapping?

First born to the house of Maub knew not.

Entering the base of the mountain through an open rock lined passage they ascended slowly. Shadowy images passed him on either side, half faces blurred as if through heavy rain, the hissing snakes reminded him that no weather was responsible. Magick was about. Before he knew it, they had entered a columned doorway, braziers lit a small antechamber, shadows danced along its marble mosaics, curtains to each side and front marked three exits.

"You will wait here." Said a hooded serpent woman, before she parted a curtain disappearing through, her tail wafting the fabric as it vanished. He stood, alone, still watched closely by the second of the two escorts.

Well trained in combat, and court etiquette, Uuk of Maub had little knowledge in wizardry. He knew the legends of his people and some of his anti-sorcery training delt with anti-magick precautions, not enough to give him confidence, not here amongst the such unholy hand maiden's. He stood.

The steady rise and fall of his chest told him that time passed, but how much he could not tell. Frescos, mosaics wore on his mortal mind, filling his head with images of strife. Troubles and tribulations, ever solved by serpentine females and their devout meddling.

Resisting their seductive sensuality, Uuk reminded himself of the epics as he had originally heard them in the temple of Kadra, for the demi goddess Helgetei and her serpentine minions had for ever been the antagonists in these tales, not the saviors as this priestly propaganda attempted to establish.

"The First Lady of Helgetei will see you now." The priestess spoke from beside him, gesturing to the curtained archway before them.

Within he found a modest temple gloriously bejeweled and adorned with the snakey manifestations of the goddess. Statuettes and statues lined each long wall, ending in a bronze, silver and golden serpentine that filled the far wall with its tail, a female body stretching skyward to the ceiling. Asps, gleaming eyes of diamond, ivory fangs, and golden tongues, watched every corner and approach, from their vantage upon her head.

The statue grasped the bow of Miss-fated Love and the Thorned Diadem of suffering in each of its human arms. Uuk guessed her to be Medusa the infamous hero of Hegetian myth. A manifestation of the demi God herself it was said.

Braziers lit the room with yellow flickering from the ends of a long low cloth covered alter. Two hooded and robed snake women lay prostrate before the craven goddess.

No pews cluttered the empty stone work of the temples floor, so the Prince was led directly out into its center of large flagstone. The prostrate priestesses rose one returned to her place flanking Uuk. Escorted once more, the third robbed gorgon turned toward him, pronouncing in a voice loud and at time shrill but ever clear beneath her hood...

"We welcome thee, first of the house of Maub
Helgete mistress, to damnation's subject
hand maiden for thy ancestor in doom,
benefactor to the tortured soul.
She who toils with incomparable trust
for thee who the gods have to Hados thrust.
Here thou wilt the noblest soul mate find,
ally in prayer, companion in bed,
mate to assuage the dread storm of undead,
for like the happily subdued steed,
our plentiful virtues, for your commandment
reins its unbridled, sorceried, passion's charms,
a dowry of life's priceless bawdy fun,
colts and mares to but thee beholden,
galleried slavery a crime to thee be none.
Our priesthood's guard, from ill to thee extends,
if with Helget's crown, extraction thou intends.
Thy predecessor diseased and raked,
did rein, a herald besieged, to Tarter went.
Escape his fate, by we, your allies make,
so bow thy proud house to thy knee, with me,
unto, the vapid worm our troth shall be,
a union of faith, before Tarter's door,
thus, through princely strength, eschew death's fell arm."
With this phrase she rotated back to the statue, her
tail moving little. And with her back to him removed

her hood, she lifted high a silvered bowl from the alter, and went on.

"A scroll for thy protection do I bless,
a heart from thy field's yew here I offer,
before my god to seal this vow for thee,
Behold thee our relic, a bow thy stock
hast wished within thy influence command,
a Bow of ever Misguided Love, is she,
to her sphere, our pledge's witness shalt be,
that from our malaise thy service is struck,
Ollisria's herald, a prince born art thee,
serve thy house long in this its cursed fate,
bondslave to none, vassal to Maub, as she."

Uuk watched the head of aspen hair from behind, knowing full well that a stair from her face would be his death. He kept his blue grey eyes cast down, looking at the floor. As allies, the priesthood was dubious, untrustworthy, but here in their lair he tried his best to think distant thoughts, thoughts as to his own immediate fate, his betrothal to the gorgeous princess of Barnaka. A pity that he had not taken their offer of a numerologist advisor more seriously, was his fate as Ollisria's herald sealed forever? the door of Tarterous, to be forever his home? or did his well-planned life on the outskirts of the Ellendei nobility still have sway? Why had not the priests of Kadra come to his aid?

Was it not their job to prepare service to Ollisria?

Donning her hood, she turned back to him. He smiled, finding his court etiquette useful in hiding his true feelings. Eyes still down he did not meet her gaze. He swallowed an urge to run, Instead, searching himself for a diplomatic answer.

Smiling again, he cleared his throat.
"I Prince Uuk of Maub, inheritor to
the curse of Ollisria, doom prophetess,
bleeder in the dark, thorned sufferer;
She that dropeth her life eternally,
that we may knowest not our own demise.
Progenitor of my line, from hence forth
thee I will serve. For in thy sufferage,
our sins do thee expunge, from shadowed life,
hast though our fate removed? Unhallowed
thy surrounds, but hallow be thy motive,
wounderous soul beyond reproach art thee,
haunted one, to who mighteous Kadra
dost willfully bend his proud vengeful eye.
Zombied, drifting, lost, animals without
hope were we, faithless, husks devoid of hope.
Till redeemed by thy tears and dropping blood.
To thee I pledge my heart from this night on.
The holy serpent may my ally be,
I know not till thy service they entend...."

Unfamiliar with speaking to goddesses, gods, demigods, and heroes, Uuk hoped he made sense. He used the high style speech of ceremony and weighty discourse.

The robbed priestess made no reply, instead lifting the bow she gestured in the air, pointing directly at him as she said in the ancient tongue of his people.

"To Ollisria thou art now joined...

...To Ollisria I thee commend!"

Engulfed by a black cloud, all vanished momentarily, to be replaced by the divine of Ollisria of the Thorned crown. A sea of death lay about the tiered pyramid of this his most famous ancestor. She sat pillowed upon her diadem's seat, the gnarled crown at her side. Behind, he saw a glowering daemon, gong, and, mace, red and gold before fungal greened gray rock, of the cavern of Ellendon.

All this he expected, but surprised was he to find a first born to the race of man at Tarterous' door. An elf, carrying the scepter of Maub, adornment as if the herald of Ollisria of the Thorned Crown. A fate to which his own doom should have intended.

CHAPTER 7

TOWER OF WIDERN

Eothan stood watch beside a tree whilst his royal companion donned pantaloons, hose, and tunic. Her simple plain cape, he thought, housed more than a commoner's pantry. She was ever drawing things forth from concealed pockets about her. The days light still oranged the sky above clouds to the north, the night was dry.

"Ready. "She piped, stepping from her improvised boudoir. Her dress reminded him of a wealthy Ellendei tradesman who had once supped with the Corserites. Noticing his gaze she added.

"It's appropriate I assure you.....Not Corser...I know.....But then nor are you.... usually keep my status a secret...remember no magick.... None...Not even your miracles. The spies of the inquisition are everywhere.. You are noticeable.....whatever you may think...As a foreigner I mean....So don't pick any fights!"

"My people are not war like...The Corsers have taught me the ways of peace..........We are not of the holy fighting orders that protect the inquisition....I can defend myself...And if I must I will."

"Yes...well I am exhausted...and since the moon is no longer full. I would love a comfortable night's sleep in human form. "Producing a small velvet pouch that jingled slightly as she tossed it upon her palm, she smiled. "I know a modest, tidy inn...that is safe...I'm buying....if you will?"

Eothan pondered. "Yes ...I believe the saint is within the walls of this town....Widern." He glanced down to the Corser rod that he held in his hand.

Snickering, politely, behind her hand, Tarese led the way. They crossed from the rivers through a cowfield, and pushing between the tangles of hedgerow they emerged to a modest cart track. The pair turned, and hurrying they approached the lights of Widern.

They found the North Gate open, guarded lightly by two Ellendei soldiers. Tarese paying a toll in copper pennies, led them beneath the large key stoned arch. Still hurrying she took Eothan by the hand pulling him along the street. A collection of small shops lined the narrow road, and there were two public houses: the Dwarfen Smithy and, the Wood Man's Cote, a choice for the thirsty. Neither looked well to do, but nor were they seedy. Opposite each other, vibrant colored signs enticed the traveler, vying for silver through engravery and bright paint.

Tarese ignored them both tugging him on. Clean for an Ellendei city thought the Northerner. He had never been to the Greater Kingdom of Arraken, although, he had both heard and read accounts of the sewage that their crowded style of life created. The smell of food dominated his senses, pig, chicken, goose, duck, lamb, and beef, he recognized all, broasted and thickly sliced. I am hungry, he thought.

The salty sausages sold ready cooked by-passing towns folk ignited his mouth with saliva.

"Muh.. They smell good." He said.

"Carnivore." The shape changer joked. "I Know a place. It has the best herbs.....An apothecist sells all manner of things there....close. The same family you see... they have herbs ..and food.."

The hubub at the gate quieted quickly and the shops soon became residences. There was less light, shuttered windows allowing only thin lines of bright heat into the night. A tired group of leather legged pike wielders moved from door to door, a lantern carried by their leader glowed on their faces. He checked each house secure, before moving on. With long well cropped beard, mustache, and red sashed blue uniform, he looked absurdly obvious. That watch will surprise nobody, thought the Norcadian, was it intended to be that way?

A left at Silvermongers Lane took them from the small towns empty market square toward an elm, maple, and grass common, land within Widern's walls. Governed by communal grazing rights, it provided the town a place where animals could be kept before they were sold for food or breeding.

Walking past a single line of houses, toward a collection of barns and chicken coups, then taking another left, they found themselves climbing up Tanner's Circle toward the town's east wall. Squires Walk, a narrow resident sided street nestled against Widern's wall, bought them, through a tight winding bend, to the shop they sort.

"You see when Primate Simmon outlawed magick the kingdoms great arcane guilds and societies went undercover...Many moved north to the more tolerant provinces of Corsinia, Tratia, Loast and West Ridge. Here in Traitia the marquis, Wirkael Ciraden, refuses to arrest spell users, but Widern is a royal town under Ottar's jurisdiction. The inquisition has spies here...The mayor, a newcomer from Arris Leon is a pawn to Sental, Ottar's Chancellor of the Exchequer and close personal friend to Illid, Scourge of Pellia... Well the herbalist I know.... She had a business in Berelan but moved it here because of the troubles. There have been no burnings in Widern nor T'bah, but the Witch Hunters have arrested people here, and there have been kidnappings, and disappearances of spell users."

"My farther does not like it. And although he still treats Ottar as a friend, Ottar is his nephew you see, he is very unhappy with their relationship. Of course the Forgiving's authority protects our house from Simmon and his lackeys...At least for the time being."

"Saint Thomas planed to travel north to consult with the Treathbaron Baron. Only he is trustworthy to the Corserites." Eothan was feeling out of place already.

Tarese had found the shop, a tall house against the outer wall. Its ground level sported a sign that read Warders of the Herb in yellow letters beneath a boiling pot. The upper stories created an overhang, under which Tarese quickly stepped.

Pushing open the door, she beckoned over her shoulder.

"Now in this place we can trust the food. "She whispered placing a hand on Eothan's shoulder and leaning toward him. He smiled back with his light green glance.

The hall beyond had been converted to accommodate dinning. A large fire crackled in a solid stone hearth, that divided the hall into a Kitchen and lounge. They stood to the lounge side, over a rough wood counter were a variety of boiling and warming pots. Drying herbs hung from the ceiling. Their aromas mixed relieving tied joints with a sharp earthiness.

Yes, Eothan liked the choice. A youth appeared from the canopy grinning widely.

"Tarese De Gent...I ...well ye are righe' on time. I just steamed ye favorit' yams n' truffles..will that it be then?"

Tarese smiled. "Yes, I'm famished. And let my friend order too please.... ...Oh.....er.... let me introduce you... Theus Dergen this is Eothan the Fair a Norcadian."

Theus looked him over, eyeing the flail staff cautiously. "peas' t' meet ye. "he said holding out his hand. They exchanged a firm hand grasp in the Ellendei fashion.

Tarese sat at a round table in the lounge close to the fire, pulling the chair around backwards so that she could warm herself better. Eothan stood directly before the hearth. Placing his hands to the stone he replaced the cold in his body with the fire's natural warmth.

Theus put some cabbage in a boiling pot. "Well er Eothan..wot nosh ye want?"

Eothan held a hand above the flame, its light danced intoxicatingly.

"Meat do you have meat, or eggs?"

"Duck we 'ave 'n we got a 'are two if ye like....An chickens're out back."

"A duck if you please." Replied the large warrior monk.

"Duck it be!" Theus chimed happily. "Oh, Ottar thee art forgiving.....to my betrothed I be pinning...." The merry cook sang to himself as he prepared the food. Now dicing, now stirring, he enjoyed his work.

"I must find Thomas."

"Yes.... and we need rest." She probed the tied features of her friend. "well perhaps, I should sprinkle some of my enchanted powder in our stew, it will refresh us....... leaving us exhausted latter.

"If we find evidence of your friend now, we will need energy. Should we not sleep here, now where we are safe....We know not what lies before us and where the trail will lead...The manatees followed the Troll's trail to the bank above Widern and since there was no trail beyond ....yes we shall.... have to explore tonight...Fine I'll keep us a wake tonight... but it can be dangerous...we must sleep tomorrow."

Eothan grimaced, Enruth had chosen his companion well.

They eat, talking little. The food indeed relieved all fatigue leaving them refreshed and invigorated. Terese wrote a letter to her farther using a quill and black ink. She folded the parchment sealing it with a ring she wore on her left hand. And stashing the extra parchment and ink secretly in the folds of her robe, that she now wore about her as a cape above her tunic.

Finishing the food she sighed and standing, handed the letter to Theus.

"Make certain my farther receives this." She said.

Then heading out into the cold night they decided to explore the dock yards. The troll was sure to stay close to the water, and as the river was the last place they knew it to be, it seemed a good choice.

A light rain had wetted the town's cobbled streets, whilst they ate, now the night lights spotting gold, yellow and silver in reflective furrows. Eothan looked into the sky, there were no stars. The lighted sky from the sun set was gone. Hoping it had rained all it would, he followed Tarese.

They made good time, the lay of the land in their favor. Tarese led them toward the North Gate, passing the small towered East Gate. Squires Walk widened into Bucket Lane, bringing them by a steeper, more direct rout to the Dwarfen Artificer, and Woodsman's Cote. From there they took three winding allies toward the river. A thick fog covered the lower, river ward side of the town, here the streets were small, and oft unmarked. Eothan found himself thanking Enruth again for his companion. Her smile inviting and pleasant for someone who was so useful.

Near the West Gate, open pubs and more dubious establishments added traffic to the otherwise empty streets. They thread their way through crowds of long boatman, bargers, ferrymen, and townspeople on a night out, farmers, thieves, slavers and pimps, blended for the most part indistinguishable, one from another, bar the occasional glance or stare.

"Norcadian...I'll trade ye three Thraition slaves for the women." Tarese looked at Eothan, biting her lower lip in anger. The tatter cloaked Ellendei winked over his brown wired beard.

"No." replied Eothan, calmly, as they kept moving.

Tarese stayed closer and moving against him in the crowd she leaned in, whispering in his ear. "You can get angry sometimes you know......"

Reaching the gate, they passed under its arch to the river. No militia collected tolls. Their only presence, halberdiers stationed far above on each of the gates towers.

Inns outside the gate, spilled their clientele onto the flagstones and earthen tracks of Widern Town's warehouse district. Men and women clung to each other to numb with drink to stand. Others lay propped against walls or flat out beyond care.

"This is what you spend your time with?" Eothan looked toward the stumbling drunkards before him.

"I spend most of my time in Corsinia....even the court of Ottar is better than this." Tarese agreed.

"The poor they have little to live for.......I am no lord do not blame me Eothan Norcadian Corser...." Then she angered. "I am already betrothed......... if you think for the length of a glass that... I would stoop to the decrepit behavior we see here..... then.... well then. we can end this friendship immediately!"

"No I...We at the monastery we have wine..but only in moderation and no one profits from it."

"Yes...you are thought to be strict....This scum sell worse than intoxicants I assure you....any thing can be bought on these streets and as you see is..."

A parade of under dressed women and girls issued from the large Inn directly south of the West Gate. They smiled and laughed, dancing in a line. People parted about them shouting in reply.

"I lov' ye darlins'" Shouted a young dock worker next to the Norcadian.

Eothan saw into them their pain. The fear that promoted their self destructive actions. Tangles of emotional torment twisted below the surface of their painted and frozen smiles. There was nothing but subservience left to them. They had been given no choice to live but survive.

He had heard that the clergy of Arraken taught that female, the women herself, housed evil. The profits of

Corser had never said such, and women among their own order were respected as equals. He instantly assessed the plight of the Ellendei, and Thratian women. They had no power. Their actions were not freely chosen but the result of the Enemy. The Enemy exacted action through fear and torture, obviously at play here. What he saw before him was the tip of an ice burgh of suffering.

If these contorting self-irreverent indignities, were understood they pointed to an underworld of criminal behavior, a sea of pain, for which its victims endured dehumanizing humiliation. An enemy so prevalent and so powerful that it demanded the continual experience of torture for its victims at the threat of increased agony if its demands were not met.

He felt disgusted. His own people, had a priesthood of women honored and respected, the Valar. They spun prayers to protect birth, a clergy more sacred than that which governed war. It felt to Eothan that the Ellendei lived in a state of war. They treated their women worse than their pigs, and every city even a small town like Widern had a teaming war seething beneath its surface.

"There is no peace here. "He said.

"You may be right. "Retorted his companion.

"If we were not busy, I would preach to this devil worshipping rabble... I feel the Imprisoned One is strong here."

"The inquisition would arrest you."

"We must leave......These people need ..more help than you a simple novice can provide...We will search for signs of the Trollen warlock...They should be beyond these buildings toward the north."

"Let us depart....." Then she added happily "You do get angry."

Eothan was confused, he did not Know why, but he found himself unhappy that Tarese was betrothed. He had expected the depravity of the Ellendei, but who was this companion and why did her eyes demand so much attention. Certainly, she showed more care and compassion than what he had witnessed in Widern. Who was she betrothed to he wondered? An Ellendei lord? He hoped her future husband was more virtuous than the lords of Widern Town.

They rounded the two fortified merchant guild's offices approaching the long boater's guildhall, a brick tower adjacent to the piers, Longboats and repair houses lay about. On the far bank, the lights of the Royal Ferry reflected in the water of the Lenerr.

Trudging on passed the Barger's Guild the most northerly of Widern Town's outlying buildings, they were again in the farmed land of Widern Valley.

Eothan concentrated, settling his mind in order to cast a quiet abjuration of tracking. Before the sand of an hour glass fell, the Norcadian had located his quarries prints where they had left the water. Two thick toe and arch prints dug deep into the steep soft river bank. From there, they turned to stalk back toward the warehouse district.

They followed their way along the outer wall of Widern, at six paces the wall was a barrier even for a troll. The troll path turned sharply as it approached the small outlying Docktown, instead it headed back toward the river and the collection of warehouses. The docks themselves lay close, to the west.

Puddles broke the gravel, mud, track separating two rows of the larger wooden warehouses, a ten-foot fortified wall blocked the road creating a cul de sac. There had been no more rain.

"That is one of the Merchant Guilds." Whispered Tarese.

The tracks became hard to follow, but with time and concentration Eothan pieced together their progress. They vanished bellow the worm-eaten wooden footings of a large Corsinian timbered warehouse. Separated from the merchant guild's wall by a pace wide alley, only Arraken's large sewer rats, watched their search, as Eothan soon located a hollow section of timber.

"If it be a portal I can open it with a powered enchantment."

Eothan smiled. Betrothed or not she was useful. They crouched next to the structure's footings while Tarese munched down her enchanted ground powder.

"After a moment it will take effect."

Then she turned and bowing her head she knocked five times solidly against its surface. An incomprehensible sound parted between her teeth, answered by the creaking of the dislodged wooden door before them. A section of the timber swung into the warehouse exposing a descending stair.

They glanced at each other, then Eothan stepped in front and down into the hole. Stairs led to a modest passage. Damp mildewed walls and floors read to Eothan with the marks of their enemy's passage. Here against the corner where a cloth surface scraped the algae covered walls, were left the signs of baggage, large enough to be Saint Thomas.

Pointing westward Eothan lead the pair on. They relied on their crafts to lend them sight in the darkened place. The passage traveled over a hundred paces, to where a wooden steal reinforced door ended their progress.

Eothan hurriedly checked it for traps or trickery, and then knocking again, Tarese opened it. To the other side a perpendicular passage led out of site. Eothan soon found the heavy mildewed print of their quarry and north they continued.

A lighted chamber sounded with spoken Ellendei, in front.

"I can conceal us, but there is a limit to the amount of powder I can consume before I get sick... very sick." She whispered.

Once more they paused while Tarese swallowed strange powders stashed within her clothing. Then when the trance was upon her she gargled uttering a second series of unintelligible syllables. Then turning she waved her hands painting both herself and her companion into the background rock of the passageway.

"Twice more I can safely eat my magick...No more."

"I have not your craft, only exhaustion can stop my prayers."

"That is as it should be."

Painted into the rock of the passage they sneaked toward the light. The corridor ended in a wider square room. The talkers, two bipedal rats, blocked their progress. One leaning heavily on a military pic, the other armed with a sheathed broadsword, and both carried shields over their shoulders, talking quietly to each other. Course hair covered them from head to foot tapering to skin around their human hands and feet. Rat heads snickered, giggling disharmonious at each other's words, as large gray tails flicked emotionally. Doors, two similar in make to that in the corridor adorned the far wall.

"The troll will provide flesh for our sports."

"Still the inquisition is far more reliable.......And entertaining....." They cackled in unison.

"Only the marquis of Tratia stands in its way......Or we would have one already."

"Yes the bishop of T'bah....is fearful enough to stay out of its way.... ye.. ye.... ye.. .ye.....ye......ye....ye....hee.!"

"ye....ye....ye...ye...ye....The Ellendei squeal so well while they die...ye...ye ...ye...ye...ye...ye!"

"We do not eat the body of the monk."

"We do not eat the body of the monk."

"Tasty though he be....Troll will give us more for free."

"Tasty though he be....Troll will give us more for free." They repeated the phrase like a nursery rhyme to each other.

"Ye...ye...ye..ye..ye....ye....ye...ye....ye...ye...ye.......ye.... eye!!!!"

Eothan and Tarese crawled back down the passage, when out of ear shot, they consulted.

"Do we attack?" Tarese asked.

"The Troll may escape if we do...If it is close."

"We can stay watch find a better time to save your friend."

"If he yet lives..the rats..."

"wer-rat..."

"Wer-rats...said body."

"Enchanted sleep?"

"I know not."

"Werrats have an acute sense of smell.... my illusion does not cover our sent completely."

"We listen from here..... I can hear from a distance..... when we learn more then we will choose."

The rats chattered on to themselves, rarely silent. Dallying happily in nonsense, and sadism, they entertained each other. Eothan found their high-pitched yipping laugh nauseating. When they talked on matters relevant to the companion's quest Eothan repeated. In this manner they learned that word had been sent to the royal barge, and that a coach had been commissioned through the Mangaran teamster's guild. It was to meet the rats party at the Royal Barge of Widern from whence it would travel by the Arraken high road to Niobia. They knew little of the details, but talked enough to be useful.

The Troll was to hand over Thomas' body to agents of Simmon Primate of Berelan before dawn. Presently the sorcerous beast rested, beyond the guards, within an undisclosed chamber. It was tempting to surprise it where it slept.

No! There were too many unknowns. They would wait.

After the length of many hour glasses, the enemy acted. They disappeared momentarily, through the left of the two doors, returning to the chamber as well dressed auburn and brown haired Ellendei merchants, their familiar personal weapons were all that told who they were. In moments another Ellendei appeared. A rotund man, light brown haired, covered from head to foot in a black woolen robe.

As Eothan gripped hard on Der Aeth, the cloaked figure changed growing to twice its size, the troll. It filled the room to the ceiling its bulk hidden behind an incantation of its foul art. Over its back hung the same heavy bag, Thomas!

The two spies, still concealed, stole down the hallway hiding behind the iron shod door. The party went on through the passage, and after they had past, Eothan and his accomplice snuck after. They traveled south ascending a stair. As before it ended in a secret passage. They watched as the group climbed, disappearing through a trap door.

Following, the monk and sorceress, climbed onto the empty floor of a warehouse. Wooden crates littered half the building. They scanned the interior, Eothan quickly finding a slight trail in the dust of the warehouse floor, it pointed them toward a door.

Tarese grabbed his arm and pulling him close whispered, "We are no longer protected by the illusion.... we will be quite visible."

They nodded to each other and when in unison scampered to the door. Eothan cracked it, and seeing the party walking from him toward a distant gate he pulled Tarese through as he started in their direction.

"Halt ...or we shoot. "Came a voice to his right.

They turned to find themselves starring into the solemn faces of a dozen armed guards. Eothan counted six loaded crossbows, a sergeant broadsword drawn, leaned against the building's wall, shining metal from sharpened pikes leered ominously over the heads of the crossbows.

"Well .... looks like we. Got the thieves don't it mates."

The men grunted in agreement.

"Why don't ye just cum with us....peac'ably if ye value ye hides....t' town constable got t' talk t' ye....."

Grabbed gruffly, their weapons were stripped from them, as they were pulled toward the same distant gate. They went along, both thinking it more expedient in the long run to let these foolish soldiery pride themselves in their capture.

"You are mistaken..." Ventured Tarese. "We may be trespassing but we are not thieves...I am a De Gent and I'll have you Know that king Ottar himself is among my family. "She did not wish these lowly men to get the wrong idea, they unhanded her, instead leading her by gesture. "My body guard and I were pursuing a thief ourselves."

"T' constable is who ye tell...Ye lucky ye not a witch.... cause if ye wuz we got a friend in inquisition...pays well fur witches 'ee does."

They stayed quiet after that, impatiently fidgeting in the gates lower tower room, attendant on the constable's arrival. The arms men had taken Eothan's bow and sword, and his small wooden shield, leaving Der Aeth. They seemingly did not notice Quareture. Not wishing them to change their mind, Eothan leaned, closely on the flail staff, nonchalant, and a little embarrassed, it was quite obvious to him.

It was light by the time the constable arrived. Blue and red emblazoned, he sported the same beard and mustache as the town watch they had seen earlier, a shared fashion. A light sword hung at his side and great plumed hat toped his head, increasing his air of self-importance. After consulting with the sergeant at arms he was completely ready to transport the prisoners. Famous as they were, but quite clearly caught red handed.

Escorted by twelve armed men, including the mounted constable. The prisoners were marched across town to the masoned tower, both, a prison, and armory for the town militia. The town hall, huddled close, housing the lord mayor and lord justice of the town.

Tarese being of royal descent, they were treated well, offered food and locked in a roomy and well strawed cell. Declining the culinary products of Widern Tower, Tarese had ordered that she be bought paper with which she intended to write to her guildhall, and to her longtime friend and relative the good King Ottar the Forgiving, she had added with emphasis. Even the swampy intellect of the Tower's constable had raised its eyebrows, and departing without delay, the two suspected thieves remained still expecting a rapid reply to their demands.

"The commonalty can feed us, we have agreements… Far to many have sickened and died at the hands of similar ruffians to trust this place."

Eothan knelt and prayed resting his forehead to Queraturre, Der Aeth the Heavy Dealer, for that was what the Corser rod had become. Like the city militia the guards noticed not the artifact of the Corserites.

A constable scribe soon hurried back with the required writing paraphernalia; parchment, pens and ink. He fished them through the bars, where upon, the only child and daughter of Irdiwin De Ghent, Genru Starborn, Keeper of the Hidden Land, composed thrice; a letter to the Commonalty, to the King, and, to her father again, via the commonalty.

The cells around were far more crowded than their own. A circle of iron they filled the towers first floor.

The ground hall had been divided between a hearing room of sorts, and the many offices that the militia and guard demanded. A stair at the towers distant wall that ascended the full 23 paces of its height, had been their path to this their dungeoned room.

Irons imbedded deep in the flint and rock of the cell's rear, told a story of treatment far worse than that which they had thus far experienced. As did a mighty rack, the rooms center piece.

They had little idea as to where Eothan's personal weapons were being held, his bow, a devise of enchanted magickal power, was already missed, fashioned by Eothan to be his tool in arcane research, a magickal storage device for his power, without it he would soon tire quickly when casting magick.

"I blame Illid Ansculf Scourge of Pellia, Ottar's Chancellor, prime minister of the Realm......A naughty person if ever such a one I have met.....He has hunted with my father. But only when a young man.....He too is a member of the same sorcery as myself....unlike the King..he coverts his art refusing to share with others.....It is he who started the revels that have so undermined the sanctity of the Red Towers." Tarese spoke low her voice reaching little beyond where Eothan Knelt.

"A violent man is he...close alley to the Primate of Berelan and the Lord of Pellia......He has a firm grip over the royal poppy fields...as the Primate controls the vineyards....They are the power behind Berelan..Ottar still maintains his royal obligations, of course, but has little true political power in the realm....I ask not what your monasteries interest in the kingdom is...I know only that my farther trusts thee.." She paused, lost in her own reverie.

"Only Toulon...and the Corserites does he mention with respect......Since the fall of the mighteous Wizard Kings the Arraken knighthood have declined losing the faith that held their early oaths as strong adamite ....words....Now bickering and the empty vows of the Primates clergy dominate Arraken. Demanding obedience from the populous through the inquisition's bureaucratic sadism.... Torture, much like the demonic villeins of those Ellendei Sorcerer Kings... from whence, the Kighthood, as succors' hero, was forged."

The poppy fields were vital economically. They were used as the active ingredient in expensive teas, wines and needed by the hidden schools of wizardry for spell casting. Ottar's poppy was one of the required substances in Tarese's powders for instance.

The adjacent cell contained a collection off ne'r do wells, in various states of health. A burly, muscled, blonde, Ellendei, that reminded Eothan of a Norcadian warrior from his own village, slumped shackled to the solid wall. Gashes on his back seeped red into his clothing, his consciousness absent, having been torn away with the pain of many lashes.

Two better dressed villains crouched using the bars of Eothan and Tarese's cell as their back rest. They dozed, the dusty frills of their shirts, and recent tears in their tunics, bore evidence that they too had been manhandled, yet to a more serious degree, than Teresa and Eothan.

Others, not as smartly dressed milled about filling the cells center.

Eothan was again thankful that he had befriended such a prestigious lady.

There were a handful of women prisoners kept in a cell opposite, but as they either could not, or chose not to move about their place of confinement, Eothan could not tell if they had been mistreated or not. After what he had seen the night before he imagined so.

On his return to pick up Tarese's pages the scribe informed them that there would be a hearing that afternoon, and that they had better be ready to "spill their brain's" he said, for they had a way to "loosen stiff tongues" as he called them, a way that was unpleasant enough that he cringed himself when he mentioned it.

Tarese swallowed.

"They wouldn't dare. "She said out loud.

They both felt it, at the same time, Tarese's powder, it wore off all at once. Curled up with weariness upon the straw, close for their own protection, the Corser Rod beneath them, they were snoring almost immediately.

Fighting drowsiness to the point of distraction, they had awoken at the rough hands of Widern's guards and had been taken under arms to the town Hall for their hearing. The lord high justice of the town, and three town jurors sat high on a tiered pew. An empty flag stone floor stretched at their feet between them and the accused. A small group of bored town's people and the accusing sergeant stood and sat to one side. A lawyer, or so he called himself, had arrived in a hurry, and with Tarese's letter in hand, attempted to extract information that would help in the defense of his exhausted, nearly catatonic clients. Obviously worried, he had a certain vested interest in protecting this minute portion of Ellendei royalty from their own corrupt justice system.

"If you could look alert......It would help your case....."

"Muhur.....thief..." is all he could illicit, he tried the body guard instead.

"Now....... your a Nocadian you better listen....Your type is oft up for brawling and battery in these parts..... are you paying attention....I am somewhat respected and have a reputation to protect....No attacking anyone...do you here?"

"I am a monk..." he managed "...Corserite."

"Likely story a monk armed with sword and dagger, and... caught red handed in Marquai merchant guild compound...we'll see about that...I like the body guard story better thank you...."

"Innocent." The giant Norcadian slurred, in half slumber.

"....Little to do with anything around here...my weighty friend....But at least two of the jurors are ours... local guild syndics you know.....The judge...worthless, too old...scared of the mayor and the inquisition...His daughter lives in Berelan you see...I wish you could look more lively....And no mention of hockus pockus....all we need now is to be turned over to the witchfinders ...and don't go believing that the free practice of wizardry is still legal....Further North you'd be right but not here ...unless you be a knight of Tratia or a son of Wirkeal himself which you quite obviously are not...So no parlor tricks....I'll try to steer you out of the wiping....Not a good day for it besides. overcast. Much to dull....be safe till tomorrow ..from punishment.... I think anyhow... Try to look awake. Please...." And with that he pushed Eothan back to the wall next to Tarese where they both strained to look alert. Propping up each other with the wall and their own weight, the stones to their backs was the only thing keeping them on their feet.

The judge, barely coherent himself peered at them over a thick lead lined pair of telescope glass spectacles, that enlarged his sagging pocketed gray green eyes. Then as they wobbled around, disconnected suspended in his face, they came to rest on the accused, magnified separated spheres of white, green/gray and, black. He smiled to himself, there even the young get tired he thought. His left hand rested on a bowl of raw grain it appeared that he shoveled into his mouth opportunistically, in his right he gripped a wooden gavel.

"Constable call the court to order." he managed.

"Silence in the name of his Majesty King Ottar the Third ..High King of Arraken the court of Widern is now in order.....Silence I say....All banter will now cease.....Court in Order!"

"Thank you....well....ye...ye...what..ye...ye...ye....do we have here...yes...burglary...ye.. ye"

The prosecutor a younger man dressed in a brown with blue emblazoned cloak, unlike the judges wore a wig in the style of the southern courts.

"Authorities of the Marquai merchant guild caught these two Tarese de Gent and Eothan the Norcadian red handed stealing a hasty retreat from a warehouse on their property your honor."

"De Gent. "The judge repeated.

"The writ of Berelan requires local prosecution prior to baronial or Royal appeal your honor.... remember..."

"Yes ..well..ye..let me say I am honored to have a member of the Arraken Royalty in my court for..ye.. ye...whatever reason...welcome." he smiled over toward Tarese, who after a quick elbow from her lawyer managed another ...

"Humph...?"

"What was that." the judge cupped a hand to his ear.

"She said likewise your honor." The lawyer piped.

"Yes..ye...ye...are...there any witnesses?"

"I call Lawrence Thashberry, the sergeant at arms who apprehended the culprits your honor."

"Humph" agreed the judge..nodding again a little himself.

"T' guard n' me sen we got em red handed...ye honor.. they 'ad just snuck out of this weare'ouse n' we nabbed em..not like 'fore cause they wuz not royal right so me un boys we just chucked em in t' riv...."

"That quite enough sergeant thank you."

"So you were caught red handed then?" A long nosed and angular featured juror jabbed.

"If I may speak.." the companions barrister spoke. "It is my clients contention that she and her bodyguard were themselves persueing a group of three thieves who had stolen from them earlier...and were only about to make an apprehension themselves but for the bungling of these Thenobal based employees were arrested under false charges."

"Let me remind you your honor that the Seat of Threnobal is a long way from here...its people are for the most part barbarians with much Kadran influence and are not beholden unto the Arraken crown. On the other hand, my client is related to the king, as a distant cousin, has many allies at court and is very....and let me say this loud slow and clearly so you can here me....Wealthy...very ....very wealthy."

"Humph? ...yes well we shall consider our verdict." A wizened juror announced, then the three huddled about the judge whispering to each other. A glance toward the dowsing prisoners, kept the lawyer interested. Then after a small hushed discussion an argument erupted, which after it calmed, the group broke with a few soft words, returning to their seats. The lawyer stood ready to shout back an appeal, if, as often was, necessary.

"Silence ..." declared the judge out of habit, although for once there was little noise in the court. "We declare that Tarese de Ghent innocent of any wrong doing and release her on her own recognizance...The Norcadian... we are not fully convinced of ..so in order to investigate the case more fully ....and free the lady de Ghent from any coercion we will hold this... so called body guard...in the Tower....Tomorrow a coroner will be free to oversea a trial by water to determine further guilt.....ye..ye...ye....... ye it is known to us that there have been thefts from the warehouse....and.....if this Norcadian is responsible we will route it out." Eothan was gladdened that Tarese seemed to be off the hooke, but the disconcerting way that the judge laughed in the same high-pitched manner as the two were rats, did not leave him feeling at ease. He could not say his own safety was assured.

"....The sentence, to be carried out on Sunday if trial by water indicates guilt is. ....ye..ye.....ye..er...a...lashing. ..One ..two er um...thirty six lashes...in all... May..you remind your client that should he be found burgeling a second time he will be branded...and ye..ye... a third.. hung...til...........de.....ad..ye ...ye ..ye..!!!"

The night had fallen before Eothan became coherent enough to consider what had happened. Having lived at the monastery, he was not accustomed to the injustices of human society. It angered him. What right had the Ellendei to condemn him a Corserite monk to the indignity of a public wiping.

The rod of Corser sat on the straw, still loosely grasped in his hand. Tarese was missing and he vaguely remembered her release, still in the same cell, he was alone, crowded conditions all around him.

He thought on the trouble of the early dawn, the fog, the disguised troll, and Saint Thomas the Young. They had nearly had him, if it hadn't been for the inept machinations of these idiotic Ellendei, was it any wonder that the Enemy had so much sway over them. They were staunchly committed to the lies that they lived by, far too blind to see the power of Enruth, The One; imprisoned as they were in the deceits of Shaitan, the Dark Enemy, the vile slanderer.

A loaf of fresh bread and bowl of apples sat on the stones inside the cage's bars, his nose told him that the fare was a great deal better than that of the poor wretches in the cell next to him. Their gruel still sat half eaten in an iron pot, wooden bowls in a heap. Tarese's commonality had helped him somewhat.

Two prisoners, the beaten though better hoseried, starred hungrily through the bars as he ate. The smaller salivated obnoxiously, his mouth a gape, viscous spittle dribbled down the side of his face wetting the frills of his under garment.

For such well-dressed gentleman, they showed a complete lack of etiquette.

Eothan polished off the plate with no effort, denying a passing thought to feed the two out of his own mouth, he reminded himself that the Ellendei were not in his best books at the moment. Instead, he decided he would give them the benefit of wise words, and finding a place against the shared wall of bars, he probed the ground examining the wooden floor beneath them. As he expected they immediately showed an interest, moving close without overtly communicating. Then he spoke the words of the evening prayer, a comfort to their souls, at least he thought.

All three rested while the Tower fell asleep, the guards retiring to a room near the stair, leaving a lone sentry that disappeared for his rounds each glass.

"We have a plan to escape." Whispered the larger of the two. "You are strong, and have friends...will you join us."

Eothan had been still, not a sleep.

"Yes I relish not the punishment these constables have ready for me."

"We thought not......Listen we have some sorcery... and can burn a hole in the floor will you accompany us? We have little physical prowess and cannot wield arms like the soldiers...."

Eothan looked at them, they had both been battered badly since the morning, blue, and scab blackened red divided their faces.

"We are foreign .." The smaller went on. "Not from here...They call us warlocks.. They poor water down our throats till we fall unconscious.....Do you know why?"

Eothan swallowed. The introduction to Enruth would wait.

"The Enemy is strong in them." he answered. "I must retrieve my weapons....If you will help, I will fly with thee."

After glancing at each other they nodded in agreement.

"We will help, a locked room in the basement holds the prisoner's goods.." The smaller went on, "...The torture chamber is there." His eyes fell on the rack in the tower's center. "The real one, not this place. "while they toyed with us there, we heard them talk... our scimitars are housed there in..as are your weapons no doubt."

"Then you agree..I also."

"This will not take long.. I will burn with my essence fire..whilst my friend keeps our cell mates asleep...When the sentinel next departs.. will we our escape make."

They watched in anticipation and when the sentry turned with a backward glance toward the cells, a last check before descending out of site, they set to work. The taller of the pair sang softly under his breath in an old language, not unlike that spoken by the Hobgoblin tribe of Gour Gareth. Simultaneously the smaller hunched over the floor boards between them concentrating intently.

Slowly, a ball of white and gold, summoned from where Eothan knew not, grew below him. Its bright light purer, than that from a naked flame flashed about the face of the perspiring sorcerer. It cracked slightly as the mage focused it into a small beam. Taking time he eventually controlled it, managing to create a thin burning beam of the magickal fire. Unlike natural flame, it cut through the oiled wood far quicker than Eothan thought possible. What little smoke there was diffused upward unnoticed by their quieted slumbering cell mates.

The two spell slingers deftly manipulated the cut wood in one motion pulling it from around its clinging prison bars, twisting it sideways and extracting it from the ready cut hole. Placing it next to them the smaller stole a glance through the escape route.

"We are above a large hall, empty for the time."

"Wait we will listen….." They heard the distant echoing footsteps of a guardsman as they tapered off…

"…he must have descended to the dungeon." They agreed with each other in silence.

Eothan did not trust these friends, though they currently seemed the lesser of Evils.

"I am the tallest I will go first. "He said. They looked to their new found accomplice.

"Very well." they spoke in unison.

He quickly lowered himself by his arms, dropping less than a stride to the lower floor: the tower's large council chamber, it was indeed empty. Lifting the two sorcerers to the ground, all three quietly drifted across the floor and around the halls edge to the stairwell. There they stooped in the dark until they again heard the sentinel's footsteps, this time, ascending. Waiting till they heard the upper stories door close and the footsteps again disappear, the guard returning to his second story post, the three crept down the same well.

Granite ribs buttressed the masonry above the heavy steps of the tower's dungeon. Moving slowly, the group passed huge wooden doors, set back each with its own steps. They knew not what piteous creatures lay beyond, nor did they have the time to investigate, instead they stalked on toward the torture chamber and the hopeful hiding place of their goods.

Still unmolested, they found the ghastly place. Chains and skewer, pointed instruments hung from the wall, and a contenting warmth issued from an ever lighted fire, its embers casting a feint red glow.

The room of prisoner's belongings lay to the side, behind a large iron enforced door, locked through a ungainly key hole. The smaller of the sorcerers examined it, peering inside. He took his time examining the door, its handle, the hinges, the wood itself, then he turned his attention to the chamber.

"I need some tools, but I can open it."

Eothan watched the passage, while his new companions searched the room for what they needed. They returned with a collection of pliers, knives, hooks, clamps, pincers, wires, a smithies hammer, and some stakes.

Enruth be blessed, he shuddered to think what the Ellendei constabulary and their coroners did with them.

The two, set to work immediately on the door with the skill and finesse of professional burglars. The tall one examined the uppermost hinges whilst the shorter began to probe the lock, they consulted from time to time sweating with the concentration the task required. Their voices hushed and hurried, strained but efficient. Large enough to allow his fingers to work within its confines, the obviously trained thief manipulated the innards with a number of the wires he had pulled from the rack.

The larger of the two finished his cursory exploration of the entire door and after he had probed in a number of places around its jam, he convinced himself of something. Then settling down he had a few words with his accomplice.

They were soon at each other's throats...arguing in hushed voices about what the monk knew not. Thinking better of trying to mediate, knowing nothing of locks or their internal workings himself, he took another step up the stairway, his ears waiting for the inevitable return of the Tower's sentry. He prayed they would not take to long at their task.

They bickered back and forth again. The smaller taking his hands from the wires and pushing the bigger back a step wildly gesticulating, at both, his unwanted consultant, and the lock. The larger stepped around him and not wanting to be bullied, explained himself again. He hurriedly tried to calm the smaller. Then as suddenly as they had argued, they settled down and both looked into the key hole talking calmer and slower. Finally, only a word or two passed between periodically.

They now manipulated the lock in unison, applying pressure here and then there. It took time, and Eothan, tiring finally sat upon the step. He began to worry, thinking it would soon be time for the watches return, then with a word of triumph the taller declared his victory.

Eothan heard the clank of gears, and as they both grinned widely with approval, the smaller acquiesced, accepting that his friend had been correct. He even went as far as to offer a quick bow in friendship.

The door was not immediately swung open, instead they craned their necks forward around the jam, then lying flat on the floor and away with the larger sprawled at his feet holding both securely, the smaller used a long iron skewer to push the door wide.

Eothan heard a door open above followed by footsteps. Someone was using the stair. He scampered across to the opened door. Standing they both grimaced wide.

"Noise?" Asked the smaller.

"On the stair." he replied.

All three looked within the door, after a pace long vestibule, the room opened into a chamber housing weaponry, and other loot acquired from prisoners. As the smaller removed the wires from the lock with the pliers, his larger comrades leapt into the room and across the thresh-hold. Eothan assisted the smaller's leap, grabbing him and pulling him across, as the other explored the room. Closing the door, in the nick of time, they hid from the approaching guard.

Eothan listened as the booted feet circled the chamber beyond, and then climbed up and out of ear shot.

"Our weapons are all here, but our money bags must be locked away inside this chest." Whispered the taller.

Eothan soon found his bow and sword, picking them from a collection of clubs, swords and falchions, arrayed in three racks. His rope and grapple he found thrown in amongst chains and grapples dangling out an open barrel, thankfully they were near the top. With satisfaction he slung the bow over his shoulder, depositing the barbarian long sword in a sling across his back, in this way he relocated it to account for his missing shield and made a space for Quarature about his waist, and the rope and grapple alongside, in this way he became more maneuverable.

The two locksmiths, or most probably thieves, Eothan expected the latter, were consulting on how, with whom, and when, they should open the large chest. Ribboned with steal, and twice their size it would take a great deal of time to chop apart. The smaller kneeled peering into its padlock, the second probed around with the same wire he had used on the door.

A slight click told Eothan that the padlock had opened. Swift he thought, apparently the smaller had not considered a lengthy investigation necessary. The thieves opened the chest's lid as cautiously as they had the door.....

"Hsssarrr! "Exclaimed the shorter.

"Coin .....and our materials. "They both dived in rummaging for their missing items. All at once, Eothan heard a hiss superimposed over a distant wurring.

"A trap!" he exclaimed. A cream-colored dust vented from the box's sides engulfing the two snoops.

Eothan covered his face, heading for the door, as a second chunk followed instantaneously by a thundering crash shook the room with its reverberations. Halting him with its shock wave, a solid granite block had sealed the passage before him completely.

Falling at its feet he held his breath. The mist diffused, filling the room, rising as it went. Rolling over Eothan watched wide eyes, as more vapor spewed from the box. What had they set off? He heard the dull clang of a bell above in the tower, an alarm, he thought!

Clang...clang....clang....clang......clang...... clang.. .clang...clang. .....clang....clang....clang...

His lungs and blood demanded oxygen, filling him with an emptiness. The slow creeping demand for air.

Clang.....clang....clang....clang......clang.....

The gas rose and leaning against the block his eyes perceived a clearing at floor level. He exhaled, distracting his body with the sensation, then as the demand for air crept back upon him, again threatening his consciousness with a black out, he looked to Der Aeth, flail staff and prayed.

As he finished the prayer, he eased air into his lungs.

So, he went on, taking in the bare minimum to maintain coherence. His head dizzied. Sounds in the hallway affirmed his fears that the guard was aware of them it would be only a matter of candles before they rose the oblong rock catching the three escapees. His first journey into Arakken proper and all he wished was that he never see the place again.

Abruptly, there was another noise, a scrapping and rapid impact. The rock of the wall beside buckled inward toward him. Earth and masonite sprinkled about. What now? an earth quake?

Clawed fury hands pulled two wall blocks back, they disappeared from site, replaced by the giant head of a badger. Its snout rotated prehensile, brown and gold stripped. Two large dark eyes followed its head mimicking the same pattern that its nose followed.

Brushing aside more brick it climbed into the tower's cache. Two others trained behind, and a fourth's head peered in.

Fleet, they scrambled about gathering up the fallen sorcerer thieves and beckoning Eothan to follow. They walked predominantly on their back legs using their articulated hands to manipulate and gesture much like people, occasionally they switched to a quadrupedal scamper, and by so doing they increased their speed and maneuverability.

As he trailed after them into the freshly dug hole, he remembered what they were: Wei'een the creatures of Toulon. A holy species talked of much in the later Corserite texts. They had first appeared during the time of the Wizard Kings. Inhabiting the thick deciduous forests of Cirwen and Loast. They had helped with the founding of the Cathedral of Toulon, becoming its sacred guardians.

Drake hated these benevolent forest creatures, and his northern barons had put a price on their heads. The Wai'een were strong, however, and although, they used no weaponry, wise and cunning, faithful friends, and bitter foes. Never a plentiful creature, Drake had had little luck in eradicating them, they protected their own.

In herb law they were considered unsurpassed, and their homes were burrowed thickets of thorned brush. These thickets were well nigh impossible to penetrate, as were the burrowed earthen dens beneath them. Wai'een thickets surrounded Toulon, protecting the city with their thick thorny cover, and accounted for over half of Toulon's districts. Their tunnel riddled masses a meeting place for the sale of Wai'een custom and merchandise.

Once in the tunnel the Wai'een urged Eothan on.

"This way .....we must cover our tracks." The Wai'een almost barked the Ellendei in its characteristic badger like fashion.

As they trailed in single file through a fresh Wai'een burrow, the Wai'een behind quickly caved in the ceiling, deftly clawing with their front legs. When their escape route was concealed, they descended quickly; the tunnel built at a sharp incline. Then as it evened out they slowed the pace.

Eothan welcomed the fresh smell of clean earth. Like many of their tunnels it meandered back and forth, and up and down, never staying straight, it was practically impossible to find your direction in a Wai'een tunnel without magickal aid.

They traveled for leagues before the leader called for a rest to be taken, he first barked it in his own language then turning to Eothan he translated gruffly.

"..You called to us Corserite and we answered .... now we must rest and have parley......why were you imprisoned.? ....and why are these two-goblin shaman your allies?"

Eothan was taken a back. Goblin shaman? But no goblins were his allies, he looked to his companions, still unconscious, each slung over the shoulder of a Wai'een. He started back a step. Bewildered, and still dazed he found himself starring at two Goblin-kin. One large like the hobgoblins of the Yan, the other small less hairy, but quite definitely goblin.

TREATIES AND HONOR

G lamawere the damned paced, his agreement with Drake had not concluded as easily as he had expected. Hoping to keep the matter within the coven, a simple transaction between Herigar Gunerson and himself, a way to bolster relations with the Wadeen, he had down played the import of the augmented profits they expected. Too tempting to deny. If the Hidden Lodge were united to the Dragon Lord, his dutchy, and the Wadeen, their's would be the ultimate power in Arraken. Rivaling Simmon the Snake. Ellendon's rule of The Hidden Kingdom could be without end. No coven would rival them.

The flask of Saint Thomas was the agreed gift, and, boded well with Glamawere. Why did those meddling Kadrons forever dabble in the affairs of mankind. Could they not leave him alone for once. He Glamawere, Lord over the Hidden Kingdom's most pivotal coven, had he not worshipped the Imprisoned One for centuries never forgetting a blaspheming? Had he not sold his entire legacy for the furthering of the Dark One's return?

It was in their mutual best interest for him to succeed in this task. Herigar had agreed through Davide de Clune, as to Gorgon wife's claim to the diadem of Mernnon, what else were she and her agents from Hados planning?

Plots, within plots, complots, and espionage did a high priest not deserve some rest? He had lived centuries, forever working toward the Kingdom's Crown, was Wicca to play wet nurse to a pack of immature demi-goddess and their pet plays to rule a dead and forgotten city? Were not the politics of Tarterous enough for them? Why did Gorgon wife obsess with such a prize? Did she not see the importance of defeating the First Born and Thornbreak, before the pursuit of mere trinkets? With Herigar securely in place as High Lord of Thornbreak they would be free to resurrect the Imprisoned One, the domination of the Ellendei and Mernnonia would be a matter of course.

Perhaps he could forestall Herigar with a marriage. Arien Olofin, Ottar's sister had not yet been with child, according to ancient Ellendei custom this meant their marriage had not yet been consummated, not in the eyes of Enruth, at least.

"Psat" Glamawer spat involuntarily when he mentioned the name.

If they arranged an accident, or if she was to sicken and die. The Coven of the Snake would be opposed, of course, the marriage never could have occurred in the first place without their consent. If they did risk open coven war, who was to be their bride choice?

Glamawere himself had not sired humans since his marriage, he cursed that day of fate. For power and a secure foothold in Mnt. Ellondon, he had given up any chance for human offspring. Gorgon Wife birthed only aspen things, atrocious to the mundane tastes of the Ellendei royalty. Glamawer smirked as he remembered her nursing their last child, a plump wriggling torso and snake.

Her female children were intelligent half snaken beasts, while the males, similarly formed were all mentally deficient, good for nothing but filling Tarterous with mindless rabble.

Was there a slave in the coven's harem that could pass off as his daughter? The Wadeen were hard to fool but knew little of the Corsinian underworld, their resources were far too stretched running espionage fronts in the West for their eyes to reach this far east. The wild states beyond Daquin, Barenrock and Thunderrock were the focus of their sphere's of influence, a myopia that he hoped would increase over the Duke's next years of conquest.

He paused, caught by the glittering green gemmed eye, of an exquisitely carved ebony statue that stood at the end of his private Kadron shrine. Much of its decor chosen by his wife, its affluently historical approach envied by most of the priestess-hood and coven.

Glamawere found the room somewhat humbling, it was hard to find a piece in the small collection that he was barely even half the age of. Likewise, it was where he did his best work, his mind alert here, more discerning, critical. All those chiseled voluptuous manifestations of Helgotei, her serpentine mistresses, and the rooms solid gold silver and aluminum Medusa center piece, in full glower, loaded bow at her side. It shuddered the soul, reminded him to take the care needed for perfection. To be exacting. To Glamawere the knowledge that the center piece was able to turn to stone any not specifically invited into the room added to its awe. The ambiance, heightened his senses, specifying his thought to a hard clarity. The natural power of Mernnoian theology, his unwilling alley, and enemy, surrounding him with the majesty that only great, divinely inspired, art could aspire.

His dry wrinkled eye lids closed with a slow scrape across his mortally strained eyes.

"Argotte of Bogwood....Master of Slaves..your priest commands you to attend on him....in his personal library.. immediately." The black speech of the Imprisoned One felt appropriate in this room of Kadron devil worship.

Argotte, the great cave troll, Master of Slaves to the Hidden Lodge would be on his way to the library, he had not disobeyed an order in his hundred fifty or more years of service. So, paying his respects to the center piece Glamawere exited down the short passage that led to the tapestried personnel scroll hall of the Damned.

Argotte had grown to adulthood in the Lodges prison caves, after migrating to Ellendon from the retinue of the hill giant Bogwood. Bogwood lorded an enclave of giants, ogres, trolls and wild goblin kin that made their living harassing trade along the great north road from Arraken to the Treathbaron's province of Darkmore. Making a good living, they were a steady and reliable alley to the lodge.

Opening the small arched door way, he crossed the library toward a pillowed ottoman, finding his armchair on the way, he chose to sit instead, grinning to himself, a solution would present itself, it always did.

"...thinking on the Elysian Fields are we.?" The caped boyish young man stood before his chair, one hand on his chin, the other moved forward to trace the desiccated face of Glamawere.

"Eserostianus.." Managed the damned.

"Stating the mundane as always I see."

"..I did not expect you for a decade at least."

"Things have changed some…. what…… where as many of the agreements for our extended litigation…. have. been ratified, the flavor of our universal commitment to mutual aid, and your own solemn ….. and let me say that I cannot stress enough how somber your oath was…." Red eyes bore through the Damned, from the serenity of a cherubic face.

"…. Please forgo the reminder…"

"…to go on…the subpoena on your soul as procured with your signature in your own blood by me ….and carrying the countersignature of the Chief, Master, General, Arch Deacon, Lord, Governor our Imprisoned most unholy reverence Shaitan himself….Is I am afraid. A, yes…a, binding…in every sense of the word….a tightly binding clause….So you take your Head of Wose the Eater, and if you wish your servitude to continue as peaceable as his then you must begin to honor the full flavor of the contract… not only its minor agreements…..Because.." The youth arranged Glamawere's scant wisps of hair as he continued.

"…Because! I do not appreciate tearing myself away from the entertainments of my people to talk to mere mortals like yourself…who are to be a boon and not…as you appear to be striving to become ..a bane."

"If you please Lord Eserostianus I am attempting to further our quest through an alliance.wi..."

"Don't bore me with details Glamawere." He silenced the damned touching three fingers to the evil priest's lips. "We...care little for your politics...I want results.... Flavor not pedantism ..Or your soul will be maggot seed before you can breathe...And don't think you can impress me with high speech I am no Ellendei or Kadron... remember I have my eye on you....and The Law is on my side.... Anon, anon, I must be gone...Grand duke of the land your wife calls Hados is entertaining me with the torture of a god...a little matter of who is to over throw...Kadra I think...they worked out a good bit with an eagle eating his kidney, or his bladder or something. ought to be a break from dueling Titans. Well, I'm the guest of Honor so I must hurry. Don't forget...Please."

Glamawere was alone again. If he still drank, perchance his skin would offer a sweat to relieve his worry, just the priest exclusively relied on prepared and spiced meats, with the odd glass of blood, as a soaking reminder, to the throat. It had been decades since he last tasted water.

After a time he exhaled, sad, his fate had been such a heavy one, still alive he thought, if only I can avoid the eternal fate of a larva. The prospect of being thrown back and forth between daemons of Hell, or Hados, or even Tarterous, as an exchange system, did not appeal. Endlessly waiting to be consumed by some minor prince or chevalier de l'enfer who could not find a less transient meal, Helgotei be praised, servitude in a Ergedhian dueling arena would be better.

Was the pact with Herigar enough, the Worms, were they willing to cut him a deal that involved a resurrection? For the Saints soul were they sufficiently trustworthy to hide this from Eserostianius? He knew not. He could be resurrected in a distant plane or demi plane, he would need the secret to be kept sacrosanct. If the legions of hell learned that he lived with new blood far from the confines of his contract, he would burn, and far worse.

The Leathered one had allies in Mernnon. Was that it? Was this last visitation an attempt to warn him of close Kadron ties, or was that what he was supposed to think? Yet his fate was not the immediate concern. This was, as he had said earlier a coven matter.

"You demanded my attendance my lord Prince."

The Master of slaves filled the doorway with his bulk. Over two paces tall, on his steal breast plate he wore a blood shot eye motif, the coven's stylized shrunken head, brown, centered in its red as a pupil. Sharpened and pointed tusks protruded from below the folds of his lips. A course brown hair tufted about its head and ears.

The rest of its body bald cracked and crusted with the rock-hard regenerating skin of cave trolls. Slits marked its nose, only water and mountain trolls had protruding human like noses, the forest and cave variety, slits like the apes of Daquin. Lose plates of uneven metal tied about its belt barbarically adorned the troll above its red kilt.

"Yes, Algotte we must peruse the harem for any young women of marriable age that could pass as the Gorgon Wife's and my offspring, also, our contacts with the Thayinian slaver's guild must be asked in, of course, the strictest confidence ..Oh, and this be a Covern matter. Only contacts of the Hidden Lodge itself are to be trusted. ....Oh, and just checking ..but have our visiting ambassadors been entertained?"

"The Wadeen has my lord."

"..and was he polite."

"Mostly my lord."

"Very well.... you may go...I must be informed of your progress. Remember on pain of forfeiture to Ollisria this be a matter of the Lodge alone."

"I understand my lord."

Then he departed, his large form and massive fingers surprisingly lithe for a creature of such bulk. Glamawere watched his armored back as it left. His mind went to the Saint, it was wise to keep to the original oath, the

Wadeen would carry him back to Ergedh, which could only expedite the release of the Imprisoned One, pleasing Eserostianous.

Glamawere felt miserable, doomed to be beholden unto the will's of others. He looked to his mind's eye, sorting through the harems faces that he found there in. Times, there were, that he had wasted years in the trivial pursuit of such worldly pleasures. His wife's priestess-hood had, in the beginning, wielded far too much power over his fledgling witches. Sexuality ever the tool of Helgotei, and her Medusal manifestation was no exception.

For fifty years he battled to establish a human harem around which he could protect the sexual power of his converts, to weed out the asps and their offspring. He had himself married a worm, but the coven's ambitions required they cultivate a relationship with the Ellendei, it was they wished to ultimately reign. For the last eighty years, the coven's concubines had replaced the snaky shape shifting Medusan priestesses, as his warlock's fleshy pursuits. In so doing the manipulative power of the Medusans had declined, whilst, the coven had become far more humanoid.

Glamawere regretted not the policy. Relationships with the Wadeen and the nations many criminal organizations had been much increased by the Hidden

Lodges dabbling in the slave trade. They imported slaves from Theine, Ergedh, and the mighty cities of the realm, the worms themselves had even contracted with them on occasion. Human women were often needed in their Kadron sacrificial ceremonies, he made them pay well for the loss of flesh. It fueled his coffers.

The Damned had at times recruited apprentice witches from this resource. In particular he examined the newcomers each year for marks, wickes that pointed to the work of the Imprisoned One amongst his people. Skin blots, shades, however slight, that spoke to him, a sign which pointed to their bearer's greater fate. These converts to the Kingdom of Wicca, he scattered throughout the princes in his suzerain. His wickes, he called them, supported his portion of Wicca with their presence.

It was time for him to face the Gorgon. Again. Sorrow for his lost freedom, what was left of his heart ached. Often, he had felt a closeness with a wicke, coveting both her smooth, soft body, and her human soul, at these times it had been hard. He had been reminded of his younger years. His life before. Should he keep her close as a slave or lose her to the distant life of a member coven. His mind usually prevailed; parting company for the wicke's freedom, was preferable to witnessing her slow brutal degradation at the hands of the Master of Slaves.

It was always the most intelligent who fought being subjugated for the sexual pleasure of others. And Glamawere was not numb enough to enjoy the sadistic rites that conditioned these unfortunates to their life as coven slaves.

Agotte ever efficient, broke their will quickly, and if he couldn't then they were soon fed to the dead. The subjects of the unwilling queen always craved life for their pitiful undeathed survival. Excessively unwilling slaves, were shown what their fate was to be, if that did not terrify them into servility, then to the dead they were fed.

At times the many agreements, and contracts of blood, or spoken vow, demanded they lose a few harem slaves. All Glamawere could do was try to keep the depletion at affordable levels. He hated watching the suffering himself, especially if the slave reminded him of an ancient love, a love from a distant human past that he now vaguely remembered. He found it irksome.

Allying the coven to Ergedh and its massive slave trade had helped. Not only were they willing to lend eunuchs or prize torturers, but the Hidden Lodge, had there found a source of submissive people. Subjected to abuse all their lives the Ergedhian peasant stock and other peoples that Drake had conquered adapted well to the resigned passivity of slavedom. Ergedhian's could live through ordeals that broke or killed others.

Even the warlike Gunerson's were not an inexhaustible source of humanity, however, and the Lodge cultivated contacts with any organization that delt in the sale of live women, the dead variety they already had in abundance.

The face of a gorgeous Thaine for who he had had a particular fondness haunted him as he made his way toward the great stair. The secret portal that hid his private quarters from the rest of Mnt. Ellendon. The entire personal complex constructed, as it was, from materials enchanted entirely, and assembled by a Dwarfen artificer from the Derem Gorin Mnt tribes, he had embedded with countless protections and wards.

It breathed ethereally, much like the head of Wose, regenerating magickal power with each sun set. Years earlier he had spent the better part of a decade learning and imbibing it with essence fire, the most powerful of the basic elemental magicks. Within the elemental realm of air, essence fire was a destructive deterrent to any unwanted tampering to his hidden front door.

The material plane, an amalgamation of the four cardinal elements, fire, water, air, and earth, lay about. Inundated by both the astral and ethereal energies. The fabric of its reality was manipulatable by those born with the power of mind that the Ellendei called magick. Essence fire was an extension of the wizard themself, it acted much like an intense combustion, literally "burning" with a voracity that normal incendiaries could not match.

The Ethereal plane acted as medium for the four cardinal elements and their manifestation into the plane of Material existence. The Astral Plane, its antithesis, was the home of lost souls, or spirits. It perpetuated the divine mind's efficacy on the Material Plane. The One, Enruth, Eserostianus, Medusa, Helgotei, Kadra, and that which the Ellendei named God, all ascended to the world through this plane.

Glamawere passed his front door and climbed the long stair that led to the Wyvern's cave, and, the lair of the Asp Society of Medusa; the den his wife called home. A hand grasped automatically to his chest assuring him that he wore his amulet against petrification. The Head of Wose and his own innate resistance to sorcery also warded him from the crystallization effect that the wife's gaze caused, Glamawere, wanting to be safe, had searched out the amulet before their courtship, and had worn it ever since.

Reaching the top of the stair, he felt the Asp Society's eyes upon him. He turned right crossing the peak of Ellendon toward the east facing lair. Not continuing to the Societies own lair, he instead climbed the private stair of the Gorgon Wife to a series of rooms and chambers that they shared together, a home, of sorts. Unlocking their door, and using a shoulder he pushed it wide. Then hurriedly strolling through their east facing and, mountain viewed, living room he avoided the kitchen, hearth space instead jumping backwards on the round over cushioned bed.

"Gorgon Wife. Glamawere be home." He called.

Davide de Clune, more than uncomfortable, sensed he was perturbed, out of place. The Wadeen in comparison was in full form, never in attendance, and as elusive as ever.

As Herigar's feudal embassy, the procurement of a protection agreement for the dozen slaves they had transported, as a gift to the Hidden Lodge had been his. The last days he had spent in discussions mitigating the concord that governed the gift.

Davide, famous for his honesty and nobility, his adherence to the strict codes that ran their life, trusted the Lodge little, and barely credited the Wadeen, when it came to it, with much of anything, more a bane than a boon. Sorcerers were ever devious, insidiously embroiled in their own counter plots. Machiavellianism, flowed in their watery blood, the Arraken Knighthood itself had arisen to fight Spell Slinging, and the perverse dictatorialism it produced.

A member of the Most Chivalric Order of the Lance, the embassy of Herigar, Dragon Lord, Davide committed himself to the protection of his word, its consistency and fame. As such, the vows and accords struck by Davide de Clune carried the weight of a readied lance, willing to prove its divine righteousness in the lists of honor, should a dispute arise.

Direct, to the point of righteousness the kniving ways of the thousand wizards, or so his master's people referred to the plethora of Ellendei spell slingers, were not his. Davide preferred the unswerving word of his mighty sword to the manipulations and unholy machinations of the Hidden Lodge, the Wadeen, and their hexicological spell weaving. After days here he was no longer sure who, or what, he was talking to, they could all be vampires or worse for all he knew.

His Squire sat to one side of their quarters sharpening the pair's weaponry. Putting down the sword he was working on, he turned to their crossbows, checking the gear mechanisms, their cord, and aim. They had enough room here to warm up and exercise, and a room down the hall had been reserved for sparing.

On edge, they had spent their first days in hours of sparing and the honing of combat skills. The room's gold inlaid pentagram and the conspicuous blood stains had taken a toll. Davide had noticed a certain unnatural relish come across his partner after a bout or more. Usually a practical warrior, his squire began escalating their combats with an unfriendly zeal. He wants my blood, Davide had thought, and there had been something in his eyes, a distant glimmer, or absence of glimmer, rather. Davide took it as a warning. He soon put their daily bouts on hiatus until they left this Godless, hedonistic place.

Now they prayed, instead. Toward evening Davide lead Jorin in a reading from the psalms, avoiding the room down the hall entirely. This bolstered moral, helping them with their nights rest.

His eyes fell on the small leaden, silver capped flask over the fire. Davide smiled he had faced down Glamawere the Damned preserving their original contract. Herigar would be glad. Far safer on their mantle, the soul of a heretical abbot, of the Corserite order, yes, a heretical Corserite. What better way to seal an alliance, than with the soul of his Duke's excommunicate foe.

The Corserites had always been unruly not only did they condone the practice of magick they sided with Thornbreak and the Elfen Highlord Serderan against the Claim of Herigar to the Lordship of Thornbreak. Eorowin Noldarkein Lord High Justice of the realm, an elf more honored by far than Serderan, upheld the Gunerson's claim through their ancestor Enerille Gunerson, Eorowin's own wife.

As Feorowin claimed right to the Elfen diadem so did his great grandson Herigar. Allies they had declared war on Thornbreak. Not since the war against the Wizard Kings had Arraken seen such an amassed military power as Herigar now represented. Dragon Lord and War Lord, he prepared to assert his hereditary right to overlordship of the entire west.

The heretical elf friend's soul was a glorious thing indeed.

It would ride at the head of their armies to hearten the disquieted, a rally post for the might of lord Herigar of Drake.

Seraus, Lizard worshipper of the Wadeen, Seraus the Babbler, as he was named within Drake's household, slipped quickly into the chamber from without. Ssthaithich hung about his neck, the miniature dragon, a lizard grin pulling its lips backward to expose a set of short sharp fangs. Its forked tongue darted along their surface, its wings were folded against its hide it used its long prehensile tail and limbs to cling about his master.

"We that toil in thy behaf ...thus return...."

"...this be true ....wee..haf..." Ssthaithich answered snickering.

Davide looked solemnly toward them, great, the Wadeen are back, he thought.

"What haf thee to report Wadeen?"

"That we art amongst our friends Sir Davide... Absent do we find the tardy rabble....of which thy slandering rumorers whisper....painting our allied kin in a bloodied humor..."

"Thou art not in court Wadeen talk plainly."

"Thy mind be speedy as the serpents tongue....What do thee in thy metaled might despair...to see the Arraken sun unhindered...No mountain of death betwixt it and thee.."

"Enough Babbler I said cease!"

"Me thinks thy keep a heavy pondering heart."

"Be that as it may...." The knight countered, "we have a lordly conduct to bare hence..doth not thee Wadeen cherish...our crusade? We are to Ergedh. This holy shrine of heresy to be our charge" He had crossed to where Thomas' soul jar lay on the mantle. "Ellondon hast nor sway on thee or me...Herigar Dragon Lord is to the fray...No dallying on his strength will this his servant be."

"There yet be talk I would have on this..." Seraus placed his hands stretched open together in front of him. "Our hosts are not unaccustomed in our arts ...we think they have learning that given time we can carry hence."

"Tarry we would... if thou master give us leave..." The tiny dragon flew above the Wadeen's head, arresting a somersault in midair to bow deeply before the knight.

This creature is as crazy as its priest, thought Davide. Seraus had ever been considered unstable, wild even for a Lizard Worshiper.

"If thou must ...a single day longer we will stay.... Though at sunrise day after the moro we wilt depart... Thus I command." Davide was final.

Seraus bowed to the knight, as had his familial dragonette. They tittered back and forth in the tongue of Great Drakes, circling the room toward the curtains, that, covered their particular bed. Davide and his squire shared the only other bed in the room, one standing sentinel as the other slept.

Davide slept first, fitfully tossing, snakes swarming around his unconscious mind. They slithered, hiding the ducal crown from his view. They rampaged burning elf, and, Ellendei alike. Drakes sat ancient beyond compare, beneath Giants Pass they bread, amongst the Plateered hills they thrived, snakes, worms, drakes, half women asps, many armed twisting forms, gorgons from Kadron myth, and the lizards of the Wadeen. Wriggling, writhing, abhorrent massed undulations.

Noldarn searched the face of Uuk of Maub interpreting the lines and flickers he found there. Ollisria, his love, stood behind. She watched the two new comers ever quiet. The dooms of earth and Tarterous met on her preserved mortal form, the one who offered tears in the dark, who watched the passing grief of man with ever readied waters to bedew the door steps of hell.

"Thy services I dismiss...begone mortal.... I first born accept thy doom...your lady dost my soul hold dear.... why then? should thy life be ought but free?"

"I be Uuk of Maub...." the prince had not expected this turn of events. "To the Thorned Queen have I my life time rendered...not to another. Then who art thee? Elf .....dost thy usurp a doom unwanted. Or art thou an apparition. Foul hell birthed spawn?"

Noldarn smiled. Exhaling, he cleared his face of the thick air issuing from Hados. Then, with a clear voice sometimes shrill, sometimes, melodic, caressing the stones and ears about with its deep, sweet, Elfen chimes. He spoke. He spoke slow, purposeful, and with the power of the diviner. Never had he tried to lift a curse as deadly and omnipotent as the doom that he now sensed. He a first born attacked the human spirit of death. Its ever presence in their fleeting lives. The reaper, the boatman, grey Hados, known by many names he petitioned them all substituting himself as Maub's surrogate.

"Fear not Uuk, no spawn of Hados be I,
sired in towering ancient oaken stands,

life times of age bosomed within their charms,
calm turbidity the fluid sways,
a breeze of love wafted dangerless trees.
Before thy maturity did begin,
two score ten, and three hundred years more,
haft I for Enruth strived here,
lonely in life no companion found,
an immortality without true love,
eternity to no issue propound,
a thankless void intolerable fate!
Lo to this starless night a star resounds,
beacon of joy thee be! contentment true!
enchanted with carrion, hell confound.
For thy mistress, thy kin, forlorn be I,
smitten in life I ever will serve her hence.
From thy dread Hados doom I release thee,
begone thy fate will be better spent,
with my soul price, I thee thy curse dispense.
to this tier leave thy execrated piers,
accursed progenitor, dutiful slave,
washed tiers at respite in the enemy's plot,
grease on the chains of man's vile quietus."

.....The words still echoed, carried deep to the earth, through the gates of Hados they flew, flitting about the banks of the Stix. The Titans of Tartarus, imprisoned by Kadra's tyranny, looked up with hope, as a moment of forest song carried to their banished solitude, on a hope born wind, scented with the breeze of ancient wood.

Mnt Ellondon shuddered with the un-quieted murmurs of their protest, the ground shook, rocking those of the tiered pyramid. Ollisria stood, Noldarn beside her, two first lights in the starless night of death. The prince aghast, at the return of his mortal life stumbled to his knee.

"Prince Uuk of Maub I am again once more,
not a pawn of Helgotei's snaked gorgons.
As thou hast upon thy head my fate placed,
then elf, do I, to thee the same pledge make,
to the first born of man, Earl Serderan.
a vassal I shalt be. Thornbreak's alley,
the heaths of Mernnon in my lifetime be.
Thy name I know not......"

The mortals voice small and insignificant in Ollisria's great hall of death, lacked the weighted power of the Thorned Crown's new herald, as it muted lost in the silent throng. The movement sounds of the dead. To the prince it was the most honest speech of his life, not lengthy, it intended no subterfuge, no politics, there were no young Mernnonian princesses, or ladies to impress, only the heart felt vow. He was grateful.

His mortally had been stolen and returned in the space of one night. Now a prince once again he sensed the effect his simple words had caused. Something in his chest, a pang, a desire, an unfinished charge. Thomas he must save the Abbot. What Abbot, he had no thought. Then he had. Saint Thomas the young. The abbot he had known for years. He saw his face in his mind. The flask! of course the spell the troll he had to be gone. Must continue his quest. Start the quest. The Saint would be saved.

It was then he caught the gaise of Ollisria. Her dark eyes filling the elipses of crescent white that lined her pupils, long lashes an outer frame of black. He beheld her, his ancestor, the advent of his house, she who weapeth for eternity, that those who came after may not foresee their death. The mote at the door of Hados. White and green in the light of that room, she seemed as the forest moss, that hung thick as the beards of Mernnon.

Her lashes black night, circled the black in brown eyes filling their face with the shine of compassion. A smile suggested itself on her lip, and for a moment a solitary line dimpled her cheek. With her blink her chest rose with an inhale and Uuk noticed her slender nudity revealed beneath the thick blanket of thick gloss hair. Her breast, nipples, a reflection of her eyes, dark round and pointed.

"I speak for Kadra...Tyrant God..Farther,
Uuk of Maub thou art free. Noldarn Asen,
the Herald of Ollisria serves me.

On three thrones as judge the Tyrant climbs,

Hados, Tarterous and Olympus high,

his word condemns mortal, devil, Titan, and God,

if thou his servants help in thy flight wish,

then to Ellendon's peak hastily flee,

there with the Saint to the sky can you soar."

Her eyes closed, as still as marble but for the slow heaving of her chest, she appeared fragile. A slave of fate, her frozen legs flexed in a strong motionless dance, separating the sea of black that lay smoothly about her. She gave him her blessing.

Slender steps glided her to the divine where she sat, the herald stepping forward, wielded the staff of his office. He struck the stone floor thrice and spoke in the Elfen language of his people. Then when he had finished, he traced a circular outline on the pyramids summit with the herald staff. To Uuk of Maub he went on, returning to the Ellendei, a language fluent to them both.

"I summon a spirit that will accompany you on thy quest. As you will need help retrieving the saint's soul here be a spirit that will take my place with you." He had drooped the high speech talking as if to his brothers in the monastery.

Within the circle a small white glow formed, growing as it did so. Soon it sprouted white feathered wings and a humanoid torso with muscular legs. The deamon behind them hissed, snarling at the unruffled white wing beats. Noldarn's angel beamed back a golden glow issuing from its body.

"I be Aserren. "The sound of many voices spoke its words in their heads.

"You will accompany the Prince Uuk of Maub, aiding him in his quest to rescue the soul of Saint Thomas the young. He will release you on its completion."

"So be it." The voice answered.

"An angel. "said the prince.

"a lesser angel.." clarified the Diviner.

"Ye of little faith.." Chortled the voice.

The low growl of the daemon hastened the elf.

"Now afore thee be detected leave...remember this is not your home."

The angel grappled the prince and holding him firm winged upward toward the halls distant ceiling. Uuk stabilized the carry by grasping his hands, entwined together around its torso. They glided above the shuffling dead below them; the prince felt a water of tears splash against his strong arms.

The angel cried quietly, dipping through the north most tunnel of funneling death. They flew above shadowed nameless tombs, the catacombs of Ellendon.

Veering east and sweeping to the ground, weeping still, the angel darted through the center of a giant wooded door, emerging onto a spiraling stair they climbed upward on the strength of his wings. Soon at another door, the pair stopped.

Speaking and chanting in a language Uuk was unfamiliar with, it painted them into the masonry environment, covering their outer forms with magickal colors and lines. When invisible, it turned to the wall. Here abutting the door, it took time opening an invisible passage in the stone. Beckoning to Uuk it stepped, stooping through, Uuk followed.

They were in a plain square room, in its center a massive rock stair lead up into the ceiling climbing toward Ellendon's peak. The angel led him quickly on toward the adjacent wall. It again opened a hole in the masonry through which they stepped. Finding themselves in an empty, but Uuk thought, well used passage, the angel took a moment to decide which way to lead the prince. The smells of a distant meal, and the heavy smell of perfume told him that this part of the complex was inhabited by life. They went on, the yellow, gold glow from the angelic guardian lit a number of side corridors, and doors, which they ignored, instead approaching a naturally illuminated area ahead.

The flicker of naked torch outlined the end of the hallway. They crept closer, the features of a distant wall coming into view; decorated sparsely with two gigantic tapestries, the wall marked the far side of a large chamber. Empty for the moment, the end of a passage could be seen to the right, and a door in the wall to the left, both at right angles to the two explorers.

A yellowed eye, webbed with blood shot red veins starred at them from the opposite tapestries, a shrunken and crushed brown head as its pupil. The heads expression was not maniacal, rather it had an air of calm, serene in calamity. The second wall hanging depicted a daemon much like that he had seem on Ollisria's Dias. It glowered at them with the contempt of its unnatural race.

The angel turned left leading his charge toward the door in the south wall of the chamber. Braziers built in the wall lit their way. They once more passed through the wall beside the door with the aid of the angel's dweomer.

In a short brazier lit passage, that ended paces ahead in a large door, they paused the angel closing its eyes and concentrating. A corridor and door lay opposite each other in the center.

Its hands stretched wide feeling the space around, it turned in a complete circle. Then moving, it honed in on the passages center door. The angel looked to Uuk, whispering.

"The Saint's soul lies in a chamber, it is on a mantel within.....not far...but ..there are guards..three.... no four.

You wait here I will sing them into a deep slumber... quieting the sleeper's dreams...You stay guard."

The angel looked up and down the short hallway, checking its intersecting passage. Finding all still, it stepped through the wall toward the saint and away from Uuk.

Muffled sounds from the door at the far end of the hallway, told him of an imminent approach. Seeing nowhere to hide, Uuk stole his way down the smaller passage, camouflaged by the angel's power he crouched. Sounds further on warned him not to move.

There he sat, as the voices came closer. Seven red masked, and shrouded coven members filed passed along the short hallway. They talked light heartedly in Ellendei. Those with their masks pulled back, looked sweaty and tired, relieved after a long work. They left quickly toward the tapestried hall.

Uuk breathed in relief.

The wall that he flattened against was painted top to bottom with scenes from Hados or the Ellendie version of it, Hell. Tortured souls burned in vats of fire or froze in icy catacombs, were herded by winged and horned forms, a countless sea of humanity.

A pained groan from deeper down the side passage told him he was not alone, uneasily he hastened back to the where the angel had disappeared. It reappeared through the wall, the flask containing Thomas in hand.

"I left an illusory image of the flask…if you are lucky they will not notice….shall we depart?"

"Yes let's." answered the prince.

The coven's lair irked him, its walls were filled with a sense of dread. They waited then retraced their steps to the large room with the upward spiraling stair. Here the angel handed Prince Uuk the flask saying,

"I beseech thee Prince of Maub release me from thy service…as I have retrieved the soul of Saint Thomas for thee..If thy leave now Kadra will help thee fly…To mnt. Ellendon peak thee must climb… past Gorgon stair and hippogrif cower…. up up up..! thee must climb escaping fate and doom in Ellendon tower…"

"You are released", he said.

Before the Prince had finished the phrase, it was gone, and Uuk was truly alone. He stood on the stair above the square room thinking on the Angeles last words, he had to hurry. Climbing, step after step he trudged upward toward the peak's summit.

Kadra had promised aid, Uuk praying to himself as he continued, hoped the patriarchal tyrant of his people would not forget him their first prince in this his time of need. Shivering at the place around him, he wished the aid was not to be long in coming. His legs were strong, he was the inheritor of his father, Sarkhen the Mighty, in strength of sinew, bone and muscle. The steps went on and on wearing the mortal muscles that battled him toward their height. An endless chore he thought, the spirit had implied hast and Uuk wanted nothing better than to get out of this place of decrepitude and death, a dark, lonely mnt. It had costed the lives of countless nobles of his line. Thus was the curse of Maub; losing the first-born son of those generations doomed to serve Ollisria, there at the doorstep of Hados.

The air thinned as he pushed his ascent on, losing a degree of its oppressive thickness, it became harder to get enough wind. He tired, easily, slowing to a crawl, in his attempt to reach the top, and whatever help waited there for him. Forcing on, he collapsed often gasping for breath in the accursed place. His muscles held up better than his lungs. Ever, he staggered back to his feet, pulling upwards along the roughhewn walls, a never-ending circle of pained exertions. The nagging pull of muscles struggled to lift his heaving legs. Cold now, his panting breath hung about him. Wet with its sweat he huffed on.

A cavernous corridor broke the way, its incline slight, the Prince thanked the respite it offered. Following its course, he left the stair and Ellendon's core behind him. He must be far from where he started, close to the summit. The cold had replaced the dusty dry of the lower mountain. The thick odor of manure, disguised under the freezing air like his own stables. Beasts were close.

The incline bought him to the base of a second stair. A wooden door, marked with a image of tangled asps, filled the tunnel from here. Avoiding the door as best he could he resumed his upward journey. The bestial stench abated and relieved he finally reached a landing. The air had warmed slightly, and resting he noticed a collection of doors to one side off set from the landing by a short passage. Across the landing from these a single stout door bard any progress.

A great deal of his ascent had been made in the pitch dark of Ellendon, using touch, but since, he had reached the caverned incline, a gentle light, had grown. Filtering through the cracks from he knew not where, this light hinted at the walls.Tinting them a slight gray at first, he was now able to see without straining. Waiting for his exhaustion to die, he perceived the intensity growing about him. Heartened he moved about, somewhere a dawn was to be found.

The doors bore no distinguishing designs or motifs, and finding no other consideration he chose the segregated portal. It was latched from his side, through a visible complex set of gears and devices. He was no locksmith so hoping for the best he turned the latch, pulling sharply toward him.

After a loud snap, the portal swung in with the blinding light of the new day. Clambering out to the windy, snow tufted crag, the forested mountain hills of northern Corsinia giddied him with their distant tops, miniature at this great height. The sun had begun its slow daily trek and still low its rays found a way under a thick western cloud to dazzle Ellendon and its foothills. North and east lay wilderness shadowed in the long light of mourning. Caron Crag and its gigantic neighbors were visible through a second bank of cloud, their height too much for even the early autumn weather to hide. In this way a section of the north shinned in the yellow of the sun, Ellendon in its center, an island within the gray blue brown of a wet sky.

It was freezing, and about to retreat back into the mountain the prince was startled by an unexpected voice.

"Sooo...this be the First Prince of Maub...does it? ...tichy.. I say..Yes I must say.. ..tichy.."

Turning against the cold, Uuk noticed a monstrous beaked eagle head, gold, and yellow brown against the snow. With a quick shake, a blizzard of frozen water was thrown into the strong wind, buffeting about the sheltering basalt peninsulas. The giant eagle lion body of a griffin, had been lying prone on the rock. It appeared a large pile of snow before it emerged. It stood. Its taloned front claws scratched the feathers of its neck, lion tail swishing. A second shivering shake cleared off the remaining snow.

"I hope I did not surprise you..but with so many hippogriffs and wyverns about I thought caution was the best bet...Speaking of bets you wouldn't care to make a small wager..would you?......say we..oh but I can't tell you that can I ..Oh well say we save the sportsmanship till latter shall we?"

"If you say so." Shivered the prince.

"How cold you look! Here I bought something for that... yes...... here we go."

Picking up a rolled woolen package it handed it to the prince, with a talon the size of a mighty shield.

Too cold to answer, Uuk unfolded a thick white fired robe, and leather tunic, in their center he found a pair of woolen hose and two great white boots that reached to his knees, lashed from the same white fir as the robe. Rushing against the bitter air of the mountain top he soon felt heat returning to his body, soaking out from within his bones, and kept close by the thick-skinned fir.

"Now hurry on up we must make hast."

The griffin bowed its long neck, as Uuk grabbing the soul flask clambered over its folded wing to a place behind. Wiggling between its huge raptor feathers he found a good grip on the messenger of Kadra. He looked up into the huge eagle face, turned back to front on its malleable neck as it watched its passenger.

Winking, largely, it turned forward, and spreading its wings it leaped from that cold wind-swept summit into the Corsinian sky. They flew directly south picking up the unfriendly shadow of two Ellendonian hippogriffs. Half horse half eagle these fliers were smaller than the griffin. Uuk thought that they could carry a rider a piece whereas the beast that had rescued him could manage three- or four-man sized riders.

Laden as he was the griffin still out paced the pursuit, and by the time the Prince and Kadran steed reached the southern cloud bank the hippogriffs were well back, two specks in the clear sky.

The thick cloud was wet, Uuk stayed dry, pulling the fir closed around him, and hiding from its icy fingers within the repellent feathers of the griffin's back. They sailed south until the cloud broke; bracken and heath lined hills of Mernnon meeting the Uuk's expectant eye. He recognized the central forest that divided the hill land of his people's province. They were steering their way to his families own dwelling, the House of Maub.

He saw the hard covered road that had stood centuries before the war of the Wizard kings, and which Choital I reconstructed to commemorate the passing of the wurm 500 years ago. With its completion the renovation signified Mernnon's incorporation into the Arraken feudal system, the house of Maub was then raised to the stature of the other Ellendei royal families. Choital I made the oath of fealty becoming the 1st Barron of Mernnon. Their house was all that remained of the original houses of Kadran heroes, all well seeped in their own blood and treachery.

The House of Maub had been faithful vassals till the civil war, four hundred eighty years since the passing, when Oritand III sided with the rebels against Meleg the decrepit. Meleg died when surprised by rebels in the wilds past South End, his son Ottar, protected by the Arraken clergy during his turbulent youth managed to bring these rebels to bay.

Oritand was captured by his brother Sarkhen I, and executed in Y.S.P. four hundred and eighty four. Sarkhen II, Uuk's farther, the first son of Oritand being adopted as heir by Sarkhen I, thereby carrying the diadem of Maub to a new generation. The priests of the Acropolis had urged Sarkhen I, successfully, to maintain the lineage of Maub. The curse of Ollisria sited as a primary reason, Sarkhen I had fathered no children of his own, marrying his brothers wife, Uuk's grandmother, Artimi Trengotte, on the execution of her husband.

Breiyr wood nestled against the well groomed road; curving, it filled the land between a line of Mernnonian hills and and the steep flat peak on which the House of Maub lay. The road cut a winding spiral round the hill to reach the house after two circles. A two towered gate met the wall here. Across a paved and grassy courtyard from the tower, the blocky keep with its tall ornamented house carved a ragged and buttressed horizon from the rolling terrain of central Mernnon.

The air warmed as the griffin dove toward the house. They glided, slowing, as the beast dipped. Close, Uuk got his best look ever at the marbled and rock sphinx decorating their houses tallest tower. A face in its window, a serving man he recognized stared in wonder as they passed. Not familiar yet with flying, Uuk resisted an urge to wave.

Banking around the south of the house they flapped slowing to a hover, before the lion legs jolted to the grass. Wings folding they had landed. A small crowd was gathering at the steps to the house, and Uuk saw loaded crossbow men, on the crenelated roof.

He jumped off the griffin's back elated to be home, a place he never thought he would see again in his doomed enclosed life. He had so much to discuss with his farther and their advisors that he knew not where he would begin.

"I be Horatius steed to Iandredar the fleet... First Griffin of the Circle.. Thank thee Uuk First Prince of Uuk... Thanks be to thee.. thou waited till a complete stop...I dist reach... Remember fate be not through with thee"

Then it leapt to the sky and with Three wing beats it disappeared over the house's outer wall heading north. Uuk looked after. Soon rising above the wall's height, it winged upward to the distant cloud.

Happy Mernnonian reached his ears, and turning, the hermetic advisor to the house, Ajaxus Trengotte greeted him with an Abjuration, a ritual banishment of evil.

Worried gray eyes, examined him till content. Assured that the Prince was intact and uncorrupted, he bowed welcoming Uuk home in his most polite Mernonian etiquette, an asped caduceus held at his side.

They walked toward the house, home to the curse of Maub.

She stood by their glass windowed living room and starred north toward Darkmore and the keep she Knew to contain the Treathbaron, Aterol Aterolson. She was angry, as always Glamawere had been hard to please. His obsessions had become so involved they took time, energy and in their climax total concentration of her thought. They had started well with her aspial obsession to smother and engulf.

That was how their relationship had always been, a jealous craving for each other's devoted and undistracted thought. The asps of her hair hissed harmonically with her mood. It had ended as last time with phantasmal excursions into their own psyches. Some were hard to remember. How much time had they wasted? Had they learned anything? Why had they both develop a fascination with deluding each other?

She had asked Medusa that question before, but the goddess ever wished them to continue the union. Was there a dearth of Gorgons, or was it Glamawer's intellect that the prietesshood craved? A slight smirk lightened her glaring face. Her children were intelligent, brightest of Tarterous, well close, there were those boys she had birthed, still they always had a place in the coliseum.

It had been that temple mistress again, her images were coming back to her now, that fantasy always attracted Glamawere. That wrinkled old warlock, who did he think he was fooling, though he did create a believable, if somewhat lusty high elf lord. He used a disguise spell augmented by phantasmal illusions, she laughed, what had he looked like. And parts, she thought he borrowed from a certain Bachan sub daemon she knew, at least she guessed that was where he got that elf's lower torso from. Not a bad attempt. Had that all been for her? He had made her think so.

But the temple dancer, she was sick of it. So mundanely revolting, and enchanting, but how? Why should she want such a thing? All those clandestine meetings, the agreements with lords, and of course the vows, Glamawere loved those vows. Complicated promises and sworn fealty, and the frantic attempt to ever comply. Something close to a romantic Mernnonian farce was the result. One of those Satyr comedies from the extinct Mernnonian festival of wine.

The athletically voluptuous dancer, and her serious heart felt commitment to escape, and betterment, overwhelmed Glamawere. Of all the personalities she adopted to attract her mate it was by far his favorite. Was his obsession something to do with his own contract with the Devil, and its many subclauses. Shaitan, rather, her imagination corrected her in her husband's voice. Or did he have a crush on one of his slaves? Was she filling his desire for another? Was there further minion she would have to murder? Probably not, she thought.

Those days were long gone.

What bothered her mostly was how intellectually demanding their sex had become. How it demanded every crevice of her mind leaving none to follow distant events that she did not wish to lose track of, even for a flicker. But when she and Glamawere loved it could take days, or even weeks of absorption into each other's mind. Did she dote? No there was a thought, an anger, a thing forgotten, something searched for. She was not consumed.

Her life had lasted so long already, generations of mortals faced death in her eyes. Their temple in Tarterous was decorated with her most prestigious victims, lords, priests of Kadra, and the recent Arraken knights. A time would come, she told herself, when these stoned victims would adorn the Helgotei temple in Mernnon, a fitting seat for her throne. She would reach her true ascendancy.

Yes, there was a thing that angered her. If she could only remember. They had both wanted each other and now she knew not the cost. Still irritated, she left their quarters descending to the Medusan halls. She would prey, she knew not how long the rapture of love had taken, nor could she remember what contention had motivated the liaison with Glamawere in the first place. She had to follow back in her thoughts. Had she wanted something from him? A price? Did she get what she wanted? She seemed satisfied but there was something.....

CHAPTER 9

PINNACLE OF PARNASSUS

The Waieen browsed on a collection of nuts, grubs, and root, some they had picked up on the way, pulling them by hand and tooth from amongst the thick tuberous growths that knotted into the tunnel. And others that they had bought with them in their packs, the only possession each carried was a plain leather sack, slung loosely over their badger-like shoulder.

They spaced evenly along an earthy rough dug tunnel. It was not wet, though clayey and at times it felt damp. The crunch of nuts was reassuring. Eothan eat, he was hungry and their food filed his body with well needed energy. Nutritious and tasty he thought, the grubs were much akin to a larva he had looked forward to in his childhood, but his tribe had roasted the puffy white insect, these he eat raw. The two goblin kin had not come to, the gas diagnosed to be a powerful sleep powder.

The Waieen leader, a priest, or so Eothan presumed, detected a latent magickal effect with a potent natural narcotic delivery system. No wonder it was lasting.

He gathered from their talk that his hosts were on their way to Parnassus peak by way of a complex network of underground passages. The monk recalled the Lands Beneath, a never-ending cavernous catacomb, spoke of with almost pious reverence by the hobs of the Enorien Peaks. Powers, deities, and lords divided these underground domains, warring in hob legend throughout the ages, much like the Ellendei knights on the surface, he thought.

The Waieen dug and maintained their own network within the hierarchy.

The thought of the Abbot being tossed in a troll wielded sac, on its way south was hard for Eothan to shake. It was in his thoughts again. Not resisting he closed his eyes, concentrated on it. He sensed the inside of a coach. The rhythmic, thump of its wheels as it raced through the night, its brown varnished interior, the cushion of its seat, Thomas was there, he was sure of it. As he opened his eyes the vision vanished, replaced with the earthen wall of the Waieen tunnel. Der Aeath was aiding his search for Saint Thomas.

"We are to confide in council with the cult of Artificers. Gnomes of Parnassus... you needed aide.

Now accompany us. Shaitan has eyes in these depths…
we must not tarry."

And with that the troop hastened down their round
tunnel. Eothan trekking after beside the ported bodies
of his two allies. Did they belong to the sect of Gour
Garath or some of that tribes more war like kin? He
knew not.

They ran and walked, now like men on two legs,
and now on all fours. Their claws digging deep in the
hard earthen walls. The warrior monk impressed them
with his stamina keeping pace with these man-badgers.
In their gruff barking language, they sounded close to
forest speak, sharing the same sounds, and, probably
many meanings. In time Eothan began to recognize
words and understand their hushed barking dialogue.

They talked of their burrows, the Cathedral of
Toulon, their war with Drake, and the upcoming
meeting in Parnassus. Secretiveness, he gathered was
important, as they did not plan to travel directly to the
peak. Instead they discussed a rendeview to be arrived
at through a freshly dug passage. They were not to use
the established corridors. From a particular tunnel that
they knew of a concealed path would bring them to the
chamber of the meeting.

He listened intently, yet heard nothing of what
the council was to discuss. Eothan had read little of

Parnassus, he was aware that it had been the penultimate seat of wizardry at the height of the War between the Wizard Kings. Parnassus, second only to the sorcerer Ergedh, had sway over Gaobel his sorcerous neighbor, and if it wasn't for Ergedh's majority in the Circle of Flame, the Traition based Daemonoligical society, Parnassus may have dominated the entire world.

The Arraken Knighthood had succeeded first in the defeat of Traitian fire worshipers, and then had been considerably strengthened with the defeat of Ergedh and the founding of Drake. The unified Arraken, allowing a concerted un-flanked attack from Berelan on Gaoble, as his cabalistic alley fell, Parnassus sort to protect his pinnacle. Mernnon a sometime friend broke with the Master of Hexes, Choital I taking an oath of fealty to the Arrakens. Cut off, the remnants of the Circle of Flame appeared again as alley to Parnassus, Master of Hexes. They managed to offset defeat at the hands of the knighthood. A new but smaller realm of wizardry came about. It was not until the revolt of the Parnassian Gnomes, that Hex Master Parnassus was finally and completely defeated.

Many were the great troves and catches of power beneath the Gorges lone Pinnacle. Black hardened rock had soon become home to those who had slaved and toiled over eons for its owner. Imported from Derem

Goria as serfs the Gnomes learned fast their Master's wizardry. Within a generation the gondola had been built, and their skill at crafting trade goods had won them markets and allies throughout Mernnon and Arraken.

The Ellendei had for long feared Parnassus as an accursed crag, but its new and friendly stewards had done much to assuage their fears. That was all ancient history. As to recent events, Eothan had not an inkling. The Gondola still operated as a primary trade route into Mernnon, and Gnomish trinkets and carpentry were respected gifts throughout Arraken.

The Waieen stopped to clear a recent cave in. As they toiled shoveling dirt that crumbled about, Eothan again checked the two goblin-kin. They snored deeply. After a slap to the face, and water did not stir them, he offered a quiet prayer. The answering snores thickened. Well, he thought, Enruth, wishes them a quiet slumber.

They were soon traveling again, the corridor re-dug with the sharp scoop nailed claws of the Waieen. There were few side branches, the route for the most part being a straight path toward Parnassus. On occasion a halt would be called, and after discussion they would take a jog to a parallel passage below or beside the original.

He learned from their talk that it was a thirteen-league trip from Widerntown to Parnassus, a journey they hoped to complete in a day. The more often they needed to take detours, however, the longer that trip would take.

Meandering little the Weieen tunnel's structural integrity had lost nothing since its last use, although Eothan knew not when that was, he sensed that it lay empty and unused for long periods of time. Eothan got the impression that certain areas were avoided for structural reasons, whilst others housed the dens of recent migrants. Legendary beast or faunal emigre that the furry Weieen chose to respectfully circumvent rather than spend time evicting. Thus, they went on covering leagues of underground terrain in what seemed an impossibly short amount of time.

Eventually they left the Waieen tunnels for empty rock lined corridors. We must be close to Parnassus, he thought. A dark rock, it fit close, no obvious cracks between large bricks. The brick of Widern had been held by a visible gray pug, a mortar of thick gravel and sand. Here there was no such glue. Rocks, not bricks, with little more than a feint line separating individual blocks. A mildew thrived in the moist air, dankly clinging about them. He missed the loam of the earthen tunnels, the creeping mildew did nothing to replace it.

Soon they ascended stairs, silently skirting the edges of unused chambers buttressed with huge granite columns. Piles of termite invested wood rot stank in the darkness. The Waieen knew the way leading them past frescoes of unwritten histories, a record to the abominations and corruptions of Parnassus. They barked hushly of the breeding pits, an area above which they threaded their way, occasional noises beneath them told that they were still infested with dark spawn, and malevolent beings, offspring to the foul servants of Parnassus.

Ergedh too had bread foul creatures to fill the ranks of his armies. Vast was the land, and the Enemy had friends that were beyond the reach of Arraken's swords. The Kingdom spent generations irradicating these vile vermin in its first years. The works of Shaitan ever outwitted those of Enruth, man weak, willing to waist his energies in the pursuit of worldly desire. Thus, it had come to pass that much of that which was vile escaped the purges. Dwelling in the dark recesses of the Lands Beneath, and the stagnant pools of Rotwart swamp, here the evil spawn of the Wizard Kings multiplied still.

The waters of Deepwash fed a vast wetland separating Arraken from Drake, a foul river, it descended from the west through a steep ravine. It was here that the surviving hordes of corruption flourished, protected by quicksand and mire. A stone wall led for leagues protecting Drake from these spawning monstrosities.

Arraken preferred to trust in a brave sharpened sword, having many unknighted warriors willing to prove themselves. Eothan wondered whether that dread land's waters reached throughout the Kingdom, underground rifts carrying its defilement to and throw, or whether the stout warriors of the Ellendei were a match to its spread.

Rooms cleared, the mildew, replaced with a dry dust of unuse. Finding an arched anti-chamber, beside a cobwebbed and forgotten nameless tomb, the party rested. Waieen scouts moved ahead and sentinels were placed. The unconscious hobgoblin, and goblin breathed steadily, lain amongst the rest.

"From here we will go alone... You shall stay.... we are to parley with the Legislator... Wise One of Parnassus... His people are split. The Imprisoned One, Shaitan, The Dark Enemy. he moves in the mighty halls of Parnassus.... The cult of Nal Noldream, Lady of fate, Scissor of the Thread of Life. Gains strength throughout the Gnomish chambers of Parnassus. We come to seek council with our allies in the inner sanctum of Parnassus. The Legislator loses power. As our alley we have thoughts to share... Toulon must protect the faith. Enruth will preserve..." The Waieen barked out his explanation.

"You Corserite.. we must speak more on our return from the Pinnacle of Parnassus. The old Oaths from times before…. surface in the lands beneath threatening a rekindled war… We of few numbers… must know which laws will fall…and what people from beneath are free from the deceits of the Imprisoned One."

Eothan wanted to stress the importance of his own quest. The rescue of Saint Thomas and the urgent need to warn the Treathbaron, but the implied seriousness in the Weieen's voice, and his dark, worried, imploring eyes lead him to swallow his own trouble, thanking Enruth for their speedy rescue he listened instead. After they returned there would be time to talk on Corserite matters. Till then he would have to wait.

The band gathered splitting in half. Four Weieen including the priest departed, they moved in single file cautious, their ears and eyes alert for danger. Eothan sat in the dark silence, alone again. He heard the Weieen sentries, and his sleeping companions. The Abbot still missing, he felt safer than he had in Widern Tower, and allowing his fatigue to overtake him he dosed off. The empty sound of holy verse sung without care, or reverence plagued his half-conscious mind.

A bustle awoke him, hushed barks, voices in the forest speak, something was afoot. Choyuk, the Weieen priest, or at least that was how Eothan would pronounce, the bark he assumed to be its name, knelt ending on all four beside the monk.

"You are awake ...good.. we shall talk.. much has changed.. the Nal Nondream has grown in power.. Treiilelwisteralidarei Legislator of Parnassus has vetoed the Ourath..sad times are to come.."

"Vetoed ? Ourath? I Know not of what thee speak."

"The lands beneath have abided in peace since the passing of the dragon. The Ourath the oath of free passage has kept the tunnels of the Weieen and the Goblin halls of Enoria in peace..without strife... The Legislater of Parnassus is keeper of the oath of beneath. We of Toulon have traveled far through our farthest reaching paths ..Treilelwisteralidarei met us in his chamber of words.. There on the silvery throne, heir loom of his people....at who's feet they oft have served... slaves unto the Hexes of Unyielding Parnassus..the legislator hast to us of burrow spoke."

"In words of truth hast he broken the Ourath.. his people to long haft they the words of Nal Nodream heeded. Their fates untangled from Enruth the One and to the Imprisoned One leadeth..He as Legistrator does not command the respect from them to protect the Ourath. Muster...we must look to our teeth, claws, and burrows here after..No more the race of Gnomes or the peace of Ourath can we rely on."

"The Magick of Parnassus speaks on in his emancipated slaves, their hearts darken with greed kindled within the artifacts of Yor. Relics of the Master's Hex blacken the soul with ages of greed. Their own family of king haft the Gnomes put to flight... In hiding now abide the allies of Toulon, no voice to stand fast by oath or Ourath, a land of War, as in the Wizard King's prime now half we to replace our backdoors. Drake assails us from above.... now perchance we shall bleed when to our own tunnels we descend to feed.

"His beard is long... grizzled with curl, red is his face and long large his nose..his eyes thin sharp and green, yellow his hair... touched now with white.. wisped like his chin in curl.. a Legislator of the Deep.. In our songs and customs. He no longer trusts his own people to honor agreements he makes with his allies from yonder. Nal Nondream they heed assassinating their kings!"

"A spirit is growing in this ancient mountain... Though Parnassus be dead buried and gone it is he That we fear does his soul linger on? In trinkets, and heirlooms in walls, and in floors... in tombs of his victims, his slaves and servants..His hexes were ever long tangled with lies. Dost he now return through deluded magiis? The Gnomes have dwelt long studied, wrote and wielded potent dweomer filled devices... Hast this their undoing fostered before us... Put our allies in hiding... a disaster in friendship?........."

"They have usurped their King?"

"Yea.. his step brother now rules he dead.. his wife.. daughter have fled..To hiding they must flourish we will help as we can.. Foul news must to the Archbishop of Toulon we carry.. Not safe are we here.. Nal Nondream's minions are alert.. A different route with tiding and friends now to the Seat of Geobal wilt we depart."

It was then Eothan noticed the newcomers to the group. Two gnomes had returned with the party, and each of the returning group of Weieen was wounded, they had seen some battle.

"I am in search of my Abbot, Saint Thomas the Young, kidnapped in Corsinia Enruth leads me south for his rescue. If you can aid in my journey, we of the Corserite Brotherhood will be much in your debt... we are all in the service of Enruth."

"Yes ..Corserite I know of your quest... Thy art a warrior of renown... We are to travel South to the Seat of Gaobel, from thence we turn North...There is a stair relatively safe it will lead thee to the surface...Enruth be with thee...Our people will need us in Toulon."

"The Seat of Geobal I have read of it."

"It tops a crag of Niobia.. we detour via the castle of Parnassus' alley..Though it please us not... Our enemies will be hard pressed to ambush in the complex caves Gaobal and Troll-rock. The route be dangerous and shall work to our advantage. Thy sword will be appreciated.. with us Eothan the Fair.... servant to the One, Enruth."

Eothan had not told Choyuk his name and hearing it deep under the Pinnacle of Parnassus, it gladdened his heavy heart.

"My sword is yours. "He assured the Weieen.

The Gnomes, Galfreed, and Druallagall, both youthful males with cheery faces their wavy hair long and tied back in pony tail, short wisps outlining their chins, with what they hoped people were kind enough to call beards, looked inquisitively at the human. Shorter than dwarves, they wore smart hose and tunics, embroidered. One covered his tunic with a red-brown surcoat, the other wore an open many layered robe, with ruffled sleeves. The fine weave of their garments and its intricate embroidered filigree far surpassed any clothing Eothan had seen before.

He wondered at the Parnassan Gnomes, did they all have such crafted garb, or were these two nobles amongst their people. The robed had Auburn hair and a red orange face, emerald green eyes gleamed over a large nose. Normal or so the monk thought, for Gnomes the other, was quite different, with his fine surcoat and tunic, bright red hair and a dark brown almost black complexion and equally dark gaze. This dark-skinned gnome wore a shield insignia sown to the heart side of his surcoat: outlined in silver, a black pinnacle silhouetted the emblems center. They spoke easily in the forest speak to the reformed party of Weieen, their shiny black boots hard and tall.

Choyuk knelt to the prostrate sleeping Goblin kin and this time offered a prayer to awaken them. He sniffed around each, placing a clawed paw on their foreheads. Then as he leaned back to his rear legs into a sit, they stirred. Grunting at first then as they surroundings became clear they huddled together, their backs touching.

"Why wert thee a Widern Town? "Choyuk asked.

They looked about and finding themselves clearly outnumbered looked fearfully to themselves. They both wore loin straps, and fir tied round their middle. The taller, hairy but for his face clutched at one of a number of carved stones and bones threaded into his hide with twine. The other eyed a wooden clasped leather bag that he carried slung over shoulder and neck. The veins and sinews of his skinny joints showed through a naked smooth leathery skin, nobbled in parts from skin infections. A twitch along its upper lip flashed a row of pointed teeth and canine. Long pointed ears moved independently, desperately noting anything that could help. Their earlier appearance as human travelers was an illusion, that faded when the fell unconscious.

"Thy foul stench in me breeds rabid hunger.. so speak least thy throats be rent by canined jaw ....as thou well knowest..Weieen thirst well for corruption's breed." Choyuk's expressive snout twitched, flaring with hunger.

The smaller spoke first, long nailed fingers playing with his leather satchel's toggle...

"Though we art rough in birth..and under the yoke of damned arts..have struggled... me do to thee my virtues bow.................. In these kingdoms we art familiar is this but to thee not a gift.. For though we wert by the most foul birthed.. we too have by these same been tormented. To Widern by the Damned we were commanded. A pair bearing coin of and for damnation's brood. Motley we art... bastard all in kin. Unpleasant to thee in smell and sight yet un-likeing our own we can with you unite. Hold with thy rath we will with you share our fealty. Only this we ask spare our wretched lives.. and for this small fee will we our crafts alley to thee for the time till our freedom thee give...freely and willingly will this thou endow?"

The Weieen barked howling in discussion, then hushing quickly, they yelped to and throw. Choyuk silenced them with a cough...

"We 'ave skills I don't talk the speech of man well but we 'ave no lord.. only he, the Winged Damned 'ow for a vanishing fee.. 'e 'as us much faeried silver coin for portage of a leaden silver capped flask given." The goblin spoke the common in a broken unfamiliar fashion. "'e 'ow gobbles our kin and pays us well..e 'ow flaming beasts commands..it is 'ee 'ow to Widern Town commands us.. yet now we are our own and you for life can command us.. so says I. "The taller looked pleadingly to the Weieen, its prognethic face and sloped back nostrils wet with their own moisture. The long angular nose of his companion, and receded jaw, marked them both as members of different tribes and kin.

"These spawn of goblin kind haf spoke truth to thee." The Weieen priest pronounced the Ellendei clear. "Perchance we wilt need their help.. I rule that we wilt our canines sheath till they prove their wrong. If with us they serve well then to the halls of Troll Rock will we bid them part. Their people unwar like there do dwell..."

"So be it. "The Norcadian said out loud. Serious indeed did these burrow creatures sound in council, Eothan had often found the Hob's of Enoria peaceful if given a chance, he did not wish to see his companions from the previous night torn apart before his eyes.

"There are enemies about, the Gnomes of Nal Nondream and the foul spawn of Parnassus... we depart now.. before we are again attacked."

The Weieen took the front and rear with Eothan, the goblin kin, and the Gnomes grouped loosely in the middle. In this way they retraced their steps descending the path they had earlier ascended. As they reached the first Weieen tunnels they bared South heading toward the Seat of Geobal. The passages were less used, frequent earth slides barred their way slowing them as the burrowers quickly cleared a path.

These excavations held particular attention for the Gnomes, especially the surcoated dark skinned Parnassian, Druallagal. He took a small device from his pocket and peering through it much like a sailor does an astrolabe, he took various notes on their work, these he stored in a small leather-bound book that he kept locked and close, dangling on a bronze chain.

Like the day before they rested little, the Weieen finding a route less direct yet easy. With little elevation change they meandered to and throw, picking between natural caverns, that towered above or reached out ahead and to the sides, stalagmited, ored with the colors of many metals. The fractures broke the earth with their empty spaces, or small compact earthen Weieen holes pocked the cavern walls. These holes penetrated the porous earth easily avoiding areas of dense clay and rock.

For glass lengths at a time they clambered around lake filled hollows that reflected the colorful metal and mineral formations, the fruit of the Lands Beneath. Pits, great shafts, fissures in the rock, vented cold and hot as they passed, as if the earth itself lived and breathed; exhuming its heated exhaust via gapping gaps, sucking in the fresh dry air to replace the dank.

Grottoes that felt safe, glittered with crystal gems, in the color of viened metal ore. Blankets, canopies, of folded weave cream white, carried in on the tide of the under worlds seeping wet to be deposited in sweeping curtains of carbonate. Smooth were the surfaces of these sheets, slick as ice.

Eothan and his companions talked quietly as they carefully climbed through the caves till, they reached the next perforated rock, honeycombed with a maze of Weieen tunnels. The Goblinoids and Gnomes were at home, their feet and boots equipped for the slippery, and gnarled walkways. Talons on the toes of the hob and goblin gripped cracks of the rock, as they stooped naturally, avoiding stalagmites and overhangs.

The monk found it more difficult, his head bruised, and cut by the jagged rock of the convoluted ceilings. Happy he was when they returned to the soft earth and clay of Weieen workmanship, its giving circumference, far easier on the flesh than the gnawing igneous rock, that tore his clothes, its appetite seemingly craved his very blood.

It was whilst in the Weieen tunnels that Drualleigall raised a hand to his large ear and after a moment said..

"I dost here a shadow."

Eothan concentrated against the sound of the party's passage, yet heard nothing. The dark Gnome's ear vibrated. much like that of the Goblins it moved with its own volition, searching for the distant sound.

"Undeniable..." He continued. "We are followed... the earth moves..A scrape... a crushing something is this way coming... Choyuck! "he called low with immediacy.

The Weieen leader turned scurrying under his troupe as they leaped forward over him, the whole maneuver was as if planed and rehearsed. Without thought or word, Weieen moved oppositely like the eddies of the river Mourn.

"Drualleigall thee of the deep Gnomes what dost thou say?"

"We are followed my alley.. there be a follower ..I here from the earth.. a slithering that moves the ground afore it... Snake..wurm or centipede.. our enemies do pursue us with a beast of Beneath.. To arms we must least an ambush is our undoing to be... unhappy end for the lands last hope.. Gnome of Parnassus.. Corserite.. Weieen."

A series of muffled barks and Weieen hoots accompanied the groups readiment. They bunched up, ringing Eothan and the others. The gnomes talked quickly in their own high and sing songed tongue, the Goblin kin looked around in anticipation. Eothan strung his bow, loading it with one of his truest shafts. They slowed their pace continuing along the tunnel. Choyuck joined the five humanoids, a frothed saliva foamed collecting on his jowls and snout, the rapture of enchantment flickered his dark black, brown eyes.

"There be many.. the sound is close." Drualleigall spoke. He pointed his telescoped device this way and that apparently detecting the movement of their distant enemy.

The goblin unclasped the wooden toggle of his arm satchel, palming a handful of pellets suspended in a sparkling powder. Placing a pouch worth between his cheek, and gum he chewed. The hob held firmly to a large bored rock that hung from the hair of his shoulder.

Galfreed's cloak gleamed out from the dark, a tangled network of heterogeneous signs and symbols that ran from his neck to feet, they glowed blue, orange, yellow, and silver. Eothan recognized an apparently random assortment of numbers and letters amongst the jumble that meant nothing to him.

A rumbling at his feet told him that the foe was nigh. He heard little, his acute ears discerning a popping, then as the air filled with dirt a much louder crash.

"They are here!" Drualleigall shouted.

A column of earth cascaded into their faces, as a twisting pale segmented worm came thrashing through the tunnel side, round fanged maw gapped forward toward warm flesh.

A second plume of earth signaled another surfacing worm. Their segments worked in unison propelling them forward contracting and expanding, a series of small appendages aided their movement, levering the worms mass against the surrounding earth. These finger like legs were not restricted to the things underside but appeared around the entire circumference of the body.

Near the maw four enlarged appendages were differentiated into a pair of mandibular organs, that reached outward toward Eothan.

Catching it under the mouth in badger jaw, a Weieen threw the beast backward with the weight of its leap, a pale orange blood ozed out under the bite. A second and third Weieen followed latching onto the carnivore with blinding speed. It thrashed and writhed in their grapple, as Weieen taloned fore paws ripped its hardened segmented body to shreds.

The sweet choking smell of rotted meat accosted Eothan as he saw another worm thrown back under the weight of Weieen. With more earth the empty honking of a third filled the space rearing up from the ground behind. The Gnomes leaped back, Eothan spun to the ground ending in an aimed stance, he unleashed his arrow deep into its neck.

It groaned again, as the Hob stepped from beside the kneeling monk, thrusting a thick dagger in through its exoskeleton upto the shaft. The neck was thrown back to the ceiling, wavering slightly, its maw gapped, widening and closing, mandibles searching for food in the empty air.

Having no eyes they hunted by sent. Catching the smell of their quarry, in a series of thin hairs that covered the segmental form. Its mandibles searched to hold that smell more firmly, devouring it, consuming that which it felt from afar with its acute sense fibers.

Striking forward it engulfed Galfreed in its canined jaw, lifting him upward and off his feet. Screaming in pain he flailed desperately. A Weieen from the front lunged backward catching the worm in its midsection.

Eothan jumped up to draw his barbarian long sword. He saw worms and Weieen thrashing in an avalanche of dirt. If the tunnel were to close about them the worms could graise in leisure on suffocating victims.

The Norcadian slashed at its neck, though his blade did not cut through the segmented exoskeleton, he swung the sword skyward crouching to avoid the low roof, turning from the feeding worm as his arm sweeped back preparing a thrust. The point of his sword may have better effect than did its edge.

Thrashing tail battered the affixed Weieen as the worm's head bowed pining Galfreed hard against the earth. Still screaming the trapped Galfreed struggled against mandibular appendage and fang.

Eothan's point lay wedged between the segmented plates of its exoskeleton, but it went no further. Eothan threw his weight on the blade puncturing its body. He lurched back and forth pulled by the worm's momentum holding fast to his family's blade.

With a flash flame leaped from around its ravenous head. Squawking in its empty voice it tossed Gallfreed to the side, flame licking around his pulsating robe. His fall slowed as he ricocheted of the opposite wall, till he stayed suspended in midair, levitating. Blood smeared his tunic, which he mopped at with a ruffled sleeve.

Lunging the worm barreled into Draulleigall its mouth closed missing the Gnomes body, two of its mandible pincers grabbed, tugging on his arms and torso. Resisting its grasp, he struck at it with a short broadsword. Smashing himself free from its grasp.

Drug to the ground with the lunge Eothan righted himself, with legs wide flexed for stability he used his weight to crack further into its soft body. The sword slid deeper and he twisted it with all his might, sent to the ground he was within reach of the clutching pedipalps. He pulled the sword out, rolling to regain his feet, he swung the barbarian blade again.

A shout told him that Draulleigall had been bitten. Weieen and warrior struggled to subdue the writhing worm.

Eothan chopped, wielding the blade two handily, this time he penetrated the hard segmental surface first time and twisting his hands he thrust the sword's point into the wound's gash. His weight carried the blade clean out to the worm's other side, skewing it to the tunnel's floor.

Honking its protest, it turned back on itself biting at its assailant. Partially immobile the Weieen burrowed through the worm's middle section, with teeth and claw. Its head fell limp, maw twitching at the warrior monk's feet.

The tunnel was in shambles, large caved in sections reduced visibility and before them, further along, the sound of battle continued.

The Goblin stood hands imbedded up to his wrists into the side of the under earth. He concentrated, apparently holding up the ceiling above with his spell craft. Choyuck on all fours still frothed at the mouth, also lost in the reverie of incantation.

Both Gnomes were wounded, the Hob was nowhere to be seen, and a dead or unconscious Weieen lay close. He saw the rent, ripped, and torn bodies of four worms, orange puss of their insectoid hides covered the soil, and stone.

Choyuck going before, Eothan ran toward the sound of battle, slowing to clamber between the fallen banks of the tunnel and over the body of another worm, that the scrambling Weieen had passed without a pause.

In the open of a medium sized cavern eight Weieen in two lines held two more of the beasts at bay. These two, bigger than their previous foes struck forward like asps attempting to break the Weieen line. Skilled at working collectively, the Weieen acted in unison to snare the worms as they lunged forward.

Barking, a Weieen would spring forward as bait, yelping in its high pitched bark. Then as the beast struck, the Weieen leaped back as the others pounced toward its neck.

One worm had already been wounded somewhat, and its companion now attacked more fervently.

The Weieen steadied their line for another attack.

Eothan looked back into the tunnel and seeing the Goblin following, he scrambled down and out to the cavern mouth. Sheathing the long sword he loaded his bow, aiming from the back line. The plates of the worm's exoskeletons undulated, pedipalps groping the air.

The tired sinew of his bow snapped uselessly; the Tower guards must have tampered with it. Redrawing his sword, he edged around the Weieen finding a place from which he could attack. The rock of the cavern floor reminded him to take more care.

Dancing, the worm weaved then its head flying toward the taunting Weieen it struck home, pulling a struggling yelping burrower up. Mandibular appendages pulled and pushed at the squirming Weieen, as the worm's slanting fangs cut flesh and hair.

As it rose on its neck, rearing back, five of the victim's brothers pounced to the enemy, a blur of talons and jaw.

Twisting the worm fell back, its tail thrashing into the few remaining Weieen scattering them and the Norcadian. A yelp from beside told Eothan that at least one of his companions had been caught under its weight. From the side of his eye, he saw the wounded worm's maw as it shot toward him. Too late to dodge the Norcadian thrust his sword into its mouth as it bit his shoulder and arm.

For a moment he was lifted from the ground, the mandible's arms scrapping along his back and legs. He saw the point of his sword sticking out from between the head's exoskeletal plates. Fighting the pain in his chest, he pulled his sword, cutting an arc through its head toward the apex of the worm.

His leather booted feet cushioned the momentum that bought him back to the surface of the cave floor, folding under they scrambled for footing. The beast heaved and groaned, falling dead unable to raise itself. Without energy, it twitched. Taking his hand from his sword he lifted his leg to shoulder its weight carefully pushing open the needle toothed maw.

Cuts through his skins left dagger like wounds along his chest ending in a small puncture in his right thigh. Extracted from the worm he lay on the ground next to it swabbing at his wounds. Flinching with pain he reached over his shoulder fishing the Corser Rod form his back harness. The bandages were already red with blood, not able to move he closed his eyes and prayed. He prayed for the bleeding to stop, he prayed for the energy to complete his quest, to save Saint Thomas, he even found himself praying for Tarese's safety and an opportunity to see her again.

Sounds around told him that the battle was over, the Weieen bayed and yelped in joy, their forest speak rattling disorientatingly off the hard wall of the cave.

The talking quieted and Eothan feeling better, opened his eyes. The bleeding had stopped the white glow of Enruth replacing his torn skin. An upper rib hurt, when he moved, a throbbing in his leg told him that the muscle was in pain. He clenched his teeth pushing up to sit. His prayer would keep him alive but he had been damaged badly in Wyre Wood hold and though he had managed a day or two of rest since then, his flesh still needed time to recuperate, he doubted that prayer would hold his abused body together any more than it already did. I will have to show care, he thought, avoid injuries.

I need rest, real curative rest.

The body of the two worms oozed orange puss from gaping holes clawed in their middle by the Weieen. The two Gnomes sat close to on a pedestal of deposited rock, the tunnel's mouth beside them. The Goblin crouched hunched close to Eothan, and the Weieen conglomerated in a scatter of groups. The wounded gathered about Choyuck, receiving his clerical craft, an assistant helped by applying bandages. A pile of two dead Weieen marked the battles casualties. Two others examined the worm corpses and still others scouted out the cave, acting as sentries. The Hob-goblin was still nowhere to be seen.

"Where is the Hob...our friend? "Eothan asked the Goblin.

"I know not. "He replied. Eothan saw through his lie, yet he also knew that the Goblin meant him no harm. Perhaps they do not trust the Weieen, he thought. From the fragmented corpses of monstrous worm, he understood why. The tuned destructive power of the Weieen fighting unit touched the Norcadian warrior within him, worthy allies for any crusade, not a people he wished to anger.

Wandering down through the cave back to where Galfreed, and Drualleigall waited he and the Goblin stopped to drink clear water collected in a stalagmited troth. They drank deep, thirsty from the exertion of battle.

The two Dwarves were merry enough, Gallfreed drew from an ornate pipe blowing rings toward the ceiling. There was no sign of the blood Eothan had seen about him earlier. His exquisite filigreed cloak, worn now clasped, no longer pulsating with the color of enchantment.

Drualleigall sat next to his friend his note book on his lap and with a pen of manufacture unknown to Eothan scribbled in the script of Gnomes. From a diagram across the margin, he gathered that the dark Gnome recorded the creatures and battle, a history.

"Death worms...we have called them... Not know this far east..not this near the surface that is. A few smaller specimens from Parnassus provide the bite in the Wizard Kings traps... We eradicated them for years... Now the worshipers of Nal Nondream, cutter of the thread, she who resurrects the oracle, they have begun to breed such foul denizens.

"To the East above the falls of Parnassus there lies a sacred well, a healer to our people through the perilous times of the Wizard Kings, its waters bring dreams of the future to those who imbibe of them... The Noldream cult ever protected and interpreted these water's Oracles to our people. In those days the muses of Mernnon and the the three weavers of fate were common visitors to our peak of gladdened song.

"Our plays wrote in the low crystaled caves of our Kingdom Beneath entertained the Princes of Maub, in their Acropolis, and the arts and crafts of their ancient priests and priestess mingled with our own in the smithies and forges of my people. Flying ships of many types and the Great Gondola of Parnassus were in this time rendered.

"Our people chose a king from the most skilled of our artisans. Ssanitelleitalodor the First, a great orator and performer of the legends of our people. A legislater was elected, soon there after, and the many laws and agreements designed to fight the Imprisoned One developed. The races of the Lands Beneath entered an age of cooperation in which the arts could flourish.

"But omnipresent was he of Hex. Parnassus, penultimate of dweomered power. His ages of darkness and foul corruptions spawning, a great unfathomed dark about the peak had he left, an inheritance unlooked for, unheeded and malevolent, unprepared were we for the enemy within. From the catches of his treasure, hex craft caught in device, the spindle worn hand of fate was again supplanted. The shadow of oath breaking, spite, and crime, crept back from the crannies and holes that Parnassus had prepared for its hiding.

"Now the spirit of Nal Nondream is worshipped, darkest of the weavers of fate. She that chops life short has inherited the sacred well of our oracle. Now the visions of the well are dark, they trick the spirit deluding with wealth and despairing with predetermined death. As mankind before the gift Ollisria of the Thorned crown have we, under the priests of Nal Nondream, become.

"Two score years afore haft they our king usurped... Now the legislater loses influence and cancels oath with allied races before the agents of Nal Nondream can cause discontent breaking them. The Lands Beneath are falling back to the agreements of the Imprisoned One. The constant state of war and tribute paid to Shaitan, he cast out, the Imprisoned One."

"Nobles like Galfreed and myself must flee into hiding, our cousin, daughter of Drestelliedar the Fift' is rightful lord of Parnassus, but when the Lady of fate foretold her death though a foul plague she fled. We are two of the last in line who have stayed now we too flee to Toulon for safety. The Weieen our allies of old will our blood lines savior be."

The dark Gnomes words carried timber, their tones bouncing naturally about the grottoes of that war grizzled cave.

Eothan was filled with the lore of these little people, their troubled land of Faerie, pawns of Wizard, deity and Dwarf. Protected by their innate and well-studied sorceries, their strength, it had also been their downfall. The hexes of their dread lord Parnassus reaching them from the grave, with the spindly fingers of his dark bewitchments.

Many of the Weieen had drifted toward the sound of this skilled Gnome orator, his words caressing attention out of all who listened. He varied his voice in pitch and timber captivating his audience. Now Chouyuck stood and addressing the group announced that they would soon get under way…

"It will two days to the Seat of Geobal take… Not for a decade haft we these tunnels taken … corruptions spawn hast grown…Bellow the benevolent Sweda Morte, ruined peak from times unsullied… shall we repose many glasses of the hour hence… Come we must be gone…least more worms of hell ascend upon us."

Scampering through his people he set a pace out of the cave and back into the Weieen holes. Eothan and the humanoids followed, the Goblin stayed close. Where the hob was, he knew not.

They gained altitude from the cavern, traipsing along behind the fast-moving tireless Weieen. Even the Goblin had trouble sorting out which direction they were traveling, only the dark Gnome was totally at ease. He laughed at his companion's inabilities, happily chiding their mistaken estimates as to their where abouts, and the honeycombed passages they wound through.

Their beaten wounded bodies craved rest, and when Drualleigall mentioned that they were finally climbing into the rifts, and canyoned fissures of Swede Morte, heartened they all picked up the pace.

Catching up with the Weieen in a small grottoed cave, that according to the reports of their fury comrades had the sweetest water this side of the Meer, they collapsed. Sleep came early and easy that night.

On waking he thought they had slept long. The Weieen had found a gathering of nuts, fungus and dried fruit, to coerce the muscles of their charges along the trail ahead. They all drank quietly begrudging the fatigue that came with abundant mourning chatter.

The paths were silent, smooth and easy. They descended early to level out along a series of tunnels with few natural formations. Their pace was slower but they still made good time. As the third day of Weieen companionship drew to a close they were once more climbing steeply, this time into the halls and catacombs of the Seat of Geobal, cohort of Parnassus, Hex master of the Ellendei.

Stairs dusted by unuse, sealed vaults, and mine shafts maized their treacherous path. Choyuck had warned them that many of Geobal's ancient portals still carried traps and wards. They were to keep their hands from the walls and to touch no door unless directed to do so by the Weieen.

The Weieen priest had looked directly at the goblin when he had said this, who shifting uneasily had glanced toward Eothan. There had been no mention of the missing Hob-goblin and Eothan sensed no ill will from the remaining Goblin. He had not died in the battle, so he must have fled.

The Weieen erected a long wooden ladder that had lain hidden, since their last foray, beneath a clutter of cloth and fractured timbers. Hand over hand they climbed one by one through an ancient but sturdy shaft. Its winch operated elevator hung in disarray, squawking at them as they disturbed its rest.

The ladder was study and held for the party's mount.

Collecting in an empty workspace, the ladder was lifted to be used to descend later if needed. Eothan did not bother to count the side passages and narrow remnants of excavated veins, there were too many, and he was not the best counter.

A huge gallery that faded out of sight for all but the eyes of the Dark Gnome, spread from around the mine.

Close, two arch ways led to empty guardrooms, piles of wood rot and metal told the tale of ages of neglect. Huddling together against the blackness the party found comfort from the yawing expanse of black that swamped in at them.

"Beautiful it is! "Drualleigall said, his whisper reflecting back to them from an impossible distance, still whispered.

"Stop Boasting. "Gallfreed replied.

"Well, it be not as the mightiest of chambers nor the fissured rents of Deepest Earth, yet for the work of humanity it surpasses all. "

Staying close to the wall, they crossed to a gigantic double door of hard stained and polished wood. Its hinges attached, iron bar sized handles, its rough cross work hatched a decorative design along its border. It took three Weieen working in unison to open and pry back the hard wood allowing the party to slip through. Beyond, a long wide hallway reached in both directions, and a wide stair in front dissected the corridor leading up and out of sight.

Inside the door Choyuck told Eothan that the stair would lead him to the streets of Geobal, if he avoided detours and moved upward. Wishing them well the monk took his leave crossing the wide corridor toward the stair.

He had reached its first step, when the unmistakable sound of crossbows, and Weieen barks stopped him. To his right, toward the north, or so he thought the direction to be, he would have to ask Drualleigall, there was a fight. Though his craft afforded him a limited vision he could not see well in the pitch of the Lands Beneath. Drawing energy from his bow for an enchantment, the immediate surrounds became clearer. He drew his sword, and wishing he had time to fix the sinew of his bow he went after them, stalking through the dark. If his friends needed help, he would not leave without offering the succor of his sword arm.

Toward the end of the hall way, he found them. The Weieen in disarray hurried to order themselves, under a volley of arrows. The Gnomes and Goblin huddled in discussion protected by scrambling Weieen. Choyuck near the back barked orders to his troupe. The third volley felled two of the brave badger like creatures before they reacted in an attack. Simultaneously Choyuck leaped to the center front rank, his assistant with him. The Gnomes and Goblin tagged directly after, a slight haze grew from around the five focused sorcerers.

Eothan thought that they must be protecting themselves with their combined magickal-religious energies. He rushed to catch up. As a unit the Weieen maintained ranks around the spreading magickal shield.

A number of the forest creatures had fallen, they lay dead, or Eothan presumed mortally wounded.

Passing a breathing Weieen, who was pierced with two barbed arrows the monk knelt, drawing the Corser rod he placed it to the fir hide and prayed. Its bleeding stopped and taking care to extract the arrows one at a time, he filled the holes in the Weieen's hide with the same white energy that held his own body together. He noticed more their was an infection, a curse, that was it, poison! It spread from the arrow tips damaging their victim as it went.

Eothan concentrated harder, battling with the foreign agent. He had removed curses from Hob converts, poison responded to the same prayer.

"Quetera dan yall choteck... nol Nandrellar." He dispelled the poison, banishing it in the ancient Ellendei of his monastery. Leaving the Weieen asleep, he ran to catch up with the war party.

Eothan saw another volley of arrows, this time more than half were deflected before they reached the Weieen, what few did break through the shimmering almost invisible barrier lacked the momentum to strike home, falling harmlessly at their feet. Was it a trick of the darkness, or did he actually see an arrow turn back toward its source?

Nearing the end of the hallway he got his first look at the attackers. A dark arch in the end wall, gleamed with the yellow of eyes. The spark of fire alerted him, lighting reptilian snout and white tooth. A line of crossbow armed bipedal lizardmen blocked the path. Their fiery plumes reached yards afore them lighting the hallway's end. The reptiles front line filled the ascendant passage there with three, halberd wielding fire breathers, the crossbows were not visible, only an intermittent volley plaguing the Weieen hidden behind the row of polearms.

Eothan could not tell how many more hid further down the corridor. Taking the lapse in the arrow shower to their advantage the Weieen halted their advance then suddenly they charged headlong toward the reptilian battle. Weieen pounced and leaped in unison falling over each other in a furry ball of teeth and claw that smashed into the reptiles, sending them realing.

Focused to the far right, the pile swamped a halberd wielding, man-sized and a half high, lizardmen. Folding under their weight he disappeared from Eothan's view. Choyuck with the sorcerers staying close behind deflecting a combined blast of snorted fire. Weieen scattered, leaping willy-nilly in a berserk rage of gleeful war.

The Norcaidian rushed to catch up. Reaching the corridor he brandished his long sword. The Weieen had forged on ahead, into the the dark and past the bipedal reptiles.

He looked quickly about. An angry lizard, halberd in hand lunged toward him, smoke trickled from its venting nostrils. The monk dodged back and into the hall from which he had come. The halberd missed, clattering along the stones of the wall beside him. Cut off from his allies rather than pursue Eothan decided to led off the attacker, he could at least save any wounded, opening the corridor for their escape.

He backed further, and as the large reptilian gathered breath for a fire blast he turned and ran. Heat seared the monks back as he continued toward the stair.

Unburnt he bowed his head and turning his feet in for added power he cut into his full pace. Pain shot from his thigh, but he fought its crippling desire for the leaps of a runner's full stride. The lizard panted behind him, caught off guard it had lost ground, but its larger size and longer legs gave it the advantage in the open, it crouched tail counter weighting head, arms and halberd.

They sprinted the length of the hall, Eothan leaping up the first ten steps as the enemy behind him again vented a plume of hot fire, it spattered on the steps at his feet. He panted, heaving air into the bottom of his lungs, his body crying for more oxygen, muscles threatened cramp. His hands hit the steps before preventing a stumble, swallowing he pushed on up the stair. Not looking back he held to his sword, leaping upward as best he could.

The pursuit continued. At a long thin landing the Norcadian found a smaller spiral case.

Upward, Choiyuck had stressed and hoping for escape the monk pushed on up not wasting time to determine where he was. The stair ended in a door that he threw open, running on without care.

Almost passing an upward side stair, he halted took a step back and leaped up again. A snarl told him that he was still followed. He heard a preparatory inhaled breath, and flattening against a passage wall, fire shot passed. Eothan thudded on.

He smelt the fresh air of Geobal, a clear stared night awakening his light sensitive eyes to its sudden expanse. A grating beside his head, he was in a underground sewer. Dry underfoot it was not, thankfully, in use. A further light showed the passage's opening before him. He was close to escape. Running out into the night he found himself on a steep grassy slope, towers of a mighty gray citadel sprawled about.

The saurian growled from the sewer mouth. Dry now, Eothan had escaped through a part of the Seat of Geobal's moat system. He stepped out of the moat where he stood looking down to the small town.

Growling again it loitered around the sewer mouth, unwilling to leave the Lands Beneath. A light in its nostrils showed him where it stood.

Turning he pulled the Rod Corser from his back, and as it transformed into Der Aeth, the heavy dealer, he strode back toward the foe. It had lost the halberd, in pursuit, barring rows of sharpened fangs glowing with the yellow of its fire it threatened.

Swinging the flail around his head, Eothan bounded forward, stepping to the side, as the saurian breathed fire. Der Aeth glowed absorbing the heat. The fiery blast was completely swallowed into the flail staff.

Eothan crushed into its neck and body with the strength of his weapon. Looking surprised it recovered, biting ferociously. He was nipped under the wrist, but did not get a hold of his arm or hand.

Eothan bled, as he bought the flail upward smashing it under the chin,. Battered backward, it crouched on its large legs. Fire held within its throat.

Not willing to pursue into the close quarters of the tunnel where he would have to use his long sword Eothan faced it down from the entrance.

Der Aeth sparked with silver star light. Grumbling a low growl, it backed off and disappeared into the dark, taller and heavier than the wounded warrior.

He sighed.

After a time Eothan convinced it would not return dropped his guard and bandaged his arm. Finding no one about he lay amongst the long autumnal grass of that waterless moat and slept.

CHAPTER 10

CELENT

Peaceful, it was all far too peaceful. The house, even the servants, who were usually at each other's throats with some rumor or intrigue, were all quiet.

It reminded him of his father's house in Berelan, silent still like a morgue. The weather in Berelan, the sun and the imported palm that grew in the solarium, the mechanistic click of training warriors, these were missing, but there was something in the Mernnonian mountain air that triggered memories of his childhood in that grand house of Berelan.

Sarkhen Heath keeper, reputed to be among the best swordsmen in

Arraken, had ever maintained the dignity of such a honor. In the personal surroundings of his home in the nation's capital this was visible in the frozen faces of his collection of statued nobility.

Sarkhen had lost two of his over thirty knightly combats, one to King Ottar, the Forgiving, and the other to the Duke of Drake, Herigar Gunerson, Elf kin. Friendly bouts, they had thankfully not been contests of honor. It was said in Mernnon, that those too should have been victories, and that, Prince Uuk's farther had bowed lower than he should to the Arraken nobility. The Pilloried Prince, Uuk had heard him called while in disguise enjoying the back streets of Mernnon. Not a name to use to his father's face. Placing first in the javelin, discus, and martial arms, at the annual games for a full decade before assuming the Mernnonian diadem. Sarkhen was not a warrior to trifle with.

Uuk sat on the throne he would share with his farther until Sarkhen abdicated or died. On the second floor of the house, a well ornamented council chamber, empty for the time spread around him. Sarkhen had always been close to the De Vishi side of the house of Maub, the fates and festivities of the Red Towers more attractive than those of Mernnon.

Uuk on the other hand preferred Mernnon and Kadra to the jousting and God worship of the Ellendei. The commandments, and their monk's hypocritical castigation of sorcery as a manifestation of Shaitan, turned his stomach. Being kin to Ollisria he found it hard to deny the reality of the heroes and deities that his people worshipped. Now especially he felt a keen connection to the acropolis and its priests.

The histories that had guided his people through peace and war.

He had talked to Ajaxus, and they both had trepidations about informing Sarkhen of the recent incident. Neither wanted the royal court discussing their curse, the house was already the subject of far to much Berelan chatter. Being the grandson of Oritand the Great, the Ellendei did not need reminding of his family's intimate relationship with deities outside their own myth structure, or recent well-known traitors.

Simmon the Snake had created a far more repressive bureaucracy since the revolution, and though Uuk was secure amongst his own people. The memory of the grandfather, alike which he was said to look and act, was not a thought the older priests wished Simmon to think on. Silence was in order. The soul of the saint Abbot Thomas the Young, would stay stashed securely among the heirlooms of the House of Maub until Ajaxus received word from the Corserites themselves.

Uuk had given Ajaxus instructions to communicate with both the Herald of Ollisria, and the Corserite Monastery seeking advice and offering friendship. Sometimes Kadra's reliance on the deity of thieves, messengers, and diplomats profited the nobles of Mernnon. The high status of the Hermetic order in the Mernnonian pantheon, as their tyrant's herald, placed an artful community of priests and lay worshipers in the hands of the Mernnonian nobility.

Kadra remained Uuk's house patron deity, though, most of their dealings with the rest of the pantheon was conducted by Ajaxus Trengotte, Hermetic advisor to the house. It was Ajaxus, for instance, who had taught Uuk his court etiquette, and his apprentice priest the acolyte and poet Palamydes, who had instructed the young prince in the arts of anti-espionage. Both choose Hermes as their patron deity.

Uuk inheritor of his father's muscles and build had won weight lifting contests since the age of thirteen. Herodus, marshal of arms to the House, trained the First Prince regularly in the accepted weapons of the Arraken Knighthood, like Sarkhen, Uuk was strong enough to break through most parries, over powering his opponents with force, he as yet, lacked the finesse of Mernnonian's most renowned warriors, but the sheer weight and strength of the young prince was often able to beat experience in a fair fight. An impressive fighter the marshal often boasted of his young pupil.

Leaving the marbled throne, he meandered, his sandaled feet slapping on the smooth tile of the Hall of Councils. Kadra sternly assessed him, caught in bronze, with gold hour glass, and spear. Had he not been worthy to share the fate of Ollisria? his progenitor, or had Kadra another fate planed? He knew little of the first born and their history beyond their relationship with Drake, and the Eororwin Lord Justice of the Realm. Was Noldarn to serve for ages as Ollisria's Herald, as the elf's kinsman had served the King's of Arraken? Should he send word to High Lord Serderan, Lord of Thornbreak, were Elfs to be a bane or ally to Mernnon? And he Uuk the First, would he make Choital I proud?

There was nothing but condemnation to be found in the forehead of their deity king. And perhaps even devout glee at his mortal follower's chagrin.

Needing a rest he retired to his private quarters, where his personal man servant Tethon greeted him, with a curtious nod.

"Tethon draw a bath and bring fruit." He said. "Later I would see a dance in the theatre."

"My Prince." Tethon replied. Tethon was half Norcadian, the black hair of his farther dominating the blond from his mother, a wavy auburn tinted brown that he held back loosely in a tail, that crept down his vertebra.

Finding a small silver miniturette of his betrothed on a round table Uuk lifted it and held it gently. Swaying he strolled to the curtained west window. Thrown back shutters helped the unusually warm sun heat the sill, its white wash beaming the heat back up at him. He sat placed the statue on the sill, and waited for the servant's return.

The family of Catator of Barnaka was a good choice. Not only because his first daughter was beautiful, but, being Barnakan she would surely know numbers better than most. Yes, their island Earldom was blessed with trade, and their tolerance of Mernnonian worship put them in his favor, already found of fish he anticipated no problems. There had been ancient relationships between Barnaka and Mernnon, before the Ellendie migration.

From the flowing dress and sprightly pose his mind went to the sacred dance of Eurynome the spawning of sea and sky; did it described his humor? A local cult of Terpischore, who worshipped with Ajaxus and whom's supreme talents in performance rivaled even the lusty leciviousness of the Dyoniasians were the best choice as producers.

He had at times in his youth felt a particular fondness for a Daene, a reciter of sacred poems. One of Trengotte's apprentices, they had met during his tutelage in fine arts, and crafts. He smiled to himself; they had become quite silly with their mutual obsession. Notes, flowery poetry that she could always out craft him with, and even for at least a year a master plan to elope, to become traveling sages in Norcadia, a wild but romantic land.

Pangs in his heart reminded him that the scars of their misguided love were still with him. His jealously for the Malponian who finally swept her of her feet.

When his duties kept him away, far too long, at the House De Vishi, and Mernnon, she had finally and he had thought then spitefully, written him an eloquent manuscript declaring their relationship void. The whole thing embarrassed the Prince now.

He hoped the performers talents were available for tonight.

Palymedes had dabbled in the art of thamaturgey and was often called on to play the part of Ophion, the great serpent; a second flying dancer in feathers, played the dove that hatches Ophion's and Eurynome's world egg. He would remember to tell Tethon that Palymedes' services were required, the rest he could leave to the Muses of Trengotte's retinue.

There had been a time, according to myth, when Apollus the banished friend to Nal Nondream, God of prophecy, had a following in the house, it was from his worshipers that the Hermetic Muses had originated. They joined the priests of Hermes after their own god fell into disfavor. Banished to Tarterous the God no longer boasted the following he had once. Unwilling to predict and warn Kadra who his eventual usurper would be, he and his entire faction were in disfavor, banished from heaven to Tarterous until they divulged the secret.

Oritand had been a great lover of the arts, overtly a worshiper of Arus the Mernnonian God of war, Uuk wondered whether he had secretly converted to Apollus. A large temple on the Acropollis dedicated to the banished deity made offering each day in his name. There the Muses had not deserted their benefactor for the knavish messenger of Kadra, but honored the dissatisfied and estranged faction of Titan and God.

Visions of Tarterian amusements filled his mind during his bath, deamonic gladiators battling the issue of Helgottei. Hundred armed monstrosities and serpentine women, Medusa and her foul sisters. The harpies and gargoyles that plagued wrong doers carting their souls to Hados for judgment by the visiting dignitary Kadra.

Perfumed, and oiled, and bathed, he returned via the kitchens where he added bread and dried fish to the fruit he had eaten in his rooms. The air charged with anticipation as to the evening's festivities, was alive with talk of his abduction and return at the hands of Kadran steed, or that is how they saw it.

The Griffin, according to presently bantered gossip was an undeniable sign that Kadra's was acting himself and not working through Hermes. Ajaxus had added a few words of his own to the commoner's chatter, steering the word of mouth away from the volatile subject of Ollisria by implying that some personal rite of passage after such a good showing at the games was the motivation for divine intervention.

The servants and artisans of Maub all hailed it to be a great omen of things to come. Ushering in the lordship of Uuk Griffin friend of Maub. Let them talk, after attempting to remind four or five of his friends and advisors that Sakhen Heath Keeper was very much lord and regent, Baron of Mernnon, only to be ignored for a more exciting insistence that Mernnonian births were far more plentiful this year, and that the importance of Berelan in the world economy was greatly overestimated, he relented. Let them gossip, there were worst things they could do with the time.

Soon they were all filing into the theatre and he congratulated himself at coming up with the idea. The forming of the world egg and the birth and banishment of Ophion the great wurm would occupy their minds instead. Soon they would forget their blather. And what better way to celebrate his return to Maub after the week long Mernnonian festival than the most sacred birth of Gea, the world?

The Prince sat close to the stage, Cleatous ambassador of Maub, recently returned from a trade council in the earldom of Rodenwack; he had saved a number of seats for Uuk and any who should accompany him. Idiaos, the inheritor of Farech, a friend with him on the acropolis during the kidnapping, sat to the right. Idias had searched out Maub before the rest of the Prince's retinue, he found him before the doors, and would not leave his side, jostling to say close.

Phegus and Pherusia, dancers for the cult of Eros, who were not performing tonight, they also joined the Prince. Unpredictable, these two flighty busybodies messed with everyone.

Uuk considered it better to stay close to the cult, they more than any in the household, had connections in the Royal Court of Ottar, the Dandy. Often busy entertaining foreign visitors, it was best to placate them with attention whenever possible, in this way things went far more smoothly about the House.

They sat to his right giggling with anticipation, real theatre was something they found somewhat embarrassing. More reverent than the passion demanded by their own Muse, it left them nervous.

Cleatous, and Idiaos sat to his left. They discussed a particular dancer of the acropolis that they were both infatuated with, unfortunately for the intellectuals she was married to Artimus Senasor, a high-profile priest of Hermies, who's first apprentice was wowing her sister. Uuk scoffed keeping to himself. They talked on.

Smiling politely, the prince assured all in attendance that he was in good health. Kadrus Nineus, Chief Orator of Themis, oldest and most respected of the Sages of Maub walked out from the vomitoria, floating on a stately stride crafted for the greater part of a century to impress its witnesses with its wearers poise.

Turning he quieted the house with a slowly shifting gaze. Like a game the audience murmured till his eyes put a stop to their chatter, moving on to their neighbors his silence spread. Like a virulent plague its quietness weighty as a room of the Mernnonian oligarchy in heavy session.

There had been a good turnout for the week after the year's Festival. The House's large indoor three quarters, thrust stage, could seat up to five hundred, in three steep sections. This evening over half that was full, the houses around would be quiet most everyone is here, he thought. Noticing a few soldiers who had attended in uniform; their breast plates shined out from the white, gray and creams of the other spectators, helms carried, and placed at their feet, to keep the colorful plumes from obstructing vision.

"We Muses of Maub give you Mernnonian's our people, ancient stocks from before the Ellendei..... the birth of Earth..Gea.. Banishment of Ophion, wurm... farther of earth. "Walking backwards as he spoke, the old Mernnonian who felt his age more than an Ellendei of the same years, faded into the dark.

Chaos, a stilted threesome of actors, who lofted gigantic masks of carved light wood, gold and silver inlayed, painted with ochre, and black, flew from the black behind the stage. All was dark but the twirling mass of streamer and train, the three gruesome heads glamoured and glowered, amongst a mass of custom crafted Mernnonian silk and fabric. Hidden instruments beat a heavy discordant rhythm. Drums, gong, cymbal, obscuring a misused string.

Feint at first and then growing a soft husky laugh, accompanied the cascading din. Growing in intensity as the laughs became distinct, three, male voices, each with its own flavor. Five times the noise built to a crescendo to fall back to silence, the beast undulating to its ebb and flow.

Maniacal, troubled, disquieting in its demand on ear and mind, the chaos from which all was born crashed about at the feet of Prince Uuk.

Finally, a single clear and high female voice broke through the furry with a steady clear note. Rising in volume she fluctuated slowly, a stark contrast to the random disharmony of Chaos.

Eurynome, the dancer, appeared in the midst. Bursting from within the swarm of colored fabric, she stood, still, swarmed in brilliant white silk, satin laced in a halo.

Chaos split, and as she began a slow ballet, an awakening, its separated parts cascaded about the stage. Uuk recognized her, a strong dancer of the house. Her muscled legs rose slow, elegant, on massive thighs. Stretching she held her leg upwards, then after a pause fell to her knees twisting in laments after Chaos.

Her voice, sung from the blackness, warbled a wordless falsetto, wailing its lament at the early void. She cut through the clangor, leaping into splits, as she careened, closing the fragments of chaos with her path. Dancing with each, she was lifted and thrown, one to another. Defeated she struggled poetically moving herself back to life, then vaulting back to her feet she was at them again. Climbing up their height to descend again. Frantic then calm, a dervish of tumultuous order.

Divided, Chaos became sea and sky, the third suspended between waves. Always she danced moving from one to the other, then settling, wave and Eurynome danced. They danced long, wave losing its chaotic violence, bent his will to her's. He lofted her high suspended above all, then swung her low to the ground. As they danced her silks vanished absorbed into the waves, tufting them with tips of white.

Naked, the dance continued her muscles froze, painting her curved bones with an interwoven band of sinewed flesh. Then she moved again framing the figure of wave, circling. Sweat gathering in droplets shimmered within her back. Her eyes focused, the intensity of a supplicant in the reverent state of worship.

As a rattle sounded through the melodic accompaniment, the green and orange, wurm grew from the waves. The mask vanishing, the fabric blue and white remained. A meeting of the planes of Air and Water. Spouts of blue, white. Fabric droplets, cloth in space, and time.

Golden, its white teeth gleaming, red tongue flicking along its mouth, snaking to the audience and back, the wurm emerged. From Erynomes dance it came, responding to the friction she evoked in wind and water. A snaking beast of old, glorious, reptilian, red hair wisped on its chin, and behind its ears, that rotated, hearing all that passed in the early void.

As fire issued from its grinning mouth it unfurled two impossibly small wing and took to the air. Palymedes, was outdoing himself, thought Uuk. It soared above the audience while Erynome danced in its fire as she had the waves. The flame pranced and flickered washing her nakedness, her rhythmically, contorting, body in a writhing light.

The serpentine wurm flew above the gapping crowd, till in a mighty dive it ended prone, supine, at Erynome's feet.

She flexed her upstage leg and lifting it gradually she placed on the beast's snout, flinging her down stage arm up and head back, in triumph. There they froze while the music continued. No applause was necessary. The audience sat in rapt silence.

Then slowly, they circled, erotic. Cascading patterns between mistress and wurm. Music followed, building with the serene movements of their love. Gaining in momentum, Erynome began leaping above her serpentine mate, one leg out straight the other held bent, as she apexed with each leep. During the jumps a planet was formed, and endowed with male and female deities. Each spun off to stand at the edge of the stage, forming a chorus of sorts.

Pipes and harp grew audible, adding a more melodic tune to the percussion.

The Titans of Kadran myth. Soon they too danced again, and, finally when all were exhausted with sheer spectacle. The Wurm revolted against his mate, imprisoning her in a contortion exercise of excruciating slow back bending, that left the dancers hands intertwined beneath her strongly arched back. Now the new born titans rose to aid her, returning from the edge of the stage, they tossed the wurm between them before they cast him out to the void.

Thus, the universe was formed before their eyes. The music continuing on, far more melodic than it had been, a single female voice crying softly, harmonizing to the sounds. No word had been spoken, yet it had been the most moving rendition they had seen to date. Stunned the audience sat absorbed in half dark.

The priests and priestesses who had performed did not show themselves, but after more time and only a few departures. Daen, Uuk's boyhood love appeared from the darkness. A blinding white silken gown covered her to the floor, and breaking the now gathered quiet, she recited the Tyrynome, an old poem of the Universe's birth in a clear flat and unemotional voice.

The hushed crowd told Uuk that he had made the right choice, the plain-spoken poem adding the depth of understanding to that which they had seen. After Daen was through they funneled slowly out the large double doors, that lead onto a gray stoned walkway, connecting to the main house along its north wall.

Groups formed out on the grass laughing and passing Dionisian jugs. The Prince walked, taking his time to greet and share a word with friends and vassals, alike. He had noticed before that the creation myth often had a soothing effect, to him it provided perspective.

The Helgottei gorgons of mnt. Ellondon floated about the eye of his mind. Their creepy tails and bewitching ways building roads of unwanted desire.

"Dost worry knot thy brow m' lord. "Pharusia leaned toward him her pink short cut tunic hung lose. Smiling broadly she bit the end of her tongue, holding it between her teeth. Pointed canines hinted danger behind her face. The tip of a white enchanted trident stored in the cache of Maub was blunter. How many had she impaled? Her green eyes searched his innocently.

"Kadra hast left me with thoughts. "

"Wine m' Lord. "

Phagus, her male companion offered him a jug. Cleatous and Ideos chatted close.

"No.. I thank you... I haft supped deep with Dionius in Merrnon."

"Well m' Lord.. Thy pleasure is mine."

"I think they out did themselves .. a creation to remember. "Called Ideos, lagging further behind.

"Yes, my friends the performance was astounding I hope you tell all that I said so... and now if you will forgive me... I have pressing matters to attend to... May Kadra be with you."

Nodding he turned and hurried toward his quarters. He had a copy there of the full poem from which Dean had recited, a browse through that sacred work, pushed him on.

The vast council hall was empty apart for two cuirassed yellow plumed guards, that leaned on their pikes heavily. He stayed close to the statues not wishing to bother them at work. He knew how they would act, all proper and pumped up.

Dionius smirked carting his large carafe, and Faerie, wife of Kadra, looked down with smug contempt. The prince troubled, overwhelmed by the ceremony he had just witnessed, hurried on. As he neared the far side of the hall about to turn onto the staircase that lead up to his collection of private rooms, a voice caught him from behind.

"My prince I would humble myself to you.." Turning he found blue eyes under brown auburn hair. The dancer of Erynome.

"Care.." she said razing a finger to his stunned lips. "..Things are not always what they seem..." Robed in silk her full strong body curved into the fabric invitingly. Children from such a women would have strength, he thought.

"Do I please you prince.. Uuk." She stepped away from him turning and opening her silken gown. Flexing her torso, muscles snugged about her pushing forward her exposed breasts, with a soft breath.

He refused to allow the pull of their circular beauty to draw his eyes down into her natural depths.

A triangle of doom.

Instead, he looked deeply into her blue eyes. He found enough there, the lighter rays of blue highlights, alternating with darker rays, starlike and sparkling. Was there a Norcadian in her family history? Such eyes were rare in Mernnon. Blue, light and dark, with specks of black, then a dissolving, no not eyes at all, but, lizard. Asp. They were the eyes of Helgottei, Medusa. The Wurm. He wrenched himself away covering his face with the back of his muscled arm. Had he been leaning in to kiss her?

Nothing. Silence. Looking back there was only the empty hall, the distant mumble of the guards. A statue to Hellgotei had never stood in the hall as far as Uuk knew. The want for the dancer fatigued him. Kadra frowned in supreme tyranny.

Stumbling, he slumped on the base of Apollus, the banished Lord, patron of art and craft.

"Strength.. my young Uuk.. It will be through thee that Kadra and I are to be reconciled... If the Banished are to return to heaven thy must the saint reassociate... A soul to a body, on earth as it is in heaven... For, if thee fail, an eon must pass 'afore heaven can sing again... Be hardened brave and virtuous... Mernnon trusts in thee."

He looked about but there was nothing, only the statues, Hermes, Helogtei, all of them.

The voice had been clear, loud, but the guards noticed nothing. Lifting himself up he saw the Appollus effigy silver, its lyre and bow plated gold. Like Mernnon it was disembodied, an art without a people. A temple God, worshipped here, but from heaven banished.

His night's sleep was passioned with battles and romance, the lyre a constant, a ribbon to follow through the neverworld, faerie.

The Wadeen were precise he gave them that, uncouth, violent, crazy, even undisciplined, but they knew their craft's specifics, yes, he did give them that. So, they waited in the great hall of Celent, the cathedral sprawled around them. His farther had been a monk in Clune not far from here, the brown robbed figures that moved from candle to candle seemed familiar to him. Less rain than Drake and low in elevation the weather was far milder, sunny for two days in a row already, and though early autumn, it was warmer than many a day in Ergedh during the summer.

Celent, nestled on the lower slopes of the East Downs within the heart of the new Kingdom's agricultural center. It depended predominantly on the export of wheat, from its well supplied granaries situated both here, inside its twenty-five-foot walls, and at Saint Loth along the banner's major port.

A small castle whose Lord Herbar the Cogent, Keeper of the Vale, charged and commanded a hundred of the Most Renowned Holy Order of the Knight Defenders of the One. A holy fighting order, who's close relationship with Primate Simmon was matched only by the Knights of Mealandei.

Traditionally at odds, the Wadeen and the Knights of the One had become allies under Simmon, indeed their reconciliation had been a major step in clearing the way for Drake's claim on Thornbreak. Without their support and the apathy of Ottar on the matter, Drake would not have safe, secure, boarders. With his standing army abroad attacks across the Meer from, either, Pellia or the Traition Lands would be devastating, Ergedh could be crippled within weeks.

The dispute over Toor Slope timber access, and the Duchies south boarder with the Marquis Daquin, plagued the defense of Ergedh as always, the marriage between Illid Asculf's first boy and Herigar's daughter had insured a constant friend in both the Primate's and the Kingdom's Oligarchy. As Chancellor of the realm, Illid's role as Arraken's prime minister afforded Drake a military alley with the might to protect them in the event of a crisis.

A new town, Celent's towered outer wall, ringed in crowded streets and a dwarfing domed cathedral. Small parks and walkways filled the streets with the smells of initial autumn wind falls. Churches, shops, markets, stables, and cattle barns crested the dimpled, undulating city.

Davide leaned against a rippled marble column, no word yet. He tipped his head staring down the steep steps that ascended to the glitter of the ornamental cathedral. Named after the Saint Celent, decisive in the peace reached between Arraken and Drake soon after the passing of the Dragon, its multicolored windowed dome, mimicked the style of Berelan. Scenes of the great profit and his persecution at the hands of Wizard King and Ellendei alike, decorated the building. Not until the oath of Arraken, concluded the unification of the Ellendei, did their race begin its rise to power.

Saint Augusta now stood on the site of the Ancient warlords citadel where the Profit of the One had finally met his demise on the cross. Of course, there had been an eon in the history of the faith since then. The Wizards had rose and fell, to be replaced by an age, that the Lord Chief Justice of the Realm, had named the time of a thousand witches. The ancient elf, who administered justice for the free courts of Arraken resided in the Summer Hills, a hall old in the stories of the Mernnonian's even before the first Ellendei sailing vessel touched the sands of Arecia. It was he who had fathered the first Dragon Lord of Drake, and together they began the battles against Wizard King Ergedh.

The prominent Cathedral covered the highest ground in Celent, with its sacred rooms and chambers of prayer. Davide waited to see the archdeacon Yieaval of Celent, Cardinal Verallari, had carried news of the Corserites excommunication, deeper into the great cathedral. Davide knowing the de Vishi's influence in the area, thought this the strategic location for a council on the subject of the Excommunicate Abbot Thomas' soul.

Arriving on the tail of the news Davide hoped to gain impetus for his cause.

Supreme Primate Simmon, pronounced the ceremony of excommunication, accusing the Corserites of murdering his envoy, and protecting witchcraft, the illegal practice of magick. The halls of Berelan and the Crown Hold had again rung with his words.

Seraus, the Wadeen had tracked their charge with divination declaring it to be in the hands of Uuk de Vishi, prince of Maub. Having the local commanders and marshals of the regions puissant holy fighting orders on his side Davide planed to challenge this young prince to mortal combat over the soul. His claim to the excommunicate Abbot would be decided before God and King alike. Not even the Treathbarron could deny his right to seek trial by combat. Uuk grandson to the traitor of Mernnon was nothing more than a petty thief.

Not holding a large standing army Drake feared little resistance, from Mernnon, as long as their families Abydosian side was behind Drake's claim. Sarkhen had never been a one to interfere in major political actions, although, his family's strength in mortal arms was famed. The son Uuk was unknown to Davide, if he was assured that the military might of the Abydosian de Vishis, was behind the Primate then he was clear to make and demand a challenge.

"The Archdeacon will see you now."

The older habited monk had returned. Davide pushed off the column with a gauntleted fist, the afternoon sun burning silver in the metal of his plated armor, blinding the eyes of the unarmored cleric. Turning they passed rows of candles, walking toward a audience chamber far near the back of the Cathedral of Celent.

A chant filtered about the halls, vibrating throughout, harmonics humming up and down the dome. They stopping before a carved oaken door, and, the monk gestured.

"The reverend farther lies within. "He moved off toward the Cathedral arch, as Davide de Clune knocked upon the heavy oak with his gauntlet.

"Enter Arraken Knight. "The voice rasped old with chant and prayer uninhibited it reached him through the door's small open priest hole.

The Archdeacon sat on a stool before a double arched and plain leaded glass window. White tufted ears, wrinkles told of years of service for the One. Gray eyes, glassy, worried, flicked from the knight's sheathed sword to his face then back down to visored helm carried tucked under his arm. Offering a hand, the knight bowed and kissed a conspicuous ring, one among many.

"Thou art welcome Knight of Drake..Commander in the Order of the Lance. My hearth is thine, Arraken... May God's grace bless thee.."

Rising he found a bench near the chamber's only furniture, a small desk adjoining a white washed wall. Bound paperwork cluttered its Toor Slope timber surface.

"Venerable Sir Drake humbly greets thee,
I am to consult with thee concerning
the traitor Thomas Abbot of Corser.
His soul by primal law be condemned,
a cankered ooze, spawning nought but ill,
haughty, violent, breathing villainy,
out spoken critic of all that sprouts,
from Berelan, our beacon purposed.
Who whence an embessage to he wast sort,

did in hasted, unconstrained, dire, hand,

the trusted servant of our God do dead,

no compassioned quarter our ally shown,

no tender care for a patient fellow."

The archdeacon sniffed, and scratching his nose he stared through the outer metal of the knight. Flesh and muscled bone, willing to fight for his Duke, to death, if the cause demanded it.....

"We haft the Primal decree perused,

for this rank murder are the Corserites,

deposed, from that high place to which they,

their ancestors to them did inherit.

Be that so, yet the Pope's true voice be still.

Cardinals haft a duty to Berelan,

a seat of near, armed, regal, power,

home of holy fighter, King, Primate, lord.

A bastion from which our devotees hail,

no resistance to thy true policies,

shalt we of diocese, Saint Loth offer."

Davide rested his helmet and arm on the small desk. The Knight continued.

"This be just cause, we should in Celent Vale,

a trumpeted, nobal, meeting make,

holy knight, chivalric order, monk, scribe,

a gathering of gracious Arraken.

To thee do we request a vaulted hall,

a curtained, metaled, gilded, tier round,

stool for rest and clamoring space abound."

Yeiaval nodded slowly..

"Yes the greatest hall of Castle Celent,

wilt the tidy precepts of thy request meet.

Monks of Celent Cathedral, send I hense,

to Holy Order, and Herbar de Vishi,

coalesce fighters of Arraken crown!

Parl, long unto this day's bewitching black night,

feast with thy peers in God and holy Sword,

a tribute of Ellendei, legendary,

to new songs long historic reverence.

Families of note and many warriors strong,

excommunicate fiend be thy enemy!"

The ancient cleric rose and wandering to the door
pulled a bell chain that hung close.

"We will escort thee.......... "

A sneeze caught the Archdeacon throwing his head
forward with its blast. Smiling he pulled his habit closer
about him, smoothing the white of its apron.

The knight left, trailing behind an escorting
novice. At the Cathedral's steps he met his squire and
their steeds, pulling himself to saddle, his spurs urged
Torell his charger out through the crowded streets of
Celent.

"Perfumes sir knight.. "

A clean houppelarded, young women, cream doublet, and smart townsman's breeches peered up toward him. Bags, and sacs hung about her, a gentleman stood close a collection of woven baskets around. Straining she lifted an unbottled, flask, a strong fragrance similar to rose petal combated the dusty smell of market fish and manure.

Reining brown splotched white steed, he scanned the market crowd about. It was some way to the distant buildings, and the warm day had brought a throng to Cathedral square. Linen and canvas covered stilted structures, hung colorful fabrics and wares for the silver sovereigned passerby.

Around the market's outer edge, a ring of beverage, and food could for the parting of a few copper pennies provide meals for a day or a week. Davide de Clune heard the jingle as Jorin his squire counted a cache of shilling and penny he carried about him.

"Tis not a time for such paltry confectioneries Celentian."

Her large brimmed hat bounced behind her head; a pale thong held it tight around her long elegant neck. An Ellendei her light brown eyes danced about his, fencing for an in rode of her wares. Long straight black hair, contrasted with her white pink skin, red from the Abydosian sun, her hair gave her the look of Mernnon he thought.

"Please sir Knight, a pretty smell for your lady..." Her eyes widened at the green and red blazing dragon spiked tail of his surcoat.

"A gift from distant Celent to Ergedh ? "She asked.

"No my good women we be in hast. "

He steered by her.

Areander his betrothed, a lady of Vournas Wake, in upper Olen, leaned from her balcony to look out on the rain and drizzle of Drake's new autumn. Her brown wavy hair sparkled with a similar flowered fragrance. The sooner he returned with the excommunicate's soul he could run his fingers through that thick growth.

They sorted through the crowd picking up the pace as townspeople and peasants began to part, scrambling out of their mount's way. Reaching a road the knights continued down a steep slope terraced with a double row of well to do, residences. They crisscrossed, switching back to give the chargers a break as they hoofed along the dry cobblestones.

The houses thinned, becoming separate structures. They dismounted and watered the horses at a quiet welled plaza, before the massive timber columned town hall. Then re mounting they rode around and through the twenty-pace tall gateway of Celent's castle. Clattering over a loud draw bridge, the slabs of the bailey received their horses' shod hoofs. The ten-pointed banner of

Abydos flew high above the castle's round keep, silver against blue and red, the red poppy of Berelan beside it.

A free town, Celent hailed to king Ottar the forgiving, the castle held by Herbar de Vishi, Lord Defender of Celent Vale, Ottar's sheriff. As champion, it was Herbar who kept the peace, protecting the cathedral, the monastery and its pilgrims from the bastion of his own castle, set some way off, nestled in amongst the surrounding farms. Town law was the decree of mayor Adolf Wittlebread, enforced by magistrates and the town courts.

They dismounted, the squire leading the chargers to the thatched stable. Davide walked against a slight rise toward the second gate, and the castles wood beamed brick hall.

The thick bitter smell of heated iron, billowed from a small smithy. A separate thin wood stair climbed the side of the huge round keep, that towered from behind the hall, buttressing the entire structure. The keep riveted Celent's East most corner, in a formidable defensive structure.

Before he reached the hall's door a flutter at his ear told him of Seraus' return.

The Wadeen priest had shrunk to the length of Davide's finger, and rode upon the back of his Dragonette, Ssistathich.

"Sir Davide I return thy servant as ever."

"Seraus."

Leaping from its back Seraus grew to full size, alighting on the ground next to the knight. Ssistathich flew about his close-cropped brown hair, Wadeen's dark-green twinkling eyes gleamed humorously at the tinned man known as Davide de Clune.

"Art thee resolved to play against death Davide... for our Duke's prize is thy life so cheap?"

"What dost thy know of honor spell weaver, worshiper of lizards."

Ssistathich hissed his complaint.

"Take care knight.. least thou escape the fate of princes only to become food for the Wurm of Kantor."

"Enough Wadeen hast though returned to aid or goode me?.. my blade can drink thy blood faster than ye can hide in prayer or cantation...What be thy report?"

"As I expected the saint's soul is held by Prince Uuk of Maub in the temple of Hermes. Too guarded for theft... Your challenge bist the way most direct......Sir Knight."

Ignoring the smirk in the priest's voice he led Seraus, Ssistathich now perched on shoulder, through an iron enforced outer doorway into the castle's great hall. The smell of cooked beef and the panting of lounging dog, filled the galleried brick oblong.

Five large tables stood side by side, a smoldering fire in the far wall provided some heat. Two other fires lay dormant, given a reprise from the mild autumn. Ssitathich blended the color of his skin to match the black robe of the Wadeen, black on black, he was now hardly noticeable, a broach blending to his master's cotton.

A monk sat with a group of children teaching letters. Chalk and boards in hand they perched around on bench, table and floor alike, listening to the robed farther. Servants cleaned with brush and straw.

"Go fetch thy master serf... Davide de Clune Knight of Ergedh has need of him! "Davide shouted to the nearest.

"I am not a serf if it please you sir... but a vassal of the house... I will carry your words to chamberlain Eric. "Leaving his brush and a pile of straw he left through a small curtained arch, in the hall's long outer wall.

More uppity than the castle slaves of Ergedh. Angry he looked to the Wadeen, flustering, searching for a complaint, nothing coming to mind, he stayed silent.

Seraus grinned back, his gray green eyes involved in a personal joke that he ever maintained with the world about him.

Rounlet splashed with folds of velvet, silken doublet, leather grieves, and tunic, Eric almost ran around the corner. A hand reached about his head holding the top-heavy hat in place. In a gesture he swept it from his scalp bowing deeply and as he rose placing roundlet back to crown.

"Good Sir knight our hearth be thine, share the nar of our man.... Greeting to your lord the scale filamented lord of wurms Herigar Dragon Lord."

Timarr's house was amiable at least. The chamberlain dressed modestly enough, the leather of his uniform carrying a small banner of Abydos over its heart. He looked willing to don armor over the soft leather, padding on joint, to smooth the pain of hinged metal.

Not as hard as the style of Ergedh's court the fancy roundlet reminded Davide of the Red Tower's of Berelan, here he was more as a herald than a chamberlain.

"We be here as supplicants to thy hearth.
The need of honor drives us on to thee,
pray thou wilt our declarations abide,
flattering, descanted, holy friends,
to this hall we should our pilgrimage make.
A time to council, under thy allied,
cragged, and divinely wizened towers,
that we through talk our tribulations shake.
With grace of God and right reverended lord,
the bold flagrant metal of devout warrior,
to this timber, raftered hall shalt descend,

congregation of knightly puissance,

a sight to terrify the traitor's friend,

Arraken's holy army brought to sword."

The chamberlain looked about clapping his hands. A worried grimace had crept onto his cheek.

"If thou art to call a meeting here of holy fighters, monk and knight I must needs prepare a feast... Order meats... prepare dish of fruits... To cutlery my happy retches... Our master is to host an unlooked-for party... Villien, vassal, yeomen, serf... waiting slave... to bowl, to cauldron, to soup to pantry... fetch thee the slaughter... Call back our chefs... to kitchens I will toil till the knights have supper. "He spun, sending orders every which way. Three maids appeared from the gallery and leaning over they shouted down to Eric that they were far too busy to help with the cooking.

"How many holy knights dost thee expect Davide de Clune? "He said as the clamor of his muster ebbed to quiet.

"A hundred honored Knight ..I know not if there be more. "Davide replied. "I be not a numerologist... my bloody pilgrimage haunts my mind entire. Go to thy lord tell him we be here I would with he a word or more."

Exasperated, Erik spun the hall twice, before leaving in search of Herbar, the twitter of laughing children hounded his busy heals. The new comers sat at the closest of the five tables, and as the schooling took a break to ogle at them, a servant brought a plate of bread, fruit, and cheese. The Knight eat ravenously, the Wadeen little.

Jorin returned to his knight from the stable, he had removed his chain hauberk, carrying it slung in bag over a weighted shoulder. As he sat and took an orange from the plate, Ssithathich crept, slinking, down Sarus' outer arm toward the bowl. Snaking, it kept head low, its shoulders the highest of its wurm body, tail twitched in anticipation as it neared the fruit plate.

"It hast been time since I supped on orange. "Jorin offered as he ripped the fruit in two. No answer, he ate watching Ssistathich as it adapted from black to the dull brown of their table top. Soon, it challenged an apple, feigning trouble like a playful cat. Catching it in jaw it rolled once and freezing when it felt Davide's eyes on it, it yelped, bounding in a winged flash, back to its shoulder perch, prey firm grasped in back claw. Secure, and growling low it began to guardedly devour the trophy.

They had eaten, before Erik returned with news that his lord Herbar had been sent for from Vale Keep Manor. He had also sent word to East Keep and Trilliam monastery, as they were close. The Knight Defenders of the One would attend in numbers, and if any of Davide's own chivalric order, the Order of the Lance were within the message's ride, then they too could be looked for.

Erik arranged food for more than a hundred, moving a table to sit at the head of the other four creating a space that would be filled with Nobel testimony. Davide wanted no entertainment despite the obnoxious protestations of Seraus.

Three clerks of the Cathedral had arrived in the early afternoon to help in any way they could and before Herbar arrived the council was planed to the last till late.

Red hair and beard flaming, blue grayed eyes sternly booming to his commands, Herbar wore a chain shirt with plate leggings. Ouras his pure white horse had been stabled with the rest, blazoned with the red and blue of Abydos' silver poniards, bright in the southern sun. It was rumored to be of the stock of Seofar Flame Hoof, the legendary steed rode by Ruik de Gent, Warder of the White Plains; Earl of Justice Hall, his home lay to the north east, the word of the crown for the wild lands of Norcadia, and Rodenwack.

Knights of the Purity of the One, practiced arms in the paved courtyard and bailey, spilling into the streets before the castle with their martial practice. Brawling was at a minimum, with less drafting of beer than these gatherings of Arraken puissance often entailed.

After inspection the Town Hall's grass park was deemed dry as a bone and able to accommodate the horsed flourishes of Davide's sparsely represented Chivalric Order of the Lance. Towns folk cheered and laid wagers, as friendly challenges and pas des arms were declared and fought. Herbar himself took to the lists at one point, and after proving his worth upon the plated torsos of three contestants, then, rushed off on Ouras to purportedly, have weighty words with Davide de Clune. The visiting Ergedian, who, for his own honor, did decline combat, preparing, or so it was said, to meet the Prince of Uuk over the matter of a devil, or deamon protected by this upstart of Mernnon.

Brave was this Ergedian to challenge the ill-fated House of Maub, who the rabble remembered, had threatened Holem and Celent with the rebelling army of Oritand, Uuk's grandfather. The crazy Prince held the soul of a dangerous enemy of God; a deamon of hell, an anathema, slayer of clerics, excommunicate from Berelan by the word of Primate Simmon. They cheered wishing the knight well in his quest to bring the unruly Prince to the justice of God, the Maker, builder of Arraken.

As the evening approached, bruised, and wearied knights drifted into the Great Hall of Celent castle for a council on the subject of the excommunicate, and the Prince of Maub. The tables filled with more than a hundred knights and their squires, gobbling food and laughing with the pride of displayed wound.

Music played while they eat; lute, drum, flute and lyre. No wine was served, and as the hubbub died, Davide de Clune addressed the assembled body of Abydosian's Holy strength.

"Yee that live in holy God's honor,
a sworn brotherhood barring sword and word,
thee that haft traded brazened burly knocks,
those proud badges of our shared Arraken faith,
wilt thou now listen, lending me thy care,
for to thy high virtue do I need plead.
Chivalric Order of Lance commands thee,
and as thee me. To arms! List bound am I!!
For from my crasp the foulest fiend was snatched,
imprisoned in holy enchanted flask,
blessed in silver and capped hard in lead,
a sealed tomb for a murderer's doom.
Once
a saint reverenced Corser abbot,
fell to witchery, wicca, Saitan's brood,
vilest, dweomer craft, hexologies,
traps invisible, imprisoned weavings,
from their long damned arm shalt I us cleave.
What shalt we who Oritand near assaulted,
gladly sit by wilst his grandson steals,

that which through devilry in power grows,
to strength, in threats for their neighbor near.
Challenge apon the strengthy Uuk place I,
who in the lists of Ottar Eadiawin,
faces knavery, with broadsword and I.
Thy loves support in arm do I beesech,
to lend my claim weighty force's demand,
a show of holy, angered, deadly, men,
a threat in field and Mernnonian town,
an assurance that leads the Prince to me,
least through deviled trick Uuk should fate escape.
Then to me pleadge thy true hearted lances,
to Maub with a debt of honor go I."
The knights, cheered in agreement with his augment,
swade by the ideals of their oaths. He clenched his hands
in a gesture of union, returning to sit at table, to the
patting of shoulder from charged peer. Herbar de Vishi,
rose from beside him, and without walking to the space
before the table he spoke from where he stood.
"Honor of Celent we welcome our friend,
compatriate in vow and armored bout,
his charge hast honor, by Simmon's decree,
I be de Vishi with Uuk's kin lineage,
I doth share, a collection of mariages,
for a century or more. Yet with Oritand,
I would a decade's bloody length brawl.

To Uuk then, smite his youthful boasted pride,

for much like unto his grandfather, and not,

the passive graceful, Sarkhen Heath Keeper.

So to thee, I ask for a yea or nae,

wilt we follow Davide son of de Clune,

give his cause the incentive of weapon,

insurance to draw Uuk to the King's List?"

He raised his hand, to still the individual clamoring voices, then when silence returned, he sat. Stepping from the wall the herald of the local order of the One, took the open center space. He turned in full circle examining the faces of the hall, the single silver circle in black of his holy order covered his lose worn surcoat, chain visible beneath.

"Nobel peers of the Lance and Holy One,

I ask for your vote, how many say yae..."

A great shout filled the room, ringing the metal of those that attended clad.

"And now for the nae, any thus inclined?

A few of the monks and a smatter of knights whose obligations fell further across the Mernnonian boarder than the rest, spoke up.

"The most Nobel voters in agreement sound...
the Yeas..... Have ...IT !!!!!!!!!!!!!!!!!!!

Shouting the hall sang its opinion. Davide relaxed, he would take a brigade of his own order, twenty knights and squire to the House of Maub, there to deliver his challenge. The order of the One, under Herbar were to deploy at Awel keep, the combined puissance should persuade the young Prince that the challenge was serious. Davide smiled for the first time since he left Ergedh. Fighting he was familiar with, no doubt, he would soon have the saint's soul back in his grasp.

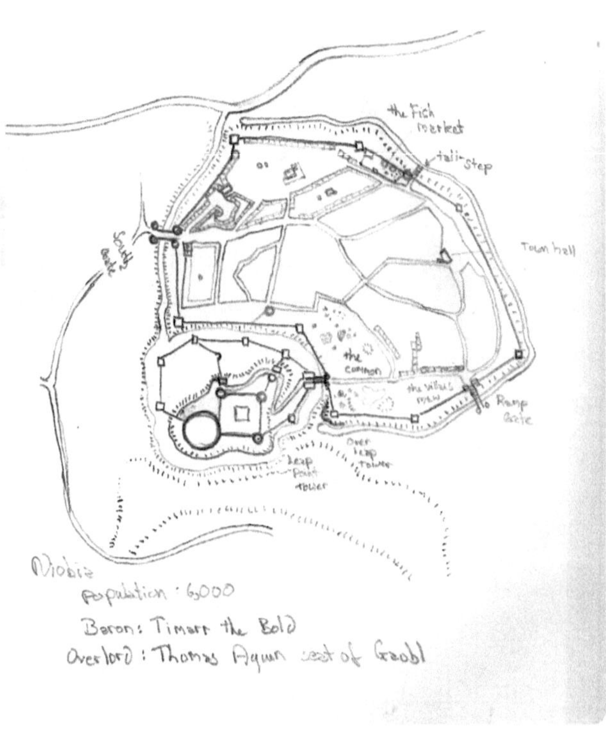

Niobia

Population : 6,000

Baron: Timarr the Bold

Overlord : Thomas Aquan seat of Graobl

CHAPTER 11

ROTWART

Tarese sucked her lip, Widern had never seemed so small. She longed to be running free in the hills and forests of Corsinia, her hoofs pounding the ground, cutting the earth, a fresh woody breeze cooling her through course prickling hair. The Durgens had been exemplary hosts as usual, with piping stew, homemade bread, and a spiced cheese from Toulon, across the Wierd.

According to the lawyer, Eothan's trial by water would take most of the weekend. He was strong, she hoped the militia would treat her barbarian monk well. He reminded her of a young boar she had befriended in her youth, unsure of the world, less confident, yet willing to act far more brazenly than most. They had made happy playmates, tusking for root in the rich earth of Corsinia.

Compared to the aloof Genru de Gent, the Unkown Land and the stoic, empty, tiring, studiousness of the

Irdewin Lodge, he was much easier to be with. Not guarded and ever manipulating, but willing to see what she had to offer for herself, and grateful when she had an idea.

Ottar Ediawin, the Forgiving, ever beside himself with greetings and salutations showed little real warmth she thought. If he and his advisors were not so pedantically lascivious, she would have spent more time in the king's court during her youth.

Her father too was weary of this Ediawin king and his constant bowing to the wishes of the Primate Simmon's clergy. The Snake, or so she had heard her father call him on occasion, bought more than mere favor from their relative the king. As the older brother Genru had been the ever studious acolyte of the Hidden Land, he had no time for the Arraken Knighthood and Ottar's pursuit of the Ellendie Crown.

The time she had stayed in the Red Towers for the celebration of Ottar's birthday, the phantoms that haunted the evening mask had so confused and befuddled her that she had crept deep into the protection of her own mask. Not knowing what was real and what illusory, the steaming, leering, demanding, faces of Ottar's court drug on her defenses. Circles of vile wealth and its hench men, that formed with an unspoken command, preventing passage and walling her in. Their leud remarks urging, exposure and fornication. Deamons she had thought. Pushing past their crude debaucheries, her status protecting her, she had felt nothing but revulsion for their abusive "party games".

The poppies of Berlan abounded and through a haze of tiring enforced gaiety, that threatened to destroy all that stood in the way of its narcissus, she combated the unhappy waves of sadistic laughter, that reveled in debauchery either stolen or coerced from its victims.

Phantom shapes intermixed with the real, half-clad dancing girls from Nabroth Aries, and Thaine distributed elixirs and potions on trays, their deep green and brown eyes lifeless, detached, from years of will whittling abuse. Her own phantoms had appeared, guarding her from the screams and female shrieks that echoed from within the closing circles of nobility and their oiled and scented paramours. Few Ellendei women attended, she had noticed, a privilege she herself wished she had exercised but, being the most eligible royal maid she had a certain obligation to debut herself.

The brutal panting and thumping of these corrupt Ellendei, the emptiness that king Ottar surrounded himself with, was everywhere, it pervaded the room, absorbing to the walls till the foul reek of their bodies demand for the power of forced lust was too much to bear. Visions of exhaling, grinding, subjugations, filled her mind from behind the impenetrable walls of giggling meaninglessness, a threat to violate all that was sacred, condemning it to perpetual oblivion.

If she succumbed never again would she be master of her own fate. Protected by the watchfulness of her own phantoms, phantasmal protectors that issued from the magick her farther had scent with her, appearing first as friends and now butlers and finally an armed guard, she had warded herself from the abuses of the court. Thus, she had warded herself from a humiliation beyond redemption at the hands of those tyrannical egoists.

Visions and frights of that night still plagued her dreams at times, warning her of a close relationship with the crown, and its poppy worshipping decadence. Genru de Ghent and his daughter took the powers of their enchanted intoxicants far more seriously. Death and addiction were often the side effects for the careless practitioner of such arts, Irdwin lodge, avoided such mishaps with great care, the Unknown Land.

She looked around the comfortable room that hung with herbs and vegetables the fabric of the Communality's fare. The earthy aroma of vegetation, friendly, comforted her, erasing the memory of that hellish night.

The door opened and a hurried looking Theus Drugar pushed in with an arm load of the days fresh produce. A sack round shoulder and head carried a clay jar of fresh milk, with a cloth wrapped collection of river fish. Lettuce heads, cabbage, and onion filled his arms. Placing them on the bar, he turned to Teresa.

"The Norcadian has escaped..... I was buying daily supplies at market....n' t' cook for ye Barrister was there n' all .....n' ee comes up nn' says that .. ye body guard had scarpered..Long with two other prisoners... two thieves who they caught day a' fore you..."

"Escaped!" She almost jumped to her feet. "Is he safe? "

"Well I's donna know that m' lady... They be a looking for 'im an town guard was about....wot would ye 'ave me say?"

"Nothing.. not a word.. I must find him."

"Best be eating ye breakfast first I think, me lady.... Norcadian 'unts go much be'ter on a full stomach...'sides word is they dug out through bot'em of Tower ye see... probley lost in lands beneath b' now..... 'alf way t' Pinnacle of Parnassus I warrant ye... If they're not dead that is..eatten b' one em.. spawn of the Hexecologist... least that's wot we calls 'em ...Horrible worms... n' t' like... nasty critters they got down there... I's been in 'em caverns me self... looking for enchanted materials, scales n' bone n' what not for the Commonalties coffers. not alone mind ye'... first time I went it was ye farther im self who showed us way.. old Genru Starborn.. Good trip that introduced me to t' Gnomes of Parnassus un we traded some scale we got frum t' Waieen for these beautiful gems, n.. some mold that worked wonders for sleep powder.."

He boiled water while he spoke, throwing in the cabbage and onion whole. The lettuce, and fish he set aside for latter. Then presenting Teresa with half a loaf of Bread and a big bowl of mourning milk, he sat as the soup boiled behind the bar.

"Fish'll be ready afore lunch."

"Yes well ....I may stay ... till then...then." She thought on Ceroth the Good, a Ciradan, bastard brother of Wirkeal, the marquis of Traitia, chamberlain to Ottar, he was still a friend of her fathers. It was he who had arranged Tarese's betrothal after the dismal royal mask to Tholrin first son of Atrol Atroson, Treathbaron and Earl of Darkmore. He was considered to be a good tentative first choice.

Sentenal tower, Southern most of the Red Tower's and domain to Ceroth, overlooked the entire citadel of Ottar Eidawin. Surrounded by its majesty and there alone in all of the king's castle did she feel safe. Her chambers had lay close to the Sentenal's and she and Ceroth had had a number of fine talks. It was over a game of chess one afternoon that he suggested she begin a search for a husband, and though she had acted shy then, after council, her farther, agreed that a match would be sort.

She studied the black-haired, green-eyed servant before her, freeman and trusted member of her father's secret order the Irdewin Lodge, Friends of the Unknown Land. A plain, ordinary looking Ellendei, he was trustworthy, their long-standing friendship did not carry the threat and danger that mere conversations did in the Red Towers. Ceroth had stayed close to her after the mask, and warded her from many of the Towers less savory courtiers.

The brother of Wirkael Ciradan, Warden of the North Marches, and marquis of Traitia, he had a keen interest in jousting and weaponry. His collection of exotic arms and armor filled the lower two floors of the tower, and was one of the most popular sights of the entire citadel. In his late forties Ciradan had reached the prime of his races life, no longer a bachelor, he had recently been married to the lady Ansculf, only child of Rand Lakedweller, Baron of Corsinia. She, in her twenties was young for an Ellendei bride, but with the political termoil of the last decade, and the strained marriage between Illid's young boy and the Gunarsson's heir, an alliance between the Northern Marches and the king's chamber was favored. Besides Ceroth was an even keeled and amiable fellow, he was a good catch.

She recalled the marriage, a splendid event in the halls of Ellentroth, ceremonial hall of the Red Towers. Her father had accompanied her that time and they had not stayed in Sentanal Tower, rather, the Chattelei's of Mangara, Saeredhra the Elder, had put them up in their modest Berelan manner house.

Surrounded by canals, and barges; longboats, brought traffic, and wares to and throw. On the weading day itself Earl Hasalblad of the Gray Lands, sent a petite yellow and black ship, a replica of the latest dromo. Pulled by three giant golden sea carp, the boat arrived to pick up and triumphantly deliver the guests to the island of the Red Towers.

The common people of Berelan lined the channel cheering and waving as the procession was drug around the city's water ways by the monstrous golden scaled fish, eyes rolling in their huge heads, gulping emptily in the air. The Berelan Clergy were suspiciously absent the wedding, conducted by a cardinal from Aricia, not Simmon the Snake. The Ciradan's had attended, Wirkeal and his three boys. One an Arraken knight, Arinbeorn of Darkmore, the vassal to Atrol Atrolson Treathbaron of the Ellendei, wore his heavy plate armor polished to a sheen, a massive battle axe hung silver and gold on his back. He it was said, was betrothed to the beautiful Melisande of Edmire, a noblewomen of

Darkmore, who's plaintive muse carried the rare gift to charm her listeners. A pity, he was already betrothed she had thought, the Wirkeals were well respected enemies of Berelan and as her peer and a knight, he would have been a suitable choice for her. Of his brothers, the youngest was far to scrawny and pale, and the other carried a distant look to his eyes, and he smelled slightly of some essence, frankincense she thought. Tholrin Atrolson nor his farther had attended too busy in their own businesses.

She heard it rumored that, Herigar Gunerson, Dragon Lord, was smitten by the same Melesande of Edmire, and although already married, the Duke ever impossible to dissuade from tasks taken to heart, wowed her also. Arinbeorn and Herigar were bitter enemies, and had both sworn to retrieve the skull of a mighty Griffin from the wilds as a gift for Melasande. Romantic she had found the tail, the young enchantress and her rivaled suitors, both noble Ellendei.

The decrees against spell weaving, had not been as serious then, only the flagrant worship of the Imprisoned One, and the odd Deamon summoner were punished by death. The church had still frowned on magick, however, especially when used for a frivolous or personal gain. Teresa curtailed her own wishes to add prestidigitation to the festivities when she threw multi colored confetti.

In the Northern Marches, the Ciradens, Ansculfs, and de Gents had managed to protect the rights of virtuous spell usage in the wake of a steady and rising opposition from Berelan, acting through the clergy. Her best choices for a mate would be found among the Arraken Earls, the sons of Berreck Theine, Atrol Atrolson, or Ollentia. Her own brother Ruick de Gent was Warder of the White Plains, a wild and poor Earldom that stretched along the distant slopes of Northern Derem-Goria. An uncivilized land, the White Plains were famous for their independent and hauty horse stock, and the fanatical devotion of their lord to causes of true honor and decency. The rival state of Rodenwack, run by Remarr a corrupt Arraken Earl lay to the White Plain's South East. Remarr used the arts of deceit, and slander to control his land with a net of crime, extortion and other tactics, all without honor, ruling his land as the Web Master.

Since Orlentia, an island state, was ruled by Marent Halkinson, a young Earless, with no apparent heirs, Marent being younger than Teresa even, and as yet unmarried or betrothed, had no apparent offspring, that left Teresa a choice between Berreck Theine's or Atrol Atrolson's male children, both heirs they would be well sort after by others. Tholrin Atrolson, a good-looking man she had watched joust in a tournament held in

Darkmore's largest town Arnhern. He was younger than she, and obsessed with Arraken Knighthood. Richard Theine another fine-looking man, according to reports, and lord of the citadel of Theine, was a more accepted age for her mate, being a little older, closer to thirty she thought. The Earls of Zymosia, were not true Ellendei, darker skinned they were, and their age expectancy was likewise a little shorter. The Ellendei had always been blessed with long life.

Richard was then close to the age he should marry. Theine a city that rivaled Berelan in size and wealth, hated the Ellendei religious bureaucracy, although Richard ruled in Ottar's name, the religious cults of Nabroth Melzanos and Brahilia guided his people. The Alabarque of Theine headed the cities religious courts. Richard worshipped Enruth she was sure but he was bound to be much more worldly about the practice of magick. In her mind she pictured him as a better choice, for she knew he to be, like herself, a probable practitioner of arcane lore.

And if she was fated to marry a noble, then why did the face of this Norcaidian warrior monk haunt the back of her mind. Yellow hair was rare in the Ellendei nobility, only a few of the northern barons of Drake, had truly blonde hair, there were lighter tones, of course and her brother Rand's hair was red, like the kings.

Eothan's almost blonde, was rare, it appealed to her somehow. Would her farther anger if she was to marry a commoner? What was best for Irdiwin, the Unknown Land? She knew not. Eothan she had befriended and all she could do was worry for his safety, where had he vanished to? And what of his Abbot, the kidnapped Saint Thomas the Young?

She needed advice, someone close. Then it occurred to her Nariono Mentrene wife to Ngrath Mentrene, lord of Rotwart Swamp dabbled in the art of Astrology. Not Ellendei, she had come from a land far to the North beyond Darkmore and the Wyrum Tongue Plains. As a foreigner, perchance she would have untainted advice for the confused Teresa de Gent. They had met, she remembered, at Ceroth's wedding. Not many of the Ellendei would talk to such a foreign looking woman, but Terese, hoped to travel North through the wilderness herself one day, and was glad to find someone who had been born and raised in such a far distant place, and, to whom spell weaving was not merely a matter of man talk.

Rotwart Manor, was not the most savory of holds, standing as it did on a dry valley bordering the fens, of Rotwart, A fertile but dangerous region famous for its wild game, duck, antelope, and gator. Once one became used to the boggy rich smell of the drying peat, and the warty growths that plagued the area's common people, it could be an attractive region of Arraken. The mourning sun as it burnt back the mists that issued from the Meer, and the bog's Dark Woods had been the subject of some well recited ballads.

A horse! she would need a palfrey. The nobility of Arraken reserved the rite to ride for themselves and a few designated servants. The Ellendei's fighting sergeantry in particular, were a horse mounted common people. Town magistrates and certain guild syndics were powerful enough to circumvent the law, they carried letters of permission, avoiding the ten lashes that welcomed a commoner found ridding. In the realms distant reaches, like the wilderness fiefs of Corsinia, horses were ridden, with greater freedom, but in Arraken's major cities the repeated offense, was punishable by death.

"I am to leave today... do you know of a palfrey I can purchase?"

"There be a stable a t' royal ferry m' lady.. I shalt accompany thee.. .but prey thee.. wouldst thou.. eat fish stew a' fore we leave?"

Teresa looked distant, preoccupied.

"Yes fish .. that will be.... nice..." Then snapping back to the comfortable lunching chamber of the commonality she noticed Theus, and seeing the concern in his face she smiled. And patting the back of his hand opposite her she said.

"Thank you, Theus."

He smiled back, then returning to the kitchen he returned to his stews and soups.

"Got some cabbage w'ter ere ..m'lady... right good fer ye this stuff... mel'ed but'er in it... n' all... Fill ye bowl if ye like."

"Humh..Yes."

She filled her empty milk bowl and drank leaning propped along the herb cabinet's, boiling cauldrons, and the plants drying in the steam. She waited for the stew to cook, and ate, lumps of large river fish scalding nutritiously on the back of her tongue, softened potatoes, and cabbage filled out the dish. Theus prepared her a bag, cheese and dryed fish, he joked, as he included a thick loaf, reminding her that the Ellendei were particularly found of pork.

"Ye watch 'em market venders... ye could be goblin' down a friend else. "he smirked. "Lots of Pig they sell ye known... Oh n' they say it's anything... Cow.. bull.. even fish.. but its mostly pig, 'un boar salted... much frum up north 'un all.."

Taking the bag, she threw it over her shoulder and hurried down Squire's Walk toward the North gate. There she left Widern and taking the first left she headed along a worn cobbled road to the Royal Ferry of Widern.

Being mid-week, there was a little traffic waiting around the two storied white washed structure, a short tower, she supposed. Carts pulled by smaller relatives of the massive Corsinian barge ox, and some petty nobility milled around on horse, and a group of foot traffic, that huddled behind the building sheltering from a strong, brisk wind that blew across the river chilling with the water's cold. These were to be her across river companions. A high cloud covered the sky, but its brown streaked bland gray, threatened no rain.

North she could see the yellow and brown leafed oak of Southern Corsinia and Traitia, and tall hills to the East and West. The river Lenerr large with rain and its confluence to the Mourn, meandered wearing a wide fertile and farmed valley out of Arraken's West Downs. Villages, hamlets and thorps presented brown fences to darken the fields around Widern with their specks.

Moving fast she had not yet felt the cold. The heat of her sweat warming her throughout. Across the river she spied the turrets, and tower of the Royal Ferry, a traveler's lodge, and stables snugged the outer wall of the small fortified structure. The ferry drug on chains that stretched across the river to wind around a winch, fixed into the roof of the towered building. Drooping down to the water midstream the chain was lifted high at each side, providing a space for the multi oared Traitian longboats, to make their way up and down stream.

A cranking from the chain told her that the ferry had started its monotonous voyage across the river. Clanking, the winch wound, propelled by a distant force that reached from an oxen driven wheeled gear system housed in the buildings on the far side of the Lenerr. She cooled, watching the long barge like ferry as its chain tugged it toward her bank.

When she finally felt the cold, she searched out the other passengers, hoping to hide from the valley's strong and biting wind, somewhere. The group of wool and linen covered peasants, huddled behind the stone building, and she wandered toward them. They watched her slowly with a collection of pleading fright, and deadly venomed appraisal. She was either a savior or victim and from scanning their faces she did not know which, they implored her with images of both.

As they parted to allow her a place in their mutual heat she stopped, their was an over powering smell, a stench, their closeness carried, something in their cloths and bodies. Like the filthy pig stalls of Corsinia, these pitiful people carried the reek of their livelihood about them. She grimaced and holding down a retch she went to stand with the horse, at least they did not smell like a festering Widern sewer.

She pulled a woolen scarf from a pocket in her cloak wrapping it about her neck, then covering herself from head to foot in its expanse, she warded off the cold wind. The horse breath, and perfumed nobility was an improvement from the stench of poverty and the toll it took on the frail human form.

They watched quiet as the ferry unloaded. A Mangaran stage coach, two cart and oxen and a similar group of peasants, itinerant workers, she expected, those poor and unliveried peoples, that for lack of work were forced to travel as far as they could, desperately seeking sustenance before starvation took them. She wished them well, not knowing what she as a de Gent, and relative of the king should do. She had always been well provided for. Were they better of than surf? She knew that the surf were bought and sold with the land, they did not have the right to move from place to place by their own choice.

Snorting the mounted party loaded first, a gray haired and bearded gentleman, wearing a square hat, with folded up corners, leaned down to the ferry master paying for the whole group. Two younger men, and three women one with a child covered and held before her on side saddle, they all wore the same thick black cloak, the women their hair in woolen scarves, the younger men, scarf and hat less, shoulder length brown hair blowing in the wind. A traveling syndic with journeymen she guessed, or an extended family, farther, sons, with wives.

Following them onto the barge she paid a seven copper piece toll, two thrupenny pieces and a single penny. The ferry man wore wool, over his light chain shirt that ended bellow his sword belt. The bare flesh of his legs between the frill of his kilt and his pair of high knee length furred boots shone pink, chaffing in the wind. The other pedestrians were close behind Teresa, paying, as the ferry's assistants, began to load the two well ladened carts.

The trip was quick, and before she got any colder, they were unloading onto the Lenerr's west bank. A sewer emptying into the river, washed manure from the ferry's hidden winch house. Muscle to be lost, diffusing in the river water. Finding the stable amongst the mercantile rows that had grown unwalled around the fortified ferry headquarters, she brought a small reddish-brown horse with bridal and saddle. And not wishing to waste time, she paid the steep price of a single gold sovereign, quickly climbing into the saddle refusing the stable master's offer for a side saddle.

"Dost Saeredha the Elder ride side saddle."

"Well no m' lady. "He had answered.

From the ferry, she rode south along the king's highway toward T'bah, a city in constant political turmoil. Its wealthy streets lay on the boarder of four of Arraken's states. The Lenner impassable to sea vessels, that could not pass the waterfall of Parnassus, was bridged at T'bah by a fifteen arched stone structure, built after the fall of Parnassus, by a now defunct union between Corsinian Dwarf, Ellendei, and Gnome.

The Lenner divided T'bah in half, the West bank dominated by the Chattellies that hailed to Mangara, the East looked to Wikeal Ciradan, Warden of the North Marches, and Marquis of Traitia, as over lord. Between the Lord mayor, the Lord Chief Justice, and the nation's two rival merchant guilds, both of whom saw T'bah as their primary seat of operations, this central market of Arraken, was rife with espionage, and intrigue, that often erupted in armed civil brawling and worse.

The cold day kept the high road empty for the most part, three Manganran stage coaches cantered past on their way north, a group of peasant field workers walked the stone track from village to village. She kicked her horse to a gallop passing their troubles without allowing its misery to reach her. What could she do to feed and warm Arraken's people?

Closer to T'bah, long stone walls dissected the land, into gated fields. Stables and barns, bleated and bayed with the sounds of animals escaping the cold. As the afternoon stretched on Teresa began to shiver, with the wind chill, swallowing a pinch of her powders, her vision blurred the bleak, hilly, horizon blending brown into the gray sky. When her eyes cleared a warmth had passed through her body. Braving the wind, she let the palfrey trot along the hard road. The mare would earn a meal of oat and hay, and a warm strawed stall by tonight the shape changer thought.

Letting her eat what was left of the summer's grass at a cross roads, Teresa read the many carved wood and stone sign posts. To the south she could see the outer walls of T'bah, a murky black smoke hung over the city darkening the gray sky. Sorting the villages, and hamlets, from the chapels, monasteries, manors, towns and cities she found a short cut, if she took a hard dirt path directly south, she could avoid T'bah all together, picking up the King's Highroad South of the city. Much better, she thought. Reining up her horse she turned it down the hard earth surface toward Tineral Spring.

Passing hedge and ditch guarded hovels, and farms, they wandered through the Elm, and oak of Chappel Wood, till she found the road she was looking for. Then, gaining elevation out of the woods, she stopped to appreciate a Northward view. The entire Lenerr Valley swept below. Widern Town and T'bah clung to the banks of this giant wandering river, the swollen banks filled patches of green floor with the blue reflection of evening water.

The day had cleared, the gray brown cloud now shadowed only the East hills of Southern Corsinia. And as the day was darkening, the opening blue in the sky did little to lighten the valley. Chapel Wood lay behind her, seven brown clad monks sang as they walked the trees edge; to the North, a top the horn of the West Downs, marking the boarder of Traitia, she saw twinkling yellow light in the windows of the distant Mermont Keep, a single gray tower in the night.

Cresting the first climb of Arraken's central highland, the latern lit walls of a wayfarer's inn shone before her. Built on the side of a tall mountainous hill, to her East, a snaking gray line of stone, the king's highroad, disappeared uphill, behind the four squat shacks and one multistoried structure. The unpaved road stayed exposed and without losing elevation it found the paving stones before the inn. A standing stone at the cross roads told that it was four leagues back down the mountain to T'bah.

Clopping in through the inn's small gate, lanterns warmed the cold from her eyes. A stable boy soon took the steed and after a tip of a copper thrupenny, promised to feed and treat it extra nice. The courtyard, cluttered with two tarp covered wagon and a cart, told her that business was good. The Iron Cragg, read the sign above the wood framed door that led into the inn's main house, a sprig of fresh pine hung beneath the sign scenting arrival.

The common rooms smelled of a thick brew sold from kegs stacked behind the bar. A collection of round tables half fill with guests huddled around a blazing wall hearth.

"Need a room does ye? "Said a middle aged... mousy hair and beard, Ellendei. She looked at him tiered from the day on horseback.

".... Just the one then?"

"I have a mare."

"Of course, ye does..... That 'll be three silver pennies then... if ye wont t' eat that is..... M' lady." His eyes found the small badge of her house that she wore over her breast.

"Yes please... "She looked quickly about the room, a handsome looking, black hair, clean shaven faced soldier, she thought, by the look of the heavy leather jerkin he wore, gleamed a suggestion of company into her dark eyes. No obvious heraldry displayed, she presumed him to be a mercenary, his weaponry probably hung with the modest collection the bar keep kept hanging beside the stair well. Her eyes fell to the bar, then back to the keep.

"I would like my food in my room please."

"As it please ye.." And leaning close he whispered. "But don't let 'im bother ye... That just be a mercenary... we got this merchant here now see.. carries stuff a value.. not turnips an spuds if ye know wot I mean... Yea 'eees harmless enough.. Most a this group is with that merchant.. On 'es way t' T'bah see.. Always 'as same lot with 'im.. Got some Berelan wine an that... Furniture from Thornbreak is what he brings back this way... Dont let 'em fret ye that's all."

"Thank you I will not.. I still think I'll eat in my room if you don't mind. "

"Please ye self.. I'll have Lisa send it up.... That's me sis... Alright?"

"Yes."

"Boris... heh!" He shouted through an open door behind him. "Get out 'ere 'n show our new guest 'ere to that single bedroom near top.. Ye 'ear... put down that chow .. 'n get a move on."

A young boy child scurried quickly under his father's arm and into the small stair well, skirting Teresa with the dexterity of one who knew his homes layout like the back of his hand.

"Com.. on then or me nosh'll get cold ." He piped in a high clear voice.

The room was snug, barely large enough for the short-stilted bed and desk. A water tub and camber pot fit in the cabinet space under the stilts, and a notched tree trunk provided a single step to climb to the soft, linen wool, and downy, fluff of the hill side bed. She eat on the small desk, an old barrel as a chair. A thick potato and, rabbit, stew, with some chicken to spread the stock, and a large loaf of porous white bread to absorbed the broth.

Locking the door with a latch from the inside, she crawled to her bed, full and tiered. Straightening sore thighs from the ride she slept.

The next morning, she rose early ridding into an early fog that lingered in the steep ravines and gorges of the rocky hills, turning into tufted cloud as it blew up the hill sides separating around the inn. The air was cold, but the hills blocked the wind, and the mist dampened her horses' hoofs on the flagstones.

Peacefully, they wound three leagues through a long hilly pass, the squat flint stone farms, and cabins of herders scattered the steep valleys of that border land. Woodland sprung up to the road's west, as their path flattened out. The tents, and carts of a encamped party were to the East. Teresa did not bother to find their business pressing on south, instead. The thick aroma of their stews and roasts had her fishing in the bag Theus had packed for her. She browsed her food she rode.

Leaving the fog behind they traveled through rolling farm and open grassland, to the clearing day; cloudy banks that only hid patches of the blue sky, and the air far warmer than the day before. A hunting kestrel caught her attention, as its gilding flight searched scythe cut meadows for prey. She passed monastery and village, hovel and manor. At one point, a collection of produce carts, blocked her way overflowing with hay and potato, so leaving the highroad she galloped around a hedgerow field threading her way back past a millpond, and stockade. The smells of hearth and fire, wafted from the village behind a wooden wall.

Back on the road, again, she made good time through the intermittently sunny afternoon. Close to the road's west the short walls and towers of a monastery peaked out from over the orange, and, green autumn leaves. A mob of starlings lingered above her at the forests edge.

"Can I help you m'lady. "The soft husky voice came from behind her to the East. Turning in her saddle she found herself looking into the hazel, eyes of a auburn tufted cleric. The priest wore a plain brown cloak, his hair a circle on his close shaved head. Over on a shoulder, hung a collection of snares and twine, limp hare and rabbit around his slender tight corded waist.

"Mearly a traveler farther."

"We all be travelers… tell me .. Can thou deliver a gift to my flock for me?"

Wanting to say no she somehow involuntarily agreed.

"Yes of course father." She heard herself saying.

"This be a long road to Berelan I pray that thee dost our lord god well… If thou canst deliver these arms to those of need that thou dost meet."

And with that he handed her twenty fresh caught rabbit and hare, hanging them over her saddle. Then he was gone, disappeared into the wood, toward the monastery she presumed. Seeing no more of him, she went on puzzled by his cryptic command. Was she to give the rodents to the poor? She liked that idea. Who else? His flock?

It was afternoon and the highroad ran straight through a broken wooded and farmed flat land, walled to the west by the Downs and to the east by Kendel Wood. The river Myth irrigated the land filling it with thick grazable grass, and small crops of unfelled deciduous timber. Hamlets and thorps toped the foliage with their church spires, and hungry hawks whistled above farmed fields.

Choosing not to stop early at a large highway inn, the Whinnying Pig, a silly name thought she, she pressed on, instead. Her horse tired craned for grass at any chance it got.

Twisting and turning about short hills, they descended toward the Meer, a large lake and swampy marsh that's plentiful fish and game kept a stable population of Ellendei villages well fed. It was said that the Meer was the cleanest water of the wetlands that divided the land of King Ottar from his vasseled duke Herigar's. A complex network of swamp, lake marsh, bog and

forest, the area was difficult to navigate, and had proved almost impossible to settle. Its perimeter to the east from the Meer, south through Rotwart Swamp and from thence to Pressia and the sea, on the other hand supported a healthy population of fishermen and hunters. But further west the waters became decidedly dank and inhospitable. Blood worms, and long eels, ruled these waters, and the ghost of many a Wizard King's victim were thought to wander in the empty forests and swamps.

The Wyerd, or so the Ellendei called it, was to where the fell beasts of Ergedh and Parnassus fled during the War of Arraken. For a time Wurms had bread there, before Drake drove them from the waters with his mighty sword Thangbite. A gift from the dwarves of Derem-Goria, and forged with the help of Feorowin, Lord Chief Justice of Arraken, the sword boasted the tooth of the legendary drake of Ergedh for its blade. And it was said that it aided its wielder in the command and friendship of drakes both great and small.

To the west a long stone wall, blessed and mixed with the bones of many a noble soul, stretched for fifteen leagues, guarding Daquin from bestial incursions that issued from the foul swamps of Wyred. Berelan, on the other hand, trusted to its fleet of war vessels that rolled the navigable waters between Prassia and the Capital, to keep the monstrous spawn of those swamps at bay. North the stone wall became a mighty palisade of timber, from the Toor slope forests. Towering evergreen striped and buried deep into the ground, circled the wild forests of North Wyred. Built in the time of the Dragon, when Clortherregge the wurm of Ergedh had retreated to Old Nede after the fall of its master.

Now 500 years since the passing of the drake, the thirty pace tall barrier to the Wyred was still maintained and patrolled, an important tool in the protection of the farming peoples of Arraken. A cause way linked the north between Mirris and Waken, built above the trees, it allowed safe travel through the faerie rich forests around Old Nede, the Wyred's single mighty mountain. Built within the last hundred years its garrison at North Lake kept a watchful eye on the movements and habits of the Wyred's enchanted fauna. A series of standing stones, depicting the many tribulations of the Ellendie's,

Profit of the One, blessed and maintained by Arician Clergy, formed a line along the West Downs, from the causeway to the Meer, warding the populous baronies of Mangara, Pellia, and Arris Leon from the foul breeds of Troll Rock and Old Nede. In this way, through wall, palisade, patrol, and standing stone, the Ellendei protected themselves from the wild in their midst. This Wyred also dissuaded any open conflict between Drake and Arraken, being impassible to a marching army.

A knight of the Holy Order of the One watched a small bridge carefully, visor back he nodded to her, black curls peaked from under metal, ruddy cheeks told of recent exercise, burning with heat. He steamed in the weak sun of the late afternoon. The silver circle of his order shined in the black void of his shield. Crossing the bridge, she rose from the thin valley toward a fortified chapel. A manor of the Order of the One, or so she thought. Topping a second rise she saw again the Meer its blue water covering leagues of the swamp land to the south.

A line of north south running swamp and forest, blackened the horizon, afore. Light reflected the brown green foliage skyward from the clear water of the autumn swollen wet lands. She rubbed her tired road weary eyes, and from the darkening gnarled growth of Rotwart picked out the light gray sliver of road before her. Lights were visible in the fog of the deep wash's land, darkening. Though it was not yet dark enough for these land bound stars to show clear in a black sea of invisible thorn and bog.

Not wanting to waste the little light remaining she hurried on. There must be a traveler's inn soon, she thought. They descended to the Meer, the road built up above the ground, was swamped and gnarled, crisscrossed with stunted oak and hawthorn. The trees here had lost their leaves already, struggling in the wet for life. Geese honked in the distance, and the bog stank, rich, rotted a putrid ooze. She pitied those who lived here amongst the mud, frequenting the sparkling stockades that she could see occasionally in the mist.

Shapes, dark moved in the fog, there and then gone. Was she being followed? There again, a movement behind twisted stump. She reined up the steed. Looking about her. The stench was all, no sound but the geese. She urged on, the weary palfrey resisting a trot. Then they were there again, on the road ahead. Shadows in the night. She strained forward making out the dimming far fog. Shapes, people, the commons of Bogwood? Why were they want to show themselves?

On the road ahead, three or four she thought, yes, as boulders in the fog when they moved not. Then there again, their movement deceiving them.

The face shocked her lunging from the road side as it did. Eyes grey brown and blood shot, hair black long straight and straggled with mud. He had a hold of her reins in a moment, glaring at her silently a third of his face covered with a green billowing growth, that inflated the skin with blistering sores. Scabs, dry, red in the lumps of creamy pale green. Other shapes appeared around her. They stood silently along the road side blocking her before and behind. Her hand found a pinch of enchanted intoxicant in the folds of her robe.

"You have entered the land of Rotwart..... what dost thou offer? least we who are the eyes and ears of the bog... take that which we desire..." The voice graveled and husked a loud whisper, almost a wind in the mists of Rotwart. A thick robed figure to the front she ascribed it to. It was he; his arms rose wide as if he meant the swamp its self. The others were frozen, they moved not, empty faces, pleasureless, mouths open in numbed hardship. They stared at the royal lady before them, unable to comprehend her healthy vigor. How was such luxurious bounty possible, she looked as one who had never experienced hunger or disease, the daily deamons that these spirits of the swamp contended with.

"Yes, I do have an offering for you in need. "She pulled forward the rabbits, and hare holding them out, an offering. "Here is that which will feed thee heartily... blessed meat from Myth Monastery."

They fell about the pile dividing it between them. She was left alone untethered, breaking herself from their miserable spell, she shook her head, and digging her leather booted heels deep into the side of the horse they shot away down the road. It was dark before they slowed to a walk and she had found the light door of a highway inn, the Willow's Wisp.

Three gold lights hung in the air above a brown weeping willow, blue water and black night, surround, a skilled painter had rendered the design on a deep mauve-stained hard wood.

She dismounted and lead the exhausted, frothing horse, into the Wisp's compound. Finding none about, she tethered its drooping head outside the common room, climbed its steps to enter the house. Parting with four silver pennies, she found another clean warm room, and directions to Rotwart Manor, a further eight leagues south.

From the Willow's Wisp the road ascended a series of small hillocks, away from the wet of Rotwart. Dragon Wood to the east was often the site for the King's hunt. Not like the week-long hunts for boar, and stag that Ottar and the household retreated to Irdiwin lodge, and the hospitality of her farther for. No, here game was released to be tracked down immediately, small dragons delivered by the Wadeen, trolls, from Rotwart, witches from prison and, lion and tigers, from the jungles of Brahil. The locals ever complained that these creatures lingered in the wood and were not always dispatched. Lord Illid of Pellia, contended that with Rotwart Swamp so close, it was incursions from the Wyred that stemmed such rumors.

Illid Manor lay within the confines of the wood; a strange mix of imported evergreen and the natural Oak that grew East of the King's highway. Constructed from beast cages, and an ornate Mernnonian style architecture, but surrounded with an Arraken retaining wall, and moat, the manor was unusual looking to say the least. A retreat for the King and his minister it lay a hard day's ride from Berelan.

The Tower of the Sword in Praessia was pledged to eradicate any troubling monsters in Southern Mangara, and Pellia, their Knights Errant patrolled from Toll Fort to Dragon Wood, where they operated under strict orders from the prime minister. These noble warriors bolstered the mundane troops, crossbowmen, and heavy soldiery, with which, Berelan guarded its Western fields, vineyards, and poppy fields.

It was afternoon, by the time, her foot heavy mare, carried her, over the moat, into the manor of Rotwart.

Its open gate house, a black timbered, glass windowed, house sat above the small stone archway, built more for comfort than siege.

Paintings of the Profit, covered the postern's portal with a thick layer of bright color. Here he hung on the cross, there he preached of the One in the streets of Thaine. Saint Augustia revenged him along one wall, while the union of Arraken pleadged their believe in the One. On the ceiling, there were other works too, diagrams, devices, circles and lines that Teresa recognized not, woven hexagrams, symbolic geometrics, all colored and interpenetrated with metal, jewelry. Diamonds, she was sure, glinted back, buried for eternity in the fragile rock of the ornate gate.

Off the high road, and eastward, by half a league, the villages there abouts were picturesque in the extreme, far tidier and quaint than the stoic mud and thatch dwellings of the swamp land. A higher land still lay behind the Manor, ringing the cultivated fields and thorps with a horizon of empty meadow. Canals and streams irrigated and trafficked the fields with plentiful peasants, who ran in the fallows, and working along the banks and hedgerows filled the county roads with livestock. The wet lands of Rotwart lay a league or more to the west beyond the King's highroad, brown, and green, ugly for the farmer, yet a welcome hunting ground for yeoman, and serf.

A chapel lay inside the gate, carved leaves crisscrossed a steep pointed arch around its jarred door. The morning had been cold, and she found her way to the main house, that, lay above all on an inclined pedestal of large hard stone, timbered and white washed. It was without the towers and stone turrets that adorned the walls and manors of the warlike northern castles. Far more palatial, she thought as a voice caught her from behind.

"I welcome thee Teresa de Gent, daughter of Genru Starborn, our hearth is thine... Yet before thee enter my lord's house.........thy must take a blessing in the house of the One. The foul dank of Rotwart must cleansed at our door step."

"You knew of my coming?" She questioned. The plain black robed chaplain wore a silver hemmed red apron, similar to the clergy of Berelan.

Light brown hair, grayed with age, circled his head in the fashion of Aricia.

"The things we of the One know are many. "He led her close, into the modest chapel, un-shuttered windows pored sun light onto the flag stoned floor. A plain wooden cross lay behind a low alter, decorated with a satin cloth and golden candelabra. There were no benches, but a pile of mats provided knee rests for worshipers. Turning full circle, he rose his arm pointing to a pedestaled cistern inside the door. Thin windows framed the holy waters.

"Here my.. child kneel and I will bless thee. "After she scooped up a mat and kneeled on it he sprinkled the waters on his hands placing moist fingers to her forehead.

"In the name of the Profit, the One, and the sacred covenant of Arraken I bless thee. May the hand of the Imprisoned not touch thy heart with his corruption... There... now you may rise. I am here at all times to bless the visitors to the house of Menterne. Lord N'grath orders that all be blessed when they enter his hearth place. If you should leave be sure to be blessed on your return.... whatever time of day.. or night, it may be... If I am asleep then one of my priests or a deacon will be here... Do not forget. "

His last three words carried the weight of command, she felt them become part of her. Yes, I must be cleansed from the outside she found herself thinking.

Rising she also felt a little rested, as if some of the trail's fatigue had been lifted from her shoulders.

"Now go to the house my lady Welen awaits you."

A set of tall steps lead up and around a sentry platform, to the top of the rock on which the large wooden house stood. Beams and wide columns supported the triangular shaped overhanging roof, the gable above the steps contained two rows of wood frame shuttered windows, and massive round pillars sided the steps down to its lowest level. There were three levels, an attic and two floors she guessed. Painted in a bright gold, stylized lion heads looked out from atop the giant dark brown beams. Many smaller beasts and shapes adorned the peaked roof tops.

"You have been expected. "The voice was high and clear carrying a hint of accent. "It hast been time since the wedding of Ceroth the Good.. hast not? .. Our hearth be yours daughter of de Gent." Welen stepped to the upper step a thick quilted silken gown covered her against the chill day. Her long black hair held back off her face, fell down her back, to end around her hips in a thick bunch. A gold badge sown over her heart, carried the withered branch of Rotwart.

"Come we will sit ..sup tea and share the talk of our class. "Teresa reached the top step, and taking her by the hand Welen Menterne lead her into their house. Leather armed and halberd wielding men at arms parted standing to attention at their posts, stern faces held front.

Bare, stained deep brown wood walls divided the interior into a variety of spaces and rooms. Statuettes stood elegantly in the corners, Berelan, and Mernnonian workmanship of high quality. Gods and heroes from legends that had been old before the first ships of the

Ellendei had landed. Priests and monks from Arician religious history, and an assortment of personages that Teresa did not recognize, they bore the round, circular, features and designs of her hostess, imported from the lands far to the north, where Welan herself had been born.

Near the back of the house, they took a flight of stairs thick with a latticed, wood lacing, to a series of small rectangular doors around a hard wood-floored landing. It was comfortably warm on the second floor, coals glowing in iron braziers. They walked around to the last door where Welan reached down removing her wooden sandals.

"These are my quarters and I ask you to remove thy boots, before we enter. "

Teresa obeyed leaving her leather walking boots outside the door step. Inside was well lit, glass lead banded windows open to the afternoon sun. Weaved mats covered the floor and a short knee-high table with pillows sat beneath light that poured in to them from outside. Sleeping mattresses rolled and stored against the wall, aided in the spacious feeling of the room.

Welan's outstretched palm told Teresa to sit as the lady of Rotwart tugged a wide yellow, gold frilled, bell pull hanging in a corner.

Teresa noticed, tight, muscles flexing along Welan's calf as she moved, weighty, tall for a woman, the fold of her robe showed that her shoulders were also well built stocky as her legs. Lowering onto her arms, Welan crossed her legs joining Teresa at the table. The soft features of her face, round nose, not long and angular like the Ellendei, and the smooth unwrinkled skin around her eyes, set her apart from those the young de Gent had grown up with. Teresa had never been surrounded by many people, the lodge, was used rarely by the court of Ottar, not like in the days of her father's youth. At that time, magick was respected and the King did not dabble with intoxicants, for his own entertainment, the art itself had been honored, the Unknown Land.

The powerful women before her smiled, dark brown eyes flicking from Tarese's to role low and inquisitively back again. The Ellendei grinned, there was something friendly, inviting, hesitant in the gesture.

"Our tea will be here shortly," she said.

"I know you are informed as to the intrigues of court... and are versed in the powers of astrology... that is why I have come..."

The muscle of her forearm bulged delineated with a ripple as she leaned forward extracting a velvet silken bag from within her opposite sleeve. Placing it heavily on the table, she undid a pull, revealing a browned and stained stack of cards. The black gnarled stump of Rotwart wandered across their back, blending with the stain.

"Yes I am a student of the Master Gordel Elerendil, and, a week ago I saw your arrival here in the ascent of the great constellation of Apollus, who my people name, Sueslar, thus the lives of mankind are played, reflected, in the cosmos above them. But these observations take time..and the stars develop their patterns slowly.... For matters concerning Royalty... and their hearts the Tarot of Rotwart, an heirloom of the house into which I have joined myself, for life, in marriage hast been accurate. Its predictions expedient, not the ponderous precision of the sky, yet more enlightening somehow. More human? It speaks more to our land, the swamp and that of Arraken. I consider myself a student, my interpretations are at times faulty, but this deck it is truly the master."

"If Teresa de Gent thy hast a question then phrase it in thy mind and shuffle that which hast been with Rotwart since before the passing of Tien Mienor the Omnipotent, Drake of Ergedh."

Pointing to the cards with a palm, her hands fell to the table, with a thud, there they lay quiet.

Teresa picked up the deck, and as she shuffled, she traced the form of a question in her mind. Who was to be her mate among these royal Ellendei, was it Eothan, he who's light hair, and sparkling eyes, plagued her mind's eye? A Norcadian, not an Arraken at all, or did she have a girlish crush, nothing of import? And what of his quest, his kidnapped abbot Saint Thomas the Young? What was she to take this to mean?

The cards pulled on her question, and as she folded them one on top of each other, memories of her childhood, surfaced, to drift upward leaving her for the oblivion of the Rotwart's rafters. She played about the empty rooms of the Lodge, remembering, studied with Edward of Clune, a scribe her farther had imported to teach her letters and histories of the Ellendei. She had received her first lessons from Erabia, an acolyte of her farther, it was he who showed her the first elixirs and intoxicating powder's, of her art and had reminded her that she and her father had a boar manifestation to their spirits. She had spent years after that studying how to control the transformation from human to boar, her first incantation, self-mastery.

Uncontrolled at first, she gradually grew in the awareness of the transformation. It was considered her first great work Erabia, had said, her first step toward magery.

"To be a sorcerer," he said, "we of peace must master self-control, for you and your breed this is more complex, you can consider your curse, a gift, an innate pentagram that you must study and unwind. An enchantment that you shall master as your first step on the path toward wizardry."

It had taken years of her life to master, but now the monthly change was a desire not an uncontrollable possession, the moon an invitation not a demand. In sun light the change was less mutable, if she was caught in its direct rays the change was impossible, but in the dark, she had full mastery, meta-morphing at will. Antithetically, when in direct moonlight she desired to be a boar, during full moon this was an almost irresistible compulsion.

Nor did she have memory blanks, as did some lycanthropes, her mind was the same in boar and human shape, she had integrated the two halves of her personality, fusing them into the amalgamation Teresa de Gent.

She grew galloping through the deep Oaken groves of northern Corsinia, ever, turning her back on the tame Parnasian Forest, leaving the Lodge for the Boar dominated lands that lay north. Druids and wood people had been the friends of her youth. Hermits and isolated homesteads that shared the same love for grove and fen as Teresa de Gent.

Her rare visits to court, reminded her of the cards and the spacious, warm room of Welan Menterne. Her shuffling finished she returned the deck to the velvet bag setting them atop the empty fabric.

"Tea. "her hostess offered pouring from a pot into two oval cups. Not the large mugs of the Corsinian dwarf brews, or the bowls of the Ellendei, but dainty petite vessels, that invited slow drink. Teresa had not noticed the tray arrive, Welan returned the ornate pot to the flattened steel, passing her guest a full cup.

"The pot is full if you desire more." The accent, singsong in her words, soft a gliding, rhythmical speech. Teresa drank a light leafy taste with a hint of bitter. Their eyes met, again. Dark Ellendei, to the dark ovals of the far unknown North.

"We will start with the cross of the profit... and your present influences."

Welan took the top card in her strong fingers turning it in a simple motion as she placed it on the table. Seven swirling cups met Tarese's eye, wurms, serpents, jewelry, appeared in each, peeking above the rim to disappear from sight. She saw men of beauty, castles, the Seat of the Wizard King Geobal, or so it seemed, and from another cup emblems of honor, wreathes of Mernnon, and the Chivalric Orders of the Ellendei. They swirled about each other in a red and yellow mist. Like the powders and smokes that filled the halls of Berelan during, the mask she had attended. Skulls and devils reflected in the gold of the floating goblets as they spun about the mist. Within all a veiled figure, herself she thought, struggled to find which cup was for her, which untainted.

A second card filled her mind, as Welan's fingers fidgeted it across the face of the cups, adding more goblets to her view. Two individuals bearing ladened goblets exchanged the vows of love beneath a pair of struggling aspes, one white and one black. Eothan filled her mind and then the demands of her station and the pawing ogling nobles of Berelan. Like lions they slavered at the thought of a kill.

Three cards? She knew not, the lion like nobles had grown staffs, wands, branches that freighted her, accosting her as she was about to exchange goblets with the young man from the second card. She dodged and ducked, assailed on all sides, she struggled on bravely, her full vessel at her feet.

Her mother Maltitia Aquin, robed and wearing the crown of her family sat on a lion decorated thrown, staff in hand, flowers blooming at her feet. Having not seen her mother, but once, since she left the family returning to a nunnery near Saint Loth, Teresa was surprised, startled, her face held the same sad kindness a distant, out of the world look that she remembered from her childhood. She appeared as she had before she under her long journey. Maltiita had become a pilgrim, first retreating to the nunnery then, traveled to the White Plains, where she now lived with her son Ruick, Warder of the White Plains, Defender of the Halls of

Justice. The women on the throne smiled benevolently, speeding Teresa as she warded herself from the staffs. Holding out a hand the Queen of Aquin handed her daughter her own staff, the wand she herself carried. Teresa no longer dodged, blocking and parrying the attacks instead.

Wielding the staff she gained advantage, soon accompanying a metal clad knight as he nobly protected a new chalice, much like the goblet she had begun to exchange with Eothan, beaten once, the staff wielding attackers became pursuers as they allies fled before them. At times the knight was Eothan, at times someone else. Tarese's proficiency increased, the staff transforming into a knight's broadsword.

"That was the cross of the Profit... do you want to go on... a trace into the future?"

Teresa blinked she was again in Rotwart, the cards on the table paralleled the vision. The page with five swords, the knight of chalice, and the Queen of wands.

"Yes I wish to know more she said."

Welan turned over the next card, lying it close. Teresa celebrated, as she spun, holding goblets of wine high, laughing with friends she knew not.

A feast, a celebration, revolved about, her mind a celebration for her Teresa de Gent, robes were bought, a red boar emblem flew on high. Pillars all about alternated in white and black marble, imported from where, she did not know. An acolyte placed a silver moon at her feet.

"Priestess of Moon and Night! "Called her followers. Then she toiled alone and wandered in shadowed lands far to the north, and deep in the bowels of the earth. Papers, parchments, scrolls, and, bound books, tombs through which she poored, hexes, spells, rituals, and, pentigrams, an endless work. Gathering them in her arms, she struggled to return to the safety of her temple, as she made a steady but difficult progress, the vision faded.

Welan smiled, her eyes gleaming.

"The cards, speak." Her hands wafted above the line she had built along the side of the cross. Teresa, caught the three dancing chalices, the enthroned priestess, and many wands under her, not wanting the vision to return she smiled back to her hostess steadying in the gaze of the diviner.

"Come we shall walk. "

Welan grasped Teresa with one hand and lifted her to stand. The lady's grip was solid and she lifted the royal Ellendei with a force that left Tarese's joints with no work to do till they found themselves locking into place, upright. Still distracted Welan lead her out of the room. Slipping into sandals, they walked around the landing to where, behind another door, they climbed a tightly spiraling thin wooden stair.

On the floor above a series of windows in the roof lit a sparse workshop, here an assembly of astrolabes, telescopes, and one long table were the only furnishings.

"Now we find your chalice knight... his name? "

"Eothan the Fair.. he is a Norcadian... A Corserite monk from Corsinia."

"Tonight we will know more yet there is work...I need preparation...........Now about that walk. "She spoke as she scribbled notes in ink on a parchment lying across the table. "We have some nice gardens about the manor... shall we see?"

They left the house, Teresa re-donning her leather boots, strolling about the confines of Rotwart Manor, autumn turning trees, drooping willow, and a great variety of bush and herb to please their eyes and noses. Rock was used to a pleasing degree, arranged into benches, boarders, and a trickling stream bed. A gravel garden of sorted size stone created a calm refuge from the distant sounds of the manor's yeomanry.

After walking the entire layout, the two noble ladies found themselves feeding giant carp in the moat. Here the garden fed out through an arch, to creep along the water's edge. The great fish wallowed in the shallow water floating slowly to the surface, to gulp down lumps of doe, then disappear in the brown blue haze. The sun, sinking, passed under the canopy of high cloud, and here, in this southern lowland it warmed Teresa de Gent, daughter of Genru Starborn, Keeper of the Hidden Land.

The messenger was out of breath when he found them. A boy from the Manor. An official from the King, a herald of Ottar awaited them in the Rotwart council chamber. Ngrath Menterne away, they wished Welan to receive the guest.

The pair walked back directly taking a short cut across the manors grassy yard, finding the ornately dressed and baton carrying herald standing patiently in the manor's comfortable wooden hall.

"My steed remains ready lady Welan Montana... I ha' a message from Ottar to deliver and many leagues to ride before I rest.....

Hear then, that our grace, King Ottar the third
of that name, he that is most forgiving,
a mighteous lord, of tower and sword,
dost me, to thee, his subjects thus disperse.
On all Saint's day, a week and Friday hense,
to the Red Towers, a trial of combat,
there for thee to witness, Uuk de Vishi,
and Davide de Clune, contest in arms,
a point of honored Ellendei law,
excommunicate or saint? By the sword,
a Corser Abbot's fate shalt stand or fall!

The blood of Arraken disputes his life,
Primate stands with Drake, Prince Uuk with Corser.
Maub a house of repute, dread doom curses,
in a traitor's nest. Mernnon's first warrior,
wilt thou like rebellious Oritand be?
Or, dost thou stand for honor and true God?
A heart for the blessed, wrongly accused,
with sharpened blade canst thee face down Davide,
a knight of Drake, Chivalric Lance Order,
wise in years, and meated with war's vanity,
a rumored soldier of Ergedh's battle?
Chivalry contends with nobility,
the primacy with monastic abbots,
beneath the forgiving's gold diadem,
to high God will the judgment deliver,
Saint Thomas the young, or foul murderer?
To the Red Towers we call thee Ellendei,
a combat of arms, our honors true call."

Welan and Teresa looked at each other, Teresa scratched the dark hair on her head, Thomas was Eothan's Abbot, what was going on?

CHAPTER 12

PAS DES ARMES

With hundred knight supported by squire and sergeantry stationed behind them at Awell Keep, Davide and his forty mounted personnel rode confidently along the winding road to The House of Maub. Dry aspen forests, filled the valleys between shrub tufted hills.

The northern road followed the clear shallow watered Dowen, that bubbled from the ground West of the East Weald, to cascade into the gorge, opposite the Pinnacle of Parnassus. The Dowen was just a trickle compared to the mighty falls of Parnassus, that called to it from across the gorge's mighty chasm. According to travelers who tasted from its waters, its clear refreshing cool was preferable to any water to the west. A dwarf built overlook provided a place for the thirsty wayfarer to dip empty flask and water skin, before mounting the Gnome Gondola, that rode the steam cable across the Gorge.

Dowen Manor had almost certainly reported the Abydosian troop movements, and scouts of the troop had ridden ahead on fleet footed steeds to watch for an armed resistance. Without armor, their needling explorations should warn of any trouble. Davide's men displayed the banner of their order, a golden lance on blue. Personnel arms were worn on shield only, softening the violent appearance of their incursion. Flying, no state's flag, the Order of the Lance trotted past Mernnonian village, and thorp, to the frightened, bemused, and even jovial faces that peered over fence, hedge, and wall.

The darker hair and eyes of Mernnon, and their less acute features followed closely the out numbered knights, as they traveled deeper into foreign territory. A generation earlier, they had been at war, the able bodied of these peaceable hamlets toting weaponry in the ranks of Oritand.

Davide rode in front, Jorin close behind, the dark blue of de Clune's order blanketed Toretell's surcoat. The green dragon tailed spike of Ergedh clearly told all that he rode for his duke, Herigar Gunarson, Lord of Drakes. Yellow and black plumes feathered in the wind, capping the crest of his visored helm. He joked as they rode, and was clearly happy to be on his way to an important example of his own honor.

Sheep and goat were rounded up, kept well off the roadway. By lunch they had left the winding dirt and rock tracks of the border land and reached the pathed "Way of Maub".

The Heathen Tyrant, a large travel inn had prepared for them. About a league from the Rwellia Bridge, the Inn had set up tables in its enclosed courtyard, meats, bread, cheese, fruit, and carrots, a cold fare for knights willing to part with a silver penny. A light mead was included, to wash out the dust of Mernnon's autumn.

The Inn ran by a family of Mernnonian's sprawled like many Mernnonian structures, saving second and third stories for a gatehouse, and two modest corner turrets. The Inn flowed from open garden space to columned and buttressed chamber, then toward its back wall a long stairway led to a collection of separate hut sized dwellings that cluttered over the roof. All rentable for another silver penny.

Knights eat heartily many paying the inn for the commercial fare. The squires less free with money, managed an occasional jug of mead, dipping into their saddle bags for dried meats, bread and cheese. Davide himself stayed apart without entering the Inn's compound. He and the sergeants and knights of his order discussed their position and various contingency escape plans should they by chance meet armed opposition.

Their flags not being those of conquest, they expected none.

Mustering the metal clad Ellendei, Davide thought of his youth on the island of Clune, to the south. The isolation of the island, and his early training as a monk. His father, Robert, had pushed him into the life of the cloth wishing him to follow in his own devout footsteps.

Davide rebelling against the confines of the Arician clergy, found solace for a time in the Most Holy Order of the Knight Protectors of the One. Then, finally, he left the church entirely to fight alongside the knights of Herigar Gunerson. His early training had prepared him well, and familiar with the traditions of the church, the Duke of Drake, soon found him invaluable as an ambassador. Less war like and violent than his home-grown warriors, Davide de Clune represented the closest thing to a holy fighter that Drake could count amongst its vassals.

Mounted, the knights resumed the journey East. Forests of aspen, beech and alder, stretched to the North, interrupted by dry heather, and brush covered hillsides. As the afternoon turned toward evening and the falling sun elongated the hills of South central Mernnon, they came into view of the Mouse of Maub.

Silhouetted, a crest a lone hill, that grew within the long Maub valley half covered in dry forest, its height easily equaled the hills that ringed the horizon. Lights glinted, shooting along the statues and gargoyles that decorated the prodigious house, brightening their glowering visages, a threat to all who challenged Maub of Mernnon; embedded glass or jewel eyes? They clopped on, the heavy iron ladened steeds, slow after a hard day of work. Chaplain of the Order of the Lance, had encouraged the most lagging of the troop with a few stiff words and a prayer. In this way none of the horse had needed rest, the whole troop could stand behind their champion, making good time toward their goal.

The road spiraled about the mount of Maub, three complete times, tracing leagues with each curve. A massive stone tower round and blocky, straddled the road at the second circle. Steep, jagged cliffs and rough rock made an assault from the road nearly impossible, artificers, war machines, magick or trickery, were all that could conquer the first House of Mernnon. Any army on her roadway were sitting ducks for catapult, ballista or arrow.

Forming a double line, knights and squires beside each other, they ascended. Stones rumbled, clacking down the rock of the steep sided hill, reminding them they were not alone; spears, and helms of Mernnonian troops appeared above the line of rock, to disappear, a cascade of lose pebble, evidence to their vigilant watchfulness.

As they marched the slow sun left the valley below, rounding a great circle about the hill they crossed the shadow of the sun back into the dull autumn burning light. Silver shined and glinted from their armor, blinding back toward the bronze and gold of Mernnonian cuirass and shield. Along their towers and cliff tops, crenelations full, they watched the steady progress of the Ellendei beneath them. Their progress was slow after the day of ridding the dark line of night threatening to catch them again before they reached the tower gate.

High, the hill of Maub remained caught bright and warm in the mild autumn rays, as around all darkened. The sphere of sun, chariot of fire was now descending to trace its plumed course through a tortured path of the lands beneath. Unsurpassed in height the mountains of the far north cast great shadows along the valley. It lay far to the north the cavernous entrance to the underworld that Apollus would steer his divine chariot thorough to emerge in the southern seas by morn.

As the troupe rose above the hills that ringed the vale of Maub, the collected Ellendei spied the golden globe, the last day's sun again. Low in the sky, near it must be, by now to the monstrous cavern that chambered its voyage down and to the south-west. For the night it would warm Hell with its passing light, before furious it would again climb to the North-Eastern heavens by tomorrow again.

The hammered iron doors lay bared, gray and white stone of the tower's thirty passes of height, cold, immovable, in the dark shadow of dusk. The chargers snorted, steam and fume, rose from their hot hides, as the soldiers of Maub starred down from the gate. Arrow slits before watched quietly.

Davide stiffened pushing up on his stirrups and looking up toward the house far above them. He was sure that soldiers stationed on the shear rock above could dispatch his whole band with falling rubble, without even reaching for a weapon. Toretell, pranced beneath him, when he settled Davide lifted both hands to his helmet and removing it, he placed it under his arm. The plume sat snugly against his forearm's plated chain.

No wind, the strength of Maub remained still, quiet. Cold, the night's creeping shadow caught them there, darkening the roadway and gate then swallowing the Ellendei in its black. As the scouts moved along the marching order lighting torches against the dusk, Davide broke the calm of the shuffling hill side with his voice.

"Go to the bronze and bedeviled Maub house,
clamor with trumpet and drum, here lies,
the soul of Thomas, excommunicate!
saint no more, he wilt boil in foul Hell.

Thee of Mernnon, thy too be circumspect,
a traitor's brood of princes reins thee in,
then call Uuk hence, to my arms long embrace.
Here stand I, true Chivalric Order attends,
armored in silver, teethed with steel,
beckon thy prince away to royal court,
now he must prove his stout Arraken soul,
be he a knight, then, answer me, he must,
in royal lists of Berelan Towers,
afore our king and God to judge our war,
the saint a devil, demon or hell spawn?
Simmon Primate of Arraken, say yea,
a vile murderer, traitor to the faith,
excommunicate, by blessed decree.
Then here stand I, God at my sworded side,
the flame of Arraken to smite thy lord.
Summon thee thy prince, that, his ears might,
consume, this, the chastisement of this peer,
to Berelan field I draw thee Prince Uuk,
the day of all saints blessed to our lord,
there and then do we settle this with sword.
Go to Uuk, this message take, least Abydos,
with released hate, dost ravage to thy cost.
Go, go, be gone, for though thy haft dwelled,
in these hills long, with war they be swelled.
Is Uuk to lose his land for this abbot,

or meet the case in arms at Ottar's foot?"

His voice bounced around the rock, in the new clear night sky, stars twinkled bright and crowded. It was tumultuous the sky of this age. Not knowing whether the constelations noticed the machinations, that crawled below them, the celestial sphere was ever unfathomable, it embraced Davide's attention. There, high above the valley, the solus was close enough to touch, he felt, if he steered his horse they could ride in amongst the deities, themselves. The educated saw changes in the celestial dome, noting their patterns as symbols of upcoming events, but Davide knew not the meaning of the burning gold and silver sparks that so demanded his attention.

There was no other sound beside the panting of the horse, and birds who were not yet to roost. They waited nothing came from the Mernnonian gate, no horn, no word. No offered silver jar. They sat in silence till bats began their nightly feeding, then signaling the troupe they turned and descended the hill back toward Celent.

Ottar was not amused, his new shirt had been late and now, he found himself almost resorting to phantasms to pull in the drooping gut that appeared unwanted, brazenly shouting to all that the kitchens of the Red Towers held the king's attention more than the jousting ground. He who had managed to beat Sarkhen heath keeper in single combat, could not face the honesty of his own doublet. Pulling himself in he twirled, yes it was a twirl, he did it again, just to check, yes definitely a twirl. Maybe he should decree a ball instead,

"he who danced the better, was to hold the saint."

Or, demon what was it?

Illid had been adamant, as to the Corserite's guilt no question in his mind. Then, Illid was like that.

Arching, his back didn't help, nor did slumping his shoulders. Hmh? There, he had told himself to stay off the drugs, but already his hand was in his bag of enchanted powders. Of course, he could appear as he wished, with the right powder. What if he altered the glass, and yet, that wouldn't prove a thing. Or? Enough!

"Fetch the ruddy gown."

A smartly stockinged and hosed servant nodded, slipping through the partially open double doors to make the long trek from the king's private chambers to the palace's secure wardrobe.

Ottar examined himself again in the long glass, Sardraciea Aquin, his Queen, the princess of Aricia, would be attending him in the court of Ellentroth, perfumed, handsomely, clothed in the latest Arician fashion, the stern look that crept onto her face on these occasions, freezing her lower lip. Her stare had become crystallized in his memory. Was that love? Doubtful.

He saw something else.

It told him, or so he presumed, that he was not the lord that Arecia expected. Well, what was he to do? It was Meleg not he who had appointed Simmon. He hopped the servant was quick, none of that normal Red Tower dawdling. Finishing the thought he had earlier he tossed a lump of poppied, essence powder, to the back of his throat and swallowing a wave of elation spread through his body.

Invigorated, he threw his mind out to the searching dresser, 'Hurry thy king awaits thee."

He felt the thought seek out and find its target.

As he had expected the servant was busy in gossip with two maids and a palace watchman, one of Ceroth's men. Startled the poor man broke of the conversation with a yelp, to continue his run toward the wardrobe.

The ochre was a good choice in stocking, sensible for such a somber occasion. Draken knight verses the first Prince of Maub, and for the questionable soul of a Corserite. The whole historic pride of the Corserite Order was in dispute, not to mention the lives of two noble Arrakens.

He doubted either fought with the light sword that he, in his younger days had made popular. Being a knight of

Drake, Davide de Clune was most like to use the traditional Two-handed sword that the duchy favored. Not fast, but it inflicted a deadly amount of damage with each strike.

And Uuk, what did the Mernnonians use in battle these days, the spear and short sword of Oritand the Traitor, or something more practical, the broad sword and shield like his father. Sarkhen Heath Keeper and his family were mighty warriors. Uuk, according to gossip, was nothing less in strength and prowess, the well-known and experienced Ellendei made a good match for the young prince. God would guide the outcome, as he always did in the lists of Ellentroth.

The columned and gilded hall of Ellendei reckoning, loomed, white above the shaded stone of the Red Towers. A top, the supreme peak of the citadel's island, its twenty pace walls, and forty pace turreted keep, and dungeon, looked down to a rocky south east bay, two hundred paces bellow. The apex of a great triangular cliff spur, that protected the Red Towers' inland port, and dockside, supported the blinding white majesty. The Ellendei, had named the hall Ellentroth, hall of truth. It was in these chambers that the sacred oaths of Arraken knighthood sounded. The Oaths of allegiance to the pontiff of Aricia, to the Arraken King, and the oaths of Duke and Earl, had filled the columned chamber throughout the age of Arraken.

A single marble throne sat on a carved, granite dais, a network of Arraken, warring with the foul brood of the wizard kings intricately traced the dais in deeds of glory. Here he Ottar Ediawin, the Forgiving would hear the pledges of the combatants. The lists stood before the hall, and in that tall walled enclosure, that the sun only warmed from late morning to early afternoon, challenges were fought to the death. In the height of summer, the space was well suited to the hot exchange of blows, but now with growing winter, it was a cold, unpleasant place. Especially for those watching, poor souls, the King thought.

The court was kept by the sworn Order of the Treathbaron, Aterol Atrolson's personal appointed masters of Heraldry and Arraken law. Though Aterol, far from hence in the wilderness Earldom of Darkmore, his well-chosen marshals and constables served the king in his stead. For matters of knighthood, Ellentroth and the lists were the last ground of appeal. In civil matters the Lord Chief Justice Eorowin presided over the royal court of appeal, from his province of Talchoel.

Only matters involving the king directly, as either plaintiff, or accused, required Aterol's presence itself; the king or Aterol the only Arrakens that could preside in Ellentroth.

Noble and baronial courts throughout Arraken looked to Ellentroth as the symbolic head of their judicial power, a structure parallel and beside the courts of hundred, sheriff, and justice, that were governed by Telltale.

Affixing the long robe with a silver clasp, the man servant's green eyes stayed low, an apology to his liege. The king shoed him away with a brisk hand, and after assessing the look in his long glass, he walked to an adjacent chamber, choosing a talisman from an enchanted and locked chest.

Curved metal designs ringed the exterior with Thaition symbols and devices, the Zymosian ambassador had made a gift of the strong box at Ottar's wedding.

Returning to his place, before the only real mirror in his chambers, he sized up the talisman's effect. The carefully prepared and Gnome crafted full length glass reflected the two pace tall liege in his gold adorned stocky glory.

"Crown. "he said trying to put chagrin in his voice.

Taking it from the maroon gold hinged pillow, that the servant hefted with the utmost reverence he placed it securely on his head. A band of gold, sharp filigreed lace work pointed skyward, gems and diamonds from Derem Goria imbedded throughout. He had worn it since the death of his farther Arandar Eiadwin, twenty years earlier. A feeble cripple, Meleg had fought revolt and war his long sixty year rein, marrying a Gunerson late, he saved the thrown, and increased the strength of his line with Elfen blood. Virile as a youth Ottar had consolidated power, avoiding revolt by supporting the Primacy, and bowing to the wishes of his warlike duke, Herigar.

Pushing, at his hair, he pulled the curly auburn locks back from blue green eyes, that he had inherited from his mother. Lines, deepening on his face showed him to be in the later prime, for an Ellendei, thrice a score of years. It was considered a blessing that his people lived longer than most. Ottar proud of his sixty-six years, resolved that it was time to rule. Why keep them waiting any longer?

No matter the outcome there would be trouble, Illid, his Chancellor, alley to Simmon, was bound to be hoping for the Corserites excommunication, Ceroth the Good, on the other hand disliked Berelan, he always urged caution, much like the Pope in Aricia. No matter what God had in mind, they would soon know, and he, and the treasury, were sure to be left with some bill or other, especially if Berelan was unhappy. Things always cost more when at odds with Berelan, it had become the theme of his reign.

He thought of the first Arraken king placing the crown on his head, after the defeat of Traitia, the first of the Wizard King's to fall, over eight hundred years ago, and his present exchequer steadily marking of the expenditures of his, Ottar III's reign. The feudal bureaucracy had grown no end since the Wizard Wars, now more a stock exchange than a fighting brotherhood.

The Corserites were an order long before the wars, evolving with the worship of the One. According to legend, they started as the Course Writes, those who passed between ships of the exodus, carrying directions from vessel to vessel.

Simmon, Primate of Berelan, must know that, and more, Ottar presumed. Illid Scourge of Pellia, often touted the primates wishes. the king had politely listened to his chancellor, while the Scourge explained his thoughts on the matter, that the realm was taxed already, what with Drake waging war to reclaim his land of Thornbreak, disputed with Serderan, and fighting men of Davide and Uuk's caliber rare, he urged constraint perhaps Ottar could decree that the Primate should arbitrate the matter. Ceroth had not agreed nor had Thomas Aquin chancellor of the Exchequer. Sentol the Great, keeper of the privy seal, remained silent on the matter.

Ottar was not willing to challenge the authority of Ellentroth, and the traditional power of Ellendei nobility, to stand before the hall and God to circumvent law through his aging sword. Rare, in the rolls of history, were cases in which the king had intervened, and then he had the consent of the Treathbaron. In this case Ottar was sure that Aterol was to side with the Corserite Abbot, and if he Ottar followed the primate, it would be he and Aterol clashing swords. In the minds of the people, he might be the finest swordsman in the land, bar Herigar, but Ottar was not willing to chance his luck. Not against the Treathbaron, and not on an issue that could very easily be fought to the fatality of the loser.

Knights who fell unconscious defending their honor, were sometimes drug from death by the attending physicians, and the work of monk and chirgeon, yet they were never quite the same again. The scars of combat in Ellentroth far deeper than the marks born on the skin. Like prime cockerels beaten by a lesser cock for the first time, they lose their will to life. Or to win in life. It depended on the knight.

Davide and Uuk would decide this one, Illid could rant to his hearts content, there was to be no challenge to Ellendei feudal law while he reined, not with the duchy, amassing the largest army to be seen since the Wizard Wars, and on their own west boarder. It was true that the Wyred protected his demesne but Herigar had dragons and ships could be bought.

Buckling Boreshelek, Flame Sword of the Arraken crown, about his waist he departed his chambers. The servant hurried after catching the kings long silvered, gold rimmed maroon train, lofting it from imagined snags in the stone work of the palace floor.

Deciding to walk, they made their way through the palace grounds, well-groomed trees and hedges, past rose bushes in autumn's last bloom, and private lines of the royal poppy swarmed in over flowing beds. The poppy, a symbol of his family for two hundred years, was a commodity well-guarded and controlled by the Ellendei Royalty. Mixed with the highest priced Berelan wines, and also the basis for a popular intoxicating mead, the poppy was both valued for trade and effect, the relaxing trance it induced, craved by scholar, monk and noble alike. Working people were dissuaded from its use, it was considered to make them lazy and distant, but not so the trading class, who jealously relished and bartered the plant. Not like the sunroot, a drug imported and sold on the underground throughout the south. Addictive this drug was common and used much among the commons, reducing the tedium of their lives, also considered to make them lazy, it was politically unpopular.

Sunroot was numbing, stupefying, not the visionary elixir that the royalty cultured. Considered illegal and a threat to productivity sunroot never the less found its way into the streets of manor, village, and, city alike. Ottar had worried little about it. Illid had persuaded him early that the clergy were better suited to fight the problem than was he.

Through a small door in the palace garden wall, they ascended the stair of one of the citadel's lofty red towers. Staggering to the top, out of breath, they rested under the eaves of an arched court yard, who's cobble stones often rang with the chimes of sword and shield practice. Then crossing the stones, they came upon the hall of Ellentroth from behind, avoiding its gate and descending into its catacombic basement where generations of Arraken king lay beside Treathbaron, in never ending sleep.

The mosaicked walls of Ellentroth, flashed with the flicker of torch, casting the war grimaced faces of its ancient knights in a dim half-light. They debarked from exodus ships, to protect the Ellendei's first priests, calling a crusade to punish Thasia, after the murder of the Profit. And after establishing the city of saint Augustia they fought the centuries of war against the growing malice of the Wizards. Forging the Oaths of Arraken Knighthood, and battling wurm and monstrosity. The Mernnonian princes pledged their fealty unto Arraken, and the dragon passed with help of the dwarf forged Thagbite, bane of wurms.

His eyes glanced about. Then they took the short stair that took them into the Courtyard of Challenge, that housed the single list, and dueling ground. How long had he kept them waiting. Most were already seated and no one was still arriving. Too long for a king of the Ellendei, his inner voice chided him. The stair ended out of site directly behind his list-throne. Walking from behind, he paced the edge of the dais, the servant moving aside his train as he swished back to sit. A raised hub-hub indicated that his arrival was anticipated.

The throne was cold, uncomfortable, not a bit like his throne that stood aside his Queen's in the palace conference chamber. The martial of Ellentroth frowned somewhat, not launching into his ritual greeting as spiritedly as Ottar hoped. It was Ottar's citadel, but the keep of Ellentroth was ruled by Darkmore. Brown eyes, jet black hair feathered from beneath the gold conical helm, read him with contempt, and not thinly masked. Humph.

A strange breed these strict dark haired Ellendei from the north, hardened by their years of war with the spawn of the Imprisoned One, or so it was said.

Queaidell Chattelie, Marshal of the Realm, lord of the king's army caught the uncomfortable glance of his liege, and finding support there, Ottar stayed feeling reassured that he commanded more than this historic hall. Illid stood close, his blue gray eyes bright in the long curls of graying brown locks.

The blonde of Ceroth, drew him to the assembly's rear, where he recognized a collection of Ellendei, Terese de Ghent, daughter of the master of his own order, his older brother, Genru Starborn of the Irdiwin Lodge, why was she here? An attractive young woman, he wondered why his niece did not tend him at court as much as she could. His brother's commitment to the Unknown Land and its chemical research had precluded him entering the Ellendie knighthood or accepting the crown. It had fallen on his to be the diplomat and warrior. He looked about at his peers, she had not able to keep pace with the revelry, no doubt. Ottar III smiled, even the youth had trouble keeping up. Thomas Aquin he saw there talking, next to his niece.

The nobility was decked in all the finery of their strong boxes, gold, and silver trinkets hung, thick. Amulets, and ornaments of state draped from shoulder, and eyes looked back and forth settling between he and the stalling marshal of Ellentroth.

Why didn't he get on with it?

Fine he had made the point Ottar the Forgiving had been late, well was not that his prerogative, being king. The two knights stood still and quiet at his feet.

Prince Uuk wore a bronze cuirass, with plate leggings, a shining gold shield hung on his arm, the sable sash and high left square of Mernnon broke the shield from under the coronet of the first-born son. Davide, somber in the traditional chain plate strengthened hauberk of Ergedh. No shield, a single two-handed great sword hung on his back. A squire, Jorin, Ottar thought his name, carried a shield for the knight, painted with the lance, emblem of his order.

Ottar knew Davide, he was the champion Drake used as ambassador, and had often carried news between the king and the noble bellicose Herigar. Raised across the bay in Clune, a distant and barren monastery, the home to a hundred monks and the peasant families that supported them. He was far less wild, than many of Drake's knights, rarely resorting to arms in the pursuit of diplomacy.

"Hear hearts of Arraken heed my summons,
for dost thee sit on Ellentroth's high height,
sea blown peak, in wind that haft brought thee nigh,
to litter the soil in thy fertile blood,
brood of kings, sons of lord, God thy sovereign,
for truth we stand, Treathbaron's chosen few,
marshals beyond court, justice, sheriff, tax,
Aterol Aterolson, Ottar Eidawen,
thee we plea, afore holy God to see,
a bout of honor, contest in drawn sword,
declare to God, these Arraken shall here.
Davide de Clune appellant art thee,

state thy case clear, brave, true, and resolute,

for thy challenge is met on Uuk's sharp sword."

The marshal had finally begun, Ottar noticed that his name was given the second billing, not always the case. Spying his unhappy queen in the crowd he tried not to let her notice his attention, she was with their unmarried daughter, Tarren. The fairest of their children, she could be called blonde, though a red tint showed her to be more Ellendei than Norcadian. Beginning to reach the Ellendei age of maturity he was searching her a husband, Ottar had no male children, as yet, and his wife was angered he could tell from here, perhaps because he and his vanity had missed another fine opportunity at diplomacy with some of the more distant, and better respected Ellendei families. She wanted him here shmoozing before festivities started.

Stepping forward toward dais, crown, and marshal, Davide de Clune stared up at the lords, then, brazenly he spoke his oath.

"Davide de Clune, a knight commander,

of the right most Chiveralous Lance Order,

subject of Drake, and true Arraken King,

for God, ready in arms do I here stand,

an issue of honor in Arraken law,

betwixt noble rivals contentions lie,

and to God, Ellentroth, the Treathbaron,

pledge I, my cause be just, weighty true,
in the name of Drake, Simmon our Primate,
demand we our charge the damned Abbot.
Thomas the Young, a saint be he no more,
but dark murderer his soul condemned,
vilified spawn of the Imprisoned One.
His flask be mine by right of primal law,
an imprisoned demon for mighty Drake.
A double hand sword wilt cleave this traitor,
Uuk of Mernnon, of miscreants coffers,
for Oritand and Corserite dost he here die."

The marshal looked to Uuk, who though the larger built of the two knights, was inexperienced compared to his opponent. His black hair sweat wet against his forehead; he stood tall, confident that he was fighting for right. He offered a small prayer to Appolus, with whom he had talked in the throne room of Maub before his journey south.

"Uuk de Vishi, first born Prince of Mernnon,
state the case that thee Arraken, defend here,
or, to thy oath, thy youth, do we all call,
your God, Treathbaron, King, and we thy peers?"

Uuk gave the crowd and King a quick look, and without moving he uttered, his reply, the words warbling slightly with a thick Mernnonian accent.

"For my gods, and thine, Enruth the holy,

here stand I afore the king and marshal,
to defend this gracious, reverend abbot,
Thomas the Young, wrongfully accused,
imprisoned perforce, by cruel trollish hands.
He held aloft the silver lead capped vessel.
Deliver I to thee this blessed shrine,
to guard, whilst I with callused might,
a noble of Drake's misguided violent arm,
to free a fine pure soul happily fight.
No quiver of fear, no timid retreat,
but, craven opposition to evil's blight.
Noldarn first born learned me god's true sight
Seek not for me till the battle be done!"

Stepping up to the marshal he knelt on bended knee, offering the silver flasked prison of the saint into the safe keeping of the Treathbaron's men. Rising, he followed a herald of Ellentroth out of the great hall to the grassy listed enclosure, that lay at the foot of its columned stair. Similar to the steps of the Kadron temple of Mernnon, Ellentroth mimicked slightly the architecture of Uuk's people, adding the flavor of the ship bound new comers to its ancient reverence.

The small throng of nobility and sergentry that attended the challenge assembled, covering the gray stone of Ellentroth's steps. King and Queen, now together, took their places in a wood framed stand that abutted the great East wall, opposite the hall. The royal Ellendei collected around them filling the small stand. In front stood the marshal, the lists laying lengthwise between them and the crowded steps.

Well drained, and guarded by high walls from the onslaught of the driving autumn rains, that blew in off the sea, the field of Ellentroth, was damp from a morning shower evaporating to mist. A light fog that clung about gray columned towering stone, softened the light. Uuk and Davide stood at opposite ends of the lists a herald of the Treathbaron escorted each. As the gathering settled, Marshal, Thomas' prison jar under his arm, turned, the carved oak baton of Ellentroth lay nestled in the crook of his elbow.

"On pain of banishment no Arraken,
be so reckless, insolent, to brave the fray,
nor, to touch the field and lists, less be he,
of Ellentroth's proud service. Hail Aterol
Atrolson! Treathbaron of the Ellendei!"

From their place beside Ellentroth's massive granite gate, two of Ellentroth's sergeants rode forward on heavy brown white face lined horses, dressed in light armor, and to the flourish of trumpet, they each bore a set of three lancing spears. Hoofs thumped dully in the moist ground of the immaculate sod. Thudding to a stop, they bowed to their sovereign and turning, about with a shower of earth clod they presented their weapons for inspection. The marshal touched each with the baton of Ellentroth saying, as each dismounted to present personnel arms and armor.

"Go bear these lances hence, to Arraken,

that God may settle the declared dispute."

Trumpets sounded again as each knight mounted to receive his first lance. Jorin stayed close baring his master's arms, the great two-handed broad sword ready.

For Uuk, Ajax Trengotte, had donned the incongruous garb of a squire, Sarkhen had not seen it politically appropriate to attend, he was to prey in their local house de Vishi, shine, to protect his son from afar. Ajax fumbled with the spears he was handed by the mounted Ellendei, passing the first to Uuk.

"It be blessed my prince. "He whispered.

"I trust in Appolus. "Replied Uuk.

With a crescendo of trumpet, the combatants hefted lances and urging their steeds on they charged, picking up speed on the soft clod of Ellentroth scaring its surface with mud.

Steady in the saddle Uuk aimed his lance to the upper center of his opponent's shield, the chief pale or so the Ellendei named it.

Davide the more skilled jouster, leaned away from his opponent aiming to the dead middle of Uuk's sable dashed kite shield, the fess pale. He hopped the full force of his horse would knock his younger opponent back and out of his saddle.

Both lances shattered, the tips splintering a third of the way down the shaft.

Rounding next to the opponents' squires, they recovered shaking off the shock of impact. Spurs wheeled the chargers back down the lists passing each other on the way to their next lance.

The combat would be to the death, till one either passed out, died or, recanted, before the assembled Ellendei. Snatching the next spear they again charged, the gallop of their destriers, fast, cushioned and sure in the sodden grass. Uuk's mottled white and gray stallion brightened the dark courtyard under the overcast Arraken sky.

Toretell's stern snorts challenged the Mernnonian steed for his master's charge.

Pulling his shield low and aiming high Davide's lance impacted Uuk's throat gorget knocking him back, Uuk had leaned away from the attack, and though his own shot struck home to the far side of Davide's shield, shattering there fess, he fell. Flopping precariously along the back of his horse, one foot lose from its stirrup, he flailed the air with leg and arm.

Beneath him the destrier moved to counter act his momentum, anticipating the motion. Bouncing from its back, his strong stripped leg pulled the weight of his fall, armor and all back toward the saddle, as a gauntlet hand clutched under saddle pommel, leg and arm together flexed against the fall pulling himself upright to an answering gasp from the crowd.

They passed each other again on the way to the third and final lance.

Thundering around the lists, Davide was ahead, reaching a faster velocity than his opponent. Uuk had steadied himself center in the saddle and managed to aim his lance at the outer fess of de Clune's shield. The tested knight aimed to bellow Uuk's visored helm, hopping to repeat his late success. The faster horse rose high above the grass clod, sending his rider's shot wild, remaining low and clam Uuk shattered his lance into the shield of his enemy. Both remained calm, low in saddle, Uuk had shattered three lances and Davide two, but Uuk had been unseated, almost falling.

Ridding at a trot they returned their horses to their respective squires and without wasting time switched to foot weapons.

Uuk drew his Arraken broadsword, and hefting his shield forward sternly returned to the lists. Davide had snatched a Draken two handed great sword and already began his brandished approach. They stayed to the king's side of the list, quickly closing the ground between them.

Both wielded heirlooms, the great sword from the dragon catches of Ergedh, and Uuk's broadsword from the ancient troves of Maub. Enchanted silver, and iron to meet itself, in the field of Ellentroth.

Stalking about, they feinted, skilled warriors looking for an opening.

Ducking and leaping forward with a stride the two-handed weapon struck first. Davide had lunged toward Uuk's shield side and then dipped smashing into the shieldless side of the Prince's cuirass. Uuk was driven back deflecting a sequence of follow through with shield and sword.

Finally, getting his feet under him Uuk met the power of the two-handed sword with the great strength of his mighty legs, refusing to be backed further he took the sword on his shield cutting into the back of Davide's chain hauberk with a slash from his broadsword. Davide twisted back, spinning to crash through the single biting sword, but the great two-handed sword was deflected from the bronze cuirass, protected by his houses enchanted metal. Uuk, pulled up his shield to again block a shower of blows from Davide de Clune.

Readying his sword defensively, to deflect a reply attack that the prince directed to his upper body, Davide faltered, as Uuk broke the defense, deftly out maneuvering the slower weapon, to reach down, with a sweep, slicing the plate of Davide's leggings.

Pulling the great sword down the Ergedian followed Uuk's blow, twirling the sword circularly through the air, and then thrusting it up, and inside Uuk's shield arm. He smashed into the bronze cuirass, denting it as he again drove the Prince back, a number of paces. Pushing the advantage the knight spun a blow sailing over the shield, then continuing on at the Mernnonian they traded blows back and forth as Uuk retreated backwards toward the stand. The two-handed sword flu fast back and forth as David alternated with parrying with slight flicks to the left and right. Uuk's shear strength was able to neutralize the strikes to his shield and blunt the sword when it parried.

Changing tactics, Uuk stepped forward and in a controlled thrust he impaled the out stretched and exposed arm of the two-handed sword wielding Arraken. Blood spurted about the epuliere and rerebrace of his armor. The crowd shouted with empathy, grumbling, then excited its assessment bounced about the arena. Both combatants had supporters. Shouting a growl, Davide answered with a double handed swipe that cut deep into the Prince's cuirass, cracking the metal carving it back into soft flesh. Recoiling they both breathed heavily.

Little blood showed along the Prince's torso and red gushed from the deep puncture wound in Davide's arm. Their eyes met, Davide flinching as his arm dropped leaving the hilt of his two-handed weapon. The point of his sword fell, digging into the sod at the feet of the King's stand.

Davide stepped back fighting pain, he drug the sword with his one good arm. Uuk pulled himself tall and as he fought pain wracking his own chest he struggled after the retreating knight. Davide did not look well, blood now covered his left arm, and he preyed out load as he backed up.

"Oh lord show the benevolent glory of thy.."

Uuk screamed, and lifting his sword high he spun grasping it with both hands to increase the force of its momentum. Davide still praying lifted his sword parrying the attack as he retreated.

".....supreme omnipresence ....cure.. me.."

Speaking, each word he stepped back parrying a swarm of blows from the prince. The great sword was held close in a diagonal defense across his body, and he tried no offensive moves. Earlier he had held it vertically, blocking with a sideways flick and attacking with sweeps and downward thrusts, now the blood pouring from his arm took his attention.

".....thy eternal servant ....Davide de Clune...knight of the Order of.....Lance."

Attacking with both hands on his broadsword, Uuk drove the Ergedhian still further, backward, they had almost reached the wood beams of the list, the King's stand lay far behind, Davide stumbled backwards twisting on his ankle, and falling to one knee. His great sword knocked back by Uuk's shield the Prince descended with a two-handed sweep that cut into the middle of his chain hauberk.

Grabbing his chest Davide stood, and taking his great sword in two hands he traded blows weapon to weapon. Blood had stopped pouring from his arm wound.

Uuk side stepped, and as two blows from the great sword crashed against his shield, he cut into the chest of his opponent's armor, Davide's hauberk was sliced down to leather and quilted pad, absorbing the red of knight's bleeding. Falling back two paces, and holding his great sword vertical, he parried more blows from the advancing Prince of Mernnon.

Davide halted and mustering, he parried the broadsword clean out of his way as he struck Uuk's shield resoundingly. The Prince stepped back. They faced each other, knight parrying every attack as Uuk took any blows to sneak past his sword's guard harmlessly on shield. Dented it held firm, a worthy halt for the enchanted sword of Ergedh.

They Stepped back and forth, moving little as they each wore the other down, with blow, parry, and counter blow, a tiring rhythm.

As their energies spilled about them, they slowed, and began circling. The knight kept the Prince at bay with the length and speed of his weapon. When their positioning allowed, Uuk thrust his shield forward, neutralizing the great sword, and launching a series of blows with his broadsword, to be blocked by the defensive use of the great sword. On the fourth of such a flurry, Uuk broke Davide's two-handed stance, and pushing back the sword wielding arm he got inside. The knight was forced to spin, flipping about to pull his sword back uselessly before he could attack.

Simultaneously, Davide swiped upwards, as Uuk thrust toward the spinning knight at close range. Their weapons hit at once, the broad sword digging through the Ergedh's chain gorget, to cut into the bone and flesh of Davide's neck, whilst the great sword pierced the bronze cuirass, punching a hole into Uuk's lower chest and stomach. Uuk was thrown back to ground, Davide froze in place swaying slightly. Blood covered his armor, great gaps and rents, lay red, and tattered, about his neck and chest.

Uuk pulled himself backwards along the grass, trying to get his feet under him to stand, his sword held loosely and his shield limp. Davide remained still swaying as he lifted his great sword skyward.

"Uraaarrrrrrrrrrrrrrrrrrrrrghghhhhhh!"   he screamed, his utterance bouncing around Ellentroth. A fragile misted rain descended from the sea ward wall, or so he thought.

Sweeping around and down, he spun toward the retreating Prince, who rose to his feet to meet the weighted blow. It crashed upon the broadsword almost wrenching it from the young prince's grasp, pushing through its weight, hitting him in the upper chest and again sending him back.

Keeping his feet, the Prince parried again blocking the following rain of short blows that rapidly struck at him from the great sword's neutral vertical position.

Slowly now, they again poured into each other, with a series of blow and parry, nothing conclusive, but the creeping weakness that had begun to take root in their bleeding bodies. Each struggled against death, if they did not gain succor in time, they would both bleed out.

The early sounds from the onlookers had ceased. The echoing battle was all.

Davide parried a strike from the Prince, to attack with forward thrust that compacting the hardened surface of the bronze shield bounced back with all the momentum of Uuk's strength. Knocking his sword up the blade side of the handle flew, smashing his ventail bending into his visor, and crushing it against his skull.

The knight was blind. Leaping backward he struggled pulling helm from his head.

Uuk swiped the air twice pursuing the blind knight, neither thought rationally now. The cheers and shrieks of the Ellendei urged them on. He smashed back Davide's out stretched great sword and as he readied to thrust his broadsword straight through the Ergedhian, the helm fell at their feet and Davide's sword once more swept Uuk's out of its way to descend clanking on to the dented Mernnonian shield.

Stepping back again the wounded Prince tried to break past the reaching great sword to damage his foe. Catching on shield he lunged only to miss the knight as he side stepped toward the Prince. Both within the blades of the other, Davide dropped his good hand from sword, smashing the gauntleted weight into the side of Uuk's helm. The clang resounded through the silence of the courtyard. Sea mist glistened, beading on the struggling armored forms.

Staggering back Davide parried a weak blow to step around behind catching Uuk in a tight grapple under forearm and shoulder. The knight held him bringing his great sword one handedly toward the Prince's neck. Uuk desperately pushed it back with gauntlet as he turned again to keep Davide to his front. As his hand slid along the length of the blade the enchanted steel severed his little finger and the most of his third, completely. They fell to the grass unnoticed in the fray. Gauntleted they lay as two thimbles, Uuk bit his lip to control the pain.

Drawing his arm in behind shield, Uuk jumped at his opponent with all his weight, hurtling into the Ergedian who fell backwards.

Uuk kept his feet, standing. He waited for more.

There the Ergedian lay, his shallow breathing the last movement Uuk noticed.

Davide de Clune rose no more.

Uuk slumped without kneeling. He twirled on tired legs. Yes, a slow methodical twirl, Ottar was sure of it.

Uuk de Vishi, first Prince of the House of Maub had defended his honor and that of his people. Thomas deserved salvation.

Appolus could be proud. He dropped the shield and sword standing to his full height.

Physicians attended the dying Davide, as Uuk slumped toward the waiting and horrified Ajax. Who ran out to meet him.

The battle had been close. Yet, the young prince had been victorious in a pas des arms against an experienced Arraken knight, the priest hoped there would not be many more.

Uuk surveyed the onlooking nobility as, Ajax applied cotton and cloth to his bleeding.

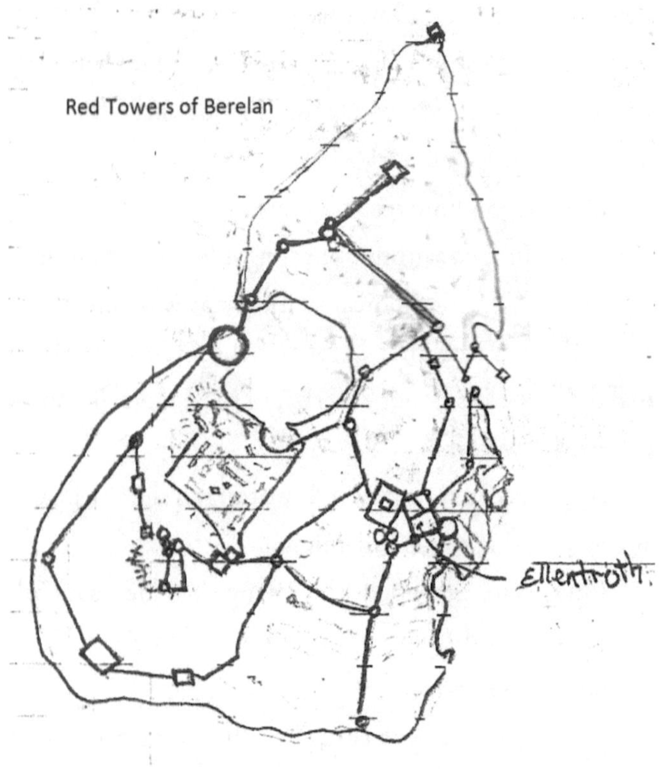

Red Towers of Berelan
Ellentroth

CHAPTER 13

BERELAN

The dew awoke him, the early dawn growing clear and bright about the buildings and walls of Geobel. He could hear distant sounds of the adjacent town floating up, burbling on the early morning wind. Shouts as milk and water carts delivered supplies from the outlying farms, and the crowing of restless chicken cocks.

Geobel a quaint and peaceful town was the royally bestowed charge of Thomas Aquin, treasurer of Ottar's Exchequer. The ancient buttressed hold of Geobel, cohort to the wizard king Parnassus, and king in his own right, towered over its small citadeled town.

Eothan found his way off its slopes to a ruined rocky wall, that rose and fell as it lead him into the town's center. Ending in a over grown and half eroded tower the warrior lowered himself from the crumbling rock to the hard dirt of Geobel town.

The street was empty, and Eothen watched the slow arrows of geese flapping quietly to the distant waters of the west. From the heights he saw the line of the king's high road dividing the land from north to south, disappearing into the foliage of Pellia. Close at the base of the mount, and on an outcropping of its hardened granite grew Niobia, sister city to Geobel. Here, Eothan could see a full three quarters of its sprawling network of buildings and the gold painted lacework of its cathedral. The large fortress circled apart in the shinning morning crystal blue of its masonry, reflecting a dark moat.

Pain from his days of battle stiffened his moves as he paced through the awakening streets. Sulfur from the towns famous spar prickled in his nose, reminding his sensitive hairs of the spiced brews mixed by the Norcadian priests of his youth. The priestess who had named him oft added her unique blends to that of their village's priest. Finding the main gate he left Geobel, descending the three leagues of roadway that crisscrossed the mountain till they reached a road before the town. He rested, stretching tight awakening muscles. League stones marked the juncture, and following a compunction deep in his heart he turned south, striding toward Arraken's capital of Berelan.

The visions of a stage coach had faded, and now the spires and hymns of Simmon's Primacy filled the sights and sounds of his mind. Thomas was there he could feel it, the awareness crept up his arms from the staff of

Corser, demanding his attention, dwelling in the recesses of his thoughts, now rested and alone they urged him on toward the hub of the snake's power.

The towered gate bridge of Niobia stood behind him, Leon forest spread north from the city, a green and gold turning blanket, the brown weathered rock of Swede Morte, breaking its waves in the morning light. The sky was mottled, thick banks of cloud pushed south along the chasm of the great gap to collide with banks gathering in the west above the marsh land of Rotwart. Here north, there were patches of blue in the middling morning but toward Berelan the banks converged sending themselves plummeting upwards into the stratosphere. Blue gray yellow and black thickened the banks, and their rumbling convulsions threatened an autumn thunder shower.

Not cold for Eothan, he established a pace that would rapidly take him out off the hill land of Niobia and down into the plains of Pellia. Heather, bracken and course scrub turned to the dry dead golden barley corn, and grasses that provided a staple diet for Arraken's growing population.

Looking south the king's road stretched toward the sea in a long arc. Little but a group of hills between him and its wide unknown expanse. To the east a yellow brown line that marked the great gorge dissected the land following the moving banks of cloud toward Berelan. The tree tufted hills and valleys of Abydos marked the distant horizon beyond.

Eothan chose to leave the high road here and instead run at time and a half pace through the plane lands of Pellia. Pellia's many and varied thorps and hamlets were clear to see, dark spots in a well farmed plain. The lack of tree cover allowed him a relatively straight route toward the capital. He marked good time.

Passed fences of farms, skirting behind animal stalls carrying only his weapons and rope, he maintained a steady pace. He followed footpaths worn for centuries by the simple folk of Pellia. At one point he took a jog over the arched stone bridge of a village, and ducked down the narrow cart filled alley before the mill.

"Stanger!" came a shout from a boy sitting in the driver's seat of a large cart. Before he could call again Eothan had ducked amongst the small trees that grew along the village's river bank. Emerging south, by passing buildings, he again ran, out into cut fields that stretched here across Pellia. Avoiding tracks and what few roads he found, and occasionally hiding whilst a passerby or group of farm laborers crossed his path, he traveled across the miles of land surrounding the northern approach to the capital in secret.

Before nightfall he had climbed the scattered hill land of central Pellia, from where he got a good view of the buttressed basalt pillars that comprised the hundreds of feet walls of Arraken's great gorge, north the thin line of Parnassus Pinnacle visible dark against the gray sky. He had run quickly through the southern flat lands to reach the olive and orange orchards of southern Pellia.

Here he rested and sneaking amongst the huts and stores of the fruit pickers he stole for himself a meal. Their happy voices lifted his heart, as they married with the famous mead of the area, sang to the night. The fine Berelan crafted flutes, and lyre imported from Mernnon glided their tunes through the leaves of the orchard. These sounds pleased as he listened tunes boisterous and fun, full of glee from the past harvest.

The orchards smells were new to him, apples being the only fruit to grew well around the monastery. Orange, he was unfamiliar with, it played upon his sinuses, awakening his face with its hungry tingle, pleasant.

Not full, he satiated himself from the trees. The last of the harvest he thought as he walked on toward Berelan. The Gorge loomed to his east tapering the mixed orchards as it approached the sea. Here the broken cliff dwindled to a mere 30 paces, fragmenting about the earthen beaches north of the city.

Eothan walked out onto wind-blown course grass of the mainland, cresting the last of the gorge's highland, the orchard trees did not grow here on the unprotected slope of sea ward descending ground. Salt collected in the barbarian's blonde hair, too much for the plantation trees the sea facing highland was cropless. From this vantage point the Norcadian surveyed the lights of Berelan that stared back at him reflecting double in the sea water channel that surrounded the island. Overgrown with rock and marble the capital island was concealed on all but its west side, here great cliffs descended to narrow pebbled beaches.

A causeway linked the mainland to island across the channels shortest span. He was startled never had he seen such a mass of human dwelling. Street lights, buildings, domes, the impenetrable fortified towers, all shuddered his Norcadian sense of wild expanse.

Where he stood the water course was close to one hundred paces wide. A many domed palace covered the lumpy rock of the opposite promontory. Silver and copper covered its structure's spotted with the lights of cogs and triremes in its protected bay. He had reached Berelan.

Countless towers guarded a ten-pace tall wall, surrounding and sectioning the city into its many districts. There was a rise to its twisting undulating streets that ascended away from him to the west. He perceived towering cathedrals elegantly adorned with circular collars, brown wooden warehouses, and work houses for the city's townsmen, Park land, and to the center the massive stone walled dome of the Crown Hold, where sat the power of Arraken's civil court; presided over by magistrates chosen from among the clergy, and Ellendei nobility, with a healthy sampling of important guild syndics and other prominent towns people, the Hold conducted the Kings business, including the trial of cases of law that fell within Royal jurisdiction.

It shone golden copper, above the white wash of its star shaped interior walls. He guessed that half the city was in view before him, the small northern port that he saw opposite, nestled along an elbow between the palace of Simmon the Snake and the well to do, and, fortified district of the clergy. The famous sea ward port and Berelan's floating city must be to the south, behind and below that which he could see. Its channels and tributaries wound about the city's southern half, or so he had read. A sight to behold. But his mind did not draw itself hence, instead the huge towered and domed palace opposite called him on. He knew, the saint lay somewhere there within, the reverberations of hymns and chants reaching the abbot's paralyzed form.

Looking east to Berelan's causeway, he followed along the walls of Sanorr the capitals sister town, home to many holy fighting orders and the renowned race track of Sanorr. Penultimate to the Court yard of Ellentroth, the track had tasted the blood of many a fine joust.

It was late now, and the Norcadian had walked all day, but not wanting to approach the palace by light he arranged his weaponry securing Der Aeath, Queratare, in his empty back holster, and his sword still at his side, then walked out on to the muddy sand bar.

Cold sea water washed about his calves, and in moments he was submerged. He swam low, the weight of his belongings pulling him below the brine. But a strong swimmer he managed to flip between his back and side, always a head above the sloshing waves. Fighting fast against the current, the momentum of the Gorge flow pushed him on in the direction he was going. Soon his feet scraped along the slick rocks below the palace.

Not climbing out immediately he washed around to a thin unmassonried cliff face, and using his skill as a climber scaled into the palace of Primate Simmon. Ending on a troughed roof he pulled himself to lay flat upon the wooden architecture. There he rested for the time of many glasses, but rousing before the dawn, as the dark hinted with early light, he scrutinized the roof way looking for an easy place to penetrate the palace.

Occasional guards walked the walls, and Eothan remained in the shadows working his way about its beams until he reached a darkened nook at the abutment of a corner tower with the outer wall. No sentry stood above so drawing his knife and longsword he cut and scraped as quietly as he could to whittle a hole through the roof. His acute ears alerted him to any noise, the boots of an approaching guard, and the rasp of their metals. Freezing to the opening tower door above he waited till the sentry had made his way across the battlements to the next tower before resuming his work. Deepening as it widened, he soon broke through.

Peering down he saw into a brazier and candle lit hall, statues of the profit and scenes of the Ellendei migration mosaiced in vibrant ceramics and inlayed with valuable metal and gem. Using grapple and rope and resting his weight on one of the great halls beams he lowered into the early dawn chapel. Not wanting to be discovered by vespers, he was quick. Dropping behind a row of candles to release the grapple hook, which he caught deftly as it fell past him.

Winding up the excess cord he stashed it back in his belt and stooping ran along a line of candle bright saints. The benevolent Profit of the One stared at him from the halls end blood from his crucifix dripping red. Away from the statues, and along the opposite wall from the profit, he found wardrobes of ceremonial robes, white, black, red and gray, he continued to search until under a pile of sweated launderable red, he found a few plain brown habits, thinking them less conspicuous, he donned one of a suitable size.

Vespers, the songs of the blessing of the land and the journey of exodus, sounded quietly in the hall. Hiding his skins and weaponry beneath his new habit he, slipped in amongst the brothers of Simmon the Snake.

They chanted and sang the Quenderoth, the blessing of the land, substituting 'The One' for Enruth in the ancient Ellendei scriptures. A red robed deacon conducted the hymns, raising a golden chalice before the profit's statue. Holding it high he repeated his verses to be answered by the thronged chorus. Over a hundred monks crowded in the center of the long chapel lined beneath the plaster, and painted saints, and the ceramic profit, his benevolent face highlighted with silver and gold. Blue gem emeralds sparkled in his eye sockets, adding life to his frozen pain.

As the blessing went on a low trill eased into Eothan's consciousness. The humming of bees or crickets he thought. But why here? It seeped within the thick song of hymn caressing the monks to a musical rapture. As the Berelan congregation walked forward to take their blessing from the red robe the Norcadian moved in amongst them pushing forward to join the queue.

They were in a form of trance, singing but unaware of their surrounding their eyes out front, blank, blinking very rarely, and then at such a slow pace as to seem comical. As if dozing off to sleep on their feet. Before, opening, after a pause, the closed lids began their upward climb back into the upper eyelid flesh of their sockets. Stange it was, un-naturally slow.

As he reached the congregation's front, where monks were kneeling, he saw the red robed deacon the giant goblet now pulled from the height of two out stretched arms to descend and hang level with the heads of the brethren.

Eothan balked. From the chalice a tendrilled, snaking, cilia covered tentacle reached grippingly above the rim of gold. Red, lobsteroid an exoskeleton lurched up behind the leg. Almost horn like in shape. It flexed awkwardly whilst its ciliated tentacles reached towards the closest monk. In horror Eothan watched as it swung from chalice to the back of the monk's head. There it hopped to the adjacent monk and so on climbing along the line.

Silver horns rose to meet it like spines from the nape of the worshippers' necks as in their trance they sang. The trilling continued as the ciliated arthropodic crustation touched horn to spine working along the line. Finally, near the lines end, the encountered spine emerged erupted from the back of the monk. With a spatter of blood on the ancient Berelan flagstones the paused crustacean leapt into the vacated place, in the back of the raptured monk's neck.

He went limp, convulsing as his body accommodated the new parasite. The second crustacean now groped to the outside of its previous hosts robe, and after a pause it climbed along the line, disappearing back into the chalice, from whence its replacement had come.

Eothan heard a slosh and slapping of liquid in the vessel, as the chalice was again lifted upward to arm's length, another set of cartilage appendices appeared above its side. The kneeling monks did not move spines protruding from their necks vibrated with the harmonic chirping. He recoiled from his place in line and as all around were lost in their trance he pushed back through the throngs toward the cupboards and anterooms, the vestibules of the outer cathedral.

Hurriedly checking in a collection of doors, and around the robe cupboards he found a spiral stair leading both up and down. Wishing to escape the intoxicating racket of the incessant hum, and following an inner sense he bounded downward. Three steps at a time, the large acolyte covered the stair quickly and nimbly.

Leveling into a passage he lay his head against the rock wall and listened. He knew Thomas was close. There was a thick smell. Tart, stifling, rancid, but covered again with many layers of chemical and solution. He followed it descending it seemed, past arched wooden hard worn doors and thick granite buttressed pillars. Visions of an interior crowded with bottles and vessel filled walls, told him that the saint lay prone glass tubing about his form. A robed figure moved silently at a distance. How close? He could not tell.

Slowing he concentrated following around the corridor for a fix on the chamber's location. It must be further down, carved into the granite footings of Berelan's rock somewhere. Moving silently, he examined the doors of the hallway finding none that could lead to the chamber in his head. He offered a prayer, concentrating to add a little of the magic he had been taught by his tribe, now he probed with his eyes for any secret passages or portals, walking the tunnel slowly to its end.

At the corridors dead end, he found one, a large man high sliding door disguised to appear as the snug fitting slab stores of the corridors. This must be it he thought, now to find the trigger. There were no permanent torch attachments, and no brazier to light the hall. Eothan was beginning to tire, concentrating to perceive through the dark, and, search for concealed portals. His few hours nap had not been enough to reinvigorate him from the long walk and swim of the day before.

He fumbled around its outline and pushed his weight against it. A golden white light flashed about him warming his back and shuddering the portal before the Corserite. Hunching he stepped through. He knew not precisely where the rod was leading him, but felt that his abbot lay very close. He could not have opened the secret panel himself. Queature was leading the way.

Finding a rouge hewn and ancient worn passage he pulled the flail staff from his back, staying close to the water smoothed rock. Even here, behind paces of Berelan rock the salt of the sea tasted on the skin of his hand and lips, unique from the salt of his sweat, catching in the hair of his sensitive inner nose.

Edging along the hidden corridor, sliding bearings sounded under the panel behind as it returned to a closed position. Occasional steps took him farther into the Lands Beneath. He wondered what regions an entrance from Berelan could reach, what if the warped legions of hell had found it a contractually allowable outlet for their debaucheries? Simmon the Snake had taken unspeakable liberties with the primacy, and the sight of the infected congregation above was still fresh in his mind. Not in the legends of his own people, nor in the bestiaries of the Ellendei had he ever heard or read of such a creature as he had witnessed within the acolytes of Simmon. He considered how many of Berelan's people were infected by such foul monstrosities and from whence they had issued. A brood of a pit of hell itself, the offspring of the Imprisoned one, a servant of Shatan's dark power indeed, but, in what way were they to be fought. In every aspect they appeared as normal Ellendei, and yet their thoughts, their actions subservient to the foul machinations of a foreign being.

Where they perhaps, a remnant of the Wizard Kings? An abhorrent side effect of Magick and bestial sorcery spawn? The Elfs of Corser would be a better source of this knowledge than he, yet they nor Thomas had mentioned such creatures.

Emblems, designs of the Ellendei Primacy, recent in the history of Norcadia, and even the annuals of the exodus, covered the time and water smothered crevices in the passage. Holy gold inscriptions brazenly and starkly painted over with bold bloody reds and sickening yellows assaulted the sensitivity of the monk. His chest ached at the sight. Intestinal scribblings, in a harsh unwieldy script that was unfamiliar to him, the black speech mentioned by the converts of Gour Gorath perhaps, he knew not. Here a heart, there a human, stomach or kidney the notes to some catastrophic, atrocious operation were here brightly obliterating the holy sepulchre of Ellendei Primacey. This that had been its inner sanctum?

Faces, eyes, mouth, noses mankind fragmented and presented in a dissected, mutilated form in the foul ochres, that he hated to imagine the source of. But judging from the oppressive and growing reek of the place, they were animal in base, and hung half dry in a perpetual rot, mixing with the salt water, and penetrating his holy protected body, dragging him toward unconsciousness. He fought the urge, to sit and rest.

The list of the Ellendei's ten commandments, the way of the course wrights, had been craftily placed in gold inlay along the wall. Thou shalt keep the way of the Corse Wrights read the first. Bestowed through ten great visions, during their long exodus, the vile minions of the snake had corrupted theses with their rancid graffiti. Where the phrasing read shalt an ugly not had been scrawled along the top and where the course wright phrase read not it had been blackened out, with the same abhorrent paint. Sacred engravings had been usurped creating this obscene epitaph to he knew not what?

Spiraling through the rocky promontory he finally found himself at an iron reinforced and plated postern. A hand above his height, its surface carried a hammered copper design, a circle inlayed with silvered pentagram. Vissions from Querature filled his head. His abbot lay beyond the door, it was certain. White from the flailstaff lit the corridor streaking the walls with rays from its transmuting form. Circles and curvettes radiated out cascading around the acolyte, a rainbow of diffracted light to combat the reek of red and black stained designs.

He reached out a hand, as the light sprayed from his fingertips. Reddened copper silver pentagram fought with purity, as the flails staff energy diffused into the lock and hinges of the portal before him. The door's device and Querature sparked, hissing in universal debate. The truth of the Corserites against the infinite deceits of Shatan, the vile deceiver, to whom information was merely a contrivance, a method to an end. An end that justified all means. An attempt to manipulate through words. They had fought since the dawn of the Ellendei exodus, those that slander with the desperate union of the course wrights. Those that truthfully carried the messages of the journey from ship to ship. The rod had been with its people for eons, carrying the bones of many of its abbots in the cleric forged handle. Now once again called on to deflect the manipulations of the Imprisoned One, the great enemy whose corruption ever threatened the coherency of its people.

These divine ideologies struggled one with the other, truth vs. lies, along his hands and throughout the metal enforced structure of the wooden door. As the pentagram was worn by the eroding strength of its longtime foe, the door shattered cracking inward, crumbling under the acolyte as he stepped across its threshold.

An oppressive heat hit him in his lungs and about his face, he gasped. The chambers air was hot, scalding his lungs, so that he pursed his lips cooling its heat to breathability with the passages of his face. Still on his feet, he looked about, peering through a misty haze that radiated up from a thick blanket of burning sand. The body lay across from him toward the chambers back, on a block of marble, an altar of sorts. An alter behind which a vessel and jar filled shelf peered at him in the soft red light of the place.

Hunching he leaped forward his stride widening as he lunged across the scalding divide. The white crackled about, Quaretuar defending him from an oppressive affixation. His leather boots smoked with embers propelling him for another jumping stride.

Reaching the alter he checked the saint's body. It was predominantly unscathed, the abbot's skin red and blistered with the heat, but his chest slowly heaved with a slow repeated subconscious breath. Though his awareness was absent he was still alive. Eothan knew not what enchantment had stolen his abbot's consciousness and thinking only for his safety he lifted the body to his shoulder and turning he retreated, spilling vessels and tubes, shattering as he headed toward the door.

The smoke from his boots blinded his eyes, and exiting into the passage, he stamped through their fraying smoldering hides to cold smooth worn rock. Feeling safety from the untraversed direction, and thinking that he would soon be discovered he spent no time before he hastened toward freedom.

Running he curved within the Berelan rock and panting covered in sweat he found himself at a small exit overlooking the smaller northern dock.

Galleys, biremes, triremes and cogs shared the palace side of the queues to be replaced by cogs of all types and sizes to the northern mercantile section of this the smaller bay. The Primal palace supported by its own naval force, was surrounded by an ornate and wealthy hexature composed of the fortified military engineer's guild, and, a collection of supporting building and brick manufacturing guilds. The houses here stretched away from him across the small north bay providing a habitat for some of Berelan's richer and better-connected citizens. The chief syndics of the primacy's affiliated scribe and physician's guilds lived here, as did many of the Crown Hold's bureaucrats.

A great and decorated tower rose behind him from the western wall of Simmon's palace. Daring to hope he was not pursued he never the less spent no time deciding what to do. He ran down the slope toward the city lights that huddled about the harbor below him. In the protected northern alcove, the water was calm, losing its furry in a repeating trebled thud on the rocks to his north and east. The noise of the breaking sea faded, and keeping along the palace walls edge he avoided walking the bright lit street that circled the bay. Day would return soon, and if he could only rest and catch his breath, then he hoped to plot the next stage of their escape.

A shadow against the earth bank, he dashed two hundred paces, the saint becoming heavy on his back. The ground worked for him, its slope propelled him down toward the scattered buildings and ornate row of houses that filled Berelan's palace hexature. Lofty, towering, buttressed, domed, crenelated and decorated, four mighty donjon sized structures marked the corners of Simmon the Snake's primal palace gate. Like a mighty barbican for giants or a hall to an ancient deity it dwarfed the civilian structures that grew about its feet.

No sound told him that he had been discovered, and although the towers rose the hair of his neck, and urged on his run, he turned not nor gazed toward the entrance arches of his foe. He had reached the residences and workshops of the North Bay and glancing about chose a street that led from the palace, Cobblers Wax, read an iron wrought sign at its corner. The sky above had begun to lighten, and Eothan knowing how conspicuous he looked with his comatose abbot draped over a shoulder, drove himself on hurrying against fatigue.

He passed three large row structures that's upper floors protruded out into the street creating an overhang. Much bigger than the houses of Widern Town each must provide space for many families and their offspring, he thought. The gutters smelt clean and well managed. To the streets other side two buildings lay independent and separate a residential structure, and a large factory with adjacent warehouse. A cobblers by the look of a great wooden shoe that hung above its street side door. Between the constructions Eothan caught a glimpse of the bay the light spots from its many vessels, and their sails that glowed white and folded, tied in the early day's darkness.

To his left a second street, Horse Shoe Lane marked a ninety-degree angle in the large residences of Cobblers Wax. Here, between a second large factory, that Eothan guessed from the smells of wax and perfume, to be an illuminators, and Horse Shoe Lane, a crop of well grazed grass surrounded a collection of oak and elm, banked, from this side, by green mounds of rhododendrons.

Elated to find cover he was familiar with; he hobbled in his exhaustion to his first spied cover. Once in amongst the greenery he lay Thomas gently to the dry leafy bed of humus and rested. Not allowing himself the oblivion of sleep he concentrated holding his consciousness above the luxury that sleeps surrender offered, the weight of saint Thomas lay beside him.

Horns and distant bells alerted the warrior that it was time to move. The dawn had not yet chased the shadows from Berelan's narrow streets before the long twilight faded to morning. He again gently lifted his abbot, and traveling in the same direction passed the back side of more factory buildings to reach a larger track of tree and scrub decorated common. All the grass was cropped, and the scattered trees offered little in the way of cover. A large turreted wall ringed the east of the park and a Berelan channel cut through it to the north to empty into an enclosed lake. The strong smell of fish pervaded the air, issuing from a sprawling building and warehouse that abutted the man-made lake at a small dock.

Cogs filled the lake waiting in line to take their place at the dockside. Crates stacked along the shore unloaded and carried inside by the early morning workers, emptied these vessels of their catch, for their return to the open waters. At least the smell of fish would cover their scent thought the Norcadian. He wondered at the heavy ladened low lying vessels and their lighter, departing kindred, these fishermen were delivering enough food to feed his, and many more Norcadian tribes many times over.

Eothan found a tight shrubbery of country rose about the base of an old wide-reaching oak, a tree that resembled the specimens of Northern Corsinia, rivaling them in size, unlike the countless smaller trees he had passed between here and the palace. Bells had joined the horns sounding, they moved through the streets around him, Berelan was waking quickly, early milkman, food and water sellers found themselves crowded and ordered to halt for the pressing business of an early armed guard. They were looking for him.

Across the man-made lake he saw a mounted platoon ride away and toward a neighboring hexeture. The dock side workforce continued to unload fish, as if, such disturbances were common place. His craft kept the thorns of the rose from snaring their skin, and Quereture nourished his appetite. He dozed, the rod replenishing his empty stomach, better than the fare of the Weieen, even, his muscles would have resources to call on in their next day's work.

A horn close and to his south brought his head up. The captain, a knight by the heavy plate he wore, his shield bore the plain single ring emblazoned gold on white carried on the left. He urged his brown charger through a well-manicured garden that lay between two separate and strong built manor like buildings into the park land where they hid. He was getting close.

Troops of pike supported the knight and his collection of mounted sergeantry from the road as a group of white robed red skirted Berelan clergy filled the gap between two other manor sized buildings. A hubbub from the road beyond the inland bay accompanied a house-to-house search in progress. His rescue had been discovered and they closed a noose about his position. The thoroughness of the house to house told him that they did not yet know his exact location, but at this rate it was not to take them much time.

The abbot breathed slowly the air easing in and out of his lungs at a pace far below that of even the deepest sleep. What enchantment was on him Eothan knew not. He was not versed in the ways of Arcane Lore, unlike many of his brethren. He knew the tree they hid beneath was over four hundred years old, and had seen this Hexature of Berelan grow around it. But when it came to matters of human magic the hexologies and pentologies of the soul, and the commanding sorcery of the spoken word, then he was little better than a peasant at its identification and practice.

The knight on the charger drew closer. Using his lance, he poked the bushes and shrubs of the park, paying particular attention to a low hedge that separated the ornate manor houses from the open common park land. Breathing deep himself, Eothan's chest vibrated with each intake. He was alone and fatigued, denying himself sleep had taken its toll, Querature replenished his fluids but, the nagging exhaustion of his brain was something it did not cure. For too many days had been raked to perform at his utmost. Pure natural sleep was what he needed. Desperately!

The acolyte approximated that five score pikemen, at least, with an additional two score horses, rummaged the foliage looking for him. Across the inland lake another five or six score, with others involved beyond that, all steadily approaching. Fighting his way out with a comatose saint was out of the question. Well hidden by his craft for the moment he grasped the staff Courser, and bowing his head till his forehead rested on the rod he prayed. His tied mind did not grasp his training in the ancient scripts of the Ellendei, instead he fell into the tongue of his own people. He called on Enruth in a language native to the land before the Ellendei colonization, before the war against the Imprisoned One. A guttural sharp voiced talk that had echoed the hills of his home with laughter, song, and ballad, long before the first Corserite sails had caught sight of this fair land.

"isick yarch hidien ni choucharte bein nal harsch…". He lamented his plight calling on his god, Enruth. Seeking for succor in this their order's time of need. Oudan, was the name used for the all-powerful in the script of his childhood and here he used it too, being to swayed by exhaustion to care, the words synonymous to him in his plight.

Comforted for the moment he looked out again brave with the power of the rod. The single gold ring dazzled with the light of the early sun, glaring bright in the sea of white that covered his enemy's shield. Silver his armor, visor tossed back a clean shaven and scared face peered duteously about, as his charge scurried below him, moving as it searched for their quarry.

Obscured by a flurry of chain mailed, mounted sergeantry, Eothan's eyes crossed the field to where the group of white smocked red skirted priests engaged in a collective prayer. The acolyte sensed something unholy about them, as if they were merely shells that appeared clerical, but were actually something far less pure. A haze came upon them in their rapture as if clouded by a light swarm of gnats or other insect.

Then beyond the golden domed and blue crested spires and decorative fortress of the Primal Palace he saw a shape, something moved red before the blue sea and green headland. Great wings he glimpsed and then more, a serpentine body with four massive taloned legs. The reptilian form of a great Wurm. Snorting a vent of black smoke it flew. Circling twice in the air, fire flecked along its quadrupedal form, long neck snaking around on itself, as it apparently fought to follow its keen sense of sent, and hearing. Eothan had read much of its kin, to a wurm even the strong smell of fish would be discernible from his own. His enemy would soon be upon him

A full three score and ten paces long, the beast's talons, maw, and fiery breath were easily a match for

Eothan and his unconscious abbot. After one low flight around the perimeter of the ever-closing armored snare. The mighty wurm tossed its head back and peering around grinned showing off its double sets of razor-sharp teeth. Then with another wing beat it giggled in fluent Berelan accented Ellendei.

"We have our renegade monk and the excommunicate Thomas the damned... May the lord God be praised. "And with that it folded his wings, pouncing onto the crop in which Eothan crouched hidden. He smelt the thick brimstone of its breath, but its body was surprisingly clean for a creature of such a size and temperament. Was it truly a drake?

Then it was that Eothan's mind was caught by a churning within the waters. The channel came alive before his eyes, as a host of mighty fish leaped and jumped from the brime. A frenzy of fish designed to catch his attention. He scooped up the abbot and evading the Wurm by appearing unexpectedly beneath its bulk and from a portion of roses thick and impenetrable. He ran from under it, dodging a desperate slash of scaled tail, he bounded, the abbot hefted close about his shoulder, head long toward the waters.

Giant carp, salmon, sturgeon and a host of their smaller brethren stormed the dock and waters, tossing the crowded fishing cogs wily nilly on the small man made lock. The Wurm leapt to the air turning instantly, and, like a cat dropped from tree height, yet, before it could recoil and prepare a strike, Eothan had weaved amongst two elm and was nearing the fish filled, churning, waters.

Cursing, the monster flew above the trees and as its tail and back talons crashed within their foliage as it struck again. Feeling the heat on his neck, and trusting his instincts the Norcadian leapt carrying the bulk of his abbot with him. The great jaws snapped behind them and a fiery stream of smoke and flame spewed after. Before it could burn the fleeing Corserites with its magical heat, a plume of water erupted from the channel forming a wall swallowing the power of the wurms breath.

Eothan and Thomas fell into the water and slippery fish that now crowded the lock. Eothan felt himself borne, carried, both above and below the salty brime of the ocean filled channel. The Corserite felt safe. Something in the tradition of his monastic order was awakened in him. He had no trouble breathing and worried not for the abbots body he knew they were safe. The writhing smothering school carried them at a furious pace, through the channels of Berelan and out into the open ocean far beyond the reach of Simmon the Snake and the drake into the safe waters of Arecia.

EPILOGUE

I t wasn't the workmanship of his comrades in the monastery at the foot of Corser Mountain., but it survived. For a Norcadian warrior turned monk it was hard to match. The lettering, ornate and layered with all the usual curls, divided and set up the titles and narrative of each page. He dared to attempt no pictures being only a well-practiced novice, not the skilled artists that the Corserite library had to offer. None of the monsters or animals they had encountered to stare back at the reader, but, his practical straight forward prose would outline their journey for those future Corserites who were sure to show an interest in their troubles.

Boxes surrounded some of his most meticulous work, filled with the similar designs and motifs that had been the hall marks of Elendei liturgy for over two thousand years. For his own personal edification, a collection of his birth clans appeared alongside the leaf and vine of the Elendei.

Leaning back his head cast a shadow in the Barnakhan sun light flooding through the Length of windows in this sea ward wing of the Hall of Numbers, its sacred library. Polished glass panes lay open suspended in a lattice of lead and tin, the sun mellowed by a fresh sea wind cascaded about the place.

The Barnakhans had mastered crystal reflection, he presumed from the gnomes of Parnassus or some similar group. Coloured mineral globules in bedded in the ceiling and about the tall shelves and cupboards of the library resolved the incoming light to its basic colours, then recombed it above the scattered tables. The light both brightened and beautified the dusty stacks of tomes, scrolls, binders and books.

The silhouette of his head outlined on his paper, round his hair pulled back tightly in a wavy pony tail. It was two weeks since they had been found deposited on the rocks south of the Castle by the flock of pician rescuers. Weary and happy to be reunited with the Ellendei Tarese, he had spent most of his time working at the liturgical record of this segment of their quest, interviewing personages that had knowledge pertinent to the events, and recuperating from the many wounds he had received.

According to Soedewhen numerologist of Turumbur and chief advisor to The Catator, Earl of Barnaka, Saint

Thomas was the victim of a possession spell that had not been completed. His soul, retrieved by the son of Sarkhen Heathkeeper, Uuk of Maub, had been imprisoned in a silver, lead capped flask. They would be reunited by the wizard priests of Turumbura, but these things took time, and conciltation. The astrologer Gordel Erendil from the far land of Hervan Myriel was to be consulted as to the celestial wanderings. Things must be in order for such an operation. When Gordel returned word, the final preparation would begin.

When Eothan had rescued the body of Saint Thomas, it had not yet been possessed. The first stage was completed and they had imprisoned the abbot's soul with a Magick Jar Incantation. He thought that the body may have become a vessel for one of crustations. But what Soedewhen indicated pointed more to a certain spell slinger intending to dominate the priest and use his personality and prestige.

Uuk, who promised to spar with Eothan when they both recovered from the internal wounds that they had suffered, was here courting his betrothed Neidein Eiadawin. It was he, that had accompanied Tarese to the island, bearing the vessel of Saint Thomas' soul, the jar, that he had wrestled from the grasp of a Draken knight, through mortal combat. Now the saint's innocence had been proved to all of Arraken in the sacred lists of Ellentroth, and before the gathered weight of Elendei royalty, Simmon would have a harder time discrediting them. He was vindicated and would not be excommunicated. Eothan did not know what plans their enemies had, but it was clear that Primate Simmon was not their friend. The Kingdom was dividing into fractions.

Naideen was intelligent, and she got along with Terese, they had both formed a friendship over the last weeks. He often came upon them talking in the gardens. He was happy for both Uuk and she, he had been blessed with friends in his troubles.

Quantities, and figures were the subject of the days here in Barnaka keep. The hall of numbers presented daily puzzles solved mathematically and through the participation of their priests and wizards. These daily shows worked to keep the mind and thought open, its symbol system pathways exercised, this enabled the intellect to see patterns and numerical associations. Digits, functions and integers were the talk of each day, and puzzles kept the commonality entertained. In this way they stayed well practiced. The numerologists searched to find order behind the natural processes manifesting themselves into events and objects of the prime material plane. Mathematics was the key.

From the flight of doves all in one, the murmurations of autumn, to the awkward balancing act of some of the Arraken's heaviest circus clowns, each presentation enlightened as to the divine "equations", as Barnakan priests called them. That sums governed the principles of the agreed upon universe is self-evident. Eothan thought. There was no doubt in his mind that Uuk's future wife would turn around Mernnonian's unproductive border marshes. They could rival even Abydos in agricultural output. It was good they were allies.

As for him, Tarese and he had spent much time walking in the gardens of Nadan, and even climbing some of the small peaks along the Barnakan's island coast. Sometimes silent in peace, and sometimes awkward with a silence of expectation, they had laughed, and talked about their own adventure and imagined exploits to come. It was clear that Tarese was in search for a mate, and Eothan, not being a relative of the Ellendei royal families, from which she traced her lineage, felt put off, out of his depth; nor was he ready to give up his worship, but priests of his own people often took wives, and she did show a certain fondness to the large Norcadian. He knew that a marriage between a son of the Treathbaron had been discussed, but as they did not know each other personally, even Tarese did not take it seriously.

He glanced back to the work spread before him on the gnarled and smooth worn pine table top, and closing his eyes he banished the smell and sight of Tarese's dark brown wavy hair, and those beady when joyous, and sure with some unknown superior knowledge, eyes.

Sighing deep.

He reached for his now thick with ink quill, and studying himself for more concentrated work began another scratch.

This will take a while he thought.

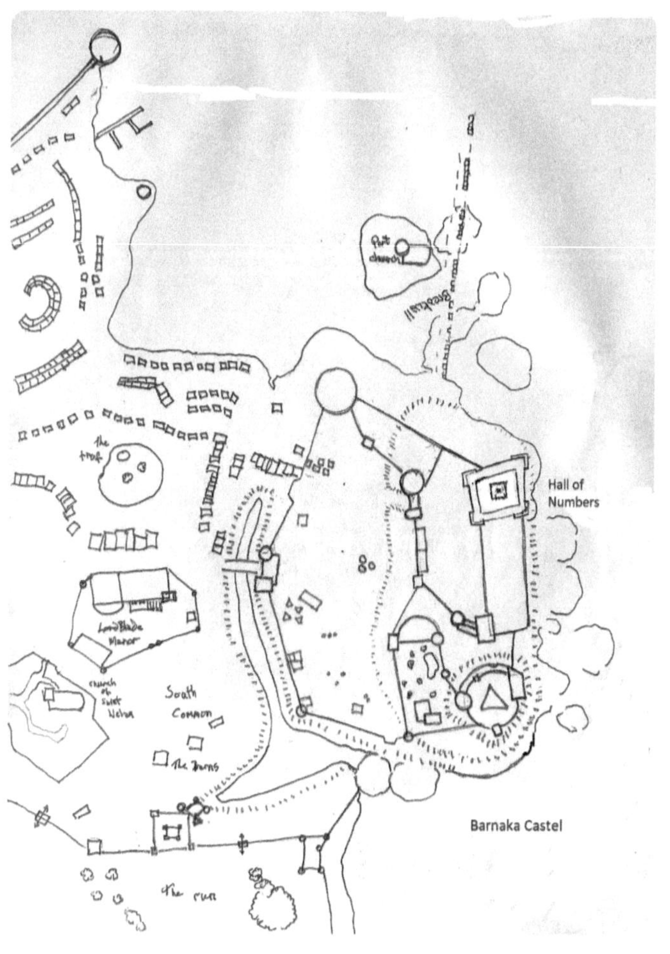

Port chuuorl
Breakfull
Hall of Numbers
the trof
LordBlade Manor
church of Saint Neban
South Common
The Barns
the run
Barnaka Castel

AUTHOR DESCRIPTION

The author started work as a puppeteer and then an actor which he did for a number years, earning a masters degree, before he became a teacher. He has taught for about 25 years now, and lives in London UK. He has travelled working in both the USA and China. He wrote this first novel many years ago when he lived on the west coast of North America. He has studied many subjects, has a Bsc. degree in anthropology and archaeology, and a MFA in theatre arts and drama. He is an avid fan of board, card, miniature and role-playing games. He started rpging in the late 1970's with the dnd white box, and still loves that. During covid he spent much of his time running and playing online games with other gamers.